About

**KALYAN RAY** is the author of the novel *Eastwords* (published by Penguin India) and has published several books of translations of contemporary Indian poetry into English, including *City of Memories* (Viking Penguin India), which has a preface by Allen Ginsberg. He has recently hosted a twenty-six-part series of interviews with writers, musicians, actors, and directors for a popular prime-time TV program in India.

Educated in the United States and India, Ray directed the India Program of the International Partnership for Service-Learning, which was affiliated with Portland State University in Oregon. He began teaching at St. Stephen's College in New Delhi and has subsequently taught in Greece, Ecuador, Jamaica, and the Philippines, where he was a visiting professor of comparative theology. He has long been associated with Indian social service organizations, and collaborated with Mother Teresa, doing the translations and voice-over for the first documentary on her work (directed by Ann Petrie). He currently divides his time between the U.S., where he teaches, and India, where he has acted in several films. He has been married for the last twe… …parna Sen.

# Also by the author

*Eastwords*

# NO COUNTRY

## Kalyan Ray

**BLOOMSBURY**

LONDON · NEW DELHI · NEW YORK · SYDNEY

First published in Great Britain 2014

This paperback edition published 2015

Copyright © 2014 by Kalyan Ray

The moral right of the author has been asserted

Bloomsbury Publishing plc
50 Bedford Square
London
WC1B 3DP

www.bloomsbury.com

Bloomsbury is a trademark of Bloomsbury Publishing Plc

Bloomsbury Publishing, London, New Delhi, New York and Sydney

A CIP catalogue record for this book is available from the British Library

ISBN 978 1 4088 4334 5

10 9 8 7 6 5 4 3 2 1

Design by Aline Pace
Printed and bound in Great Britain by CPI Group (UK) Ltd, Croydon CR0 4YY

*For daughters, lost and found*

# Family Tree

Jemmy Aherne = Maire Finnegan = Lord Palmerston
*(b. 1796, d. 1823)*     *(b. 1804, d. 1847)*     *(b. 1784, d. 1865)*

Brigid Shaughnessy = Padraig Aherne = Kalidasi Euphonia
*(b. 1825, d. 1843)*     *(b. 1824, d. 1901)*     *(b. 1840, d. 1876)*

Jakob Sztolberg = Maeve     Brendan Aherne = Susanna O'Reilly
*(b. 1834, d. 1885)*  *(b. 1843, d. 1911)*     *(b. 1868, d. 1931)*     *(b. 1877, d. 1909)*

Brigid (Bibi) Sztolberg = Frankie Talese
*(b. 1885, d. 1911)*

Mrs. Swint = Padraig Talese
*(unknown)*     (aka Archie Swint)
*(b. 1910)*

Melisande (Sandy) Swint     Billy Swint
*(b. 1956)*     *(b. 1964)*

Doorgadass Mitra
*(b. 1797, d. 1848)*

Ramkumar Mitra
*(b. 1838, d. 1933)*

Krishna Chandra
*(b. 1878, d. 1916)*

Amala Basu  =  Robert Patrick Aherne    Santimoy (Monimoy)   Monimoy
*(b. 1927, d. 1986)*    *(b. 1905, d. 1993)*        *(b. 1911, d. 1964)*      *(b. 1911, d. 1931)*

Mary Aherne      Dr. Seetha  =  Kush         Laub
*(unknown)*        Rathnam    *(b. 1940, d. 1989)*   *(b. 1940, d. 1940)*
              *(b. 1940, d. 1989)*

Neel Aherne  =  Devika Rathnam Mitra
*(b. 1965, d. 2036)*      *(b. 1967, d. 2045)*

Robert Aherne
*(b. 1990)*

# Prologue

## I

*Those dying generations*

# Chief Sandor Zuloff
## Clairmont, Upstate New York
### Friday, November 25, 1989

They lay together as if they had just disengaged from a long embrace. His right hand was stretched across her breast, his head thrown back, seemingly in laughter, pillow tossed aside. Her right leg was flexed at the knee, and her curved instep showed pale and vulnerable from where I stood at the door, looking at them in silence. The curtain stirred in the slow light, a fall afternoon that had the crispness of a seasonal apple.

The bed was streaked red, deepening to brown around the edges. Her eyes were half-open, as if she were about to speak to the man beside her. The cut on the brown skin of her neck was easy to miss, for around it was a slight necklace, its garnet beads vivid as pomegranate seeds, and her open palm next to it, covered by a film which I knew was dried blood. There was a damp pool in the gather of the bedsheets. The man had less blood around him, although the kitchen knife was impacted in his chest. A thin pencil mark of red ran from his left temple to his right jaw, as if someone had swiftly canceled his face before burying the blade.

A window by the bed had been left open an inch, but there was no sign of its having been forced from outside, nor any footprints or ladder marks or signs of entry from outside. The only prints clearly matched the man's.

"Chief," I heard someone calling me from the stairwell. "They're waiting, the morgue guys." Young Delahanty, first week on the job, uniform crisp, his manner earnest and uncertain. He'd be talking about this day for the rest of his life. The photographers were done. The fingerprint people had come and gone.

Her secretary had called the police when the female victim, a doctor, had not arrived for a scheduled morning surgery, and no one at home had answered her repeated calls.

They had died together, the husband and wife, unclear in which order. Tomlinson from the medical team had told me the approximate time the homicides had happened. About eleven.

The grown-up daughter was downstairs, brought in a squad car. She had seen the bodies, then stayed downstairs with Caitlin Roach, our female cop on duty. She hadn't spoken a word.

"I'll go talk to her now," I told Delahanty, "alone." He left. He didn't babble. I liked that about him. I lit my sixth cigarette of the morning, careful not to drop the ash on the gray carpet.

Nothing was missing from the house, nothing shifted, except the knife from the kitchen below. The daughter sat still as stone on a brown hassock in the study, her bare feet on the hardwood floor, her hair uncombed, her shoes lying forgotten beside her. Outside the window, the deck lay sepia in the afternoon light, octaves darker than the garden behind it.

"What did you fight about?"

She looked absently at me, as if surprised to find me there.

"We didn't. I was angry. I left the dinner table."

"Did you have dinner?" I had seen only two smeared dishes in the sink.

"I left before it was over."

"Who did you quarrel with, your father or your mother?"

"It wasn't a quarrel."

"It wasn't?"

"I was angry with myself."

"And they end up dead in bed?"

She looked at me, eyes growing wide. Then she said slowly, "You are so wrong," as if to herself.

"Did I say it was you?" I whispered, shaking my head.

So far we knew that she had stopped for gas on her way home a little after seven thirty and paid with her credit card at Bailey's service station three miles away. The gas station attendant had recognized her picture. She rented an upstairs apartment in a two-story detached house, like many graduate students in that university town a dozen miles down the road. Her mother, a gynecologist at our nearby hospital, returned from work a couple of hours later, shortly before ten.

The girl, Devika Mitra, had slammed her bedroom door at around eight. Mrs. Sharon Nolan, her landlady, had heard it and asked her to come down for some pumpkin pie of which she was very proud, but Devika had refused. Her car sat in the driveway for the next few hours. Mrs. Nolan had to wake her at around eleven, apologetic for doing so, but Devika's car was blocking her son's in the driveway.

Mrs. Nolan had gone to her bedroom, which was right under Devika's room, and she heard Devika pacing about for an hour after that. She read for more than an hour, unable to sleep, because she had had coffee after dessert, which always kept her up.

5

She thought she might have heard Devika crying, but decided to let her be.

I had let her talk, hoping for some scrap of information: She rambled on about how bad she had felt about Devika, all alone for Thanksgiving. How could these Indian immigrants let their daughter spend Thanksgiving alone! Even the boyfriend was away—gone to New York City to see some relative—she thought Devika had said. Mrs. Nolan was fond of Devika, who was usually cheerful and had helped her rake the fall leaves a couple of times, unasked.

The boyfriend had taken the Greyhound bus to the city on Monday and had not yet returned. Devika had said that he was staying at the Chelsea Hotel. I had NYPD check that.

I stepped outside and, fishing around for a cigarette, realized it was the last one in the packet. I lit the Camel carefully, exhaling in the evening air.

No motive, no unexplained fingerprints, no witnesses. Yet, inside this house in a drowsy cul-de-sac, a husband and his wife, both born half a world away, lay dead in each other's arms, in my hometown. Three months to retirement, I did not want this case to go cold, to enter the lore of small-town police in upstate New York, and become a private burden I would carry into my quietest moments, knee-deep in some trout stream.

I remembered, as a rookie in the city, what canny old Detective Jim Henderson used to say: "No more than two degrees of separation—if that—in murder cases, unless burglary is involved. Often the unlikeliest connections."

I felt I had been left one of those old books whose pages would have to be carefully slit open, the separating of each page a deliberate act. I whispered to myself in Hungarian, the only language I knew as a five year-old when I had first come to America, *"A konyvek nema mesterek; világos, nint a vakablak . . . feher liliomnak is lehet fekete az ámyeka." Books are silent masters; clear as a blind window . . . even a white lily casts a black shadow.* In this book I knew how just one chapter ended, the last one. The preceding narrative was still terra incognita, its geography yet unexplored.

## II

*Whatever is begotten, born, and dies*

# Brendan
## Mullaghmore, County Sligo, Western Ireland
### 1843

I was a small boy when the landlords' tax men came to deal with those who had fallen into arrears. I remember the fire. So lovely and terrible a hue. What God creates such beautiful color and flickering shapes as it leaps and rules upon a cottage, completing its unroofing and ruin? It is the landlords' weapon, a different thing altogether from our humble potboilers, grey embers where we cook our potatoes. Its red eye appears, jolly and heartless, as black smoke wreathes and twists about it. And those who lived below that roof—some for generations—stand clenching their futile fists, their cold sweat of defeat warmed savagely by it. Odd it is, this burning—with the hard bullyboys spitting and watching—and the man of the house clutching his woman, the children fearful and openmouthed by the suddenness of it all, waking into a nightmare long predicted.

These are the landlords' lands, these cottages built stone upon stone, the soddy thatch, all theirs. But it is our tenant lives that are on fire. When they battered and torched our mate Fintan's cottage, his da stood grinding his teeth, his ma on the ground as if lamed, and Fintan with great round eyes, crying and forgotten, watching the chimney slide onto the broken earth.

From under his cowlick, my best mate, Padraig, watched silent and narrow-eyed as our Fintan's cottage burned. The fire was the colour of dark rose and madder, climbing rose and gorse—all our Irish colours. And then—for it was our Ireland and our times— everything turned to ashes. The evening mist settled. And there was nowhere to shelter the head in this land that all belongs to the landlords. There were only some planks close by, pulled up and out, to be hauled away by the bullyboys. They would trundle them away next morning when they came with the carts, for they did not want the fire to spook the horses. The planks would turn soft and soggy-like in the blue evening dew. For the last time the family would sleep on the floorboards—at least the children would— Fintan's da too full of bitterness to lie down under the hard stars. From that day, my friend Padraig and I never saw Fintan or his small brothers anymore.

On that selfsame day I first saw that hard glint in Padraig's eye, his small palm clasping a stone, eyes taking in that destroying fire. In the following years I realized that his hand would forever seek that hard rock until there would be no holding him back from striking a mortal blow or, in the attempt, fall off the world.

• • •

I AM BRENDAN McCarthaigh of Mullaghmore, County Sligo, seventeen now, as addled in love as ever by words and books, and already in a fair way to becoming Mr. O'Flaherty's apprentice. It's odd how I became that, with nary a word spoken, as if my love of books and learning found its natural harbour right here, under the old schoolmaster's benign eye. Even when we were wee ones, Mr. O'Flaherty would open unexpected windows for us. Together in our one-room hedge school, Padraig and I would listen entranced to Mr. O'Flaherty's tales about the heroes who traveled far, bravehearted, but broke their own hearts forever, Oisin, and Finn McCoul. He would talk of Cuchulain, or about the battles before windy Troy, telling us about our Irish Brian Boru, about Drogheda, about the Druids. He had us staring into the sloping afternoon with wonder in our eyes, imagining ourselves into those old worlds. He would hold us enthralled with the doings and sayings of our own present-day Daniel O'Connell, as if we ourselves were at the very edge of a great beginning in our history.

The Sunday harangues of Father Conlon washed over our nodding heads like cold seawater, and we knew his relentless yellow eye was forever on the collection basket. But the centre of our young lives was not Father Conlon or the gathered prayers of the elders and the black-shawled bent women. That was a habit, like our miserable tithes. No, for us it was Mr. O'Flaherty's school. A hedge school, it would be called by the English, 'tis certain, for it had no halls and mighty rooms with great benches and a high table for the master. Although our great Daniel O'Connell had brought about the Catholic Emancipation, for us in this far western village near Sligo, there was no other school to attend. The priest got us on Sundays, but the rest of the week we went to Mr. O'Flaherty. Old Malachi he was called behind his back by some fools in their liquor, but to his face, he was always Sir or Mr. O'Flaherty, to one and all.

Our great landlord Lord Palmerston—who extracted his ample income primarily from his vast Sligo lands—came to our

Sligo just thrice, each about a decade apart, and seeing no schools the first time about, set one up. But our priests told us that it was a way to turn us from our Catholic faith. No student ever darkened its doorway in Inishmurray. The English schoolmaster stood about for a couple of years, and went back, never having had a single pupil to teach.

Next time Palmerston came across our Mr. O'Flaherty, who never talks at all about his meeting with the English lord, but I have heard tell from others that the peer found a deep and quiet knowledge of books in our Mr. O'Flaherty—even in Latin and Greek. It was understood forever after by his local agent, the English Mr. Arkwright, that he was to leave Mr. O'Flaherty and his little ground on which stood his few trees and potato patch and wheat corner alone, and no rent asked for or given. This Lord Palmerston was a man of sweeping avarice, but also known for the odd act of generosity; he had a great love of books and learning. In short, as full of contradictions as many another mortal.

Mr. Arkwright took his hat off to Mr. O'Flaherty. Our Mr. O'Flaherty simply was one of those men you took your hat off to, and felt better for having done so. Nay, he'd never rant like Father Conlon, for he was always a mild one in conversation. And wherever he stood, with his quiet smile and grey unruly hair and sparse white beard, that space was his, even our poor starving Irish soil.

From many villages around, unlettered folks would walk up to our school and wait for our day to be over. Then, hat in hand, or shyly smoothing aprons, they would ask Mr. O'Flaherty to write their letters, petitions, and such. Mr. O'Flaherty never sent anyone away. His pen gave their humble hopes and woes voice to address the usually stone-deaf ears of bailiffs, the absent landowners in

London and the English shires. He wrote the letters—to relatives in distant America and even, I heard tell, to kin who had crossed many oceans to India in red coats to serve the East India Company. If letters came back, Mr. O'Flaherty would read them out privately, and nary a soul complained that her news was bandied about. The old schoolmaster was a deep stone basin, and nothing spilt from it. Rain or shine he wore his thick black coat, the collar turned up almost to his nose, just below his thick glasses. Not much escaped those eyes either.

From our school, a single room of stone-built walls, we could see the edge of one breakwater when the door was left open in fine weather. There we sat: Padraig right next to me from the first day, Charley Keelan, Mikey Williams with his tiny nose and big ears, the O'Toole brothers—Joe, Sam, Brian, Malachi—the other Brendan, Brendan McMahon, Sorcha and Saoirse Colum, laughing Molly Purdy, Brigid from down our lane, and all the other children. Mr. O'Flaherty would stroll in for our morning class from his tiny cottage next door, still holding his chipped enamel mug of tea in one hand and his pipe in the other.

• • •

THERE WAS SOMEONE else who would not be absent for a day: Madgy Finn. Mr. O'Flaherty called her by that name. Most in our village called her Odd Madgy Finn—for she used to wander about gabbling words no one comprehended—and was known to all from Dromahair and Collooney to Mullaghmore and Sligo, and all around the harbour and the banks of our Garavogue River. She was Wally Finn's daughter, the same Wally Finn who would ask to go with the fisherfolk off Sligo Bay when he could stand on his own two feet, and not hanging about in front of the pubs, begging for drinks until the publican shooed him off. With a three-tooth yellow grin on his unshaved face, long dirty eyebrows hedging his rheumy eyes, he would also hang about the poteen brewers back in the glen, hawking and spitting, begging for a swig or two. His wife had died when Madgy was a child. Padraig's ma said that she was a good seven years older, was Madgy, though shorter than us by far.

We were still small children when her father died after the ceilidh festival down in Sligo Town. He had the poteen and tumbled on the side of the Garavogue River, where his dirty head struck a stone, and he lay facedown, a few feet off the paved path, drowned in six inches of water.

The townspeople gave him a hasty burial, and the only one who attended, apart from the gravediggers, Father Conlon, and Madgy, was Mr. O'Flaherty, who stood hat in hand beside me. I wondered what Madgy understood, but she stood quietly enough until the priest finished the prayers. But when they put Poor Wally Finn in the ground and began to pour the dug dirt on him, she gave a cry and leaped on the diggers and kicked the dirt about to stop them from putting it on her dead da. She fought tooth and nail, until they frog-marched her off the graveyard, but not before Mr. O'Flaherty gave her a piece of bread which she ate with appetite, diverted momentarily from her da and her bitter fight.

Every day after that, Madgy came to sit under the tree across from Mr. O'Flaherty's door, rocking back and forth when we recited our multiplication tables, clapping with delight, as if we had sung to her. And when Mr. O'Flaherty would teach us, she would fall asleep, stretch and yawn, or wander off. But by the time the lessons ended for the day and Mr. O'Flaherty dismissed us, Poor

Madgy would sit until Mr. O'Flaherty would emerge shortly with a couple of praties, or a wedge of bread and a rind of cheese. She would smile up at him, her mouth twisted with glee. Biting into the victuals, she would amble off unevenly, though surefooted she was, in spite of one leg shorter than the other.

As a child, I remember being afraid of Madgy because of her puppet's staring head, large teeth, and splayed feet that seemed too large for the rest of her. My eyes averted in finicky disgust as I saw her phlegm depending from a nostril. It was only of late I learned to see her through Mr. O'Flaherty's even gaze.

During the ceilidh festival time in Sligo Town, she would go and dance at the fringe when the bands played. Aye, but her dance was that odd and beautiful, whirling on the balls of her feet, round and round, tottery with the poteen she would beg off people, but never falling, a gyrating mouth-open puppet, squeaking with pleasure and dizziness until she lay spent and panting in a part of the town square, on the stone itself, and sleep till the morning sun and early flies prised her eyes open, runny as they were with something like amber gum. Up she would stand and off she would go, up the slope towards Mr. O'Flaherty's school, as if she could not bear to be late, and take her place under the tree, rocking with the multiplication tables, thumb wedged in her smiling mouth, a bairn.

It was near Christmas, almost a full year before Padraig got his sudden idea to go off to the great meeting at Clontarf so far away. The festival at Sligo Town had been big and raucous with ceilidh bands and drinking and dancing and stirring about. The harvest had been good earlier and so had the ocean's catch. Many strangers had come to town, some fisherfolk from as far away as Donegal, some had brought horses for sale from the South—some even from the Isles of Aran—and there were tramps and tinkers and poteen makers from around Roscommon inland. We had no school those days.

The morning after the festival was over, and dogs wandering all over licking the paved stones where people had spilled food or offal, and all the strangers left, and the townspeople were slowly putting themselves back into their ordinary lives, someone discovered Poor Madgy Finn lying behind a paved by-lane like a broken toy, hair matted and reeking from the poteen some jokesters had poured on it, her face torn as if she had been fighting dogs. She had cuts on her hands where some nails had broken off, and she was whimpering.

In ones and twos the townspeople gathered about her in a growing circle. Padraig's ma too had gone into town that day. She went to see what people were gawking at, and found Odd Madgy Finn moaning on the ground, a drying splotch of blood on the thin dress she had twisted over her crotch.

This put Padraig's ma in a tearing rage. What she said I did not hear, but the townspeople slunk off and Mrs. Aherne lifted Poor Madgy Finn and cradled her home. She was strong. I followed her at a distance, all the way to her home, not daring to get close. She gave a piece of bread to Madgy, who curled up in a corner, chewing between groans.

A few days later Odd Madgy Finn was back in front of Mr. O'Flaherty's school. She got no more food than she always did—fruits she got off the trees in season—the wedges of bread from Mr. O'Flaherty, or the praties that Padraig's ma would give her if she showed up at her shop, sometimes a heel of cheese, and perhaps a bit of coloured paper which Poor Madgy Finn would treasure until it got sodden and sere. But one thing was changed in Madgy. Her stomach bloated and grew as the weeks passed into warming months and late summer, until time came when she could barely stir.

She disappeared for a few days as September ended. No one knew where she was. There was even some relief, I sensed, among the townspeople. But, as unexpectedly as ever, she limped her way back, her dress now filthy with mud and a rusty stain, and one breast lay open to plain sight. On her teat suckled a naked infant, large, like a diminutive man, with a smudge of pasty hair on his blue skull. Padraig's ma coaxed her to come home with her, though Odd Madgy Finn bridled if anyone, even Mrs. Aherne, came too close to the bairn, let alone tried to dress it. I once saw her trying to feed her newborn some bread. The baby began to choke. Madgy threw the lump down, thrust her teat back in his mouth, and strolled away to the woody copse of elms and rhododendron, where a thin spring burbled from the rocky ground and black-back gulls roosted under Ben Bulben.

When she sensed no one was around she would leave the baby in a small nest-like mess made of moss and furze. I saw it there a few times, returning from school, and heard it gurgling and gooing and a-staring at the branches overhead. Madgy would run off and bathe in the stream, squawking and guffawing in the chilly water, and sometimes took to the habit of hunkering down to defecate on the road itself. And once, stingy Willy McDougall was driving his flock of mangy sheep down when he saw her, crossed himself, and doubled back, and came another day because he thought it bad luck itself to see anyone parting with anything at all on his way to market day.

In a couple of weeks Odd Madgy Finn began to leave it for longer and longer. The dress about her breasts was always wet and glotty with milky ooze, her hair coming off in patches, and she spat about a lot. Some days, she took to walking down to Sligo Town in the afternoon, begging and badgering people for food or a dram, but always returned to wherever she had left her bairn, by the time the light grew westerly and long on Sligo Bay.

And then it happened. Just a month or so after her birthing, she returned one noon and found that the birds had been at it when she was gone. They had pecked and ravaged her boy eyeless and scratch-headed, cheeks torn and flesh-pecked. Madgy had put the bairn to breast, but the creature was past suckling. She set up a mighty howl, and when she stumbled into the open door of our schoolroom with a great cry, we were all that shivered and goose-bumped with horror as she held out the baby to Mr. O'Flaherty, herself smelling of blood and stale milk. The youngest of us, Charley Keelan and Malachi O'Toole, set up wails of fright. Mr. O'Flaherty rushed out, and Odd Madgy followed him—still holding out the mottled bundle. Mr. O'Flaherty, whom we had never seen flustered, made a retching sound and led her out, slamming the door behind himself, leaving us inside in the gasping dark.

There we sat, still as death itself, in the closed schoolroom. Malachi was sniffling and hugging his older brother Joe, and rusty-haired Charley Keelan bent over the dirt floor, his hands over his ears. When Mr. O'Flaherty returned, his face looked old and lined, and he went out again with a piece of black bread in his hand, the door swinging open and shut in the dizzy sea-wind. Madgy put her baby down on the rough dirt of the threshold in front of his laced old shoes, took two lurchy steps back into the yard, bit on the bread, and was gone.

Mr. O'Flaherty picked up the bundle and spoke loudly from the threshold itself, without turning to look at us, as if he were speaking to the far wrinkled sea out there, "Go home, go away today," was all he muttered.

From the next day Poor Madgy Finn did not show up at school, rocking in time with the multiplication numbers, did not lie in the dirt under that tree, waiting for her morsel at Mr. O'Flaherty's door.

• • •

THINGS LULLED BACK in a few days, as they always did in our corner of Ireland, beneath the prow of Bulben, which faces the Atlantic. To the east, a sandy pebbled arc with a stone breakwater holds the harbour where fishing boats bob beside Mullaghmore village, between the open sea and the high Ben.

From Cairns Hill you can see Lough Gill, which holds within itself isles—one named Innisfree, a calm eye in the lake. Hazel woods east of the lough whisper from early spring into the grey slant of autumn. In the twilight, you can see the twinkle of the village of Dromahair, under a purple vein still bleeding in the sky.

There was water all around us, starting with the Garavogue, right by the harbour. On the slope to Ben Bulben, a stone hut usurped the small storm-bitten green on which it stood. Out on a jaunt, Padraig and I sheltered there once, from a sudden rain. Snug, under the muttering rain on the slate and sod roof, we watched through its door how a tunnel of radiance bore its way from the Atlantic waters, through wreathed mist, until it was all clear. Far out west the Atlantic glittered under a full and falling sun, turning its waves beyond Ben Bulben into layers upon layers of gleaming fish-scales.

During that last spring of 1843, when he was still with us,

Padraig used to take me and go, sometimes with Brigid tagging along, toward Rosses' Point, where there is a small church. Turn left and it took us to seven miniature lakes. Farther along this road we could see Dead Man's Point and the broad chest of the Atlantic gleaming, the wide rocks like armour. Underfoot, the crawling tides tug to and fro, depending upon the time of day. All we could hear—above the stir of pebbly water and the sudden squawk of a seagull—was the gong of an iron bell swung whimsically when it pleased the Atlantic gust. To the right, Ben Bulben sets the scene, like the master in his house.

During our jaunts, Padraig seemed so much less taken with Brigid than usual. I had him more to myself. Brigid tried to match his carefree mood, but I could feel my sliver of jealousy, how she was waiting to be wooed, and I feeling that small pleasure of his neglect of her. He was my brother in spirit, but it troubled me how much or what I sought of Padraig. I was content with my unwillingness to delve more. I found Brigid looking at me, in unguarded moments, in an appraising manner. We both looked away if our eyes met, but I could tell I was being measured on some inexplicable scale through her woman's eye, probing to learn the weight on my heart.

• • •

PADRAIG AND I had always known Brigid; we had known her as baby and child and girl. 'Tis a mystery how Padraig, who teased little Brigid, almost a year younger, pulled her hair and made her cry, now turned and began to go silent and watchful as she grew tall.

Padraig was the one to go nest-egg hunting, the first to bring in a frog to put in someone's school satchel. He was also the first to share his praties or give away his slice of bread to a girl or boy without lunch. His flung stone was death itself to the squirrels until one day when Brigid cried, staring at the limp bodies hanging from his bloodied fist. That's when he pulled her hair, and made a face, to be friends again. But the lass shook her mane of black and looked away. Padraig, who could bear everything but to be ignored, grabbed her by the shoulders and kissed her mouth. I saw he was breathless, while she walked off as if indifferent.

The host of children with whom we had first flocked to Mr. O'Flaherty's school had begun to drift off. Many took to the fields beside their fathers, carrying their hoes and spades at dawn. Some left for Sligo or Boyle, others farther afield, leaving their carved names on tables. Declan Clooney had run away to become a sailorman. One or two would drop by after some years, blinking at our threshold, as if expecting to find their own wee selves writing on the slate, their eyes clutching at the childhood they had left behind, crestfallen that others now occupied their seats. Charley Keelan had been the first to leave when he turned eleven. Then by ones and twos they left until in the next four years none of our vintage was left, but the three of us.

Brigid mustered the wee ones scrawling the alphabet on their slate tablets which she would wipe clean with a wet rag when they were done, Mr. O'Flaherty glad of her help. They clustered around her, and she was content, away from her mean cottage, especially when her da was home, blustering in his poteen fug. Padraig stayed on, discussing Ireland and newspapers with Mr. O'Flaherty, and willingly mend the sod roof of the schoolhouse and the doors, replacing corbel stones on the mossy sides of the lane. With his sharp knife, he would carve wooden ships for the little ones, calling these

Grania's Fleet, ignoring Peter O'Connor's real one, which sailed from his Garavogue shipyard office, where Padraig said he might one day go to work. He had an inexplicable ability of calculating numbers from large columns of figures, swiftly in his head, instant additions, divisions, and multiplications and such. Mr. O'Flaherty said that Padraig was a rare one, born with that ability: He saw numbers and the answers flocked to him as if at his bidding, like a line of sandpipers flying in to settle on the beach.

"An asset he would be in my business," Mr. O'Connor had declared, but Padraig kept putting off that plodding employ. Besides, his mother with her tidy shop was glad to have him get more book learning and was in no hurry to bid her boy goodbye. My mate too was reluctant to depart his carefree days. Oh, *I* was glad he had not left.

By the time Padraig approached seventeen, I knew he was over his head. I understood it bitterly, and ignored Brigid. I watched him stare at the frail neck and the curve of her cheek, and all the letters on his page might as well have been motes of dust swirling meaninglessly, while the sunbeam lit up Brigid Shaughnessy alone.

I began to stay back and talk to Mr. O'Flaherty, so I would not walk with Padraig trailing Brigid, him answering me in distracted monosyllables. Padraig thought me considerate. Nay, angry and bruised, I was—and proud—in my fashion, noticing more than I let on.

The winter had raged into February, and tapered off in rains and mists in March, and the faint, then glorious, sunshine began to speckle and deck our early April Sligo with scatters of bluebells, rhododendron, and forsythia all the way up the Ben.

Sharp and clear as a break in a perfect crystal, I chanced to see

Padraig kissing Brigid one day under a crab apple that was at the point of budding. A week later one April afternoon, unexpectedly warm, I spied them entering a shepherd's broken hut, one of those that lie about the county, abandoned and empty. Padraig took a hurried look around before Brigid's palm closed over his, drawing him in.

Even from the far edge of the meadow above them, I could see how gentle the clasp of his fingers was—and yet how helpless—as he held Brigid's palm. My heart and all its veins were twisted within me and hurt, for I knew that Brigid was at that moment closer in his arms than any of our heedless and raucous wrestling contests which Padraig always won, pinning me to the dirt.

Yet it was not I alone who had seen this. Father Conlon had seen it too. How is it that two persons can see the same thing, from great far distances, and react so differently? I resolved to keep the sight as between the pages of my heart's book, secreted forever. But the priest, in great snorting dudgeon, hobbled fast, even with his weak knees and wheezing breath, and arrived by the longer path—not the steep shortcut we take, half-sliding down the hill—at that same broken shepherd's hut. He found them entwined, a trace of dirt on her knee and Padraig's surprised face, sweats mingled, their little dim world redolent with caresses and kisses, fondled half-words and moans—and broke that moment apart.

He dragged them out, naked and seemingly newborn, into the April glare. He was going to tell their mothers, he was going to tell the world, he was going to bellow it to the whole congregation, he would point God's finger at them. He stood there shouting on the glorious hillside, brandishing his staff, and justifying the ways of God.

Padraig and Brigid, hastily covering their nakedness, did walk hand in hand, with wandering steps and slow, and through that valley took their solitary way.

• • •

I SAT FOR a long time on a rock and looked out at the ocean. After what I had seen, I felt a tiredness of spirit. I wanted to sit on the rock and not have to go back, to my sick mother, to my shabby sod-roofed home, to the daily wants, to the smell of sputtery tallow candles under the blackened ceiling, to the barefoot dirt beneath, to whatever sanctimonious mischief Father Conlon had been able to brew.

I saw folks gathered outside their cottages, seeming to mind their own business, but I knew the ways of our villagers. Everyone was straining their ears to every bit of scandal thrown into the air, for Father Conlon certainly prated about Brigid's shameful deflowering and how he knew about Padraig Aherne's mischief. Ah yes, his red face and pimpled neck aglow, the priest was surely having his loud say. Padraig's ma was among a number of people in front of her shop. She was with Brigid's mother. I wondered where Brigid might be. Padraig was surely inside, miserable that his day in paradise had rotted so. He would be in a rage, for I knew his temper.

It was then my heart sank. There stood Mr. Shaughnessy, Brigid's father, unsteady on his feet as a heavy hamstrung bull. He came to the village on his erratic trips home from Connemara, where he worked in the boatyard of an Englishman. He drank most of his money, and people—if you heeded them—would tell you worse. Every few months he would show up on our lane and settle some of the accounts at Mrs. Aherne's shop, and then go for a drunken binge. He would wobble down to Mullaghmore or Sligo harbour making a nuisance of himself, then weave back to his cottage, spitting and retching on the way. He had been warned in Mullaghmore for public pissing. He would stay holed in his cottage for several days, making a terror of himself at home. Brigid could not go to school those days. Then he would get up, put on his shoes without even washing off the flakes of retch, and head back to Connemara, to the relief of all, but especially to his family.

Ay, but now he was back, in the worst of times.

Mrs. Shaughnessy was weeping, her head bowed. Padraig's ma had her arm around her. Father Conlon stood a little farther away from them and kept looking at the jumble of eager neighbours who had gathered as if by chance.

" 'Tis your proud way, Maire Aherne, that's the cause of all this," said Father Conlon unexpectedly. Mrs. Aherne, who had been speaking quietly to Brigid's ma, bridled at the priest's hectoring, and walked right up to the priest and stood before him. "Is that what it is, Father?" she retorted. "And when widowed I returned here, heavy with child, my young husband late gone, what help were you?"

Desperately Father Conlon looked about him. Brigid's da had reached the crowd—for 'twas a crowd now.

"Come here, Shaughnessy!" Father Conlon called out and grasped the man's shoulder. "Look at this wronged man, Maire. Can ye look him in the face?"

Mr. Shaughnessy tried to rearrange his stubbly face into the semblance of the righteous. He sighed deeply. The poteen breath made Father Conlon blanch, in spite of himself. He took his fat hand off Mr. Shaughnessy's shoulder as that man stood swaying, his eyes goggled on one face, then another.

" 'Tis that odd, Maire, 'tis mighty odd that the English agent Arkwright comes by, wringing every sorry coin from our fists, ranting and threatening to tumble our cottages—but when he comes to ye, Maire, why then does he smile and scrape, and nary a broken farthing does he walk away with? 'Tis always Mrs. Aherne this and Mrs. Aherne that, and old Mrs. Hetty Bunthorne in London did say thus and such," said Father Conlon, mimicking the English accent. "I wonder what that lordling Palmerston has to say of all this," the priest tittered. "Your son's pride is a putrid thing in the eyes of our Lord. Ye don't see it, Maire. That riddles me."

"Let your daft head be riddled by other matters then. Is not our Brigid as much a child of mine? Will I see her wronged? You hush, and let us—just we two mothers—deal with this. You prattle of taxes and gibbering nonsense."

"Gibbering?" sputtered the priest.

But Brigid's da had had enough of this. He felt cheated of all the attention he felt he deserved. He shouldered his burly way before Padraig's ma, who refused to yield an inch, never mind the poteen breath.

"Ye say, Mrs. Maire Aherne, your son is all free and clear, having made a darned fool of me?"

"I don't know, Ruairi Shaughnessy, who is making you a fool. You do it well enough all by yourself. Now hush yourself and listen. You know Brigid is dear to me. And many's the time I have stood by your wife and child—and you gone for months at a time—and she that sick last time when she lost her poor baby boy."

Mr. Shaughnessy felt he was losing ground and rolled his eyes and looked around at the people who had closed in to hear better. But the folks suddenly parted, for Padraig had come out of the cottage into the very center of the milling crowd.

"Did I not tell you to stay inside while your ma talks with all the elders?" his mother said directly.

"Aye, you did, Ma. But I am grown and I must speak."

Mother and son regarded each other as if the crowd, the ugly words had all melted away. Padraig looked at Brigid's ma, who was weeping into her worn shawl.

"Mrs. Shaughnessy." Padraig held her hand and said softly, so softly that I could barely hear the murmur from the edge of the crowd, "Mrs. Shaughnessy, will you allow me to marry your Brigid? I do love her."

No one waited for her answer. Everyone chattered, jostling each other, "Aye, aye, 'tis agreed then. A wedding, a wedding!"

"Father Conlon," said Padraig's ma, "what say you?" The priest was waiting for just an opportunity like this.

"What are ye speaking of, woman?" he snorted, " 'Tis not for the likes of you and your milk-fed lad to make up your mind in this grave matter, is it now? 'Tis the girl's da who'll decide if he lets him marry into his family."

The whole crowd turned to Mr. Shaughnessy, who felt grateful to the priest for his newfound importance.

"Aye, Father, 'tis as you justly say. I'll take my Brigid back to Connemara with me tomorrow where she'll stay out of the clutches of this harridan and that blasphemer. I'll need to think on that matter." He glared at Padraig and his ma. Then he turned and walked back towards the poteen shack which lay beyond the fringe of the village.

"That's it then," Father Conlon snorted, turning on his heel and leaving before anyone could say anything more, happy as long as he had the last word over Mrs. Aherne.

But Mr. Shaughnessy had to return to his cottage thwarted, for the poteen hut had shut down for the evening. I am certain that if it had remained open, he would have stayed up till late celebrating his success and woken in a drunken daze the next day, letting his resolve float away. But he went to bed disgruntled.

He woke early the next morning, and to keep his triumph intact, he roused his wife and daughter. When they resisted his plan, he hit his wife a hard blow across the mouth. Brigid, face turned to stone, gathered her scanty belongings and followed her father so that he would not beat her mother more.

And so our Brigid left for Connemara with her da, before the sun rose and the mist lifted, long before the dew on the spangled grass disappeared.

Before Padraig knew it, Brigid was gone.

• • •

PADRAIG RAGED AND was for going after Mr. Shaughnessy, and perhaps getting into a bruising row with him over Brigid, but his ma reasoned with him, as did I. She was still a young lass whose father could scream for the bailiff, and besides, 'twas usual for Mr. Shaughnessy to show up every two months or so, and now with his daughter in tow, did we not expect him to return sooner? Padraig was spoiling for a row, but this once, Padraig listened to us.

But this time, three months rolled by with no news of Shaughnessy, nor any small sum for his wife, which he sometimes sent with Mr. Rafferty, who traveled about on his business on his trusty cart through the neighbouring counties. Instead what he brought this time was disquieting news. He told Brigid's waiting ma that her husband had left his job and gone off with his daughter. Some said they had headed for Galway, while others thought Shaughnessy had spoken of Dublin itself. But the last bit of talk about that feckless man was his boast that no one would ever find them in America! Now no one rightly knew where they had gone, the obstreperous man and his pale daughter.

Padraig would heed no one and hectored Mr. Rafferty to accompany him forthwith to Connemara. Seeing no way to dissuade him, Padraig's ma provided the money for hiring his cart and Mr. Rafferty's familiarity with roads. Within the month they were back, no wiser. Padraig refused to speak of his futile trip, even to his ma. Shaughnessy and Brigid had disappeared, and no one knew their whereabouts, muttered Mr. Rafferty.

It was Mr. O'Flaherty who finally sat Padraig down and talked him to a measure of calm. Shaughnessy had no fixity of purpose and would never be able to stay away completely, reasoned our schoolmaster, and Brigid had the good sense to return as soon as she could get away, for Mullaghmore was the only home she had known, the place in this big world where she knew she was cherished.

In September, five months after Brigid left, Mrs. Shaughnessy stood silently inside Padraig's ma's shop, fingering the yarn, touching the wool. Mrs. Aherne took care of her customers and came and stood beside her and let her take her time. Brigid's ma found a friendly shoulder to weep on for she had need of that surely. She had got news that her only brother, Liam, was sinking, so she was going to Antrim to live at his cottage and take care of him in his last days. Mrs. Aherne knew that she had not really come for advice; 'twas only that she needed to hear, if Brigid came back, Padraig's ma would send her on to Antrim. It was in Maire Aherne's nature to offer this simple trust and support. Brigid would be safe.

But Mr. Shaughnessy stayed away, month after month.

While Padraig waited impatiently, his raging mind began to be taken over by his other passion—the news of growing turbulence in our land. I think Mrs. Aherne was relieved, for she believed Brigid's return was just a matter of time and Padraig's increasing interest in the unfolding political news kept him away from a bloody encounter should he find the whereabouts of Mr. Shaughnessy.

As the news of Daniel O'Connell's great meetings across the breadth of Ireland hit us, I could see the growling unrest in my mate. After the departures from our village—Brigid gone in April, then Mrs. Shaughnessy leaving her key with Padraig's ma—I seldom saw Padraig as fretful as he grew by the third week of September. 'Twas then he conceived of his plan, confiding first to me and then to Mr. O'Flaherty.

We expected Padraig back in a month, maybe a little more, but by the end of October surely, even if he did stop and gawk, for his head was full of stories from our Mr. O'Flaherty and many of the places of those tales lay on his path. He was planning to walk and perhaps take the jaunting car to Drogheda and then to Clontarf, which was a stone's throw from Dublin, in time for the monster meeting on October 8, maybe even meet the great Daniel O'Connell himself. I would not put that beyond our Padraig.

He did a great studying of maps, and consulted Mr. O'Flaherty, who had been to Kells, to Drogheda, to Birr Castle, and even to Dublin, where he, a young man then, had seen Swift's house. Mr. O'Flaherty's da, he told us, had seen the Dean himself, riding by on his carriage when *he* had gone once to Dublin.

# Padraig

## Mullaghmore, County Sligo

### September 1843

I wanted to strike the blows, aye, bloody and felling, to bring back the old glory days. Brendan loved stories for their own sake, savouring the sweet and sad pith of our Irish tales—but I longed for the sweat and gore of the strife itself. All our Irish songs moved my blood about, and I was so stirred, that lads like Brenfi Clarke or Charley Keelan edged closer, ready to follow me to death. But I knew I would be the first one to charge ahead.

Even our childish games sprang from everything I had absorbed of our history: I would be Brian Boru in the rough-and-tumble games, mock battles among the trees and abandoned shepherd huts as we drove the Norsemen or the English to defeat. We brandished sticks for swords, used stones for missiles. By the time we returned home, we were hoarse and bruised, but victorious.

By sixteen, I went to every last meeting in Sligo, or wherever nearby they speeched about the wrongs done to us Irish, and our undeniable rights. It was always Brendan who would draw me back to earth when I raged against the slowness of time, in our everyday Mullaghmore, and my mother wrapped me in her strong love. I was ready to take up arms in the great uprising everyone said was brewing, but seemed to me to be forever on the pot!

Just last year, I got into an argument with a sailor from Belfast who was jawing fun at our speeches, and though I was only fifteen then, I knocked him about, and he flailing away at me too. We ended in the seawater and kelp by the wharf, and I was for keeping his stupid head underwater until he had a good bellyful of our good Sligo sand, but the watchers all clamoured for me to let him go, for they feared for his lungs and life. So I did, but not before I gave him a black eye for good measure. Och, he scrambled off after his lesson, though he had been full of huff before.

Once the worthies from Dublin or Kerry or wherever the speakers came from were gone, our Sligo would slip right back to its sleepy ways, and us with our daily plod, while I chafed. Mr. O'Flaherty said that the great stir was in the offing.

"When!" I fumed.

"Very soon, Padraig," said Mr. O'Flaherty, "I pin my hopes on Dan O'Connell."

"All he has to do is to send out his call," I grumbled.

• • •

AH, BUT THERE was one more tide that threw me about. I would amble over to Brigid's, and whistle low so her ma did not hear, and Brigid would pretend some chore beyond the haycocks and trees, and I would catch up, and she, breathless and pink, would pretend I was not there. But I was there—and she in my strong surrounding arms.

One day she was near to fainting with pleasure, and after she let me touch that sweet fern between her legs, I knew next time there would be no turning back, and for certain I would be entangled with her, forever and evermore. That time I came home, kissed and bitten, branded like a steer—for in her moments, Brigid was like one possessed, and her rosy lips gripped my soul in a sweet vise of torment.

•  •  •

I WAS BORN in April 1826, some months after my da was dead, but my ma kept our Aherne name bright and ran a good shop, selling dry goods and needles, yarns and pots, wool, seed potato and other sundry things, and hive honey besides. I never wanted for warm clothes, or potatoes and bread, and milk or cheese, which I always shared with Brendan.

My mother, Maire Aherne, stood tall, her flaming hair red-gold, a marvelous tangle to her waist. On those days she washed her hair, it would hang, straight and burnished; then as it dried— and it took time in our Ireland—the natural currents of her hair would begin to crisscross each other, as if in preordained order, becoming a mass of curls. A simple toss of the head, a shake with both her strong white hands, fingers run through the shiny mane, and it was done, as if all her hair had waited to fall into place.

Ma lived as if she were from another, more shining world. Few men had the presence of mind to try her with compliments, for in her manner there was something so direct and clear, so unexpecting of any such levity, that most men who came to the shop would shuffle their feet, and buy, and take their mumbling leave. The women would talk to her about their troubles but stop if any man came in—or any grown child too close.

Oh, she knew how to laugh—aye! —and she was greatly fond of shy Brendan with his head in a muddle of poetry. Our home was not unlike other cottages in Mullaghmore or Dromahair or Lissadel. It was small, but ours was neater, with redder flowers, it seems in my memory. She would make Brendan tell all the poetry. And she, her voice deep, told her favourite poems, which I remember in snatches.

> *On every pool there will rain*
> *A starry frost . . .*
> *The herons are calling*
> *In cold Glen Eila*
> *Swift flying flocks are flying*
> *Coming and going . . .*
> *Sweetest warble of the birds . . .*
> *Each resting stag at rest*
> *On the summit of the peaks.*

That was her favourite. It was a list, a litany, and I do not truly know why it thrilled my heart so:

> *The stag of steep Slieve Eibhlinne*
> *The stag of sharp Slieve Fuaid*
> *The stag of Eala, the stag of Orrery*
> *The mad stag of Loch Lein . . .*

Brigid used to come in with her mother since her childhood. My ma would give her a kiss, and even as she spoke to Brigid's mother, smoothed the child's hair, handing her a bobbin or such to keep her little hands busy.

Since I had my first kiss, Brigid became shy of my mother—as if she thought my mother was all-knowing. In time I found her rose-petal nipples, which grew magically taut, and made me stand still and hard. But my ma said not a word, and watched my awkwardness with a smile out of the corner of her eyes, I knew I was growing up and that she knew it and was letting me grow without intruding herself in that strange and new place, and I was that grateful to her.

• • •

OUR FIREPLACES KEPT us warm, and in their embers we cooked our sod-grown potatoes, delicious as no other, cool and earthy to the touch, cooked to perfection in our very own sod-fed embers, and a lick of sea-salt dried off our Sligo Bay. That was how home tasted: The warm praties with but just a whiff of the peat and Irish mothersoil. I know it in my heart, my mouth and nostrils.

Yet it was far from tranquil in my heart. Between lessons, Mr. O'Flaherty had always told us something new about Ireland. I sat transfixed, listening to our sad and sorry history, brooding, nursed upon the history of all our wrongs.

When the Eighth Henry broke with the Holy Father in Rome, he began the burning down of all our sacred monasteries. In the past, the pious and outraged voices of our priests would be heeded—or at least heard. Our religion itself was now an anathema, another hard reason for the English Crown to send out its troops and its steel. Our very means of calling to our Heavenly Father was now a pretext to damn us as papists, our faith trodden upon.

People here still swear by the sword of our Irish Queen Grania.

She had triumphed on ship and land, around Corraun Peninsula and the slopes of Achill Island. When Elizabeth tried to buy her off with a promise of peace and a title, she was disdainfully told off. No English title could match the one our Grania had already. She died a ruler, and in her own bed, buried royal and peaceful, under the painted gaze of saints on the walls of Knockmoy Abbey. I longed for those lost days of the Irish swords. We heard the stories of later times, complete with songs, and curses: how Sir Frederick Hamilton led the British troops in the sack of Sligo Town. In his Protestant fury, with flaming brand, he tried again and again to burn down Sligo Abbey, once the abode of the peaceful singing Fathers. May his skin rot, mottled by pox, and his eye clutched with sore aches, squint, and motes.

The Abbey walls had figures carved upon them, saints holding tablets, some with gentle palms turned towards the looking folk beneath, benedictions in stone. Though the flames leapt all about, the wall would not crumble or humble, and the holy ones stood, lit by the flames as if shielded within God's holy palm.

That fire finally burnt low, the sky full of stars until the embers blurred into dust beneath the stony stare of the saints. No one had been allowed to throw so much as a spoon of water. The hard and bitter English soldiery had stood by as the flames leapt. But our stone saints remained unharmed, Daniels in this later burning. Such were our few victories in those iron times.

In dark nights here, after the stories and songs, easy 'tis to imagine the sad-faced giant Finn McCoul a-looking seven long years for his bereft and naked son, or Oisin on his gigantic horse cantering a bronze beat in the gloaming. No such heroes rode into our town to save it on that day. But I longed to be with the warriors of the coming day, among my brother Irish.

• • •

To hear Mr. O'Flaherty tell it, our O'Connell was made of the same stuff as McCoul, the great Boru, Cuchulain, with the very mien of the heroes of old. Dan O'Connell spoke for us all, and his words were fiery. Ah, what dreams these words held for us! I had many by heart, and standing on the slope towards Mullaghmore on my way back from school, I would pretend to be the great O'Connell himself and yelled the words out—as if all the gorse-tangled valley, the rhododendron bushes, even high Ben Bulben were my audience.

"Here I am, calling for justice to Ireland. Will you, can you—refuse? You may raise the vulgar cry of 'Irishman and Papist' against me, you may send out ministers of God to slander and calumniate me. I demand equal justice for Ireland. I will not take less. *Refuse me if you can.*"

When I returned home some days, still high with the brave words, my mother would ask me with a chortle, "Will Mr. O'Connell be wanting his praties now?" But she would want to hear the words too, enthralled as I was, by the sheer rightness of them all.

I went wild with excitement the day I read the announcement of our Dan O'Connell's plan, a vast "Monster" meeting on a Sunday, the eighth day of October in 1843. He had called upon all Ireland to come to the fields of Clontarf, next to Dublin, where exactly eight hundred years ago, our great Brian Boru had met the alien Norsemen in armed conflict and battered them, driving them brokenback and spentbreath into the sea. Dan O'Connell's choice of place was masterly. Whoever thought that he was ever too much of a gentleman to roll his white sleeves and pick up the hoe or cudgel for a bleeding turn now thought of the symbolism of the site, the time. My moment had come.

• • •

'Twas morning, and me fretful the whole night before, wondering how and what I'd say to my ma. Finally she brought me my glass of buttermilk and set it on the table by our window, the seaward door open, for it was balmy that September day.

"The whole folk of Sligo Bay think that you are off to Dublin to see O'Connell at his brave meeting. I was wondering if I was going to be the very last to be told." Her eyes were twinkling as she bantered me about my secret discussions with Brendan, Mr. O'Flaherty, even Woolly Rafferty with his game leg and rusty cart, and I grinned back at her foolishly.

"Come here then, you big silly boy. Give your ma a hug and tell her when you leave. Go see a bit of the world. I went to work younger than you. I don't worry about the travel. Be careful who ye travel with. And who you speak with, and what you say. The whole world is not Mullaghmore, or Sligo, or Dromahair. There are people of ill will." Her eyes narrowed. Or did I imagine that? "God keep you safe then, Son, for I can't surely keep you home forever, can I?"

I laughed with delight. This had been easy indeed. "Drink up your buttermilk," she added. "Come back after the brave speeches. Remember, Son, it's to hear you are going, not to speak."

I left on the twenty-first day of September, well in time for the meeting. I had said goodbye to the others, many of whom marveled at my plan. Brigid had been gone for seven long months. By the time I returned, I was certain that she would be back among us, her da tiring by then of his unaccustomed responsibility. If she had not returned by then, I decided to go again to Connemara.

All Brendan said was, "Come back home when 'tis time, Padraig."

As I was about to round the corner on the road, carrying the small bag in which Ma had put her best cheese, bread, a couple of shirts, and such, I turned for a last look. She stood at the doorway looking grand, and her smile lit my world. I turned and set upon my road to Dublin, not knowing how long this journey would be.

But this picture of my ma standing before our cottage, the sun in her red hair, I held in my heart forever after.

• • •

IT WOULD NOT be difficult to find my way to Dublin, for all I would have to do was to travel east, with a little southerly meandering.

Unlike my good friend Brendan, I do not worry over much. If there be something to worry about, I worry when it arrives, and take care of it after. Even when trouble arrives, I try to whistle my way. My quick temper, Brendan never tires of telling me, encounters more conflicts than a reasonable man can hope to find. But he looks up at the sky and at his cape a dozen times, and worries about not taking it. Then he decides it will rain and returns after a few steps to debate at the threshold again. More often than not, it turns out to be a bright day with perhaps a whiff of mist. For these I would be teasing him, and he chuckling at me.

If I had a fear, it was not for the money, for my mother did skillfully sew a goodly number of shillings into my coat within a hidden hem; with my shirt tucked into my britches, these were invisible. I could easily extract, when need be, a shilling at a time.

No, my fear was of the clever people in Dublin who might find me a country dolt.

I headed along the road toward Drumshanbo for the first night's stay, leaving Lough Gill to my left, towards the south of Lough Allen. I was tempted to visit the tomb of the great Turlough O'Carolan. That blind harpist's music, Mr. O'Flaherty used to say, could make the very wind stand still. I had heard that he was buried in the old Kilronan Abbey, but I did not want to stray at the very start of my journey.

• • •

THAT FIRST NIGHT I stayed at a shepherd's cottage outside Drumshanbo. When he heard my purpose, he would not take my small coin for the dry pallet and a few potatoes—though he had naught else. I slept well and headed out again next morning, pausing at the ruined abbeys near Boyle along the way. The Curlew Hills rose beyond.

As I trudged east, county by county, I would fall into a daydream. I had a wild picture in my head of an Armageddon conflict, with all the Irish aroused and that angry, stirred by the words of O'Connell, all of Dublin, the counties around, the Boyne valley, the people around Dundalk and Malin Head and down in Glendalough and Wexford would rise as one, and the great rebellion would spread along the valleys of Liffey and Shannon, along Erne and Blackwater, across the Bann, the Bandon, and the Lee. The English would flee before this great wildfire.

The very name, *Boyne Valley*, rang through my being. Every step I took brought me towards some great name or another: Newgrange, Hill of Slane, Tara, and Mellifont, and then up to

Drogheda itself. It was as if I were treading through the great book of Ireland, and not on mere soil and rutted paths between farms and working fields. 'Twas crowded with the history of my race. I knew that O'Connell would give voice to everything that was clamouring in my heart. The mysterious sacred circles on the stones I saw at Newgrange seemed to capture the exultation swirling within my heart. I was sure I would receive one clear sign of the final battle to come.

• • •

As I APPROACHED Drogheda, I began to feel in my heart that tragic core which underlay the green; how death was a part of all Irish tales, whether they are about love or any other matter whatsoever. So long as folks trod on this land and worked out their fates, there was a backdrop the colour of blood, and every step a tap on the vast drum of Irish memory.

What tales had I heard from my childhood about Drogheda and Cromwell! With his head full of stories of Catholic monstrosity culled from *Foxe's Book of Martyrs,* this Lord Protector descended on Ireland, planning mayhem and calumny. For full nine months in 1649, Cromwell devastated all he could lay his hands on. He besieged the walls of Drogheda. When it fell, he personally directed four days of slaughter. Women, children, the old, and especially the Catholic clergy were not spared.

Was this an aberration in the great man of prayer? Nay, indeed.

When Wexford fell to him, again came his bloody order to put thousands to the sword, children, women, nuns included, even in the sanctuary. "There before God's altar fell many sacred victims. Others who were seized outside the church were scourged with whips; and others were put to death by most cruel tortures," wrote the exiled Bishop of Ferns, in Antwerp.

Canterbury had had its one Becket, a name remembered. What were the names in Drogheda and Wexford? There were so many that the very numbers became a matter treated like an Irish exaggeration, drivel and hyperbole from bogs and poteen huts. Drogheda and Wexford were iron nails in our Irish memory.

When first I came to Drogheda, I made straight for the heart of it, up the steep bank of the river, up narrow lanes, from one level of the town to the next terraced stage, flights of steps that took me above the river. I touched what remained of its medieval walls and felt a great organ's chord ring through my soul as I passed through Butter Gate. In the lowering light, I had the strangest feeling that sounds from the very next lane might not have been made in this century or the last, but further in the past.

Here, in the heart of our Drogheda, I now felt I was truly standing on a stretched skin, a drum waiting to be thrummed. I was ready to wake to a different sky, a different earth. The great meeting at Clontarf was but a few days away. I felt Destiny was sending me an intimation of death or glory, and I would need to step out, beyond our usual Irish strifes and vacillation, to a Gideon's trumpet that shrilled my being, and shook me down to my shoes.

I sharpened my knife on a Drogheda stone that night. Its sheath was snug and I tucked it behind my shirt and gathered my jacket about me. I was headed for Dublin.

• • •

WHEN I REACHED the harbour where the Boyne met the sea, I found a crowd of people already in long, snaking lines. They stood about laughing, chatting, smoking clay pipes, and even a jostle did not bring out ill humour.

They were all for the meeting at Clontarf which, they told me, was a stone's throw from Dublin harbour. Soon we were being turned away, for the ships were full. The only sour note that struck me was when I heard the angry tones of an old man with his grandson trying to board the ship. "Ye are charging thrice what ye charge for this day's ferry, and all of us going to our meeting on Boru's battleground. Are ye not that ashamed, turning a gombeen's profit on Ireland's great day itself?" I did not stay to hear the answer, but it was like a drop of ink in a clear bowl of water, its snaky coils invading the surge and joy of the day. We decided instead to walk south to Dublin, and our stream of folks did grow at every village. "Aye, aye," we would sing out, "we're for Clontarf and O'Connell!"

A tall man from Armagh, his green cap at a rakish tilt, shouted, "When the Catholic Emancipation Act was passed, King George was forced to sign it, weeping and raging. His royal blue nose did dribble, his baggy eyes did so drip, he needed brandy with the warm milk." *Hahaha*, went our crowd, and the walking grew easier, for the mirth was contagious. "The right honourable Peel had to dry off royal tears with his own kerchief, and such was the quantity, he had to have two of his footmen wring out and hang it on the dozy Queen's head—which Wellington mistook for garden topiary." *Hahahaha*. At the end of the day's walk, we lay down on the meadows outside Newbridge. We cooked our potatoes in communal fires, sharing willingly with those that had none, and all was joy and cheer under the coming stars.

I slept fitfully, exultant and troubled, and had a snatch of a dream: I was about to jump off the cliff-face of some high Ben, and a great wind came and swept me off, but taking me in a different direction from where I had meant to fly. I stretched out my arms in desperation and found that I was sailing on that contrary blast—whirling away over a vast sea in a direction opposite and away from a red setting sun.

So vivid was the dream that when I woke with a jolt, I was astonished to find myself on the ground, beaded with dew. I covered my head, curled up, tired and uncomprehending, and fell asleep again and did not wake till dawn.

• • •

IT SEEMED THAT all the world was descending on Dublin. People streamed in to join us from the harbour at Howth. From the north and from the west, people from Fingal and Maynooth joined our column of walkers, waving festoons. As the groups met, we embraced and threw our caps in the air. Some came with their wives and old ones, and a good number had brought children. On a cart, one family even had a goat which the mother milked; her two small boys dipped their victuals, their faces all shiny with milky streaks.

People were coming from the south, with great huzzahs, from Kildare, Glendalough, all the way up from Wexford and Waterford, and hardy folks from Wicklow highlands. I could hear a shrill piping somewhere. I had not known what a heady feeling it was to be Irish—no, not in this way, ever before. I felt that a hundred, two hundred years, from today, the Irish across the world would remember this day. They would paint pictures, imagining this scene. And here it was, before me. Soon we were at the edge of Dublin.

Then we stopped dead.

A wall of red-coated English soldiers stood between us and Dublin, a sanguine wall. An officer came forward on his horse, and after a moment's rearing and pawing of the hooves, the beast stood still. The rider cleared his voice to announce that the meeting had been banned, so there would be none at all, not now, not another day. Far down the right and to the left, more red-coat soldiers came forward. We laughed defiantly. And then, the news broke like thunderbolt: our Dan O'Connell had backed down.

No one in that great multitude believed it. "Liars, damned liars!" Cries filled the air, "Oh no, no no."

The officer raised a white gloved hand. "Those who do not believe me, listen to the Dubliners." The crowd fell silent. "Ask the Dubliners," roared that voice again.

The line of red-coats was, at most, two men deep, for they were fanned out—not for resistance, but seemingly to spread the word. Behind them ordinary people—Dublin folks in everyday clothes, working men and women, stood in crestfallen groups. The wind seemed knocked out of them.

From our side, a tall man with a green kerchief tied about his head screamed loud and harsh into the late morning air, "What news of our O'Connell?"

The air smelt of hay and manure, trampled mud and laundry lye, the smells of a working day. Then a man stooping to pick up a shovel by a dairy cart from the Dublin side spoke, as if to himself. "He's bowed to Peel's command."

We could have charged at the line of red, horsed as they were, and dashed them to the ground and gone on to the sacred soil of Clontarf, urging the latecomer O'Connell to come to us, rousing him from his nightmare of inaction.

But the moment, suspended in time, fell with a silent crash and died amidst us. Weeping broke out, keening, as if the great crowd had just heard that Ireland itself had died.

"What strange nonsense is this?" barked the tall man from Armagh. "Our Dan has not bowed down to Peel, has he?"

The murmur which had begun in our midst rose and wavered around us.

"But," I stammered to no one in particular, "but earlier he had laughed off the Duke of Wellington to his face, and called him a doting corporal!"

"Aye, so he did, and called him a screaming liar to boot," added a man behind me.

"Our O'Connell called that Lord Alvanley a bloated buffoon—and that man the King's favourite, isn't he?" rejoined the Armagh man, twisting his green cap in his hands. Between clenched teeth, I nodded in agreement. Cunning Disraeli had called our leader the hired instrument of the papacy, but our Dan treated them all like barking street strays, did he not?

"Oh Lord, what strange malaise is undoing him now?" the man from Armagh said in a strangled voice. We stood staring at the ground, feeling our despair spreading like a fog about us. By the time I was able to raise my bent head, the Armagh man had left. The crowd began to thin in all directions. Some turned back the way they had come. Some stopped and began to cook and rest before they started for home, dejected journeys back to Cashel and Wexford, Ballyshannon and Limerick, to Cork and Kerry.

The world looked hazy and tainted. I was that tired, I could lie down where I stood and fall into a dead sleep. I wanted no food. I wanted no words. I sat where I had stood, now watching the laughing soldiers leave. I had lost all purpose. After an hour I decided to walk into Dublin, find its harbour, ask if any ship sailed to

Sligo or Mullaghmore, or anywhere to the western counties. I did not want to walk back across my sweet green land, dragging with me the news of our failure. I wanted it washed out of my memory, cleansed with Irish seawater and rough sea-wind.

I stepped into the city, like a blind man following a smell. I wanted to go home.

# Brendan
## Mullaghmore
### November 1843

Three weeks past, we learnt with dismay the fate of O'Connell's meeting and our leader haled to prison.

I could not wait to see Padraig back and to hear from his mouth tales of his travels, although he would be sorely downcast about O'Connell. But he had had his travel. For that I was elated for him, aye, and a trifle jealous, but my widow ma was so sickly and nervous that she would never hear of my going anywhere, though I already knew in my heart that I loved stories of far places more than the actual places themselves. My centre was my home, my gum to this earth. I understood the difference between bookish Brendan McCarthaigh and bold Padraig Aherne who had to touch everything, had to go everywhere, had to risk home and hearth—aye, and heart.

Mr. Rafferty had heard from someone passing through here to Donegal, who had seen Padraig in the great crowd heading towards Dublin, but had no other news besides. Mrs. Aherne was at her cottage door a hundred times, imagining Padraig's tread, restless with growing worry. By the post road, which was some distance from our village, returned another traveler on the fifth day of November.

It was Brigid, belly swollen, far gone in months.

Abandoning her usual composure, Padraig's ma ran to Brigid, her red hair flying, and held her. 'Twas well she did, for Brigid was near to collapse with that much tiredness, and her weeping was dry and fearful, without tears. There was no Mr. Shaughnessy in sight.

Brigid held her belly beneath the thin dress, her legs seeming little more than bird-twigs. Mrs. Aherne led her in, then closed the shop door for the day.

• • •

WHEN MR. O'FLAHERTY heard the news, he sent me over every other day to help out Mrs. Aherne. I could see Brigid by the window behind the shop, the long afternoon beam catching her hair, her palms folded on her lap. Each day since her arrival, Brigid put on the apron to help Mrs. Aherne around the cottage, but by midmorning she weakened, like the new November sun itself.

Padraig's ma let me mind her store and coaxed Brigid to come sit with her. Brigid would crane her head at whoever passed the road, and lost interest when she saw it was not who her eyes sought. At night, Mrs. Aherne told me, she would cry in her sleep, whether from discomfort or the months when she lacked any affection and perhaps food too. She would take Brigid into her bed, under a large Galway quilt, and hum some song to her, or tell her stories as if she were a baby again. Mrs. Aherne had written to Mrs. Shaughnessy. Brigid was too weak to travel. Besides, Padraig would be back any day, and he would marry his bride and put up another room right next to his mother's.

So the days passed, and November grew colder. It would be a Christmas baby, Padraig's ma told everyone, if asked. She gave Brigid some knitting, and herself fell to sewing quantities of little quilts, tiny clothes, socks and bright caps. But I noticed how Brigid's hands would slacken, and the ball of wool lie on the floor beside her, untugged, her knitting needles forgotten on her little progress, her head, almost a burden on her thin neck, bent in shallow slumber.

Barely another week later, Mrs. Aherne told my ma she had woken to find Brigid moaning in her sleep. She held her until the pain abated. Brigid slept unwontedly late. Maire got ready for the day, setting up the breakfast milk jug and the bread and praties as silently as she could. When she gathered her nightdress to shake out in the sun that had come out, she noticed with alarm a large scar of brown, damp to the touch, that stood out on the Aran cloth, then rushed to the bed, knocking the washbowl with a crash to the floor, but Maire was oblivious of the sound, the spilt water, or the china fragments. Brigid had not stirred. Mrs. Aherne ran on bare feet to the bed and flung back the covers. Brigid's gown had ridden up her legs and was gathered about her thigh in a tangle, and she lying like a broken plaything in a lap of blood.

Mrs. Aherne, her wild hair loose and voice frantic, called Brigid again and again. A thread of drool hung from Brigid's mouth, and then Maire noticed a tear gathered under one eye. She was breathing, small and ragged. Maire reached into a low shelf in the cupboard and brought out a bottle of brandy, which she poured down Brigid's sputtering throat. She hauled her up and sat her on the bed between pillows and pulled her dress above the waist. The baby was very low on her thin pelvis. Maire felt for her pulse but could not seem to locate it. She let go of the wrist and held her thumb gently on the bluish neck. Ah, there it was: The slow tap of life. Brigid began to groan, wrenched out of her dead apathy.

Maire could tell the pains were coming. The thin knees were drawn up, her pale feet at the end of her narrow legs were jerking up and down unevenly. Brigid's face was contorted, and she was saying something. Maire bent her head close.

"Padraig, Padraig," she heard, "O Padraig, what will happen to us?"

"I am here, child," soothed Maire Aherne, even as it dawned on her that it was still far to Christmas, a good six weeks, and this clotted blood and the ooze that had wet the bed so early was not a good portent. "Aye, so 'tis an early baby," she muttered, then to cheer Brigid up, she said aloud, "The baby's in a hurry, like his da, who is always so."

Brigid looked at her, uncomprehending, then slowly as the pain subsided, she understood. She smiled tentatively at Maire and asked, "Is the boy born yet?"

Mrs. Aherne laughed in sheer relief. "And how did you know that it is a boy?"

" 'Tis a girl then?" asked Brigid.

"Ah, child," she said, "birthing is not that easy. It's the first wave of the good pain. We will not know if a mad boy it is or a wild girl, until some hours now."

Brigid's face fell.

"Now save your strength, my girl, and don't push yet. I will tell you when 'tis time."

• • •

'Twas not till much later that I came to know about all this. It was the tenth of November. I had gone as usual up to Mr. O'Flaherty's school. More and more these days, it was I who taught school while Mr. O'Flaherty would sit on his chair under the tree in front and enjoy a bit of sun on the odd day, puffing on his pipe. I could tell he was enjoying my telling all the stories he used to tell us, when we were children.

Ever since he decided to teach me all the Latin he knew, he gave me half a dozen books in that tongue. After my teaching of the young ones was over, I would stay on for my Latin lessons, which ran into the evening, and he would offer me some of his simple dinner, embered potatoes, buttermilk, an egg—if his birds had laid. I would be that tired by then, my head full with all the good talk and smoking a twist of his tobacco. I would often take his offer of a straw pallet in the corner of his hut. But this day black clouds had swept up from the Atlantic. Once the thick sea-blown rain started, the roads would be impassable for the next few days. Already the prow of Ben Bulben looked hazy in the light as I walked home quickly.

As I was turned the bend on the sloping road into the village, I saw a clump of folks standing in front of Padraig's cottage. *Ah, he has returned,* I thought and, throwing my bag of books over my back, ran until I was nigh out of breath at his front yard, when something odd struck me.

In the way they stood about, the neighbours seemed shaken, and there was no talk, nothing lively. *What is it?* I thought, *Whatever could it be with Padraig?* There was a bit of struggle of some kind at the front door. I could see the corduroy of strained backs, for they seemed to be pulling something out—and it was surely a bad fit. Then they did get through. What they were grappling out of the cottage was a coffin. I shuddered involuntarily and stood still.

The women had broken into a high-pitched keen but Padraig's mother stepped out, pale and gaunt, and spoke urgently. " 'Twill fright and wake the baby," she said. The women became silent, wrapping their black shawls about themselves. Then all began to follow the coffin box. Father Conlon was there, his head bowed, holding his little black Bible in his left hand, the rosary hanging from it, each bead small as an autumn blackberry ruined by frost.

'Twas a small enough procession that was headed for the cemetery. I followed, numb. We reached in no time, walking through the stone gate on which leant its rusty Celtic cross. The cloud seemed lower now. The hard rain would be upon us in an hour, I feared, with the Atlantic gusts skirling overhead. The keening had started again. The women had all known Brigid from when she was born, and the rocking and the bitter cries rose from their hearts. Mrs. Aherne stood, a little apart from Father Conlon, her grief carved on her sleepless face. She had a look of helplessness. That was the last word I would have thought of, ever, to describe Padraig's ma.

Father Conlon stepped up to her. "I am that sorry, Maire, for my hard words. Where is Padraig . . ." His voice trailed off. I was amazed to see this, but Padraig's ma put her head down on his shoulder. She did not weep. Then she stood back and faced the coffin on the ground. The grave had already been dug. After the prayers, the coffin was lowered. Padraig's ma moved aside and the priest came and stood by her.

"The child's early, Father, much too early."

"You are there to take good care of it. I have faith, Maire, you will pull her through, God grant that."

" 'Tis hard, Father, for she won't feed. We tried giving her milk, but her wee face is puffed and broken in a rash. She is too tiny to keep it down and is fast sinking, I fear"—her voice quavered—"and no one here just now to give her pap. Someone heard of a woman beyond Collooney. She has also birthed, but then, even if she agrees, the weather's turning so, it would take two days at least."

We could hear the neighbours drop handfuls of sod where they fell with a hollow sound on Brigid's coffin. The wind was rising.

"Whatever shall we do then?" said Father Conlon. His distress for the doomed baby was written all over his unshaven face. His Adam's apple moved up and down, and he was close to tears. This was not a Father Conlon I had known either. "Where's the baby now?"

"Mrs. Hanrahan down the lane is sitting with her, by my fire, till I return." Mrs. Aherne clutched at Father Conlon's sleeve. "Will you . . . will you come and give her the last words, Father?"

But before anyone could say a word, there was a wild despairing cry. Startled, I looked and saw an older woman, black shawl fluttering, hobble and run, her mouth open. Her hands were flailing, but her progress was slower than her flinging arms made it look. Padraig's ma ran towards her, screaming, "Where's the baby, where? Oh Mrs. Hanrahan, where is my baby?"

The old woman collapsed on the road, panting, words choked in her breathless throat, just pointing back at the direction of the cottage whence she had come. "Aaah, aah," she panted, bent fingers clawing at her throat. "Aaah . . ." A faint welt, as from a hard blow, was beginning to form on her face.

Mrs. Aherne stood transfixed for a moment, then took off. She was a tall, strong woman, and two nights of sleepless vigil could not slow her. Holding her wide skirts up with both hands, she ran, her feet flying over the stones, and everyone else followed, the men, Father Conlon grunting with effort, the women, and I. But ahead of all of us was the desperate speed of Maire Aherne.

She raced into the dark door of her cottage, her skirts trailing up a swirl of dust from the yard. Motes whirled in the doorway, and then the crowd burst in, jostling to get inside. I stood packed with others.

In the silence of the room with its low red fire, we saw Padraig's ma on one side of the bed. Then on the bed, as our eyes became used to the gloom, we saw the baby, held in grimy hands, its tiny mouth suckling the nipple of half-naked Odd Madgy Finn, whose eyes were closed in bliss.

# Padraig
## Dublin
### October 8, 1843

As I walked into the unknown city, I realized how one could lose one's identity here. One could wear any face in its hurrying crowds.

Even such a wondrous variety of bridges to cross the Liffey every few streets amazed and consternated my head. I drank in the sight of the many manners of houses, arches, painted doors, and the variety of colourful awnings.

I spied a tall column with a figure at its very top, solitary at that great height. I read the name: Lord Nelson. Aye, I thought, that's very like the English to put their hero on a huge height without the benefit of a ladder or even a skimpy rope so he could, of a misty day, fetch himself a nourishing pint!

I walked aimlessly, crossing street after street until I came across a fair building with grand pillars and grounds like a carpet around it. I read the sign in front: So this was the great Trinity College our Mr. O'Flaherty had told me about. It had been the All Hallows Monastery, before it had been snatched by Elizabeth. *How welcome are Catholics here?* I thought, my heart sore at our humiliation. But another thought struck me. In County Sligo where I was raised, I could name those who were not Catholics on my finger: the landlord's agent and some of his henchmen. But here, in Dublin, there must reside such great numbers that could fill such a vast college as this. It stopped me short. I looked about me, at all the crowds that flowed past. I could not tell for certain between Catholic or otherwise. The thought also struck me: neither could they.

Nearby, I came across another mighty building. On its gate was a brass plate, shiny enough that I could see myself leaning forward: Bank of Ireland. So this was where they gather our monies before they take it all away.

People loitered before gleaming shop-windows, staring at lavish displays of merchandise, ladies' dresses in many colours on shiny mannequins, large as folk. Men puffed cigars and pipes, with fine hats and thin canes, not the stout blackthorns of the rural counties. Every part of all the walls that was within reach was plastered with bills and notices. Such a strange world with so much to sell! I thought of my mother's modest shop, its simple, almost severe, merchandise.

This Grafton Street was fairyland itself. There was a large sign, *Jaeger*, on a coloured glass above, and within the thick wide panes, jewels and dazzling silver. A little farther, on a sloping awning, simply the word *Johnson* proclaimed the name of another rich merchant. Fine carriages rolled by so silently that I marveled. Then I understood: Grafton Street was paved with blocks of pine! I thought of the sod thatches and the one-room cottages that dot our counties, whitewashed or weatherbeaten, floors packed with dirt, as were most homes and Mr. O'Flaherty's school. And we Irish leave our footprints wherever we go, I thought wryly, for we live barefoot on dirt floors, and few can afford to lay boards upon their floors. Here the roads—or at least one—might not be paved with gold, but it was paved with that precious wood itself, so no slush marred the dainty ladies who might, from the looks of some, not be as immaculate as their dresses.

There were more fat people here than I had seen from end to end in an entire lifetime in Sligo, toddling about, bellies like lambeg drums, bloated under fancy waistcoats. A fierce variety of moustaches were also to be seen, waxed, in many shades, coaxed up, combed or curled. No wonder, in this big whirling city, folks could so easily shake off such a matter as the Clontarf meeting, which had seemed so momentous to me. As I gawked at the fine shops, I felt broken into fragments. One part of me wanted to prise off pieces of flagstone and fling them into the grand shops full of dazzling goods and ladies and waistcoated men. Another wanted to own a fine shop—any shop—and count the money in the ringing till. Yet another piece of me wanted to sit down right there and weep after the great failure of Clontarf. But all the parts of me were footsore and wanted a drink. Even a tramp's poteen would have been welcome, so bedraggled and low in spirit I felt, all alone in this billowing crowd.

Evening was descending and the crowds draining away, as if abandoning the city for the coming of night. I can hardly recall how long I continued to wander the now-empty streets until I came to a dainty bridge, fancifully decorated with iron railwork. I turned right to go across it, but a man intercepted me and asked me to pay a ha'penny.

"Why?" I asked testily, having just walked over any number of bridges without let or hindrance. He chuckled at me for a bumpkin and said, "Because 'tis the Ha'Penny Bridge, of course."

Not in a humour to be amused by this, I turned on my heel and walked away until I could barely see the high head of the Bank of Ireland. I cared not if I were lost. At the far end of the lane was a streetlamp with a sign that faintly read *Dame Street*. I saw stairs leading below, the blue waft of tobacco smoke, a few feet standing about on the trampled straw, and heard a hum of conversation. I knew it was a place to drink and I longed to rest my tired legs. Did not a man in a brave new city need a drink, heartsick and addled with sights as I was?

• • •

WHY I WANTED my fourth glass of whiskey I cannot tell, for I am not that kind of drinking man—as anyone who knows me from Strandhill to Sligo can vouch. I do like the first warmth of the gullet as it goes down, the feeling of ease. I enjoy the second one's savour of peat and comfort, and am done. But on this day, there was summat in me which would not be comforted. I despise those who turn over their fourth glass and roll their eyes to cry or look for a fight. But I drank as if from a thirst, and a sense of having to let go of something precious. I also knew that soon I would have to find words to defend my lost dream, yet resenting its failure. What a strange state of mind this was.

Two men were talking at my table, wrestling with words. For the better part of an hour, I paid them little attention. I had come with my drinks and sat down with a tired sigh, ankle-deep in straw. The younger one looked a dandy with mocking eyes. He was dressed in a soft brown coat with round copper buttons, his hair thick and curly under a trim felt hat with a tan band around it. The other was of middle years, with a three-day growth of beard, whose talk, as I began to listen, was clearly from farther west, from Fermanagh perchance, or from Tyrone. This older man wore worn corduroy and cloth buttons, and his hands were rough and crusty. I would not be surprised to see him at a hayrick or a threshing, or his leg pushing a spade down to square off and lift sod, or dusting the dirt off the potatoes. 'Twas odd to listen to them—the city-bred and the rough countryman—knowing that such a chance meeting of opposites could only happen over peaty whiskey in a public house. As their animosity grew, I realized I was beginning to pay their words more attention.

"And ye have an opinion of the weather and the parliament and the sun and moon, eh?" scoffed the older man.

The young man smiled and shook his head. He let his finger run round the rim of his half-empty glass, then looked up, including me in his glance. "I could have predicted today's matter, but then I am a betting man. A betting man should know his nag. And I can say confidently, I saw through that Dan O'Connell." He flipped his palm open, as if anyone with sense would agree with him.

A hard meal it was for me to digest the meaning of today, and I grimaced, despite myself. This young suave was speaking as if our failed hero was little more than a gombeen come to cheat us, playing fast and loose with our hopes.

"Mr. Blackburn," the older man said, holding his calloused palms together, as if not trusting them separately, "you are too flippant about a man who has served Ireland well all his life, but fumbles on one cursed day."

Blackburn motioned to the serving man behind the counter. "Will you join us, sir, in a toast?" he said to me directly. I was taken by surprise, not just to be included, but also that a toast was to be proposed. I could tell this Blackburn liked to hold court. The drinks arrived and Blackburn paid. What the older man had said rang fair to me: Indeed, a lifetime of service, and one wrong step; which part sat heavier?

"To Mr. Daniel O'Connell," said Blackburn, and raised his glass.

"Mr. O'Connell!" I repeated, and bolted it down. It ran like fire through me.

But Blackburn was not done with his toast. "To Mr. O'Connell, who makes politics a trade, the master of three great establishments—in Kerry, in Dublin, and in London."

I was aghast and I knew my face showed it. I had drunk my portion. The older man turned to me and, ignoring the whiskey altogether, said to me in Gaelic, "*Ni cuimhnightear ar an aran ataithe.* Eaten bread is forgotten. All that O'Connell has done will not anymore be remembered." Then he extended his hand. "Fergus Murphy from Donegal." I told him my name, and we shook hands.

"You're angry with me, I can see, my friend, so let me make amends. My name is Alexander Blackburn," said the young man to me in a conciliatory tone. "I've been sitting with Murphy here, talking over this matter. I too was going to see the sport at Clontarf."

"Ach," I said bitterly, "you would have gone there not to hear, but to tear him down later at your linen table and fine china. You went there to laugh at us roaring Irishmen."

"Why, Mr. Aherne," he said, amused by my helpless vehemence, "why do you think that at all? I am myself Ireland born. Does that not give us both the right to hear and judge—not simply high rhetoric in a speech, but what is plain sense without the rise of yeasty eloquence? Why can't we talk about it here, or on the lawns of Trinity College"—he gestured expansively—"and up and down our land?" I sensed with rising anger that he needed to have me acknowledge the superiority of his mind, and would be persistent.

I wished bitterly I had not the hedge-schooling by our Mr. O'Flaherty, but such sharp weapons of mind as his teachers at Trinity College had given him. I had never spoken to or imagined anyone like him. He could better me in argument, and I cared not to be shown up. I flung down a shilling—an entire shilling—for his whiskey I had drunk. I felt the shame of O'Connell drench me like wretched sweat.

I stormed up the stairs, into the cool night of October, and headed towards the Ha'Penny Bridge to let my heart calm by the nocturnal flow of the Liffey. The street was deserted, its shops shut fast. The toll-man had left, so I stood on a step of the bridge and leant my head against the cool metalwork. I knew nowhere in this unfamiliar city to lay down my heavy head. How long I stayed thus, I do not rightly recall, but I was rudely brought back by Blackburn's loud laugh as they came up the street towards me. *I'll just stay here and let them pass,* I told myself, as if I were Brendan trying to calm me down. Oddly enough, I had a sure feeling that quiet Brendan, our reading Brendan, would have found words to defeat this smooth city-bred Alexander Blackburn.

I stood and stared at the dark water below. I recalled what Mr. O'Flaherty had once told us. Dublin's name came from the Gaelic, *Dubh Linn*, dark pool.

"There's our Irish Hotspur," chirped Alexander Blackburn as he sauntered up to the bridge steps. "I was telling Fergus here, we need not be simply Irish anymore. We can dream—beyond our small Ireland. The East India Company will make us fortunes. I have this to prove it." He took out a folded paper from his coat pocket. He waved it about, as if it gave him the right to rule the world, then put it back. "With an empire to command, we can be the masters of destiny." I stared at him without any idea what he was on about.

"You, my friend Padraig," began Blackburn again, his smile appearing a grimace to my eyes. *Leave me alone. You belong to a different world. Let me be,* I wanted to scream, but he kept talking. As the roar in my head subsided, he said to me, "Don't you see?"

I did not wish to hear a word of what he was saying.

"Don't you see," continued Alexander Blackburn, moving in closer, an arm's width away from me, "that O'Connell is nothing but a rich landlord comfortable in County Kerry?" He spoke faster, as he picked up his theme. "Remember what your James Lalor said about O'Connell: Not a pane of glass in the parish, not a window of any kind in half the cottages, the peasants on his estate among the most wretched." His words were burning lead.

Fergus Murphy was trying to pull Alexander Blackburn away from me on this deserted embankment. I wanted to put both hands over my ears, and shut my eyes to him, but he shook off Fergus and took one more step towards me. What came over me, I will never know. I pulled out the knife behind my waist and cut a sharp arc with it before his visage. I wanted him to see that and flee. I wanted the triumph of his fear and the sound of his running steps to resurrect whatever it was I needed reviving—aye, my pride—if I have to give it a name.

But he had not seen me clutch my knife. He did not see me draw my arm back. He did not see me fling out my strong right arm in an arc. No, it did not stab him, but he had taken that heedless step, and my knife had snipped away a piece of his neckcloth. He stumbled, saying something incoherent. Fergus caught him. I had put my knife away.

"Blackburn," said Fergus, supporting him in his stumble, "steady yourself. Enough said. This is useless talk. Go you home now."

Alexander Blackburn stood quietly, looking at me with wonder. He raised his hand and lifted his finger, the other hand uncertainly fumbling with his neckcloth, which only I could see was torn. His finger was pointing at me.

"Don't you see . . ." he murmured, and crumpled on the pavement. Fergus looked at him puzzled, looked at me, and then saw the blood gathering around Alexander Blackburn's head, snaking down to the gutter. *Dark pool*, I thought. Fergus knelt by him and tearing off his neckcloth, parted his collar. There it was. On the left side of his neck was the merest gash, and with every beat a gurgle of blood was pouring out. His hands and legs quivered. His eyes had gone still, though open. By the time Fergus stood up, the man lay dead.

•  •  •

"Let me go, let me run." I struggled.

"Nay, nay, there is no time to argue, boy." Fergus Murphy had me in an iron grip. The way he said it made me stand still. "If ye run, and there is found this young rich one, a Protestant boy dead in his fine coat, the Peelers will all be looking for us. You too were seen at the tavern closest here. Listen you, for I'll say this once. Do you heed your da when he tells you?"

"My da is long dead."

"Hush and listen. I am old enough to be your da. Hold his feet, I'll hold his shoulders. Pull him into the shadow of that doorway. Get into his trousers and coat." We raced across the street with our burden. As we lurked, a carriage drove past without stopping.

"It will never work!" I said in sudden panic, "if they catch me in his clothes, it'll be the worse for me."

"This one wild chance—or the gallows for ye," Fergus said harshly. "Otherwise your best hope is Botany Bay for life. Ye'll never see anyone ye loved, ever again."

I felt my fingers trembling and clenched them into fists, my throat too dry for speech at the moment. I could feel a trickle of sweat sear my eye. Fergus smacked me sudden and hard, his hard ploughman's palm stinging me awake to my plight. My fists were up, instantly, before I knew it.

"Is your ma alive?"

I could not speak yet. I nodded.

"A brother ye love?" he rasped. I nodded again, thinking of Brendan. "There's not a moment to lose," hissed Fergus. My head was clearing now.

"His neckcloth is soaked in gore, but the shirt's clean." Fergus was peeling it off while he directed me. "Put on his shoes. Your country shoes will give you away, surely. Do they fit?"

"They're long enough, but narrow," I said, doing quickly as he spoke.

" 'Twill have to do. When you get a chance, soak them in seawater. You have a country boy's wide feet. Nay, nay, put on his stockings first." Fergus rubbed dirt liberally on Alexander Blackburn's neat white feet. I exchanged my trousers and coat, while Fergus mussed Alexander's hair and added a good part of Dublin dust to it, as if he had been traveling and sleeping in the fields. Then he propped up Alexander Blackburn by the doorway. As he was doing all this, he kept telling me all he knew about Blackburn from their evening together.

"You mustn't lose your head and run, boy. You mustn't, do you understand? The reason you have his clothes on is that you're now

Alexander Blackburn. He told me he was joining the Company and catching its ship from the harbour at dawn tomorrow. Nobody knows him there. Nor did he expect anyone. He told me his family is country gentry, from County Louth. Are you listening?"

I knew my life hung on this story's thread.

"No one will be looking for Alexander Blackburn as long as he is alive. When the ship is at Liverpool, make some excuse to get off. Change your clothes, don't forget. Beware your County Sligo tongue. Best speak as little as possible—or none at all." He was smiling grimly at me now. "That'll be the hardest for you. Never lose your temper, boy, for you'll give yourself away a thousand ways and not even know it." I slouched within the doorway.

All this while, Fergus Murphy had been readying Blackburn as he spoke to me in a rapid whisper. He pulled out a small hip-bottle and poured it on the body, and on his groin, as if he had pissed himself. There was a strong smell of whiskey. "That will buy you more time—for who'll care about another poor drunk Irish," he said. "Now we'll go out together, and turn right. Ignore the Ha'Penny Bridge. Go on to the next big one. Walk with me, neither fast nor slow."

When we reached the broad bridge, he said to me, "Cross the bridge and go right. Keep going until you see the lighthouse. Go around it towards the left. You'll see the ship-masts by then. Do not go too early or too late."

"Why are you helping me?" I asked hoarsely.

"There's nobody else. And we're Irish, ye daft fool," said Fergus with a small smile.

"I had meant only to frighten him away," I muttered, almost to myself.

"Aye, I know," he said, "but 'tis done." I began to walk away.

"Padraig," he whispered, and I looked back.

"You're Alexander Blackburn now. Remember that." Fergus whispered sternly, "Keep your wits about ye, lad. Do not write or send word to anyone at all. Remember that!"

I nodded quietly.

"Never talk about this, no matter how you're tempted." Fergus Murphy walked away around the corner while I waited quietly in the night. His footsteps stopped.

"Padraig?" he called out. I remained silent.

He chuckled softly. "Mr. Alexander Blackburn," he whispered.

"Aye?" I replied.

*"Na gearradh do theanga do sgornach,"* he whispered. Then I heard him walking warily back into the heart of Dublin. I walked in the other direction till I was close to the harbour and lurked in the recess of a doorway, out of sight, waiting for the dawn.

• • •

THE QUAY WAS raucous with people, chandlers overseeing the loading and baling, men hunchbacked under grain-sacks and boxes hauled up a wide gangplank. No one took any notice of me. Officers stood by in uniform, for this was the East India Company ship. Little matter, I thought to myself, it may be any company in the world. All I cared was that it carried Mr. Alexander Blackburn to Liverpool, where once on shore, he would disappear in the crowd. Lost for a few days and this Company ship gone, Padraig Aherne would use his mother's shillings and buy a passage, if not to Sligo itself, then to Wexford, or Galway, and walk back home, determined to forget this part of his life.

The loading of the food and materials were done. The chandlers had filled much of the hold. I understood from their conversation that more recruits were expected when we docked. Someone in the crowd laughed and mentioned that O'Connell was in the hands of Peel's men. Obedience to disband the meeting notwithstanding, the English were about clapping him in irons and dragging him for a monkey trial in London itself. I listened wearily and made no show of emotion.

A middle-aged man with a sheet of paper and a dangling pince-nez came over, calling out names. A bleak sun was rising. I had had neither food nor draught of water since last night, and my head throbbed with every beat of my heart. I heard one name that sounded familiar.

"Alexander Blackburn."

I looked around, momentarily expecting to see that young man stride up. Instead the man with the pince-nez continued to look about impatiently. I stepped up, my shoes beginning to pinch suddenly, and stood before him.

"Alexander Blackburn? Why didn't you speak up, man?" he scowled, "we're late as it is. Get your uniform on your way in."

From a table in front of him, a sailor handed me a bundle. As I walked up the gangplank, I could now see the harbour entire. Anchored beside us were a large number of navy ships, Union Jacks flying. Many of these were now weighing anchor, preparing to set sail. From the chatter on deck, I gathered that because of O'Connell's meeting at Clontarf and the dread of open rebellion all across Ireland, the English had barricaded the harbour and poured Dublin full of troops. The great uprising having fizzled, the troops and the ships were pulling away.

This very ship had been delayed for days, and Alexander Blackburn, who came down to join the Company ship, had had to cool his heels in Dublin Town. So Alexander Blackburn and

Padraig Aherne had chanced to meet, thanks to the great Daniel O'Connell himself.

The sea outside Dublin was glinty in the sun, its port far grander than our Sligo. I tried not to stare or draw attention to myself in any way. 'Twas midday already. In Dublin they surely had, by now, found a young man dead by a doorstep, smelling of whiskey. Alexander Blackburn was on his ship, his name marked present on the roster. The secret was safe, for now. Fergus Murphy had given me good advice.

*Na gearradh do theanga do sgornach.* Don't let your tongue cut your throat . . . That is what happened to Blackburn, I thought grimly. I would mind mine.

•  •  •

I COULD SEE the receding top of the Dublin lighthouse, a white finger with a red tip. Sailors climbed barefoot, nimbly among a myriad ropes that hung overhead, tugging some, loosening others, shaking out sails. A red-faced fellow stood on the higher of two decks. Shading his eyes with one large hand, he was directing the operations with the other, occasionally shouting a word or two in a hoarse volley.

"Aye-aye, Captain," the men among the ropes called back to him time and again, and "Yes sir, Mr. Connolly." So this was Mr. Connolly—an Irish captain in authority, no less. I observed him carefully and with respect.

The flag of the East India Company tossed and snapped in the breeze high above—red and white horizontal stripes with a blood-red cross on its corner, close to the masthead. I could now feel the lurch of speed as the willing vessel urged forward.

Evening fell, and a variety of lanterns were strung up in different parts of the deck. The men up in the riggings had now climbed down; they were coppery, long hair in braids, black paint on their eyelids and rings in their ears. They wore no uniform, I marveled. I had never seen men like these.

" 'Tis your maiden voyage then?" The voice behind me was Irish and friendly-like. "This is my second voyage." added the young man with pale brown hair with pride. "My name is Hanratty."

Mindful of Fergus's words, I replied briefly, "Blackburn."

"Those are the sailors from the Indies, Muslims and Malays from India, Madagascar and Penang. They drink from their own barrel of water and eat their own food." Hanratty wanted to show off his acquaintance with the ship and its manners. "They speak their own tongues, but our Mr. Connolly makes himself under-stood," he said with awe. "He is a County Cork man and a right seasoned salt. Hindu or Malay or any man from the East Indies, no matter, he can speak their jabber."

Hanratty was happy to talk on, "These brown fellows—the lascars—they are hardy, no matter how ugly the waves."

All night the big deck shivered and swayed as the great India-man swooped and rose, headed for Liverpool.

I felt exuberant, in spite of myself. Perhaps, having lived by the frothing sea for so long, I had sea legs all along and just did not know it. Overhead the skies were scarred with racing clouds and no stars. I even remembered Mr. O'Flaherty's classroom Latin: No star: dis-aster. But stars or no, Mr. Connolly knew the way to Liverpool. Then at this moment, I realized that I had not retrieved my mother's shillings when I had hurriedly exchanged my coat for Blackburn's. I had not a groat with me for my journey back to Mullaghmore.

*Ach, I will find some way once I am on dry land!* I thought.

I planned to wear Blackburn's clothes under the Company's uniform—which in any case was baggy and hung about me. Once on shore, I would moult from these garments and become Padraig Aherne again. Nothing would keep me from going home.

• • •

WHEN THE NEW recruits had come to our part of the hold, we were shown where our respective trunks, which each one had sent ahead, were heaped. I waited till the others had hauled theirs to their own corners to see the last one: a small trunk marked *A.B.* I had to shake the idea of dead Blackburn watching me, but there was no help for it. I decided to retrieve "my" trunk, otherwise it would be odd indeed. It had a simple padlock. I put the trunk away, but at night I prised it open with a boathook. Inside were some shirts, two pairs of trousers, two novels, one by Mr. Fielding and the other by Mr. Sterne, and a number of embroidered hand-kerchiefs. Underneath these was a small oval portrait of a hand-some lady of mature years, probably his mother. I felt a stab of grief for the obdurate young man and unexpected sorrow for this unknown lady. Then I thought, perhaps she is dead. But I knew I was trying to find ways to ease my burden. I dropped the portrait in the waters, unable to look at it again.

Tormented, I lay on the unfamiliar hummock among other swaying bodies. I thought of Brendan, who was surely reading into the night, as was his wont, as long as his tallow candle would not sputter out. He could never imagine what I had lived through in the last two weeks—well, in the last one day. As I grew drowsy in the sway of the ship, I thought of Brigid and our last kiss. Had she returned to Mullaghmore? Then I recalled the trickle of blood on the pavement, and Blackburn lying dead, and became stark awake, throat dry, heart pulsing. I stifled my groan.

I could not tell when I fell asleep but woke with a mighty start and went on deck. A recruit was screaming, shaking off some that tried to restrain him. But the fellow was strong, flailing his hands and legs, and his mates fell thick and fast around him. A door burst open in the upper deck. Mr. Connolly seemed to fly down the steps.

"Tell me it ain't so," screamed the recruit. "I just heard we are not to stop in at Liverpool. My mother is coming to meet me there. Dammit, why go to London port direct?"

Mr. Connolly brought his hand down, and the riding crop crackled across the recruit's face. A red slash appeared instantly on his inflamed cheek, tearing his lip down to his chin. He drew his breath in surprise and his palms came up to protect his eyes. Mr. Connolly struck him again. He fell on the deck with a wheezing cry. Mr. Connolly stood over him.

"What's yer name, man?"

"Blegg, sir," he mumbled through his bleeding mouth. "Walter Blegg."

"Then listen, Blegg," said Mr. Connolly. "Listen well, all of ye," he added, raising his voice. "This is my ship and I command it. I answer to the Honourable East India Company and to God, in that order. No one else. I decide where we anchor. Your ma will have to forgo the pleasure of feeding her pap to you, Blegg. But first ye'll be whipped at the mast, ye screaming monkey." Blegg had pissed his pants, gaping with undisguised terror at the lascars standing like shadows. One of these, his long hair tied in a black kerchief above glinting earrings, smiled openly in anticipation.

I never thought I'd live to see it, my heart's blood pounding in my head: An Englishman was being tied to the thick mast by the command of an Irishman, whipped by a black man in full sight under a blue sky on a swift sea. I had traveled to a different world altogether. But if I were to escape and go home, where was I to do this—now that we were not to stop at Liverpool?

I could not take my eyes from the whipping, as if commanded by some dread magic. The crimson drops flew as the man deftly swung the many-stringed knotted flail. One bead settled upon my shirt, but I knew if I tried to brush it off, I would only smear it worse. It was the second time in these last few days that I'd had blood on me, Irish and English, though none of my seeking. Yet how ironic, green and eager as I was when I walked towards Clontarf and the great meeting which never was, I had been that enamoured of the idea of spilling English blood. Now I felt unable and unwilling to tell the difference.

No matter what Fergus had said, I would someday tell all this to my mother. She would understand, as nobody, not Brigid—not even Brendan—ever could. I missed her sorely, to the point of heartbreak.

• • •

ON THE THIRD night, I dreamt that under my hammock was a gathering pool of blood, and I could see the last tremor of Blackburn's hands. I dragged myself through the following day in a stupor. In all my daydreams of glory, shed blood had the bright colours of a printed page, but the killing of Blackburn weighed me down in a manner I had never imagined. Not once did I long for a kneeling confession in our weekly church and Father Conlon's absolution. I needed something else, but could not name it.

The following night when I lay down, I did not know what joy and despair was to assail me. Some fickle god was at his game. I had taken my shoes off and tucked them next to my head, when I heard something shift in one of the heels. Cautiously, I looked around, but everyone was asleep; some were snoring. I took the shoe and looked closely. 'Twas well-made, with a pewter buckle, compact and with a good heel. On an impulse, I twisted the heel. As it slid open, something fell on my chest, and I put my palm down to hide it, pretending to turn in my sleep. After a moment, I looked down and found it was a gold guinea! I wanted to shout about my Irish luck, but clenched one fist in another, a-quiver with excitement.

When I had control of myself, I twisted open the heel again and there were two more, wadded in cotton. I counted them in the darkness, with my blind palms and fingers. One two three, one two three. *Aaah*. Now it was the turn for the other shoe. Again, the heel slid open at a twist, though it was not easy; it was well made. Another three coins. A sum of six. This was a great amount, no one needed to tell me. Now I need have no worry for my journey back. This was also an amount for which anyone on this ship would kill Alexander Blackburn for the second time in his young life. I hid my coins where I had found them. How easily I called them *my coins* now!

By the time we came on deck, morning had broken. The English land lay to our left like a low cloud. There were clouds aplenty above us, great piles of slate, promising a drizzle. They said that this part of England gets sodden for days. We wandered about the deck, munching our bread, and saw a number of large and smaller ships lying at anchor. I wondered impatiently when we would get ashore. Some of the crew had already spied bedraggled creatures along the quayside, brazenly waving to them. I saw that one of them had an open Oriental fan in her hand, like a full deck of cards—and she fanned herself, while touching her bared breast with the other.

But first, provisioning boats arrived from the chandlers—more sides of dry beef, sacks of flour, barrels of rum from the sweetish smell, and bales of coloured cloth. Then the new recruits came aboard. There would be little turning room belowdecks. But what did it matter? Soon to be on London ground with a whistle on my lips and gold coins in my shirt, I waited impatiently for Mr. Connolly to give the order, but it was already noon and mealtime. We were given large portions of bread and dried beef. I ate with relish, as I had worked up an appetite. One of the sailors joked, "Eat up, boys—and those that can't, give me your share—for I will need my strength tonight. I saw pretty Dolly or whatever her name be, waiting for me by the quay." They clapped his back in companionable mirth.

At the captain's call we gathered on deck. A steady wind had set in from the land by late morning, clearing the clouds, and a golden slab of sun fell on the waterway. It had turned into a glorious autumn day.

Mr. Connolly, on the upper deck, looked at all the men gathered on the deck. Some lascars stayed on the rigging, listening. Suddenly one new recruit, a greenhorn in well-fed euphoria, sang out, "God bless ye, Mr. Connolly, and this ship on this grand day."

I waited with bated breath to see what would happen. He would like as not get the whip, for he had dared to speak out of turn from the deck, directly to the captain no less. But Mr. Connolly, smiling broadly, said in his booming voice, "A glorious day to ye all." The ship broke into cheers.

"I've told our steward, Mr. Philpot, to give ye a full measure of rum," said Mr. Connolly, "with the evening bread and extra beef." Mr. Philpot waved from the side of the lower deck, acknowledging the great hurrah that rose all around the ship. The new recruits were looking around with shining faces, expecting this to be a Christmas ship itself.

"My good men," continued Mr. Connolly, "do ye see all the good signs? The sun has broken through, the wind is steady—and I know the winds. We'll cast off now, men. Soon we will be west of France, then to the Africa coast and the Good Cape, and away to India. Let's drink to that with our good rum!"

I heard mutters and wary grumbling, but no one dared to raise his voice. The disappointment about the sorry wharfside wenches faded, and the lascars sprang upon the rigging to let out the sails, which shook loose, filling with wind, and the ship slid seaward.

Staring with a sick heart at the receding land, I thought how I had found myself rich and lucky. Now I wished myself shoeless and penniless on that alien strand; I would surely have found my way back, somehow, to my lost home in Mullaghmore.

As I looked, the name of this damned place, painted on a faded wharf struck my eyes: *Gravesend*. I was being taken to India, on the other side of the earth, away from my waiting mother, sweet Brigid, and my friend Brendan. I felt my heart was dying. It was the thirteenth day of October 1843.

I went down to the hold and wept.

# Brendan

## Mullaghmore, County Sligo
### 1845

A great disquiet descended on us when Padraig did not return by Christmas. Mrs. Aherne took Mr. O'Flaherty with her down to Sligo to consult with Peter O'Connor, the businessman who knew some important people in Dublin. His recommendation was that we conduct an inquiry in Dublin itself.

Everyone thought that Mrs. Aherne could not leave Mullaghmore, for the baby was too small, but she made arrangements to have Mrs. Hanrahan stay with the mite, and with Odd Madgy Finn proven to be regular as clockwork, and the baby thriving now, there was no let or hindrance for her quest.

Old Mr. O'Connor agreed to accompany us, and we made the rounds of the grey buildings where, with the businessman's intercedence, the great ones of Dublin deigned to speak to us. But it was all futile. I could think of no words of comfort as Padraig's ma's face grew more gaunt each day.

On Sabbath afternoon, I went on a solitary walk by Dublin's port when I ran into Declan Clooney, a sailor friend from Mullaghmore, just returned from a two-month sail, and quite surprised to see me in Dublin town. When I apprised him of our search, Declan became agitated, for he had news of Padraig. He claimed that a friend of his, Ben Gantry, with whom he and Padraig used to have a dram or two at Sligo, had spied Padraig in a fancy suit on the next quay boarding some ship, a large one. Surprised, Ben called out to greet him from his deck, without success in the wharf-side din.

"And he is sure?" I exclaimed.

He certainly was, swore Declan. So I dragged him forthwith to Mrs. Aherne and Mr. O'Connor, who made detailed enquiries about departing ships from that period. But since Ben Gantry himself was away on another ship, and so many others had sailed from Dublin to such a variety of destinations, that we had to resign ourselves to the prospect that Padraig would return when he did.

"He is alive," whispered Mrs. Aherne.

"Yes," I responded in relief, "yes, thank God."

• • •

BUT THE MONTHS passed.

Now when I got up of a morning and had the peat fire on the grate a-going again, Mr. O'Flaherty was the first to come and sit by it. The pupils came much later. I took the time to pray and walked upon the headland, and when I returned, the mist still smoky about my shoulders, I put the kettle on the strong fire where it began its day's work with a hiss. Mr. O'Flaherty gropes for his glasses until, like as not, I find them for him. His left eye had a milky ring around its blue centre, and the other one was none too strong. He had aged in the last few months. Although he has never talked about it, I felt, in an obscure way, he held himself partly responsible for Padraig's disappearance.

I had built another room attached to it, so that we had what space we needed altogether. He had asked me many a time, and when my poor ma died one silent night last winter, and Mr. O'Flaherty getting more slow and wanting my company, I made up my mind. What use was it trying to keep that cottage? I could not carry its tax, small though it was. Truth be told, 'twas a relief for me, that decision—for in the evenings I became sore miserable in that cottage without the putter and talk of my gentle mother. Soon it would fall into itself, and the good earth reclaim it as if my parents' lives had never existed.

With Padraig disappeared from the very face of the earth be-seems, and I teaching all the lessons at the hedge-school, I thought to move in once and for all. It had suited us both. The children came, bright-eyed with the walk, and I led them in prayer before we got down to the lessons. When we did the recitation for the tables of multiplication, in that lovely singsong way, I always glanced out the window, expecting to see Odd Madgy Finn a-rocking with glee, keeping time with the numbers, but she did not come here anymore. The tree under which she used to sit had flourished and cast a generous shadow, but it had no company all the school day.

Madgy had nursed poor Brigid's child, but refused to sleep in the cottage, although Padraig's ma had so wanted that. Mrs. Aherne would set her out some thick slices of good bread, a pratie or two, slices of cheese on a china plate, and a glass of buttermilk, but Madgy got it in her muddled head that the good plate and clean glass were for someone else. She would not touch them—but re-turned stealthily when Mrs. Aherne attended to the shop—to steal from her pantry, broken pieces of pratie, hard heels of cheese, even some rancid lard about to be thrown out.

Padraig's ma saw how matters stood and began to leave choicer bits by the kitchen corner as if waiting to be thrown out to the dogs. Madgy Finn always ate them with relish, after which she would go off, pissing behind hedges, wandering about the hills. She would sometimes be seen walking the mudflats, toes kicking up sludge near the estuary, or on a rock in the afternoon, licking a fistful of dry sea-salt, her eyes closed in contentment or hunkered on all fours, arse in the air, drinking with loud, happy noises from a stream halfway to the Ben. Padraig's ma had worried that Odd Madgy Finn would forget about the baby altogether someday. She tried to keep an eye on Odd Madgy Finn's whereabouts, but 'twas no use whatsoever. Madgy would come back, never late for a nursing, as if the feeder and the fed were tied together by an invisible cord, and one knew about the other's need, and nothing else was a let or hindrance.

Despite Madgy Finn's dirty fingernails, unwashed hair, snot-ringed nostrils, drooling yellow mouth, the child flourished, with a headful of black curls, and everybody knew what Padraig's ma saw before her eyes—she was a little Padraig, even down to the way she ran, on her toes, and the way she called out "Ma" for Mrs. Aherne, though no one had taught her that or otherwise. But her very first word was "Moomagy." It was a word she had made up and was cross if anybody else said it.

When she cried out that name, no matter when or where, Odd Madgy Finn would bare and offer her goose-pimpled breasts to the child. The infant would suckle noisily, her minute palm playing with the other nipple, which would grow moist and ooze. Padraig's ma would turn away, her face flushed with envy for mad and filthy Madgy Finn.

Maeve—as Padraig's ma had named her—was that lively and that wild, and proved as much the prideful Irish as Maire Aherne herself, screaming and scratching her way when she would not be held. But she used to lie perfectly docile of her own free will on the filthy lap of Odd Madgy Finn. One day she would let her grandmother tie her hair with ribbons and flowers and braids; the next day she might not let her come close, or so much as make a stroke with her hair-comb. Maire had met her match and was completely in her power.

By this time in 1845, Maeve was almost two, and could lead anyone a merry romp about the kitchen garden, sometimes pulling up carrots to see if they were growing, to the distraction of her grandmother. But after a long time of running and hiding and chasing the chickens, and jumping about with the village dogs, she would call out, "Moomagy, Moomagy!" and our Odd Madgy Finn would appear, already with her bare teats flopping and thwapping about her chest as she ran and stumbled, speaking some excited babble into Padraig's yard. Passersby would halt in their stride before they continued, shaking their heads.

Our children are usually edged out by their younger brothers or sisters, so at what age Maeve would be weaned was something none seemed to have thought about. By now Maeve was a romping child, and no more in real need of pap milk than I was. But there was no way to dissuade Odd Madgy Finn from showing up, or of Maeve calling and claiming her Moomagy.

• • •

WITH THE FIRST falterings of the potato crops from that summer of 1845, more and more wandering men drifted through. In the past, even the tramps that limped and begged on their migratory paths were familiar to us, but these strangers were a different breed altogether, desperate, angry, rooting all over the land, mostly men, but sometimes women with children. The older boys—not yet men—roamed, but without the softer ways of boys, harder, dirtier, feral.

Then one late autumn morning, in spite of Maeve crying, "Moomagy, Moo—ma—gy . . ." all over the village, and time rolling into evening, there was no hide or hair of Madgy Finn to be seen. Poor Maeve ran between Mrs. Aherne's room and the street a hundred times, fretting herself and crying, until she came down with a small fever. Then, as a child does, she grew to accept the first great absence in her life, a weaning from the sure certainty that all children are born with—that it was no country where loss could come their way, that nothing would ever change in that place called home.

• • •

WITH PADRAIG GONE, I really did not know how his ma would live on. She mourned him in that hard silent way that can kill people. I would see her sitting at the door of her shop, even as I turned the lane to enter the village—and she would be looking eagerly, and then her face would fall. Oh, she was glad to see me, but every shadow around that bend in the lane held a breathless hope for her. There were crow's-feet around her fine eyes now, and more than a frosting in the wild gorse of her hair.

Returning once from a solitary walk to Sligo, I paused to look at a scythe moon bent above the Bulben, when I spied Mrs. Aherne at her cottage-door, its peeping light catching a a part of her face. "Come to me, Maeve," she was saying soft, "come here, girleen, come to me," her voice breaking on itself. The child stood leaning upon the heartless white wall, seeking someone else in the dark. "Moomagy," she said into the darkness, "Moomagy?"

I left them, each to their separate seeking, and made my quiet way.

• • •

BUT OTHER HEARTBREAKS were beginning all over in our counties. Panic began to seep in like unruly tidewater the following summer. The blight had spread after the potatoes were dug. A white smear under the leaves of the potato plant had been thought the culprit. But now with the fine potatoes harvested and put away, no one expected trouble, thank God. This year's green vigour of growth had shown, at first, no sign of any milky mould among the leaves.

Whether the disease had lain dormant in some diseased potatoes which got planted—or whether the deadly spores had outlasted the winter—our hopes were dashed. The blight had grown within the shoots themselves, and the dreaded white mould reappeared. If the weather were dry, the mould would die off and no great harm done, but Lord help us if the weather was wet.

Heavy rains were general all over Ireland. 'Twas warm, but we did not know how cold a fate awaited us in that downpour. News of the spreading mould fell like night throughout the land. Rumours ran that harvests were scanty in all of Europe. 'Twas small comfort knowing about your neighbour's sore throat, when it is spitting and pouring blood you are, your chest riddled with death's pain itself.

Now came the dread news of the potato crop turning black and pulpy, stench rising as the spade turned. At first we heard news of the distant counties, of field after field of potato turning squalid and sodden-like. Niall McCabe in our village had the occasional letter from cousins in County Clare, where he said that such was the hunger among folk that notwithstanding the fear of fever, they were peeling what was putrid, eating the small stained morsels, and by so doing, dying in small and steady numbers.

At the outset, only some far parts of Ireland seemed affected, but by the end of summer, people were coming from distant parts, rooks in the failing day. In our village everyone hid his dwindling store of victuals. The strangers kept coming, wandering bleak-eyed about town and village, sat down and starved. Their stories were like black rain settling on our seaside Sligo villages. They left trails of detritus where they rested. We shut our doors and grimly waited, as did the wolf of starvation at our door.

Few pupils came to us by autumn. If a handful did come, they had had no food. When we shared what scraps we could, they fell asleep exhausted. If truth be told, they were too thin and blue-veined to make the easy climb up to the school. And what could I teach them, their faces droopy like drying flowers by midmorning? They stopped coming, except for little bright-eyed Ruairi Doyle.

There was, it seemed to me, all over our land, not the usual smell of meadow grass and Atlantic kelp by the shore, the sweet breezes by the loughs, but a strange odour of decay, as if under the green skin of earth its veins were throbbing putrefaction in myriad channels, finding the way into the fields. The potatoes were inedible foetid messes which offended all senses. Left underground it was feared that they would pollute the soil forever. Starving cadaverous figures were seen either tearing up the soil to find acres of ordure and black squelch, or sitting around in a daze of exhaustion and despair, contemplating with bleak gaze the prospect of soil gone bad forever. There were no birds left, no squirrels. The land had fallen silent.

Up and down did the skeletal strangers walk and beg, and I was reluctant to go outside now unless I had to. Mr. Rafferty, whose work took him to the neighbouring counties, came by in his cart one day and told us that government people had set up their few depots and were giving out small doles of yellow sulphurous American maize pellets, telling starving folks how to cook these.

"At least that's something," I said, resolving to ask for directions.

"Nay"—he waved his hand—"that was soon consumed, and on the morrow there was nothing. They also opened a number of soup kitchens and an uncontrollable number lined up."

"Was there enough?" asked Mr. O'Flaherty, who had joined us by now.

"No chance of that," said Mr. Rafferty, spitting on the ground in disgust. "One in four fought to get fed. The other three were too weak to protest when 'twas gone. Now these soup kitchens are gone."

In spite of what Rafferty had said, I set out next morning for Sligo to see if any other succor was available. At the outskirt of town I saw people lying down, covering themselves with what rags they had. I recognized some of the evicted ones. The children had oddly swollen bellies, and clung to their mothers' wrinkled dugs. In Sligo, I heard rumours that in County Cork some dogs that had escaped being caught and eaten had turned feral and begun to prey on people. Ned Behan, whom I met at the quay, swore it was in Limerick. He told me about his brother-in-law Sam Clarke, a bachelor who lived near Cliffoney, had been found dead, lying in a ditch and wearing his fine coat. No one had wanted to buy his fine apparel, for food or coins were not to be had. Ned also told me of a stranger who had come by two heads of cabbage, eating them under a leafless tree. Returning the next day, Ned found him lying there dead. As so often happened when the starving ate, their unaccustomed stomachs gave way.

• • •

Now we were beginning to hear that the great landowners away in England had decreed that it was best to clear out the land and have far fewer tenants. After all, most of them produced little above their own sustenance. Where their tenants would go was no concern of theirs: They were free to go where they pleased. 'Twas a free country, our Ireland, and no slavery here, surely.

One day, my last remaining pupil, Ruairi Doyle, brought news to our schoolroom; Mr. Arkwright's men were coming from the direction of Lough Gill. They had two horse-drawn carriages. Ruairi had seen a strange contraption on one of these carts.

Mr. O'Flaherty was abed with a fever and a hard cough. Having little but worry to occupy myself, I sauntered down towards the village, when a commotion greeted me. Now I saw it was a battering ram. Balanced with ropes on what was a huge timber tripod, it was a machine, true enough—but a crude machine that bespoke our own tragic ingenuity. The three logs were tied together, as if it were a stook, with a heavy log suspended from the top.

When I came down to the village, it was as if I had been transported to that day of our childhood when Padraig and I watched the felling of Fintan's home.

The men had arrived at Purdy's cottage, and were trampling about, their boots covered with mud and manure, quite unmindful of Mrs. Purdy's flowerbed and the sundial their little boys had set up from learning about it at school. Mr. Purdy sat hunched and woebegone on the dirt, but his wife was going on pleading, with Mr. Arkwright shaking his head from side to side as if bothered by a slow fly.

" 'Tis that long we've been here . . . Mr. Arkwright, sir . . . All that time that my husband was a boy himself. Forty years now. You know what a hardscrabble living 'tis here, and now the potatoes rotten in the ground. We done paid our taxes year in and year out—and look, sir—our youngest is but six months old." Twisting her arms helplessly by her side, tears streaming down her smudged cheeks, Mrs. Purdy, staring ruin in the face, and her small children looking up at her in wonder, did the ugly weeping of the desperate poor, her mouth distended, veins standing out on her throat.

The men had set up the contraption close to a miserable cottage at Mr. Arkwright's bidding for the game they called Tumbling.

Mr. Arkwright was not even looking at her when the first thud sounded. Mrs. Purdy cried out. The men grunted and pulled it back again as far as it would go. Mrs. Purdy's balled hands unwound and dropped by her sides as she watched, as if entranced by the action.

As the ram was released, it moved forward with a rude elegance, rising a little at the end of the short trajectory before crushing the wall. The roof leant forward, the sodded wall and thatch tilting. The hut appeared an animal gut-hit, fallen on its knees before lying dead. The weak wall fell, and then a lower chunk of the sill. The interior of the mean little cottage with its tawdry poverty lay open. The ram swung again, and this time the roof cracked, and the hut lurched.

There was hoarse weeping, a terrible noise—and everyone was startled. It was Mr. Purdy, squatting on the ground, beating his open palm on the dirt by the road. His stubbled cheek looked like red bellows. It is a terrible thing to hear a grown man weep, out in the open before everyone, forgetting everything. Such crying is kept muffled, secret, for it shreds the heart of the weeper and taints the sweetness of our humanity. His children watched open-mouthed as their father wept. I felt like a felon myself, but there was nothing I could do.

But one person did not feel so. Padraig's ma had emerged from her shop and, running as swiftly as she could, she flung herself on the machine. The pole she had pushed with flying frantic strength buckled and came collapsing down. Amid the confusion, Mrs. Aherne picked up a shard of broken foundation rock and hit the man who had set up the machine. Before his bullyboys could do anything, the man fell like a dropped sack.

The bullyboys were upon her instantly, but she was a lynx, sharp and agile. She had kept hold of the sharp rock and threw herself forward and hit out at the midriff of one of them. He staggered back, but then a second one took a mighty swing and knocked her to the ground. The rock fell out of her grasp, and lay under her helpless palm. Mr. Arkwright's assistant moved quickly for a large man and held her down, and the young man who had knocked her over smashed the heel of his boot down on her white palm, trampling it hard underfoot against the foundation rock under it.

What happened after, I do not exactly remember. "Let her go, let her go, Burridge," Mr. Arkwright was screaming. "Let the woman go, she is known to his lordship. Don't hurt her, let her loose!"

I must have done something too, though by God, I am not one for fisticuffs. There would have been murder if Padraig was around, and anyone touched his ma. I carried Mrs. Aherne back to her cottage, and the village so in turmoil and roaring, that Mr. Arkwright with his tax box and his men beat a hasty retreat, leaving behind their ramming machine for the time being. The silence of rural Sligo came back with the soughing sound of the sea as the wind turned. I noticed then that the knuckles of my hand were torn and bruised and that swollen, that some must have been missing their teeth in the night.

What had Mr. Arkwright meant by saying that his lordship knew Mrs. Aherne? I remembered Father Conlon's snide words, how Mr. Arkwright had never once come to her to collect taxes. There was surely a mystery here, but I would never be able to ask Mrs. Aherne, never.

I had washed her face, which was bruised and bleeding, and in one hand three of her fingers were mangled and purple, with marks of hobnails on her wrist and palm, where the man had stomped. It was impossible to see how deep the punctures were. I tried to wash the dirt from her hand but she kept it clenched. Opening her fist would ease the pain, I pleaded, opening it slowly in the cool basin of water I had got for her. But she looked lost in thought, keeping her palm tight shut, refusing to relinquish whatever it was in her mind, making a fist—it came to my mind—making a fist at Destiny itself. I added some drops of lavender, ever her favourite perfume, but she could not unclench that fist in the cool water of the basin. She was oblivious of all my ministrations. The blood in Mrs. Aherne's tight-curled fist refused to melt and remained a clotted stigma. She waved me away, went to her bed, turned her face to the wall, without bidding me goodbye, and closed her eyes. The child clung to her like a cub, silent and watchful by wild instinct.

I knew from her breathing that Padraig's ma was not asleep,

nor likely to be anytime that night. I could not get rid of the smell of blood and the faint stench of black potato rot from my head, and shut the door after her and went home.

• • •

> *And mark in every face I meet*
> *Marks of weakness, marks of woe*

The words gonged repeatedly within my head, those lines from Mr. Blake's poem.

> *In every cry of every man*
> *In every infant's cry of fear . . .*

I was haunted by the pictures of the heap of rubble left in the wake of the tumblings, knowing there would be more. For the next three days I stayed brooding at home, and Mr. O'Flaherty stayed in bed, recovering. It was on the fourth day when I could bring myself to tell Mr. O'Flaherty of the depredations in the village. He listened, with evident displeasure at my delay in telling him, and decided that we must go immediately.

"I need to see Maire," he said, uncharacteristically short with me.

I felt guilty about not having made any queries about Mrs. Aherne in all this time, for I had simply assumed that she was mending, as were my mangled knuckles, and like all the Irish of the land, we were making the best of what was left for us.

We went slowly, for Mr. O'Flaherty with his blackthorn stick seemed to poke at the world at every step before trusting his footfall. He was yet too proud to take my elbow although I would have gladly offered it. I could see his white hairs and pink pate as he bent to read the path before him. In his hurry, he had forgotten his hat.

It was a shock when we finally reached Mrs. Aherne's door to find it ajar. To be sure, I had not expected the shop to be open, what with such want and hunger all about us. I entered and was astounded, for the store had been looted. It was not the kind of wild looting as if there were a riot, but it had been emptied, trays bare, drawers pulled open. Some useless fragments lay on the usually spotless floor. It was as if thieves had come by night, and heavy objects removed—sacks of seed potatoes, jars of biscuits and sweets, barrels of apples, rolls of fabric—but measuring ladles, the yardstick for marking off cloth, were lying neatly on the counter. The thieving had been done deliberately and thoroughly. There was no spillage, no careless tearing or hurried abandon. That was the most terrible part of it all.

I could hear Mr. O'Flaherty wheezing softly behind me. I thought him winded and worn out by this short walk. When I turned and he looked me full in the face, I could scarcely bear to read the knowledge in it. He was weeping silently, occasionally stopping for air, and his tears ran down unchecked. He saw all this about him as clearly as I did. Was Mrs. Aherne alive then? I was too terrified to look into the next room. But Mr. O'Flaherty moved purposefully.

"Maire," he called, "Maire, it is myself, Schoolmaster O'Flaherty. I know you're abed, but I need to speak with you."

He walked into the inner room and slumped down in the chair at the head of the bed. In the dim room, Mrs. Aherne turned to look at him with her enormous eyes. Her face was gaunt, and it was clear that she was gravely ill; her body seemed wasted under the covers. And it was then that my eye caught the sight of her arm. It lay bare to the shoulder, and somehow it was transformed into a monstrous thing. Her nails looked now like cracked fish scales pasted loosely on a bloated claw. Along her arm, the veins stood out like black wires, twisted one over the other, or ran skittery along the inflamed skin, hopelessly distended and oozing in parts with a deadly gum.

"Brendan," she said to me directly.

"Aye, Mrs. Aherne," I replied, wondering what I could do.

Mr. O'Flaherty sat by the bed, his blackthorn planted between his feet, his chin on the hands with which he held the stick. I could not see his face, but could read the slump of his shoulders well.

"Brendan dear," Padraig's ma said again, "coax the silly child to come out from under the bed, will you?" Her voice had resumed its usual strength, as if nothing was amiss. It even sounded amused, as it used to be, by one of Maeve's pranks. I knelt down on all fours, but the face of the child was terrified. Her eyes looked at me as if she were an animal, the small creature finally hounded to its burrow's end. She had gathered foodstuffs around her, setting up house: a large piece of cheese, some sweets, fragments of biscuits, which indicated what she had eaten recently.

"Do you want to come out and play?" I asked, poking my head under the bed. She shook her head and shrank back farther in her nook, holding the round of cheese. I did not know what to do or say. I knew how to deal with children a little older, but children change so in a year or two that it was like trying to speak another language altogether. Maeve stared back, somber, and shook her head.

With the same strong and laughing voice, Mrs. Aherne said, "Maeve dear, I am hungry, and so are these two gentlemen who have come to visit us. Can you give them a plate of biscuits and make them your pretend tea?"

I saw then what effort it took for Padraig's ma to speak in her normal tone. A thin sweat covered her face, and her arm that was whole clutched the counterpane, while the other lay by her side, purple and rigid. Maeve came up from under the bed. The child seemed reassured and went about her task of hospitality. While she was thus busy and growing happy in a way children can, Mrs. Aherne spoke low to Mr. O'Flaherty.

"I knew them all, moving about the shop, Mr. O'Flaherty," she spoke in a whisper. "I knew Mrs. O'Toole by the sound of her short leg as she lifted away the seed potatoes. I knew John Shanley when he was dragging off the fabrics, for he wheezes and stops and moves again, and many others. Oh, Mr. O'Flaherty, the saddest blow was when Mrs. Purdy came in late at night and took trays of needles and my lace where I hid them under the counter, and my bundle of shillings I buried in the floor—which she must have known all along. We have been neighbours ever so long. But Mrs. Purdy and her hut being tumbled, her husband set a-weeping. I could not bear anymore."

Her voice cracked. "Look at me now. I am done for." She stopped to regain her breath. "I can feel the poison gathered in my neck and armpits—they are swollen so. My chest is full of pain and I know I am sinking. Look after my Padraig's child. She is in your hands. I've been praying you would come."

"As long as I have breath, Maire," Mr. O'Flaherty said. "And when my time comes, I know that Brendan will take care of his mate Padraig's child. Does she need worry about that, Brendan? Tell her now, on your faith, once and for all," he said. She looked at me, eyes a-glitter with the fever.

"I promise, I do," I said, as simply.

I reached out for her hale arm, to hold her palm for assurance. It was that hot and dry I never thought the human hand could be. As my thumb lay across her wrist, I could feel the frantic thrum of her heart.

The child Maeve came by, sprightly, with some biscuits and her tiny china service of teapot and toy cups and saucers. Mr. O'Flaherty and I nibbled on biscuits, and Maeve poured us imaginary tea with great ceremony. We drank and praised its aroma. The child was pleased and offered us more.

"Miss Maeve," said Mr. O'Flaherty, "will you be so kind as to help Brendan at the school?"

Maeve looked puzzled. "But I live here," she replied.

"Aye, that's a fine point." Mr. O'Flaherty was stumped, but he recovered. "Do ye think ye could visit with us and teach him how to make that fine tea?"

"But that's pretend tea," Maeve pointed out conclusively.

At great cost, Mrs. Aherne came to our rescue. She spoke again to the child in her normal voice and said, "Well, Maeve, if you want to go with the big children to school and learn to read the picture books all by yourself, Mr. Brendan's the man to ask. He has many books with pictures." Then, as if in doubt, she added, "But may be you are not a big girl yet for school."

"I am a big girl!" Maeve bridled at any suggestion otherwise.

"All right then," said Mrs. Aherne, "why don't you try it for a couple of days. If you don't like it, you can come back and Brendan will bring you. Won't you, Brendan?"

"Aye, that I will," I agreed.

"I'll get my things then," decided Maeve. "But if I want to come back, I can?"

"Aye, that's right," Mrs. Aherne and I said together.

As the child went to get her toys and put her tea service together to improve our life at school, Padraig's ma told us urgently, "Inside my pillow, I have a number of silver coins I've laid by over the years. Take it. Use it to raise Maeve." Then she turned her intent eyes on me. "Upon your life, Brendan, take care of her as Padraig would have. Someday Padraig will come back. I know. Tell him then, this was the best I could have done for us all."

These were bitter tears, seemingly wrung out of her blood, the first I ever saw her shed. "Go now, Brendan, for I will need to talk to Mr. O'Flaherty."

"Shall I ask Father Conlon to come by?" I said, thinking of the last sacrament and extreme unction.

"Nay, I'll make my own peace, through Mr. O'Flaherty here," she said to my astonishment.

The last rites were the doors to Paradise and to Our Father. She was waving these away. Did that mean she did not care to make her last confession and leave her sins behind? But Padraig's ma has always been that mysterious.

And now I had the care of Maeve, I took her back with me. She skipped up the path, pleased to be going to school and catching up with all the bigger children, for she was very like her da, and could not bear any who was ahead.

Mr. O'Flaherty sat with the dying woman.

# Maire Aherne
## Mullaghmore, County Sligo
### 1846

As I lie here dying, I think in this dark of my life and its impulses. It is, although few would guess, my mad whims that have ruled me altogether. To hide them under a strong gait, a face that holds its smiles in abeyance until I am alone: These have been my disguises. But here comes Death, this untimely visitor who touches my fingers, then my blue-black wrist, ruffles my life's blood flow, and pulls me down by my strong and impulsive right hand. He takes me in hand and refuses to let go. I wish he would hurry.

All my life I have raged against the slowness of things, how matters unfold little by little. I used to want my little Padraig to be a man soon after he was born. I wanted to speak to him, woman to man, by passing all the slow seasons of childhood. Perhaps that is why I have spoken to him as a sensible man even as a child, and now he is gone. Impulsive mother, impulsive son. Where is he on earth today, if he is among us at all? As I lie in my feverish bed, I wonder if he will come sit by me and hold my hand, the one Death has left whole, not the one in which the veins are swollen channels and my nails undercrusted by the angry coral of corruption. Yes, yes, I do want my wandering son, or his wandering shade, to come and sit by me as I go from this place to no country, so that I can tell him how my impulsiveness brought him into this world.

I had been the much-adored Maire Finnegan, my father's daughter, whose ma had died of sudden fever when I was only three. I could do no wrong, Jock and Georgie's sister, at whom no one looked with anything but joy. When my da would go off to sea with my brothers, and they were gone for days, and I growing and watching by the sea, my father decided to have me learnt and sent me up to the village with old Mrs. Byrne the widow. Three children on our lane used to go daily to school at young Mr. O'Flaherty's. One day I went with them out of curiosity, and after the first time itself, when I heard a bit of the tale of sad Isolde and the ill-fated Tristan, I came back and told my da that I could not miss even a day of such stories. I was that swayed and seized by all these tales of King Mark, Queen Grania, the lost men of the glens, the dying Diarmuid, that I was beside myself with the hearing of all the tales. When I read, the voice of young Mr. O'Flaherty seemed to tell the tales in my head. That has not changed at all. Even in these hours of pounding fever and in the sure knowledge of my grief I recall them, drifting unmoored upon my mind.

The storms of 1811 brought great wrack upon the fisherfolk throughout the region, Galway, the Arans, Sligo Bay, and even through Donegal and Connemara. Who would care to count the boats gone, and the bodies of fathers and brothers washing ashore after days so battered by the cruel sea that they were identified by the knit and pattern of their sturdy sweaters. It made the world of difference to me, and I was left an orphan, all of fifteen, with nowhere to go but old Mrs. Byrne, who used to be given by my da fish and coins for my keep, while I scampered to school all those years, and slept on her spare bed.

Now with my da gone and both my brothers, I noticed the eyes of some villagers grow crooked, and the world a-changing. 'Twas over Easter, I remember well, and no one at school for all the churchy week—when I got it into my head to run up to Mr. O'Flaherty's. I was hot and sweaty when I got there, but he was gone, perchance to church and a day in Sligo Town, and all the decorated shops on Wine Street, or among the folks taking the air by the quayside here at Mullaghmore itself with the brave ships and their pennants of all colours.

I threw off my smock and dress and splashed the cool water from his cistern behind the cottage. I had the water streaming down my face and shut my eyes and poured some more, in the delight of that coolness and the red sun filling my world behind my shut eyes with a glow of pleasure. Then it was that I heard him. I burn to think how long he had seen me, for he seemed rooted like a tree, my bosom wet and bare, and my paps pink and goose-pimpled. Then, impulsively I did another thing. I shut my eyes and poured the water again over my head and face, my bosom hard and shaking, and even with that cool water I felt a throb in me that was not at my heart at all. When I opened my eyes, my hands, these very hands, were quiet by my side, my red hair wet and trailing over my face. I stood, now with my palms shielding my breasts, but he was gone.

I stayed back for the whole afternoon, waiting. I would have just sat by him, I swear by sweet Jesus and St. Patrick and my poor gone da, I would have listened to his tales and looked for nothing more.

In all the years, we never once spoke of this, and he that shy.

Within months, it had become clear that I was a growing burden to Mrs. Byrne, and she, crabby and crotchety, complained I ate so much. Yet all her chores, her garden and potato patch I took care of single-handed, and all that cheerily done. I have never made a fuss of work. But one day, she said that I had eaten more praties than I was due, and I, in such a blind glaring anger, instead of saying the harsh word which rattled in my head and curse her and her ratty pigtail of grey, I stomped down to the harbour and thought to walk off my ire and see my schoolfellows besides. Many of the fisherfolk who came in from the sea would hail me, for I was their dead mate's daughter, and give me fish and warm words besides. All these, the fish and good cheer, I had been wont to take back to that harridan Byrne, but I was that angry I did not want to return in the afternoon.

A fine ship had hoved into the harbour, with a show of white sails and shiny bows. A great family, I thought, had arrived. But no, it was a lady's maid that had come to set up her house before the lady arrived—and her fine china and new gowns had come in the ship, which a month or so later, would likely sail away, back to rich England. The lady's maid was a red-faced large woman, smiling and squinting in the sun, and friendly-like. The boxes were unloaded on the quay and she did much counting, got muddled and counted yet again. She had to go back into the ship and make sure that all had been unloaded, bandboxes, sea-chests, and all. Why she did not have a written tally, I did not know, but she was that flustered and riddled by the count.

She saw me watching and asked my name. "Miss Finnegan," I said, as I had read in books. I did not say, "I'm the Finnegans' Maire."

She said, please Miss Finnegan, could you watch over these

here bandboxes and mirror stands while I check the ship and its nooks once more. She was sure she had forgotten the new inkstand and the writing papers, and the card table, and the decanter, and the opera glasses and on and on—for her ladyship liked to watch the sea from her house, and Ben Bulben—and the new cards and the bedroom slippers and . . . By this time, as the list grew, I laughed in jollity and said, "Why, I will keep both eyes on these, Missus."

She rushed off and came back with a number of things, and then exclaimed, "M'lady's snuffbox! I was carrying it so carefully in my hand, I declare." I noticed a small ornamental thing, a wee column scarcely bigger than a child's thumb, prettily inlaid with shiny mother-of-pearl and some dainty green stone. I picked it up from under the fringe of her skirt where it had fallen and handed it to her.

"Would this be what you are looking for?"

"Why, bless you, girl, that's what it is. What a trouble if I could not find it, for our ladyship, that is, Lady Temple's sister—she who took care of our young Master Henry after his mother died—she is very fond of her snuff and gin and cards. So thank you, Miss Finnegan."

Then a thought struck her, and she hummed and hawed. Well, I am a straight and direct one, as my da would say. I was sore vexed with Mrs. Byrne, and it would surely be an adventure, so I said, "Will her ladyship be wanting a maid to help you while you are here?"

"Why, yes indeed," Mrs. Hester Bunthorne said, for that was her name, though her ladyship called her Hetty. "However did you guess? That is exactly what she told me to do and I was worried, for I am from their house in Herefordshire and know nothing at all of this land and its ways."

"I am your girl then," I said simply, "You'll just need to teach me what to do and when."

I was told by the relieved Mrs. Bunthorne that her ladyship, the dead Lady Temple's sister, would arrive in a few days from the great house at Boyle where she was staying with her friend, some great lady or other, and she would be the one to say the final aye—but that I could come right away.

So I scampered off to the fisherfolk and told Timmy Doherty to send word to Mrs. Byrne that I was off to the big house, and she should keep all her praties to herself and the tending of the potato patch to boot, and went off with Mrs. Bunthorne directly. Timmy Doherty did that, and was all a-blush that I had chosen him as messenger, and on his own brought all my stuff in my box to the English house.

Her ladyship came a week later and took to bed with her two furry lapdogs, her bottle of gin, and her cold that she'd brought along from the high folks she was staying with. She let me stay on as maid, as absentmindedly as if she had agreed to have another pinch of her snuff or a sip of gin. In a few days she was better, and though a little snivelly—I saw her blow her nose in the sleeve of her dress when she thought nobody was noticing—she ate well enough. Then she wandered about the newly aired home. With all the white dust covers off, the furniture gleamed after the fine hard work by Mrs. Bunthorne and me. But I could see her ladyship was bored. And just as suddenly as she had come, she was going to depart—with Mrs. Bunthorne and Mr. Arkwright, the bailiff, in tow—back again to that great house at Boyle in the heart of Rockingham Estate. I suppose this was the way of high folk.

I was to stay employed for the time being. Mrs. Byrne had sent three messages through stammering Timmy Doherty that she was sore sorry and wished me back. I ignored her completely. I was enjoying all the space and novelty, and I had just met the game-keeper, a dark, unsmiling Jemmy Aherne, who was that handsome in a strong, rough way that it made me shake. I let him kiss me once. It was my first kiss. What an awkward thing it was! I had wondered about it for all my girlhood years and then it happened. He gripped me so hard, and his tooth hurt my lip, and it was over. He asked me if I would marry him. I said, I was sure I did not know.

At this time her ladyship and Mrs. Bunthorne had left, saying they might be back in a few days, and if any gentlemen came, they were to be sent on to Boyle. Aye, I curtsied, and they were gone. I was just about the mistress of the place except for the old fool, the gardener, Mr. Scully, who was deaf as a post, and would bring me fine vegetables everyday from the garden. He would leave these and the milk at the kitchen door in the back for he never would enter the house.

The next time I went to church on Sunday, Father Conlon called me aside and said, Jemmy Aherne was from the south near Cork, and a good lad, and he was glad that he had agreed to marry a fatherless lass like me with not a farthing to my name. I bridled at this, but could not retort, for Father Conlon bustled off about some matter with the vestments and the new censer, and I returned to the English house in a fury.

When I was going up from the kitchen to my room, Jemmy Aherne came in from behind and grabbed my waist, and I gave him such a sharp fist that it chipped his tooth and crimpled my knuckle.

"I am of the Finnegans, not a sack of potatoes you reach for whenever you please." He was right startled.

"I thought," he mumbled, his good looks fumbling and awkward before my flashing anger. Then he added, "I am going with my gun out for some weeks now to keep the poachers off, way near the Ben and thereabouts," trying to impress me.

"What's that to me?" I retorted and stamped off, and as I turned the corner, I could see he was crestfallen. I knew I would make up, but give it a day or two!

"Are you not my girl?" he called angrily after me.

"What if I am? I don't know if you are my man," I fumed. He was handsome, but I wanted to laugh and not be in a temper and frown. Oh, I wanted to be in love, and sweetly wooed. But he gnashed his teeth and was gone before I could smile at him.

• • •

THE CLOUDS HAD been gathering and going away and gathering again, and a strange wind had blown off Ben Bulben that next afternoon as it veered between sun and cloud. I needed to wash all the bedclothes and air them, but was of two minds, in case it rained. I thought, let me get it done, for I cannot abide not doing something and being idle. Oh, I should have—for there were books a-plenty. I had already dusted them and found some I wanted to read. Mrs. Bunthorne was amazed I could read with ease, and write to boot, thanks to Mr. O'Flaherty. But I washed all the bedclothes and hung them out to dry on the terrace at the back, away from the sea. The winds rose and the sheets were like sails in a storm, pulling and billowing at the clothes-hooks, some threatening to fly away.

I think of that wild day of wind and shadows and racing clouds, and my airy girlish mood, and what a great difference that day made in all my life. Where is that carefree girl now? Oh, I long for my sweet son, who came into my life and stepped so casually away, and all my life over so suddenly and everything passed so soon, and my little Maeve to be alone in this wide world. I feel death in my veins today. But on that day, among the flapping white wings of the blankets, I felt I could fly, I danced on tripping steps, and twirled about alone on that terrace, my eyes half closed and dreamy, and into the arms of a laughing merry stranger, who, holding me, danced and danced into my white flying fantasies, as if he had grown out of them and would vanish when the wayward winds grew still.

All he would ever say was that his name was Henry as he entered into the exact spirit of my carefree dance, and moved among the billowing sheets, just touching my palm, or my cheek, and moving away, letting me dance, strangely unsurprised by the magic, and his presence not intruding but letting me spread my wings. When the wind stilled for a moment, and the sheets stood like curtain after curtain in a white room, he kissed me on my mouth, and I was lost. I felt the winds whirling around me, madly blowing in great oceanic billows, but when we parted after the long moment I was entranced to see the curtains stilled, and his palm cupping my beating heart, I sought his mouth, and he sought what I thought was my soul itself. On the white sheets, surrounded and overhung by them, I was his, above and under him, entwined and astride him, in an embrace that was never like any earthly embrace before.

Why do I recall everything, in such ruinous detail, every kiss and surrender, sigh and shudder, ungirding and moan, when I cannot to this day recall when the sun withdrew, night unfurled, the light of the stars overhead, and late morning when my sweet awakening came, and how all that time had slipped past our closed door? In a dream I went down to the kitchen and cooked eggs, a great number. He came and held me fast from behind, as I held one last brown egg in my palm, admiring its shape, its fullness and fragility, his palm about mine, and it had a strange meaning. His other palm folded over my heart, and time went fugitive again. I stood, naked as Eve on the cool flagstone of the kitchen, marked with flour, and the honey that he had poured on and licked from me. The cool water bathed us both, and we emerged, hungry and frolicksome, to eat the scattered repast, and were transported before the great fire we had made—when?—and fell together into a deep slumber and woke inside another dream where I had become a being, oozing honey, a part of the riotous pattern of the great silk rug.

When I woke, it was to the strange reality of a morning. I lay alone, and my maid's clothes lay about the bed. Had Henry carried me back to my room? I had been so transported in that great sleep and awakening and sleep again, that I paid no mind to this waking now. I dressed with care and with sleep-sated and shining face, I thought to dress the maid and serve him. But under my garments, I was and felt naked: Thus sweetly naked I had never felt before. I stood before the mirror and touched myself and could feel just the crinkle of my nether hair under my palm. I looked at myself with quiet joy and came downstairs on cat's feet. I glided into the kitchen and cut some bread, cheese, fruit, and poured out the last of the milk.

I served him breakfast. I knew a difference lay between our stations. I addressed him "Master Henry," fully expecting to be caressed and corrected. But he did not. He was lost in a book that he read as he ate, his face keen and intelligent, wrapped in the words that he did not think I could share with him and understand—*but*

*I could have, I could have, I knew*—just as I had shared my sweetest moments in his arms.

At this very moment there was a clatter at the front door and Mrs. Bunthorne walked briskly in, pulling off her bonnet, her shawl trailing in her hurry. She breezed into the kitchen and stopped, amazed.

"Oh, Master Henry, Master Henry," she stammered. "She has been serving you in the wrong place."

Little did she know about all that, I chuckled inwardly. This young man was probably from the estate in England, or a high employee from elsewhere in Ireland. In a great flurry, she was for removing the meal and taking out the fine china, when I told her I would take care of it.

"Take care of it?" she fumed.

But he swept past us saying, "Mrs. Bunthorne, I have eaten. Now I must ride off to Boyle."

With that he was gone, without a word or a backward glance at me.

Mrs. Bunthorne had come back to gather a few essential articles which her ladyship, as usual, had left behind. One of them was her favourite snuffbox and another was a pillow that was just right for her head when she had curlers on overnight. Mr. Arkwright would deliver them while Mrs. Bunthorne was to wait here for a few weeks, in case her ladyship decided to come back to Mullaghmore. If not, she would send word for her to join her ladyship—or if Madam had grown bored by now with Ireland, return altogether to England.

The gentleman gone, Mrs. Bunthorne sat down with a great sigh to a cup of tea I had made for her.

"You look fairly glowing," she said. I smiled back. I was glad to have her back—but only because the gentleman was gone. I would not have wanted anyone in this wide world when he was close to me. I was planning to find a way to accompany her to her ladyship, where he had gone. My mind was in turmoil. Mrs. Bunthorne had been talking and became cross when she realized I had not been attending her.

"What, Mrs. Bunthorne?" I said contritely.

" 'What, Mrs. Bunthorne?' Is that all you have to say, girl?" she said with vigour. "Imagine serving Master Henry in the kitchen," she said, waving her arms, at a loss for words.

"The young man was content enough," I replied.

"Content, Lordy Lord," she said, aghast. "*His Lordship* to you, child! What did you think he was—an assistant of Mr. Arkwright here? It's the young Lord Palmerston, the Viscount. I've known him since his nursery days, and so he wants me to call him Master Henry always. Don't *you* be saucy, girl." I stood still, letting all this sink in. Mrs. Bunthorne stopped as if some thought had struck her.

"When did he come?"

I knew to avoid this question and said simply, "I did serve his meal in time."

Mrs. Bunthorne seemed to infer from that, that Master Henry had come in this very morning. One more question, and my prevarication would be tumbled.

No directives came for Mrs. Bunthorne for over a month. We were happy enough by ourselves in the following weeks. Having finished what few chores there were by midmorning, I would sit with her, knitting and talking all the long afternoons. Mrs. Bunthorne grew very fond of me over the days. I wondered if this was what it was like to have a mother. I was always told of the cruel English, and how wary we need be in all our dealings. Yet the first

Englishwoman who came into my life walked right into my Irish heart with her simple affection, and I gave her back the same in equal measure. She told me of her husband who had died, her childhood in Herefordshire, and how she would have loved to have had children of her own.

I, who had been as regular as the full moon in its coming, had missed my time altogether. I waited apprehensively for it. But what came, and that in a matter of ten more days, was not the usual ache and drip of blood but a strange swooning sense in the morning, and a mighty abhorrence for the smell of milk and oatmeal, which Mrs. Bunthorne loved and had given me for all these many breakfasts, and I had eaten in fine humour. One morning as she poured the milk, I watched the bubbling froth, and dashed out, retching blindly by the kitchen door. I wiped my face on my apron and walked away. I stole about the garden aimlessly, killing time till she would have put away the milk.

I do not know what came over me: I knelt abruptly down and scratched the black earth under the mossy cottage tree, and put that handful of the good soil in my mouth. It tasted cool and comforting. Tears were welling in my eyes unaccountably, and I felt very sorry for myself that Master Henry had strode out and left, instead of sending Mrs. Bunthorne on some fool's errand and holding me close for one last kiss, a whispered word.

When I opened my eyes, I saw Mrs. Bunthorne standing over me. Her nose was flared.

"You're done for, girl. You let your young gamekeeper in, didn't you?" she whispered directly. "Now you'd better get him to church."

"What gamekeeper?" I mumbled, uncomprehending. I had completely forgotten about Jemmy Aherne. Mrs. Bunthorne stared into my face for a long while. I looked away, back at her, then looked down.

"When exactly did Master Henry come here?" she said. I realized that the game was over.

"I do not remember," I said simply.

She caught me roughly by the shoulders and stood me up. "He is a fine young man, and has treated me always with respect, servant as I am. I have never forgotten my place, and I in their service for thirty-two years. I saw him grow boy and man, and a finer man I have not seen." She stopped for breath. "But, he is a lord, and a young man who knows how to get his way and has done so many a time—you hear me—many a time. He even has those great young ladies do the foolish things, and some older ones too who should know better." Mrs. Bunthorne's voice was low and burned through me. "He likes to write in the fancy papers in London Town and they say he is very charming and witty. But others write about him too, and about his ways. They gave him the name Lord Cupid, and not, it seems, in jest." Mrs. Bunthorne sat down on the steps leading up to the kitchen from the back garden. All that had been the natural unfolding, very like the dance of the seasons themselves in those short enchanted days, now seemed to me bare and defiled by his practiced ease and skilled hands, tawdry in this flat light of morning.

"Your Aherne, the gamekeeper," pursued Mrs. Bunthorne, "has he been back?"

I shook my head silently.

"Good," she said briskly. "Say aye to him forthwith. It's a blunder you can paper over, you poor fool," she said angrily and tenderly. "Do not turn noble, child, and say you are in love. He will never come back. Do you understand?" She took me by the shoulder, "Do not try something stupid and bleed to death in some crone's hovel. Too many have done that, by far. You can make it up to your gamekeeper by being a better wife than he ever deserved and staying that way."

I felt a wave of nausea sweep over me as Mrs. Bunthorne helped me up the stairs and into the kitchen.

In ten more days, I was married to Jeremy Aherne—poor Jemmy—as awkward in love as can be on the first night, as I wept in his arms. For fear, he thought.

I never was a good wife to him, a better one than ever he deserved, as Mrs. Bunthorne had told me to be. For a month and eight days after we were wed, Jemmy Aherne was shot and killed by poachers and his body found facedown under a flowering hawthorn hedge by Lough Gill's shore.

My baby was born and I named him Padraig Robert. Padraig for my da, and Robert in honour of Mrs. Bunthorne, who used to hope for a son to name after her father, Robert, the kindest man she ever knew. After all I couldn't name my boy Hetty or Hester—or Henry! Besides, I liked the sound of the name Robert.

I never saw Mrs. Bunthorne since my wedding day. I do not know what she had said to Master Henry, who lived in London. But Mr. Arkwright, the estate bailiff, conveyed the instruction sent him from London that my small cottage and garden that I had bought in Mullaghmore with the settlement given me on my husband's death, was free of taxes. Not that I wanted it this way, but the prudent way to stop any tongues was just to accept it—and not go into talk or wrangle. I set up a small store. Four years later, I received a small bequest from Mrs. Bunthorne, who had died a widow woman in London.

The faint beam shifts from floor to wall, the shadows sidle—or do I imagine this? I hardly know the unmoored hours, if it is night or day, as I grit my teeth and await my son, adrift on my raft of fever. Will he not return, though cruelly late? It is time, now or forever. An angry bitterness turns my breath. I try to cling to the island of hope and feel some tide pulling me away. And my lover, a great lord of the kingdom with his untold wealth, who did not hesitate to use a naïve village girl whose eyes were full of dreams? Father and son have both left. My heart is a grindstone for these hard thoughts. My father and my brothers are long dead too. Why need I live on?

Then I hear a small sound: Maeve stirring under my bed! She refused to lie with me, frightened by my swollen arm. She is singing softly, a song I used to sing for my Padraig. She has learnt it, for she insists I sing it to her at bedtime. I must stay alive for someone to deliver Maeve to what safety is possible in this world that has turned to wormwood. My head is full of strange pains. Darkness is pressing down upon me. There are moments when I am not sure where I am, or what brought me here. Then I remember Brendan has taken my Maeve with him.

Mr. O'Flaherty waits with me. There are no candles in my robbed home. I long to talk to someone who would understand. Not just stand by wagging his head and smear my burning head with the holy oil and spatter me with the church water. God forgive me if He wishes. My greatest joys came from my lost Padraig and my lost days with his father. How can I, in the eyes of God, walk away from that?

I think I can tell Mr. O'Flaherty, and he, with his great reading and his telling the brave stories of love and its miseries, will understand. As he sits quietly, I say to him, "I have something to say." He leans forward.

"I have done something the world would not understand, something I never told my poor Jemmy." My voice was broken, I can hear, a scrape upon dying coal.

"Hush, hush, Maire," he whispers, "there is no need to talk of that mad day. I was older and you were that young," he murmurs, meaning to be kind.

And I understand. Poor Mr. O'Flaherty is thinking merely of that day, so long ago, I was bathing at his cistern behind his school cottage, and in my pride of youth and beauty and a naked innocence, I had let him look at my young body and my new breasts even when I knew he was looking, and nothing did come of that. . . .

I also understand that I can never tell him all I wanted to say, for Mr. O'Flaherty is merely a man. I let him stay by my side as I begin to sink, slow as tide, into death.

I could have spoken my heart to God—or to a kind old woman—if either of them had come and sat by me. The darkness is outside my window, its palm on my pane. With its fine edge of black lace, it advances—and advancing—drinks the lees of my day.

# Padraig
## Barisal, Bengal Province
### 1844

I had begun to be impatient with Alexander Blackburn, counting my days to be quit of this East India Company ship, and this name. I wanted as few people as possible on board the ship to remember how I looked, so had left my sprouting beard untrimmed, let my hair grow so that the very shape of my head looked different. To keep from too much brooding, I sought out work among the barrels and the ropes on deck, and this hardened my sinews as the relentless sun blackened me, and the ship's strict rations made me wiry. Even my mother would not have known me here on this ship, among people to whom the names O'Connell or Mullaghmore meant little or nothing at all.

We drifted south towards the equator following the Africa coast until we anchored off Ouidah, where I saw two ships with different flags, Belgian and American, lying hull to hull. We were anchored not far from several ships. The wind turned putrid when it shifted and came across their bows. I crinkled my nose involuntarily, and one of the older hands, Tim Landry, spat over the side of the deck rail, saying just one word of explanation, "Slavers."

Over the next two days, as we took in grains and vegetables, live goats and casks of water, I saw little by way of supplies loaded in the slave ships. What they loaded were naked black people, chained neck to neck, clinking and clattering, and every once in a while there would be a howling cry with other shackled ones joining in. I realized with a cold shiver, it was not howling, but some terrible lament, for they would never see this land or their homes again, headed for death or no country they had ever dreamed of.

Landry smiled and said, "Animals." From the numbers they were loading down into their hold, I wondered where they would lie. Landry's skeletal face, crowned with yellow hair, grinning, spat out, "Spoons."

"What?" I said.

"Spoons. Side by side. Chained. Whole trip. Americas," he said, licking his sparse teeth that had black spots on them, like dice.

"Why," I said in surprise, "they'll surely sicken and many die."

"Aye. Half. More. Heathens," he said matter-of-factly. "Pitched over. Rot clamped. If rough seas." I looked on in horror as they continued loading the human cargo.

That night, on the still oceanwater, I saw four moons: The great grey orb in the sky and its twin on the sea; the other was the round light of the porthole of one slave ship, below which glared its reflection in the dead black water, looking, for all the world, like the maw of hell itself.

• • •

THE LASCARS SLITHERED, agile as monkeys, up and down the rigging, making the most of the winds. The ship sailed on smoothly beneath us, the gulls squawking overhead, splattering us once in a while with their warm splathery guano that smelt like rotten oysters. On a warm day in early February, almost four months into my voyage, we reached a port at the bottom of Africa, with the town spread along the seashore, and a plateau looming behind it, blue with height. They called it Cape Town.

All it meant to me was that it was the southernmost point I would reach, farthest from Mullaghmore. The thought of my Brigid came in a powerful wave over me and choked my breath. Did she think, in Connemara, that I had forgotten her altogether? Had her feckless father kept her back? I should myself have gone to Connemara again and brought her home, instead of paying heed to O'Connell's call. My heart was a churn of regret. Yet I knew what reckless fervour I had for going to Dublin, and I would have heeded no one—least of all myself. I could not write just yet. Letters were read by the captain or one of the officers, and the East India Company was in its own way god-like and secretive. My secret would keep, I decided, heeding the advice of Fergus Murphy. But just the same, it weighed heavily on my heart, and I felt the hard cost of my footloose youth.

At Cape Town we got a great deal of fine beef and a variety of fruits, it being summer here. The crew ate heartily. Then, with much fanfare, two large sea-chests made of fine mahogany with brass clasps were hauled up; some great gentleman was coming on board, an important colonial official. Cape Town was full of people of note going to or returning from India. Now he was to take our ship to the eastern part of Bengal, some place called Dacca, I heard tell. He turned out to be an overfed fellow, barely beyond boyhood, attempting a pale moustache on his pink face, the younger son of some great lord, farmed out to the colonies.

• • •

THAT NIGHT I dreamt I was back in Mullaghmore, sitting at a table eating praties and sipping sweet buttermilk with my ma and Brigid and Brendan. As I looked at them, unable to speak, Brendan got up and left, and in his place sat Alexander Blackburn, who pointed his finger at me before fading away. The light turned a foreboding grey in which Brigid and Ma appeared ashen. Brigid lay down on the floor as if in great tiredness. My mother held out a hand to me, and before my eyes it twisted into driftwood. I cried out, yet aware that I was asleep, trying to free myself of its tendrils. I sat up, holding my heavy head between my hands, uncomprehending, heart pounding in misery, drifting with each heartbeat away from Ireland.

Having learnt enough of being a sailor, I resolved to find a sailor's berth as soon as I could, on any ship sailing back to England or to Belgium or any other European land, whence I could sail into Sligo harbour and make it up to my mother and Brigid. At the same time, I knew how bitter it would be to return a poor drifter, penniless and full of idle stories. Why could I not make a small fortune before I sailed back from India, with my full chest hauled behind me from Sligo? I swore I would never once leave home after that. I would amaze them, telling them of the floating curtains of kelp, and days stilled by lack of wind as on a painted ocean, the surface suddenly broken by the skitter of flying fish.

We stopped next on the eastern coast at Mombasa for a week at the beginning of March, and again at Malindi for a number of days to take in curved branches of ivory, which were packed with the greatest care against breakage or stain. We cast off again and started the arduous journey across the emptiness of the Indian Ocean, seeing no ship for weeks, the sun growing sharper, nigh unbearable.

Seven months and three weeks it had taken us, from Gravesend to India, with the ship making port wherever the Company had business, delivering papers at one, loading and unloading goods at others, taking in supplies and goods, awaiting this or that high official who came from the interior. I began to sense what an intricate web the Company had spread out through the world—out from their main office in London Town. Even our almighty Captain Connolly ruled but a tiny filament of that mighty spiderweb. Each port, heavily guarded, left little hope of escape or finding my way home.

• • •

"IN A DAY or two, we reach India," announced Hanratty.

And so we did. It was mid-May and hard summer, when we hove into sight of broken land, for the force of the great river, whose estuary it was, had shattered its meeting place with the ocean into a thousand shards, each one an island, the edges deep with mud and ooze and stick-like growths up to the tide-point. These heaped trees, with roots of gnarled fingers, spread spiderwise. These, I was told, were the mangrove. Small lizards with spiny backs and hackles slithered among them. The islands appeared to float, not founded upon firm earth. At nightfall, the unkempt heads of the trees were covered with long-necked egrets and thick jungle crows that set up a white and black cacophony. Cohorts of monkeys with muddy fur, some with wizened babies clinging to them, chittered and hooted among the branches. Scattered between these were bursts of yellow leaves amidst tangles of cane-like growth. That was my first sight of India.

As I sat alone at the stern, peering into the gloaming and the passage that lay between two mangrove islands, I had an amazing visitation. Sliding through the nightwater, a moving head, the crawling powerful torso and paws, its round, furry ears tucked back, its fanged mouth drawn in a grin, the muscled glide of the yellow and black stripes. The tiger was making its easy way from one isle to another. I now knew who ruled here. We would make landfall far inland, away from this king of the night.

• • •

THE NEXT DAY, the lascars from the rigging were pointing excitedly and shouting at each other. I thought I could see a line of cobalt-hued mountains on the southeasterly horizon. Hanratty shouted that these were the monsoon clouds. So far, the breeze was gentle and smelt muddy and green. The ship moved with ease along the deep until, to our left, a great channel opened up. At Captain Connolly's order, the ship urged northward into the channel. The water turned brown, with little eddies in which broken branches and leaves spun as they moved down the estuary, pulled into the grey-green waters of the sea receding behind us.

"How far ahead is Calcutta?" I asked Hanratty, who had sailed there in earlier voyages.

"This isn't the mouth of the Hooghly at all. We're going to Dacca first with that lordling. You see those monsoon clouds?" Hanratty said. Landry—pointing, eyes squinting, mouth open and dice-like teeth suspended from his upper gum—had come and joined us. "Storm, rain, drowning," he said with satisfaction.

I stared, while young Hanratty, eager to show his knowledge, ignored the old salt and held forth. "They move slowly, almost not at all. In two, three days they'll stir. And then, within an hour they'll be covering the earth. There will be mighty shaking and rocking on deck and worse, far worse, below." Sure enough, the ship was moving fast, as if trying to escape a distant foe. "Dacca. Tomorrow," muttered Landry. That evening we anchored off a wide grassy bank where we saw villagers burning their dead. We could see the tops of thatch roofs, the smoke from evening fires. Captain Connolly let it be known that we would begin to sail again late the next day, with the tide.

At dawn we saw a growing crowd in the open space of the beach. The villagers poured in from all directions, but kept a space in their midst wide open where they dug a hole. I wondered what it was for. Perhaps some rustic play would be enacted later in the day. I hoped it would not be at night, lit with a few dim flambeaux, because I was curious. I kept thinking of the big ceilidh festivals at Sligo where I used to go with Brendan—and was homesick in a trice.

I heard a rhythmic murmur as the crowd gathered in a circle. Several men emerged from among the trees bearing a long pole, the height of four tall persons. The chanting crowd parted, and the men held that pole erect for a moment, and then dropped it into the hole at the centre.

For a moment, I felt disappointed because I was sure they would set up a tall tent about the pole, and I would be deprived of the sight of their alien festivity. But no one brought any cloth or canvas. Next, the men gathered at the base of the tall wooden stake and began to rotate it. A single rope attached to its top began to spin out, until its motion resembled a diaphanous umbrella. A glint caught my eye. When the men stopped spinning the column, the rope became visible as its speed slowed and a hook at its end, whistling about in a circle, could plainly be seen, and then with a clatter it rested by the upright pole. The shiny fishhook, or so it looked to me, hung about shoulder height.

The drums began to beat, gaining in tempo, until all eyes were riveted on the centre. All the sailors were crowded on the deck, craning their necks. On the upper deck, Captain Connolly was looking at the spectacle through his telescope. Noticing the young toff who had emerged from his cabin—no longer pink because of seasickness—our captain offered it to him. I was amused that the young lord had to stand on tiptoe. A sharp cry rang out from the crowd, and I turned back to the gathering.

Where he came from I do not know, but the tallest man I had ever seen in my life came, awkward on unnaturally long legs, through the parting crowd. Naked but for a cloth that flapped about those shanks, he was entirely covered with some ashen powder. So were the matted tangles of his hair. He raised his head, and in a great bellow, uttered just one word, which began in deep sibilance and ended in a hollow groaning cry:

*SHIIVAA!*

The crowd began to moan and sway. Amid the terrible blaring from long snaking horns, and the drums sounding in frenzy, I thought I beheld a forest of branches and shivering leaves as everybody in the crowd raised their hands and swayed, quivering their outstretched fingers, the very mimesis of a forest as a great storm breaks over the land. The unnaturally tall man—he seemed nine or ten feet tall—lunged for the dangling rope, caught the hook, and in a single movement, plunged it into his flesh near the shoulder. The pole had begun its rapid twirl, and lifted the man away in its wild rotation over the heads of the crowd, at what appeared an inhuman height. From under his legs two stilts fell away: So that was the mystery of his great height.

But the shiny hook in his flesh, his unearthly circuit overhead, his outstretched arms made nothing of that little trick. He would be dead, he would bleed to death, the sinews of his shoulder would be sundered, and he would be flung from that whirling height, to lie gasping his last breath, blood pooling about his limbs. I watched, thrilled and dreadstruck at the same time. The drumming reached its climax, and the blaring of the native trumpets tore through our senses, and then, as suddenly as it began, it stopped. The men spinning the pole fell away from it as if in dead exhaustion, the rope slowed and swooped down towards the column. Hands reached out and caught the flying man. The arms of the crowd stopped waving, fingers outstretched for a frozen instant, and then fell back. In that moment, the man was hoisted on to his stilts, and the hook, unfleshed, clanked on the pole and hung limp, smeared in blood. Everything was utterly still. The ashen man raised his outstretched hands now, and with fingers fluttering like leaves, loped off through the parted crowd, disappearing among the trees.

The hunched crowd raised one whispered murmur, *Shiva, Shiva*, and then, carrying the pole and hooked rope among them, melted away into the interior, never even looking in our direction. The ground was utterly empty within moments and the silence, except for the susurration of the river, was complete.

I stood clutching the deck rail and wondered if I had dreamt it all.

• • •

WE HAD SAILED past the village up a vast channel that bent sharply westward when we came in sight of a town. The houses on its outskirts came right down to the riverbank, huts and shops scattered about, and banks of stairs led down to the river from some of the larger houses. People in small boats were making for the riverbank. Landry leant over the rail, surveying the land, and said, "Barisal," spitting it out like an expletive.

At this riverside town we took in potable water and fruits. I was told these were mangoes and everybody feasted on them. Great blue flies flew in from nowhere at their sweet odor, and no one was out of humour. With the tide, the ship would have to weigh anchor and sail in great haste, cross Chandpur, and make for Dacca, where it would be safe when the first onslaught of monsoon came. Then, having deposited the great lord's son, the ship would glide downstream to the Bay of Bengal, make a westerly pass up the Hooghly in an easy sail to the port of Calcutta. So said Hanratty, and Landry nodded in agreement. Rotting teeth or no, Landry was a veteran.

Hanratty wanted to impress me with all he knew and held forth with gusto. "In Calcutta you'll see the might of the East India Company, its great numbers of soldiers, white and black, the red Writers' Building for clerks, and Fort William where we'll be escorted in a group."

That set me thinking. It would be far harder to escape from a fort. In the next few hours I stealthily packed my few clothes and some scanty supplies. Gathering them within a piece of torn canvas to keep them dry, I hid them under my shirt. When night fell, and everyone sank into sleep, I wound some rags around my palms and found a deserted spot on deck. Under the merest sliver moon in the sky, I slid down a rope, went into the water without a splash and, holding the bundle above my head, let the tide take me away from the ship. I drifted an hour or so before reaching a bathing ghat with its crumbled steps leading into the river.

There was nothing here except for a dim heap of a temple in

the distance and a cremation ground surrounded by trees such as I had seen from the ship. I walked to an enormous tree, took off my wet clothes, and lay down under its low branches. I would arise, Padraig once more. That night, on the edge of a burning-ground where Hindus bore their dead to be cremated by the river, I consigned Alexander Blackburn to the past forever. I stretched out under the dense banyan tree and slept like the dead.

I dreamt of Mullaghmore again and woke up with a heavy head, hungry and unsure how much of the day was gone. The tendrils that dropped from the great limbs of the tree and the undergrowth that rose from the fecund earth made a twilit world around me. From between twigs and saplings, strange flowers opened their palms to the miserly light. From my nest, I watched a line of people carrying something with great care and placing it at the water's edge, chanting in a low musical tone with a sobbing cry that was part of it. I thought back to the slave song I had heard off the Afric coast, but this was different. They squatted around their burden, singing, making no attempt to console each other, intent on completing some grave ritual by the riverside.

As inexplicably as they had come, they withdrew single file beyond the far trees, raising again the melancholy song with the cry woven within it, and then were lost to my sight. The last thing about them was the cry that rose like a fish in the surface of the quiet spreading about us.

A swift eddy roiled the trees. The heavy branches of the banyan swayed over me, and the watery weight of the air stirred, and soon a mighty wind howled overhead. I came away from under the tree canopy and saw that the sky was loaded with indigo clouds, so tumultuously low that it seemed they would crush the earth itself. A blue spark jittered across the sky, blinding me momentarily, and a gleam played upon the crashing and froth-tormented waters of the wide river. With a sharp cackle some great bird, its wings impossibly bent, crashed to the ground and, quivering, lay still. Its neck was twisted and its wings cracked by the wind. Heavy groaning filled the sky, and the close thunder shook through my body and the earth drummed underfoot. I flung myself to the ground, hands over my ears, thinking, *The monsoon, this is the monsoon.* The Company ship, caught in such a storm, would certainly have more immediate worries, unless they took me for drowned and dead. That would be fortuitous.

Rain began to fall on the hot earth and thwapped down in great drops, bursting open before my eyes. The waters were in a boil. I could see now what those praying ones had left at the bank. Something fluttered, as the wind snapped about it. I raced breathlessly to the river's edge, the rain hitting me in great slapping gusts against my face. A few more seconds and the reaching hands of the river would grasp and snatch it away. It was a long package, one end already in the black water, but what caught my eye now was the part which was not swaddled.

It was a face, its lips blue, but faintly moving, choking under the flinging rain.

Picking up the burden and throwing it over my shoulder, I ran through the walls of falling water, stopping briefly to snatch my canvas bundle from under the tree, my feet squelching, towards the broken temple. Two nightbirds skittered out, screeching into the rain. There was a dingy stony smell of the cool floor, but it was dry. The lightning lit and jagged through the riverscape of tormented trees and water, while the sound of rain heaved and drowned all else.

He lay inert, but not yet cold. I felt no breath in his nostrils.

I unwrapped the cloth. Within it lay a thin child, and I understood that those men had left him for dead. Hastily I opened the stopper of the small bottle of rum I had purloined from the ship and poured it between his lips. I slapped his cheeks gently and rubbed his palms, then gathered all my force of breath and blew into his open helpless mouth, desperately willing him to breathe. I pressed my head upon his chest, but could hear nothing but the throbbing rain. As I sat up, I saw his eyes flicker, a small light in them, as if he had seen something very wonderful and unexpected, and a tear rolled down his left eye. He looked at me, eyes dilated.

"I'm Padraig," I said, as much to him as myself. "Do not fear. I am alive."

He tried to raise his palm, but could only manage a faint movement of his fingers. I reached and held them gently. Words would not do. I held my palm to his cold forehead. After a while, I gathered the twigs that lay nearby and under the awning, and lit a fire. It threw my looming shadow on the wall. The boy looked at it with dread. I put my palms together and moved my fingers. A shadow-bird fluttered on the wall.

The boy smiled. Then he sank into sleep. Once in a while I thought he lay too still and leant over him, anxious, until I felt his faint intaken breath. This soothed my heart. The night passed slowly into a still dawn.

● ● ●

IN THE LAST entire day, I had not been able to give the child anything but a few sips of water. I had nothing to eat, though I had been quick the night before to gather a large amount of dry kindling from under the trees to keep the fire going. I sat by the still child, the tongue of fire in the large nest of ashes and ember the only thing that moved.

Inside the temple floor, at its centre, I found a strange mound, about waist high, like a black digit. On it were vivid streaks of vermilion. To its right, embedded in the ground, stood a trident. Near it I found a stone bowl, none too clean, which I scoured with the soil at the river-edge and filled with cool water. Mangoes hung plentiful from the thick branches. I knew about the tall coconuts and their nourishing milk and fruit. It was impossible to climb any of these, but one of the clustered fruits had fallen earlier that day with a thud. On hearing that coconut fall, a villager had come out of the trees. When he saw me, and before I could call him and seek help, he turned on his heel and ran off. I cursed him to my heart's content and went about my business.

I picked up the coconut, split it on the stone floor, and gathered its dense water in the bowl. I gave the boy a sip. He lay still, but towards noon of the second day he began to shake with a chill, so I fed the fire. I took off my shirt—for I was warm, what with the fire and my fretting anxiety about this boy and my own future. I had eaten several mangoes whose pulp had slopped on my trousers. I washed them, my only pair, in the river, and coming back, laid them near the fire to dry.

It was late afternoon now. I crouched naked, as the rain tapered off, wondering what to do next. Should I seek help from the nearest village? Surely the Company ship had departed, being in a hurry to deposit the young lord in Dacca. But I did not want to chance being seen, for a deserter is whipped, sometimes to death itself. In the sudden silence after the rain, I brooded about the child. Although he had taken some sips of coconut water, he did not want any food. His breath had grown very shallow, and I feared he was surely drifting towards death. The low flame lit his emaciated face. Death was writ large on it.

What instinct there lies in humans, perhaps ingrained in us from the time of unhoused Adam—or more likely, wandering ousted Cain—but I knew that there were people prowling about among the trees that ringed this old temple. Something told me not to dash out, or to show myself. I crept to the darkest corner of the doorway to peer. The shadows in the trees made a chiaroscuro before me. The sinking sun sent out a blazing shaft that must have nigh blinded anyone looking at the temple, which lay under a tangle of shadows of the encroaching wall-rupturing banyan. I spied a straggle of villagers, the group getting larger, by ones and twos, as others joined them holding scythes, spear-like sticks, a number of machetes. Among them, I saw two uniformed sailors, Hanratty and Landry.

*They know I am here*, I thought frantically, *What can I do?* The ancient wily Druid blood in me must have prompted my head, for I was not aware of any conscious thought, just a few flickered pictures.

I did not retrieve my trousers. I reached into the dead ashes which lay in a swath, holding the live embers only at the centre. With the crumbly ashes, I rapidly smeared myself. I freed my kerchief. My hair, which had grown long, and my bushy uncut beard, like my hair, spread out, plentiful and black. I poured great handfuls of ash and rubbed it into my skin, front and back, into my hair and beard. I wrenched the trident from the ground in an afterthought, as much for effect as for defense. I would not die alone, I was determined, and I had no other weapon about me. Then I calmed myself. I wanted to master the situation. I would not dart out as if I were a cornered animal and let my assailants rejoice that they had surprised me. No, I would do the unexpected.

I stepped out of the temple with a measured step, as if it were part of a primeval ritual, and standing absolutely still and tall, with the trident at arm's length, leaning on the ground, I began to mimic that cry which I had heard: "*SH I I V A A.*"

The villagers stood rooted. At their fairs they expected spectacle, but now something from their world of imaginings had invaded their waking. They began to drop to the ground, as if struck by its great force. They lay prostrate, their weapons abandoned, whispering their dread in some unknown tongue. Only the two soldiers from the ship remained standing. Then one of them spoke. It was Hanratty. There was some kind of recognition in his manner, but it soon became clear what he was seeing.

"Hey Landry, 'tis that fellow as had the hook and whirling about. I want to check his shoulder, I surely do." He advanced towards me, but the crowd seemed reluctant to wake from its dream.

"No, no go . . . holy man!" protested a man in broken English.

Landry mimicked flight in the air, twirling round and round on his feet. Somehow he made it seem comic. The villagers were now looking keenly at me, not as if at a preternatural phenomenon, but with searching eyes, while the sailors tittered among themselves.

The crowd imperceptibly gathered closer together, a wall, a very phalanx of death. They had picked up their machetes, scythes, and sharp sticks. I could sense their breath, see the flex of their fingers on their weapons. At any moment, one of them would break forward with a cry, sharp weapon raised. There would be a flailing. I would impale one or two, and struggle with another, while someone would cut me from behind, a spurting crimson slash. Then would come a frenzy of strokes, and my Irish eyes would close upon this alien Indian ground, soaked with my blood, and I would die, naked, smeared with ash, far from home.

But in this breathless moment, with my blood a gong in my head, I saw the villagers struck motionless again. In that hush, their weapons did not fall from their hands: they dropped their weapons from their grasps, as if they had been holding unclean things.

*What is it?* my numb mind wondered.

I felt my free hand clasped by a small palm. The frail boy was standing beside me like a naked young angel.

A chorus of ululation rose about us. One man spoke out, putting the seal of reality upon the moment.

"Ramkumar, O Ramkumar," he said. They were touching the child, weeping softly, greeting him back from the dead.

Tim Landry giggled. The crowd shifted and glared at him. A couple of men picked up their machetes. Landry turned tail, closely followed by Hanratty. But as he retreated through the trees, Landry screamed out, "Good luck, goo'bye," in a high mocking voice. He thought he knew it all.

But I had begun to comprehend what had been enacted on this Indian riverbank: I had once taken one stranger's life beside a river far away. Here I had been an instrument to convey some other stranger back from the dead.

I felt powerless to question destiny.

# Brendan
## 1846

It was late when Mr. O'Flaherty came back home from Mullaghmore. He walked slowly, his eyes fixed on the ground as if he was memorizing every bit of the road's surface and curve, and he was entering blindness and preparing for it.

We sat before our meal which I had prepared. Maeve wanted to say the prayer, which she did with a great sense of importance. The meal for which we so elaborately thanked our Lord was half a potato for Mr. O'Flaherty and a glass of water; one potato I had cut into squares, triangles, and one star, and some diced tiny pieces that were put into the shape of a conical hill for Maeve, together with her small glass of sweet buttermilk; I had made a mash from my potato and had poured myself some ale. Maeve was delighted with her meal, while I calculated how many more we would have before we all starved. I put what was left of the buttermilk by Maeve's pillow, on the bed I made for her near the last warmth of the fireplace, in case she got hungry at night. That, and a glass of cool water.

As I was putting the meal together, Mr. O'Flaherty had spoken in a low voice with Maeve. Maeve did not ask about Padraig's ma anymore, as she had done all day with me. As she knelt before bed with Mr. O'Flaherty by her side, I heard them pray together for the safe voyage of Mrs. Aherne's soul.

Over her head, his gaze met mine and held it. It was a bitter struggle for me to stay silent and not cry out in my heart's pain for the loss of what had been left of my own childhood. My meek mother gone, the strong and beautiful Maire Aherne dead, my reckless friend Padraig lost and likely under the heavy earth, and I, sick at heart and bereft.

• • •

WE BARELY SURVIVED 1846, with no rent to pay and only three mouths to feed. Winter set in, and with it hard rain and sleet. We knew that dread times were come to our very doorstep. We were a fort besieged.

The reports were getting more ominous across our ravaged land. Mr. Rafferty came by again and stayed with us for a day. He told us that in a village near Clare Abbey, a man with a gun came out of a ditch and confronted the overseer face-to-face. The overseer was accompanied by five soldiers just a few steps behind him. After shooting the overseer, the man from the ditch coolly told them to hold off, as he had done all he wanted, that is, to shoot only the overseer. Then he disappeared into the night, the soldiers standing frozen. The overseer, howling with pain, stumbled the better part of a mile to get himself home, around which had gathered a great number of local tenants, laughing aloud and letting it be known that far from going for a doctor, they did approve of the ninety pellets in his sorry hide. But such acts had dire consequences, for the English authorities turned out nine hundred tenants on the streets, tumbling their homes. That is, ten tenants for each pellet.

The Great Hunger was now in plain sight here in County Sligo. Half-naked mothers, shivering and pale, rooted amid dead turnip fields like flocks of blackbirds. Children and emaciated men lined the lanes, young boys crouching by road signs to Boyle and Collooney, too weak to stand. In Sligo, Ned Behan told me that every morning there was the unthinkable sight, growing more common in village lanes: the gaunt dead, and the hovering and bold morning crows.

I had begun to wake up with angry headaches. Their only remedy for me was to walk them off, alone. I would trudge down to the wharf and sometimes stare at the water for hours together. At Sligo harbour, where ships had returned from other parts of Ireland, Ballyshannon, Tralee, Killala, and Dublin, I heard the sailors talk of unbelievable sights by busy quaysides, where waiting to be shipped out from our Ireland to English ports were mighty piles, bales and boxes full of peas and lard, honey and seed, herring, wheat and rye, and butter in hundreds of huge firkins, not to mention great numbers of sheep and beef-cattle waiting to be boarded. Grain was being sent to Scotland for making whiskey. How could Ireland be dying of hunger?

By the wharfside I once found an old discarded London newspaper. Mr. O'Flaherty and I read it, every column on each page. We tried to discern from these worn pages what the English thought of the panorama of hell unfolding all over Ireland. But there was nothing about our starvation in the pages; the biggest news and controversy, it seemed, was the shifting of the venue of the Oxford-Cambridge boat race from Henley-on-Thames to Putney.

Ireland might not exist after all, judging from these pages. I understood then that we lived on a separate island, surrounded by water, indifference, and death.

• • •

FAMINE FEVER MADE its appearance now, all over the starving counties. As people fell ill, their faces swelled and the fever grew and intensified, their hands jerked about uncontrollably, and their faces turned unaccountably black. We began to hear that some of the sick—so burning with the fever they felt—jumped into icy waters. Many threw themselves from their windows in delirium. Some were sore tormented by a virulent and disfiguring rash, so many called it the spotted fever. The odour was so loathsome that even dear ones were abandoned and left to die, lying in their detritus, which smelt hardly worse. When the doors were forced open, the malodour was so powerful that the officials pitched back into the streets, a-covering their faces, spitting and retching to get away.

Mr. Scully at Sligo harbour told me what he had heard from travelers about the horrors in Skibbereen, once an agricultural centre west of the fine harbour at Cork. He showed me an outraged letter which Nicholas Cummins, the respected magistrate of Cork, had written to the Duke of Wellington, an Irishman himself, which was printed in the *Times* on Christmas Eve, 1846, about the numerous famine dead here and the state of the land. An English official wrote that where he went, skeletal figures descended on him and tore open his clothes begging and gibbering. At one point a woman, naked but for a rag around her bony loins, handed him something. He looked down and saw a dying infant, its umbilical cord still attached.

There was another odd item in the papers: Through some

quirk of nature, mostly in County Clare, children in the extremity of starvation were growing long facial hair, sometimes as much as grew on their heads, causing some mirth among passing officials from England who speculated about their undoubted superiority to the Irish species.

Back home, I had begun to dread the arrival of Mr. Rafferty in his cart. He invariably stopped by to see Mr. O'Flaherty and bring us news, all of which was bad. Now he told us what been perpetrated in Ballinglass of County Galway, a prosperous village with sixty-one houses, built and kept by the tenants. Besides, by their own labour they had reclaimed four hundred acres from a neighbouring bog. Here a certain Mrs. Gerrard had all her tenants summarily evicted although the rent money was not unpaid. But we Irish had no rights. That is why we curse Elizabeth, curse Cromwell, curse history, and our fate. Captain Brown of the Forty-ninth Infantry and numerous police constables threw them out. The women wailed and clung to their doorposts, from which they were dragged away, the children bewildered and screaming with fear. The families dug holes in the ground, roofing them with sticks and sod. There they stayed the next few nights. These were called "scalps." The ones that were deeper and wider were called "scalpeens." Ah, the depth and marvel of our Irish words!

Some blackened their faces at night and took to the killing of small landlords, who were no longer easy on their beds.

"The great ones, like our Palmerston," said Mr. O'Flaherty, "make sure they are out of reach."

● ● ●

THAT WINTER I sodded over the seaward wall, but the cold would finger its way through every crack, quivering the wick-flame of the candle. The path outside our cottage grew hard and slippery as a mirror, as it had taken turns to sleet and rain and sleet again.

One dead night, an enormous moon stood overhead and gloated on the Bulben until everything froze over, and the tree in the front yard cracked down the middle. That tree would surely die, turning skeletal. It seemed an omen.

I tried to keep a cheerful face, and in the last months spent time reading or telling Maeve stories. When she asked about her father, we told her how he had bravely set out for travel, and that seemed to merge into all the other stories of journeys and voyages to far lands. She loved to draw on a slate board while Mr. O'Flaherty wrote, and when I read, Maeve would pretend to do the same.

So, I thought, I'd turn my thoughts from hunger and slow fear and teach her to read. Mr. O'Flaherty watched with his usual twinkle. I knew he was letting me take all the decisions of raising Maeve myself, as if it were a benign apprenticeship, a vocation for life in an era of death.

I took her to church with me on the Sabbaths, but Mr. O'Flaherty in the passing days seemed not to want to go, and when Maeve begged to stay back with him in our garden and listen to his stories instead of the weekly hectoring and thundering of Father Conlon. When it troubled me, I remembered how Padraig's ma too had chosen thus.

In September of 1847, while Ireland starved, my lost friend Padraig's daughter Maeve, our joy, perfectly mastered her letters two months before she rose to four years of age.

• • •

A FEVERED FLIGHT from Ireland, the stampede of the starving and the well-nigh dead had started, and having started, became a roaring stream westward. The great Lord Palmerston had let it be known through all his wide holdings in County Sligo that he had made fine arrangements to transport his tenants across the sea on comfortable ships, with ample provisions for one and all, adequate drinking water and ale. Upon landing in Canada, we were told, we would be met by his lordship's agents, who'd give us seed money to buy fertile farmland there, masters of the land we tilled. Such tidings came to us in waves of rumour, despair, and hope.

"What better offer can there be?" I asked Mr. O'Flaherty, when I brought back this bit of news from Sligo harbour, "and why would he even offer us this?"

Rubbing his hands over the small flame, Mr. O'Flaherty explained to me, "We shall be ballasts, Brendan. The ships which bring over the Canadian timber have little to take back. If you remember that his lordship will pay the ship-owners three pounds twelve shillings per passenger to be transported to Canada, it is the cheapest way to clear the tenants who have rented and tilled his land for generations. If they were to continue living here—and he were to do his moral duty—the cost of keeping one person in the poorhouse is seven pounds three shillings per year. His lordship's grasp of arithmetic is impeccable. And if large numbers of his starving tenantry took up arms in their dying hands, it would be an embarrassment, for Palmerston is on his way to becoming the Prime Minister of Britain. Aye, Brendan, we shall have to see what fine greeting awaits us in the Promised Land."

I surveyed his unsmiling face. The coins that Mrs. Aherne had left us had gone in buying what we could at exorbitant prices. We were facing stark hunger now.

I voiced my fear. "But if we wait, things are going to get worse.

As bad as surely the ships are, they will become worse. What if the free transports stop?"

With a grimace, Mr. O'Flaherty said, "Ah, with the luck of the Irish, a gust of fevered wind could easily carry all three of us away."

Mr. O'Flaherty had been eating little, pleading lack of appetite, and I had lost all of mine from sheer worry. Maeve ate little enough. Some mornings I could scarcely get out of bed, but would drag myself to the wharfside in Sligo, for it had become the source of all the news I managed to glean.

• • •

WHEN THE FIRST of these famine ships, the *Eliza Liddell*, reached St. John, with its starved shipload, a storm of protest broke out from the Canadians. The few Dublin papers that reached us reported that when the *Richard Watson* arrived, carrying Palmerston tenants, including one woman completely in a state of nature, the Common Council of the City of St. John accused Palmerston by name for deporting his tenants completely unprovided for in the New Brunswick winter.

It was common knowledge that an untold number had perished on the high seas, thrown overboard into the swallowing Atlantic. The ships kept no account of them: The senders did not, nor the land they never reached, though there were exact ledgers for all the convict ships that left for Australia, transporting the hapless ones England called criminals, to Botany Bay. But we were free Irish, free to leave and die. If ever in the future any relatives were to make queries, there would be few answers to be found.

Upstream on the Garavogue, our prosperous merchant Peter

O'Connor's ships, which brought in Canadian lumber all the way to his great sawmills, were being used. Many other ships were coming to Sligo port. I read, plastered on harbour walls, Notice to Passengers, full of descriptions of the comforts on board. But around the ports, amid eddies of muddy water and ship detritus, floated other stories—of supplies running out on ships overloaded with all manner of cargo, water scarce or so tainted that none who drank it could remain hale. We heard of criminals who preyed upon the old and the children, the sickness that crouched waiting in the ship's holds.

Yet such was the beauty of our Sligo coast, such the majesty of Ben Bulben and the gorse-laden slopes, that I clung to our cottage, holding off the decision to leave. Aye, I was no Padraig. I was that afraid of the unknown, if my heart's truth be told. I dared not speak to myself of the time I would lose my country, tree by tree, rock beyond rock, hill after green hill. I sat, gluttoned upon grief, emaciating.

Where was the great Dan O'Connell now, him with his great talking of liberty and justice and rights, when all that we be asking are not even whole potatoes, but gruel and horse oats perhaps, or the glutinous paste of American maize?

On Maeve's fourth birthday this November of 1847, although we had little stock of victuals left, I made her a small cake with the very last of our flour. I painted a small tin box in merry colours. Maeve's smile lit our cottage that evening.

• • •

THREE DAYS LATER, I forced myself to prepare Maeve. "Do you . . ." I began, but could find no more words. I looked haplessly at Mr. O'Flaherty, who smiled bleakly at me.

"Maeve dear," he said, reaching out to hold her palm, "will you go sailing with us?"

"Do we have to?" she asked, looking at him.

"I did not want to," said my teacher, "but now I have changed my mind."

"Nobody comes here to play anymore," said Maeve. "Will there be other children on the ship?"

"Yes," I said. "Yes, I am sure."

"Where will we go?" she asked both of us. Before I could say anything, Mr. O'Flaherty said, "We'll go to America, Maeve." Well, that was easily done, I thought, when Maeve asked, "Why do people go to America?"

"I think different people go for different reasons," I ventured, not sure what I meant.

"Are we looking for something?" she asked. "When shall we come back?"

I stared at the floor.

"We don't know, Maeve. Sometimes we do not know what we are looking for, until we find it," said Mr. O'Flaherty, making it sound like a children's riddle.

Maeve did not smile. "Is that what happened to my father? When will he know if he's found it?"

We sat silently. Then Maeve's face broke into a smile. "Do you think my da is there, waiting for us?"

"America," said Mr. O'Flaherty so softly that he must have been speaking to himself.

"Shall we stop moving about after that?" Maeve persisted.

We nodded. "Yes, Maeve. If that is what you want," Mr. O'Flaherty added.

"Do you promise?" She was asking me directly.

"What if you want to travel more, Maeve?" I asked her. "People sometimes grow up and change their minds."

She shook her head, "I am sure."

"All right," I said to her, "I promise, if that is what you wish."

"You won't change your mind?"

I shook my head, "I promise you, child."

"I promise too." She spat in her palm, and we shook hands. I did not know what promise this child was making, and to what end. But for the nonce, that seemed enough.

*Ach, but Padraig? What if he returns?* whispered my tormented heart.

• • •

ON THE WATER, cormorants dipped and flew amid the rancid kelp. We stood by the quayside, waiting to board the *Rose of Erin*, probably the last ship to sail out so late this year. I would have preferred to await spring and a better passage, but knew we could not survive winter. We were shabby beyond belief. I glanced back to look at those staying behind. I spied a woman near the inn behind the harbour, gesturing to the sailors. She stood in wretched profile, her hands folded over a concave stomach, her groin protruding, a pathetic dribble of hair between her legs clear as the wind pressing into her sorry shanks. 'Twas the stark prose of what was happening to our land.

I looked at our bundles. In a pile were Mr. O'Flaherty's books and my Bible. Maeve held her tin box with a hand-painted picture of a rose on it. Its two clasps were painted gold. I could hear the rattle of her coloured chalks with every step she took. I had brought two porcelain bottles with cork stoppers for water. They promised us a fair ration of water every day, but I knew that if they failed, we would have something to store a little in—even if it were rainwater saved—for lack of water can make a child wilt and die, and an old man too. I was now, without being so, the son of one and father of the other.

Maeve played at the water's edge, her fist full of wet pebbles, while I waited for her to select a few for her little box. She would be carrying a wee part of Ireland, I thought, picking her up to walk the creaking gangplank onto the ship. Mr. O'Flaherty followed us with slow steps. Mr. Rafferty brought up the rear, and we exchanged a bleak greeting.

In the hold, I made sure to find space near a porthole which was waist-high. I knew the child needed fresh air, and the light that came in would bring what small cheer could be had in the belly of this ship with its odour of mould and foetid air. There was no sign of the rose in our ship so bravely named.

I sailed away, dry-eyed and in silence, from Sligo harbour on the twenty-fourth day of November of 1847, from this beloved corner of the earth, knowing I would not see this shore and green ever again. It was soon to become the shadow land I would walk in my restless slumber.

# III

*therefore I have sailed the seas*

# Brendan
## Rose of Erin

Every day upon the earth I had marveled at the height of the sky. Now I was aware of awesome depth. What a great, grey thing the ocean was under us!

Mr. O'Flaherty liked being on deck, craning his thin neck and noting the wind, the slant of the sun, the sails. But on bad days, with waves slapping the ship about, its bucking and swaying, heading down and sidling up, the juddery movement would bring a groan to his lips though he would sit by the porthole and, never mind the odd spray, close his eyes and doze himself into submission.

To our front and behind were the Behan clan, the father, mother, their two unwed daughters, four dour sons, their wives, and their numerous children. It was as if County Sligo had emptied itself of all Behans. When the children got restive and began to bother each other, the women would slap the ones next to them, irrespective of who was to blame, "Joe, Teddy, Molly, Jock, Pat, Willy," and with each name went a hearty smack, followed by yowls, "But I'm Jack, and I didn't," and so forth. Sometimes one of the Behan men absently swatted a whining child—"Stop that, Peter"—and the child blubbered, "But Peter's dead. I'm Davy. Molly pushed me," followed by silence and Davy whimpering.

On the other side of the hold next to a porthole, huddled three young men. I did not know all their names. One among them, White Danny as his friends called him, had hair that hung limp as kelp but ghostly white. Under invisible brows stared his eyes, which were pale blue, his lashes thick, long, and colourless. His raw red-rimmed lids reminded me of a vicious rabbit with its sharp buck-teeth, for these he had too. He would flick a pink tongue against his lips so thin that his mouth looked a wound. I noticed that he would, whenever his fellows dozed between their endless card games, piss out the porthole. This Danny would keep staring in our direction, at Maeve.

At the back of us there were other families, including one of the few Anglo-Irish families I knew in Sligo. They were two thin girls, Misses Mary and Theodora, and their mother, Mrs. Felicita Snow, who used to keep a fine shop selling lace in Sligo Town and bought the lace my poor mamma made. She nodded at me, as if acknowledging me in her dainty shop, a worn beauty, gone sad and haggard, and obviously on her last legs, but a lady for all that. Miss Mary was the one who looked after all their needs, while pale Miss Theodora, the younger sister, seemed tainted with the gaiety of the doomed.

But few looked as wan as Katie Sweeney, whose sturdy husband carried her on deck and walked with her up and down, as effortlessly as if he were carrying a baby. Even when the spray rose, and others took refuge down below, he would cover himself with a thick shawl and sit with her on his lap if she were content. He sat steady no matter how the sea rocked the ship.

The sailors, a rough lot, all blurred together for me, except the one called Will Hayward, whose bronze curls and lithe walk set him apart. I was too shy to look at him or talk, but he was among those who distributed the first rations, and more than once gave me four pieces of black bread, although we were three. The first time, when I looked up in some confusion, he smiled and moved on. I was stricken with guilt and a thrill. No one had noticed. Mr. O'Flaherty was gumming down his slice, and I hid the extra one in my shirt and shared it later with Maeve. Mr. O'Flaherty took half the day getting the best of the hard bread by soaking it in a bit of water.

We had been told casually on Sligo quayside itself that we were to bring with us as much food and provision as we could, as if in our homes we had full larders to choose from. According to Lord Palmerston's declarations, seven pounds of weekly provision per person would be provided. Mr. Behan said that this was seven pounds more than what he was providing his family on their days of starvation. But we discovered soon enough that we were to be given just two pounds or less of mouldy biscuits and such—per week. The water was unspeakably foul. Although we hated the stormy weather, we sucked on the wet canvas or gathered rain-water to drink. I was certainly grateful for my two bottles.

The characters of the people in the hold became clearer and stark in such proximity. Mrs. Snow never ate a crumb until her daughters did. She held herself that ridiculously erect, planting herself as a frail screen between herself and White Danny. When one of the Lewis children fell asleep, seasick and nauseated, still holding his morsel, Danny prised it on the sly and devoured it. It was a small enough morsel, but if the Lord in Heaven was not like another absentee landlord—for which thought let Him forgive me—then a fiery bed is made and waiting for Danny Soames.

What distressed me most were the unsanitary conditions, men and women indiscriminately using either of the slop-holes at the far ends, the detritus falling into the sea. We used as little paper as we could, sacrificing one of Mr. O'Flaherty's books for the purpose. It was John Locke's *An Essay Concerning Human Understanding*, starting from the conclusion and worked our way towards Locke's opening argument. We hoped to reach Canada before we needed to use the Dedication.

There was an unwritten sort of rule that when the ladies went, the men either did not go at that time, but if perforce they had to, would only use the larboard one. But the card players would crowd around when some of the young women had to relieve themselves, causing them much discomfiture, and themselves indecent pleasure. When Mr. Sweeney bore his wife to the back, he would spread his shawl across her, and look about fiercely, and none dared say anything in jest or look thither.

Very early one morning I heard Maeve rise and make her way to the slops. Needing to go too, I rose to follow her. Up there lurked Danny with Miss Theodora Snow. I was confounded by such unseemliness, but he did not meet my eyes and scurried away, smirking. I wondered what Maeve had seen, and resolved to keep an eye on him, for there surely was a sickness in that Danny's mind. Once in a while he would steal a glance at me, his shoulders silently shaking in mirth at this sordid sport.

The next morning was cold but sunny, so we were all on deck, basking in the mild sun and steady wind. Perched on the broad railing of the deck, I leant against some rigging, swaying lazily with the motion of the ship. I must have dozed when suddenly came a violent shove. What primordial instinct it was, I do not know, but my hands flew out, one of them finding the rigging ropes in a desperate grasp. Dangling, I could see the churn of water, and out of the corner of my eye, glimpsed a pale hand pull quickly away. I hauled myself back and crouched on the deck, shaking. Maeve caught me around the neck fiercely, weeping and shuddering, and I held her to me.

"I am afraid of him, Papa Brendan," she said not letting me go.

I knew better than to tell the child that nothing was wrong and met her eye directly. "I will be very careful from now on," I promised.

But my heart sang. She had called me what she would call me for the rest of my life: Papa Brendan, a name she had devised herself.

• • •

THE SUN DISAPPEARED for a week after that day, and we felt the cold wind's edge whenever we ventured on deck. In the hold, we were a new village now, and indulged in idle talk. Many of the women sought each other out, at first based on whether they had been neighbours, talking of old days, often about times when their husbands were just boys looking at them. They were momentarily happy, even as they sat in this dreary transit, recalling that old life now past redeeming with any coin they could muster. Mr. O'Flaherty seemed to be reading his battered copy of Seneca over and over, while some would sing, our Maeve not the least among us. But whenever Ruairi and Jamie Egan broke into song, it was a matter of loud cheer down in the hold, their voices twining like a silver and a golden cord, making their song twice sweet. Mr. Rafferty would clap and stamp his feet until well after the others had stopped. One particular evening the brothers sang:

> *On the Curragh of Kildare and the boys will be there*
> *With their pikes in good repair, says the Sean Bhean Bhoct . . .*
> *What colour should be seen where our fathers' homes have been*
> *But our immortal green, says the Sean Bhean Bhoct,*
> *Yes old Ireland will be free from the centre to the sea*
> *Ah hurrah for liberty!*

And just as they ended, we were surprised by another voice behind us. It was Mr. Lewis. His clear baritone was a thing of wonder, and the musty hold which we had all cursed seemed to cradle and caress the beauty of his voice in its hollow. The old song "Eibhlin a Run" became a haunting call of the soul, and when he went on to "The Parting of the Friends," I sank into silence.

"And are you thinking of my father?" asked Maeve, leaning into my arm. I nodded, not trusting words.

"I hope someone sings that song to him," she said. For a moment, I thought that dead Maire Aherne herself had sent her the words, if such were possible.

We were brought back to the present by the loud wrangle, for some had suggested "The Lamentation of Deirdre," but Mr. Sweeney gruffly rejected it saying, "Nay, nay, none of that Leinster mooing—let's have 'Ruairi of the Hills' right away, what say ye all?" Without waiting, he launched with tuneless vigour into the lines, while everyone shook with laughter. It would take more than that to silence him, for he sang manfully to the end.

So our merriment ran. When we finally stopped, all we could

hear was the soughing of the cold wind, the slap and cough of Atlantic seawater, as we settled to sleep.

• • •

SEVENTEEN DAYS INTO our voyage, the great swells on the ocean turned choppy, and the hold wheezed and groaned as if it too felt the cold. The stormy troughs made the ship glissade down hills of water, to be struck by some mighty hand that sent a shudder through the beams and a terror in our bones, and heart-stopping moments when walls of surrounding water seemed to be closing in on our little wooden world, before the ship like a cornered animal in its burrow turned and seemingly leapt to escape.

The hatches were battened down, the portholes spurting seawater like hoses—so these were closed off. The hold became foetid, and all of us felt like animals shaken convulsively on our way to slaughter, the floor slippery with vomit and human detritus. During this first onslaught of storm, Mr. Lewis was flung down by a sudden buffet and, losing his footing, crashed against a beam. He cried out in pain, and whimpered with every lurch. Only after the storm passed did we find that he had crushed his collarbone.

A number of us in the hold beat upon the shut hatches, called out, and banged as hard as we could with whatever we had, our fists, pewter plates, until finally they were opened. We emerged on deck, gasping and coughing, spumes of vapour trailing from our mouths because the weather had turned chill, something we had not been aware of in the crowd and close of the hold.

The air felt blessed, but the sea was not calm, resembling a vast pot of water about to boil. The clouds were looming low. The crew laughed at our discomfiture and informed us that a worse buffeting awaited us. Down we needed to go and the dreaded boards closed shut upon us again, they shouted at us, for the deck would be awash with waves, and anything not battened down swept to sea.

On deck, Mr. Lewis, who had stood quietly beside me, listening to them, breathing sibilantly with pain, suddenly began to climb the stairs towards the captain's deck. We looked on in surprise, as nobody had access to it without permission. He hauled himself on to the rail, face drawn and pale. Abruptly he turned, then flung himself into the sea and was immediately lost to sight.

Many rushed to that part of the deck-rail to see whether he would surface. For my part, I stood rooted where I was. Mr. O'Flaherty said bleakly, "Come, Brendan." Holding Maeve's hand, he returned to the hold. I followed in silence.

In less than an hour came the second storm, screaming over us, tearing at the ship with an ululating sound, and the pitch and the roll began—and with it, the retching and moaning in the hold. By noon it was the very picture of hell with all its suffering. The hollow sound of weeping filled the space. At one period—perhaps 'twas our ship in the eye of the storm—there was a strange calm.

"Mamma, Mamma," called a child's voice in a whisper, "are you dead, Mamma?"

● ● ●

THE NEXT MORNING, when the hatches were opened, I helped Maeve and Mr. O'Flaherty to the deck. The unseasonable sun erased the last of a hovering mist on the tranquil waters as if the storm had been a bad dream. The others began to emerge like the dead revived, peering into the growing radiance of the sun and the easy puff of the sails soaring overhead. Then they brought out the dead: an infant of the Behans; Mr. Rafferty, the itinerant farrier from Cliffoney, his many journeys now over; old Mrs. Snow. Finally emerged Mr. Sweeney, his wife's limp body cradled in his arms.

Once the bodies were, with a short prayer, resigned to the waters, a huge quarrel broke out. A cooking vat and meager provisions appeared: smelly, mouldy, and far short in weight and expectation. I was amazed to see Mr. Sweeney, dumb with grief at his wife's death, become vociferous about this cheating by the captain, and demand to get his due. Will, the sailor, stood casually next to me, but I turned away in a weariness of spirit. He had slipped an unspoilt biscuit into my pocket. I gave it to Maeve, who began to eat it surreptitiously.

Our Maeve had the frail resilience of a sapling, but Mr. O'Flaherty seemed dazed and somewhat deaf for the ordeal. There had been little mention of God so far, except to take His name in despair or anger. We had no one to say Mass on board, and I wondered if that familiar and comforting ceremony could have cast its soothing unction on my trammeled soul. When I mentioned this to Mr. O'Flaherty, he stared long through the porthole into the tilting sea and muttered, "Pray within your heart, Brendan, if that is the medicine you need." I was perturbed by his tone, but he smiled bleakly at me and looked away.

I always lived with faith in God. I had not examined my faith in this dark hold, or before, in the deaths and hungers: I saw only the hand of man. But now the dark night of my soul came upon me not in the depth of all the suffering. It did not come to me unawares, but like a brother who sat by me in full sight. All the beauty I had lived amid, or imagined, seemed tainted.

I sat on the warming deck and closed my eyes, worn out in spirit. The air smacked of the earlier chill, but the sun was full on my face. In my torpor, I heard the clack and rattle of the sea-heavy ropes on the board-planks as the crew worked. In that bright and hungry day I fell into a deep sleep. I dreamt of County Sligo and its hungry and the dead, and the wandering cadavers all over our Ireland. The picture of my friend Malachi O'Toole's body, wrapped in his soiled green horse-blanket, came back to me—and his two-year-old daughter too, a month after their cottage was tumbled—crack-lipped and sharp-boned in mortal hunger. My faith was faltering, whimpering for breath. The stone and dirt on which I had walked in those last days in Ireland had no part of You whatever—these had been dirt and stone itself and nothing else—and even the magical moon above, only a dead stone in Your sky, forever in silent gong proclaiming Your criminal absence.

All Your loveliest miracles, Lord, revolve around food. On the arid stretches under glittering desert stars beyond the parted Red Seawhere, stamping the Egyptian soil from their feet, the faithful partook what You provided from thin air. At Cana. On the beach by the Sea of Galilee. The last simple and Lordly Supper . . . Are we not Your children too, with equal need for sustenance?

To be deep drowned by the Flood, to be swirled by an engulfing fire—ah, that is grand, Lord, but to be eaten away by the slimy blight, its rheumy stench foetid in the nose—ah, Lord—that is a low trick. And You, our glorious Lord, are turned into a dastardly gombeen, trashing our lives and forcing our faces into our hunger-retching and gut-drool, left with nary a scrap of dignity, on a soiled and soggy floor.

Do we not try, Lord, to make our own tiny Eden with whatever we can—and do You not, dread Lord, drive us out? A safe home and a mouthful are so little to ask. Why do You in Your heaven resent our frail homes, and Your howling winds rage against our humble hearths?

I was startled awake by a shout. The seamen with the others on deck crowded the starboard deck, and then the larboard: a gigantic whale had crossed our wake, spouting its way, and then disappeared from sight.

All the sailors said that it was an omen of bad luck.

• • •

THE HOLD, AS the one futile lantern swayed in a corner, was dim. I noticed Miss Theodora Snow sitting next to White Danny, who had given her a morsel; she was pretending indifference, gnawing what she clutched in her narrow fist, while White Danny's arm wound like a serpent about her waist. Her sister sat apart, anger and helplessness written on her face. Then I saw Danny leaning, as if unintentionally, against Miss Mary. She shrank from his touch and tried to shift, but there was little room. I was startled by Maeve's angry cry. She had sprung up.

"Get away from them," Maeve lashed, blazing at Danny. "My da Padraig will strangle you dead and throw you into the sea!" Then she added in a fierce whisper, "He is waiting for me in America." Her tender childhood had fallen away from our Maeve, her small back rigid as a provoked cat's, hackles rising.

Danny slid back into his corner among his mates. I was about to speak when I felt a hand clutch me, and turned to look at Mr. O'Flaherty, who made a small gesture for silence.

"What will happen when we reach America, and no Padraig?"

I whispered to Mr. O'Flaherty, beginning to understand her wound and her sword.

He shook his head, not inviting words.

● ● ●

I OBSERVED WITHIN myself a growing dislike for food, though I needed it for sustenance. I ate hurriedly, like a man who will walk quickly on thin ice because he must, neither enjoying the walk nor the unreliable process; 'tis such miserable matter on which our existence stands. It did not escape my pale gaze that a resentful anger returns with hunger, obliterating the little pleasure of food a few hours ago.

On the days when the sea was comparatively calm, a large cauldron was set on deck for gruel to be made. On this particular day, we all crowded around as the odd vegetable, sundry morsels, various grains were tossed in and stirred. Such was the hunger that Mr. Behan plunged his bowl in, impatient of the slow boil, to devour the half-cooked slop. When three or four others did so, complete pandemonium broke out, all semblance of order and fairness jettisoned.

The captain and the crew began to berate us at first, then stood apart, enjoying the mayhem among the wretched. With the greatest contempt for myself, I too plunged into the melee and snatched some victuals. I had two other mouths to provide for who would otherwise remain unfed. I could barely pour the unspeakable fluid down my throat. But I learned a great lesson. I had grimaced as I forced the slop into my mouth, but then I saw Maeve's eyes on me. She flashed me a conspiratorial smile and ate without any fuss or show of disgust. I knew what an effort it cost the child to keep her countenance from betraying the least distaste. Within this child, there was growing a young woman with a brave heart. And all it took was twenty-three days of this dreadful voyage.

Sailing with us was the captain's prize pig, which I was told he intended to sell in Canada for a stud animal—a huge beast, gargantuan and pink. I had noticed it when I had first got on board. Also, there were a couple of goats, for the captain fancied a little milk, like a new baby. Pigs and goats were the only creatures, sailors told me, to eat any muck given them, and no matter what battering the high seas dealt, the goats could be counted on giving milk. During the period of the rough seas, the sailors had forgotten to feed them for several days. We heard the occasional squeal or snort but had sunk into such a state of the primitive that these seemed no different from our guttural oaths of discomfort. Today a hue and cry rose when one of the sailors had gone to the captain's deck outside his cabin, perhaps to milk the goats, and set off a hullabaloo. The enormous hog in its desperate hunger had turned on the goats and savaged them for a grisly meal.

It was unthinkable for any of us to climb to the upper deck on pain of flogging. But Mr. Behan, phlegmatic though his nature appeared to be, led a crowd up the stairs. Before the amazed captain could utter a word, he reached in the filthy straw and withdrew dismembered parts not devoured entirely by the pig. Amid a great huzzah of joy, he flung the meat, hooves and all, barely skinned, into our pot and started such a wild dance around it— and so savage, joyous, and threatening it looked—that the captain was scared silent, although he followed Behan with baleful eyes, as if Mr. Behan himself had slaughtered his goats. We waited eagerly on deck for this windfall repast.

As we ate the soup, some started hopeful talk about new homes in America. Place-names were spoken of—and I mentioned to Mr. O'Flaherty how many were called *New This* or *Nova That.* "Brendan, beware the names called *New*," my old schoolmaster quipped, "the newer they be, the farther they are and more unlike what they mean to recall." Aye, I thought, for Adam finished naming all he needed to name. He did not say New Eden when he arrived down here with a flaming sword pointing at his arse. He just named it Earth, for thus he found it.

From that night Captain Hibbard posted a guard over his prize pig. A stiff gale had begun to blow, and snow turning to bitter sleet. Forthwith we were ordered belowdecks, and we did obey, all except Behan, whom the captain commanded to stay on deck to help the sailors make fast the boxes on deck. Behan, strong in spite of the starving time, was glad to comply, for he preferred the heavy work on deck to being huddled in the filthy hold.

The weather calmed by the following noon, though it had grown chilly. In the hold that night, Jamie and Ruairi Egan sang for their mother, Betty.

> *The priests are on the ocean green*
> *They march along the Deep.*
> *There's wine from the royal Pope*
> *Upon the ocean green . . .*

I remembered having heard them sing this very ditty after Bill Twomey's wedding in Collooney. Young Bill himself now sat next to me, holding his pretty wife Pia's hand, enjoying that memory.

"Some of our neighbours are still with us," I mused, "and they are all that is left me of County Sligo." I also remembered Mr. Lewis's fine baritone.

When we came up to the deck, we saw masses of ice were floating upon the slate-grey waters, but no sign of Behan. The sailors were evasive when Mrs. Behan kept screeching her question. Finally one sailor replied simply that the man had been swept overboard. We noticed now that the captain and the sailors had their blades and matlocks out. Mrs. Behan and her children kept screaming that our stomachs were responsible for her good man's death, that God would curse us surely. Everyone looked away as if her words were incomprehensible. How could she blame us and not the murderous captain?

I wondered that no one thought to place the blame where it belonged, but it was easier to blame ourselves: Is that what we do with God? This question coiled and swam in my thoughts. My long quarrel with Him had only begun. The full blast of winter and a joyless Christmas were coming—if we lived so long.

• • •

THE SUN WAS a pewter orb floating in mists that hung like curtains of shadows, and the ship made little headway. The captain had shut himself away in his cabin where he had his maps. Once in a long while he stamped outside, glancing this way and that in a twitch of indecision. Though the very prow of the ship was almost invisible, we felt unseen presences. Then, we heard in the very far distance, something fall from some great height into the ocean. Chunks of ice came floating to the hull with a dull *tock tock*, then floated away.

The sailors muttered that it was impossible to guide the ship, in the fog, despite the compass though we were only a few days away from shore. But we had little food left, and virtually no water.

From the ends of the long canvas of the lower sails, I was able to gather some moisture in a bottle. Maeve drank from it, and Mr. O'Flaherty took a small sip.

The captain stormed out again on his deck. Turning around, he stumbled on the pig and fell hard, to the general cheering of his passengers. Cursing and shaking his fist—with the pig grunting its displeasure, equally aloud—the captain withdrew into his cabin and slammed the door. Our Maeve clapped her hands with the rest of us, as if she had seen the first vaudeville show of her wee life and was powerfully pleased.

As the ship drifted ahead on the blind sea, there was a startling sound, a wrench of splintering timber. I heard cries in the hold, screams of pain. The ship had ridden up a sharp rise of land. Was it rock? A shiver of fright shook through me as sailors began sliding down the rigging.

"Ship aground!" rang the cry.

The bow was pointed up, and when I leant over the side, I saw the ship depending on a ledge of ice. The strongest clawed their way up from the hold. The ship's tilt made their climb perilous.

On deck, the large soup vat broke loose, clattering headlong, and smashed against the foremast. That was fortunate, for some steps behind it stood Mr. O'Flaherty, unable to move on the incline of the deck. I grabbed him with one arm and held Maeve with the other. With extraordinary presence of mind, the child clung to her blanket.

Although we had reached some unknown icebound shore, this was no beach rising gradually, but an abrupt wedge where the ship was breaking up and beginning to go under. The ground looked icy, with just a thin layer of snow, a bleak promontory that stretched from the slope of a looming icy palisade—a flat jut, like a thick tongue out into the ocean on which the ship had foundered—at least two men's height below the steeply angled deck.

"Let the ropes down, let them down," I shouted.

That was the only way we could safely reach the icy ledge and the headland. The ship was fast listing larboard when Mr. Sweeney and Bill Twomey had the presence of mind to slash off ropes from the rigging and hang them from the deck as it loomed above the ice. I looked around for the captain, wondering how he would direct us; then I saw that he and his crew were on board the lone lifeboat off the aft, ready to cast off. The only thing holding them back was the loading of two large sea-chests, and the dragging of the pig onto the boat. One of the chests had been hoisted on the rowboat. As the men lifted the second heavy sea-chest, the ship groaned audibly and twisted, as if in mortal pain. The awkward torque snapped a jagged tear through the entire length of the deck.

The remaining sea-chest slithered down the now steeper slope, gathered speed, and smashed against the front of the railings, but remained intact. Will Hayward writhed, his chest bleeding, then slid into the water. White Danny and his friends darted up and found purchase on the rowboat's side, trying to haul themselves on board, when Captain Hibbard raised an oar and brought it down on Danny's head. A red gash appeared instantly, and his grasp loosened. Another blow—and with a hoarse cry that ceased abruptly he plunged into the freezing waters. Captain Hibbard and his crew were abandoning us. He could easily have taken a dozen women and children in his long rowboat—perhaps for a more protracted suffering—but as captain, no matter how ineffectual, his betrayal left me breathless.

There was another wrenching sound. The pig lost its foothold and rolled against the railings, and as if on a rebound, fell overboard and landed on its back on the icy ledge, where it let out a long squeal. If there be a language in Pig, 'twas a rich phrase he uttered.

I could hear the rhythmic sound of rowing as the captain's boat pulled farther and farther off. A single torch lit their grimaced effort to get away.

Many of the people from the hold had now managed to get on deck beside us. Throwing down all the canvas and blankets we could lay our hands on, we prepared to slide down the ropes. I tied one of these around Mr. O'Flaherty and lowered him, while Bill Twomey, who had already helped his wife descend, helped steady him below. Then, clutching Maeve, and she wrapping her arms about my neck, I used all haste to descend, my palms rubbed raw by the rope. Standing on the hard ice, we watched as Mr. Sweeney climbed to the captain's cabin, and oddly enough, brought out the captain's chair and small rosewood desk. He also had two bottles of rum in each pocket of his greatcoat.

"Hurry, hurry, hurry!" I kept shouting from the ridge. And it was good that Mr. Sweeney did so, for as he cleared the ship, pulling the captain's small desk and chair after him—gasping and grunting—the mast smashed down on the ledge and broke into pieces. A small part of the icy ledge floated away after that impact. Some people leapt down in their desperate bid to reach safety. I watched that with as much horror as I did the ship which was now sliding sideways, weighed down by its wet sails, and began to disappear from sight into the unspeakable depth of the sea.

Mr. Sweeney, having regained his breath, courteously offered Mr. O'Flaherty the chair, and straddled his broad legs on both sides of the captain's desk as if it were a horse. The pig was snuffling and rooting about, trying to get inside the chest. Mr. Sweeney shooed it away, prised open the heavy box with his knife, and found it stuffed full of a variety of cheeses. This was greeted with great and momentary glee.

"What part of Canada are we on, Schoolmaster? What is your guess?" asked Mr. Sweeney. Sitting on the captain's chair, Mr. O'Flaherty replied mildly, "I do not think it is Canada just yet, Mr. Sweeney. This is an iceberg, a curious phenomenon."

He gaped at Mr. O'Flaherty. So did the rest of us.

The curdling of light which I had seen to the east indicating midmorning was now gone, hidden behind the vast mass that loomed behind us, from whose shadow a chill exuded that reached our very hearts.

• • •

SOME HAD FALLEN on the hard ice, while many had nothing worse than hurt ankles and knees. Misses Mary and Theodora Snow had scrambled to get on the captain's rowboat with the crew, but were beaten back with oars. Miss Mary fell into the icy water and sank from sight, but Miss Theodora hung on to the icy ledge, a large bruise across her face, moaning that her right bosom was severely hurt. She had lost her two front teeth and bled from her split lower lip. In jumping from the tilted rail of the ship to the ice-ledge, Mrs. Betty Egan's skirt had got tangled, and she had fallen head-first on the hard ice. Her sons, Jamie and Ruairi, had pulled her to safety, but she remained in a dead faint, her face much swollen, breathing shallow and irregular, wrapped in torn canvas. They tried to keep her warm, chafing her hands, but she died soon after. Bill Twomey and his sweet-faced wife, Pia, herself swollen with her first child, comforted them as best they could.

In spite of our initial optimism that most had escaped to the perilous ice-ledge, we began to comprehend that more than twenty people were not accounted for. We feared that in the dense fog, some of the unfortunates had lost their footing, there being nothing to hold. Sliding off the steep edge, they had sunk to their death, their cries stifled, for the merest touch of the black water was numbing. Some may not have made their way out of the tilted hold and drowned, struggling to get beyond the hatches.

What cheer had risen within us disappeared. Among us sat the mourning brothers and children and sisters, themselves facing certain death on a ledge of ice, weeping bitterly for those who had perchance preceded them by a few hours.

Behind us rose the crystalline floating mountain. Who could say what portion could crack off and come crashing down on our hapless refuge, perhaps breaking it off? What would happen if this frozen bulk floated southerly for days, where encountering warmer currents, it would dwindle and melt beneath our starved corpses?

• • •

MR. SWEENEY DISCOVERED to his glee when he managed to break off a small piece of ice and suck upon it, that the melting water was not bitter with the sea-salt, but sweet as Sligo spring water.

*What a strange creature you have created, Lord,* I whispered to my-self, who will abandon his fellow man to save his own sorry hide, even when there is ample space in the rowboat—and that rowboat impossibly far away from any land or rescue. And what creature falls on its knees and praises its merciful Maker when it finds that the ice is made of sweet water when it melts in his thirsty mouth, standing all the while on an inconstant island made of that water itself, but hardened in the palm of that Maker who keeps it afloat, for the nonce, on His ocean's deadly stretch.

In the dense night, the wind whispered around the bulk of ice. The fog began to clear, and I saw the budding of small celestial lights. We huddled under the clearing sky, and before long we could look up and see the firmament, barbaric now with stars. A phosphorescence emanated from our floating ice island. The sun would rise in a few hours, but now the cold stars reigned.

No one could say what cheer or succor the sun might bring. It might speed the melting of the iceberg. But we are creatures of the sun. The very prospect of sunrise seemed to touch something hopeful embedded within us, perhaps at birth itself. Mr. Sweeney declared that when the sun came up, he would catch the captain's pig and slaughter it for one last great feast. The pig seemed to comprehend what was said, and grunted angrily. We could see the beady glitter of its eyes and hear the gnash and jitter of its teeth. Some around us laughed, and Mr. O'Flaherty, still on his chair, said, "Ajax and his rival will meet tomorrow on this windy plain."

I do not know if I slept or no. It is darkest always before the sun comes up.

• • •

THE HORIZON WAS the faintest colour of purple, like a ray that falls aslant upon a fuchsia petal. It spread in a single streak through the eastern sky. I watched spellbound, aware that this might well be my last day on earth.

We had finished the cheese. There was to be no food today, unless Mr. Sweeney won his great combat on this windy plain. I meant to absorb all the beauty I could see and feel. I was a young man. I had lived only on one island and set foot in no other, unless I counted this most temporary of isles.

The rest of the sky was still black, but no longer the many-layered darkness cradling the moonless stars. It had grown pale, and the morning star stood bright. With astonishing rapidity the sun rose, a red yolk that spilt its colours on the far horizon, and then, seemingly in a rush, urged itself above the waters in a golden spread. I witnessed, far above the sleeping forms all around me, the top of the ice-mountain become glittering gold. It reflected some of that radiance onto an area of the sea which glistened in reflected glory. One large bird appeared from near the horizon, and upon its vast wings, floated into closer view and, passing us, flew behind the icy peak.

I was startled from my contemplation by a frantic shaking, and saw that it was Maeve, her face contorted with pain. Picking her up, I felt about her, wrapped as she was in the large and unwieldy blanket. I thought she had somehow been hurt. I had heard nothing, seen nothing that could have possibly harmed her. She was trying to speak, but unable to say anything at all, except for a terrible gasping. I thought she might be choking.

At the same time I became aware of all the people around me shouting, shrilly, hoarsely, in a variety of ways. From the corner of my eye I saw someone trying frantically to set fire to a pile of broken timbers from the mast. I was jostled about, but kept my hold on the frail and tormented child. I felt her thin bones beneath my searching palms and could see her sharp cheekbones, blue skin stretched over eyes tight shut.

I knelt on the hard ice, trying to gauge if anything was stuck in her throat. She opened her eyes, which were bloodshot, a terrible thing to see in a child.

"Where does it hurt, child, where is your pain?" I screamed in panic.

She shook her head. I was now sure she had had a bad dream. How can you avoid that, when being awake itself had become a nightmare? I still could not understand the uproar among all the people. Was the ice breaking up?

Maeve seemed to have calmed somewhat, her eyes not so flush with redness as a moment ago. As I struggled to find words to soothe the child, she reached out her small palm to stroke my cheek, trying to comfort me.

"Maeve?" I asked her.

"I will always be with you, Papa Brendan," she said.

"I know," I responded, wonder filling my mind at the words of this child. I looked over her head and now understood.

There, on the captain's chair, sat Mr. O'Flaherty—as he had through the night—head tilted as if he were still reading the book on his lap, calm and dead.

• • •

ALL ABOUT US the furor grew until it turned into an unbearable cacophony. I held Maeve in my arms. Through a veritable forest of swaying arms, swinging pieces of clothing, amid logs lit and smoking like impromptu flambeaux, the pig snorting and cavorting underfoot, I finally saw it: a large ship, with all its sails bulging, bearing straight for us.

The *Beatrix* could not get close to our shelf of ice. When they lowered a boat, there had been a general stampede to the edge where they all stood screaming, though there was now no need to do so. Maeve and I stayed beside Mr. O'Flaherty on his chair.

The pig kept going back and forth, snorting, running and wheeling back, unable to make up its mind.

The ship was Dutch, flying its flag, and its passengers, well fed and curious, lined the deck, watching. Among us, many were pushing to get on the rowboat, but the officer in charge, a small, pink man in a blue coat with two rows of shining brass buttons waved them back. He chose the women with young children first. As they pushed off towards the ship, the men began to get restive. Were they going to take us all? Just the women and children? It was a slow procedure getting the women—weakened by hunger, with children clinging to them—up the rope ladder.

The captain now sent two rowboats, and he himself came out in the second boat. As he made his way to us, at the middle of the ledge, I noticed how long his shadow was on the white expanse. Maeve, held the blanket around herself, and with great compo- sure, said, "Good day to you, sir."

An enormous smile broke over his face, revealing a gold tooth which glinted momentarily in the sun. I struggled to my feet and steadied myself, holding the edge of the table. He was an im- mensely tall man, with a golden beard, eyebrows like gilded wires, and brown eyeballs as large as coins. He spoke in a strange lisp. It was clear that he thought of our threesome as a grandfather, father, and child. *We are that*, I thought and did not offer any expla- nation. I did not have any Dutch, and given his English, I doubt I could explain much.

He beckoned Maeve to come, but she did not want to leave my side. Observing this, he gestured discreetly at Mr. O'Flaherty, unsure whether I realised that he was dead. I simply nodded my head to indicate that I already knew.

*"Komm,"* he said to me and led the way. I held Maeve's hand and followed him, sensing the urgency. The rowboats came back

quickly for the last trip. The short officer was also there: Mein-herr Hoogstraaten, who spoke fluent if broken English, lightly ac-cented. He gestured at Mr. O'Flaherty. I stepped aside with him, and explained what I wanted. Then I took Maeve and boarded the rowboat.

Hot black tea was being handed to us as we came on board. One small piece of bread had been given to each, and curiously enough, a tiny lump of salt.

"Captain DeLeeuw asked me to tell for you," said Officer Hoogstraaten, "welcome on board. You eat this little bread and tea only now, because your stomach needs to get used. The salt help your health. Don't throw away."

On the deck behind us, snorting after its meal, was the pig, which had also been rescued and seemed to have chosen us, espe-cially Maeve, as his companions. We were, we had just been told, only two days' sail from the mouth of the St. Lawrence River, and from there it was but a short way to Grosse Isle, Quebec, where the *Beatrix* would disembark us.

From its deck, as the *Beatrix* sailed away, I began to discern the shape of the great white mass from where we stood: Its height, its great level top, and the steepness that led to it, was exactly Ben Bulben itself. And below this floating and evanescent Ben Bulben, in the now deserted and temporary sloping valley, on a chair facing the open sea sat Mr. O'Flaherty.

On his lap lay the book I had seen him read so often in my school days, his battered copy of Cicero. I had picked up the book to glance at what he had been reading: *et ex vita ita discedo tamquam ex hospitio, non tamquam e domo. Commorandi enim natura devorsorium nobis, non habitandi dedit.* I put the book back on his lap. I have often thought of these words in later years.

Hand in hand Maeve and I stood by the deck rail as long as we could see Mr. O'Flaherty on his chair, until the receding Atlantic withdrew him from our lives. She was too young yet to understand the words our schoolmaster, Padraig's and mine, had been reading: *And I quit life as I would an inn, not a home, for nature has given us lodging for a sojourn, not a permanent residence.*

•  •  •

HAVING BEEN RESCUED from certain death, we should have thrived on this hospitable ship. But almost a dozen of our rescued shipmates could not get up even for their meals the next day. Their febrile faces pale, all dangers seemingly past, they began to falter from something within themselves. How strange it is, I thought, that had our goal been the far end of the new continent, these doughty ones would have trudged doggedly on, across hard mountains. If the aim had been the Pacific edge, they would begin to wither as they approached that far coast. I wondered if I were making a fool's observation, or whether we are all allotted the full measure of journeys that will exactly wear us out.

I could not help but wonder every so often where Padraig could have gone. He might have gone heedlessly to see England or France perhaps, but why, in heaven's name, would he not send word! He knew surely that Brigid would return. And what of his mother? Nothing could ever come between Padraig and his ma. Nothing, I thought with a shiver, but death. If he is alive, he will have a heartbreaking journey when he thinks to return. Brigid gone, Mrs. Aherne dead, his world swept away, and he not even knowing all that—or his own daughter.

•  •  •

A LARGE AND twittering flock of birds came winging, and rested on the masts and halyards. I could not tell you how pleasing and strange at once this felt. It was as if I were Noah of the old times. I observed the gabble and clucking of the great seabirds, ogling quietly from the riggings high overhead, the oozy splat of their guano, their yawping cry when I could see their pink open mouths. Behind the masts was a sky frizzled with clouds, and the morning breaking like milk over the waters. It seemed inconceivable that it was the same sky I had looked at the other night, with the stab and twinkle of the stars overhead.

I cannot say how many times I opened my mouth to speak to Mr. O'Flaherty, and then remembered. But Maeve was full of questions at every turn, and all that I could, I answered.

The weather turned in the evening. The fever and pitch of the waves brought back all the dread memories. The strong Mr. Sweeney was stricken by the fever. Perhaps the first time I saw him, big-boned and mighty, carrying his poor wife cradled in his arms, his innards might have been turning mouldy with the eating of black potatoes, boiled or no. He had been taken with a sharp turn, and his great frame now looked hollowed out by the misery, yet he laughed at my look of concern and said, "I'll eat that pig yet."

As we were nearing the dreaded Mingan Rocks which lie at the mouth of the St. Lawrence River, we heard a commotion on deck. Maeve went in a flash—and there was the pig, cornered by three Dutch sailors who had begun by pestering it, and when that obstreperous beast snorted and turned the corner on them, were determined to make sausage of him. But Maeve's shrill protestation must have reached Mr. Hoogstraaten's ears, for he appeared in his nightshirt, but hat in place. He said something rapidly and angrily to the sailors, who slunk away. Then Officer Hoogstraaten told Maeve in his stilted English that her pig was safe, and he was guaranteeing its safe passage. At that moment, the enormous stud pig became the child's property, and no one did challenge it.

• • •

THE NEXT MORNING we saw Canada. The land unfolded before our enchanted eyes, richly wooded and green. The northern bank seemed more rugged, but both sides remarkable for their beauty, with a sweet slope visible along the southern bank. Every once in a while a church steeple rose from the surrounding green, white farmhouses, and there was a palpable sense of peace. In front of us and behind, the wide and majestic river gleamed under a sky of sunshine.

From the deck I saw what looked like charred timber floating past. Then I realized these were cadavers consigned to the river. The bodies looked wasted and contorted, utterly naked. I made some excuse to draw Maeve away, and she quietly said, "I do not want to see all this." How much had she seen, I wondered, and how much resilience are we born with?

We had reached the island where we were going to be quarantined. This was where all the Irish went. I could hear people speak the name Grosse Isle in tones of dread. The Dutch passengers would stay on board, to be taken directly to the City of Quebec, where they would be received in a very different manner.

Some of my fellow Irish were beginning to excoriate the captain, but it was hardly generous to hold him at fault, forgetting that without him we would all have perished. His Dutch passengers had become alarmed with all the fever deaths, and had insisted that now the sea rescue was over, we Irish were to be put on land at once.

So we arrived, Maeve and I, accompanied by her pig and little else. The officer, Meinherr Hoogstraaten, had stepped over to us before we disembarked and spoken very formally to Maeve.

"I would like you to this doll have," he said gravely. "Is something from Delft, nice place." With that he handed a small figure, a doll-like object, to Maeve. Then he bowed. Maeve took it from him without shyness and coyness. She bowed back as formally and said, "Thank you kindly, sir. You have been a grand gentleman to Papa Brendan and me." She shook his hand very properly and returned to me.

On shore with Maeve and the pig, I got a better look at the figure. It had the exquisite porcelain face of a white-haired old man, with a genial half-smile, dressed in quaint Dutch clothes; on his feet were wooden clogs. But the face, the posture, had a familiar, unmistakable likeness.

"He is very like Mr. O'Flaherty," said Maeve.

• • •

THE DECREPIT LANDING dock stood on long legs as unsteady as any seasick man's. Around it swirled swollen straw mattresses discarded overboard, human ordure, and other putrid matter. One ship, obviously from Ireland, was waiting to unload its human cargo. I noticed with horror a sailor lowering a bucket into this filthy Lethe for an impatient group on deck who were obviously at the extremity of thirst.

We were the talk of Grosse Isle. Our time on the iceberg had made us famous. But as long as I live I shall think of this island as the native place of Death itself. The isle lay in the middle of the St. Lawrence River, damp and rank, its greenery extending down to the water itself. In the interior, on higher ground, a church building was out of bounds. Although we were not allowed to step off the perimeter of the quarantine, men from Quebec came to ogle the strange and sickly Irish as at a zoo.

Beyond the rickety landing dock were two long sheds which housed a series of bunks. No fire or any such provision had been made. In dismal rows, people lay in different stages of their journey to death, off ship after ship from Ireland.

One of the first men to meet us was an Anglican priest who gave Maeve an apple. Alan Chisholm was a Scotsman who had come to Canada many years ago, as a child. He had a thin, ruminative face and a shy smile, and was so disarmingly gentle that I wished for more of his kind among our priests, with their hectoring rant of sin and damnation.

Mr. Chisholm told me that the hale lying among the sick in the sheds quickly fell ill. This was simply spoken, an observation. I know an intelligent man by his quiet talk and had learnt to listen, and so I resolved for us to lie at the far long end of the second shed, away from the crowd. There were rows of empty bunks between us and them. I soon understood the reason for this crowding when they brought in a small cauldron of soup. They began distributing it from that end, and it was gone before we got near it.

Maeve and I tried to sleep while the pig went off to root somewhere but came back soon. It seemed to have realized that if it was captured out of our sight, it would end up cooked and eaten, and its best chance of survival was to put itself under the patronage of our Maeve. We woke after a fitful and hungry slumber. Mr. Chisholm appeared, tending to the gravely ill. By the time he made his way to us, it was past noon.

A naturally reticent man, he had the habit of a half-smile and a pursing of his lips before he spoke. "You would not take it amiss if I offered you a piece of bread?" he said.

"Sir," I joked grimly, "you might ask me if I would be offended to find a piece of gold stuck to my shoe. Introduce us to this piece of bread, if you will."

From the large pocket of his old-fashioned peacoat, he took out a brown packet which held two thick slices of brown bread with a bit of butter between them, for he had realized we had not had a crumb overnight. The pig stirred and sat up with a lively show of interest, much like a dog at a supper table.

"Merry Christmas," Mr. Chisholm said, for so it was, and Maeve and I ate the kind Anglican pastor's bread, the first morsel I had on this land.

"Are you a farming man, Mr. McCarthaigh?" he asked me.

"Nay, sir," I said between chewing the bread, "not much of one. I used to be a schoolteacher."

"Is this your pig, Miss Maeve?" asked Mr. Chisholm.

"No, sir. He likes us for company because most people want to eat him," said Maeve.

"Ah," said Mr. Chisholm, who did not have the look of a pig dealer at all, in spite of this line of talk. I thought he was making small talk. "Tomorrow I will ask my friend Mr. Josiah Braithwaite to come. You may find him interesting," he said.

"Any friend of yours, Mr. Chisholm," I said cordially, "will be welcome at our residence." I realized my humour was being affected by my sense of despair. In the rising fog, I wondered how long it would be before Maeve and I would fall prey to the miasma.

• • •

MR. JOSIAH BRAITHWAITE WAS an enormous man, pink and rotund, with large upturned nostrils. He twinkled his eyes at Maeve and said, "Fine Fine Fine Pig."

"Good morning, sir," responded Maeve.

Mr. Braithwaite tickled the pig and ran his hand on its haunches, and made snuffling sounds, while the pig wriggled with delight. After a point I was not sure who was making which noise. And to cap the absurdity, Mr. Chisholm and I spoke calmly about the weather. Mr. Braithwaite continued in his adoration of the pig; he looked amazingly similar to the creature, although he was in human clothes and enormous shoes, the bottoms of which I could see, since he was kneeling.

Abruptly Mr. Braithwaite, still kneeling, addressed us. "I would . . . ahem . . . I would like to offer you a Happy Proposition." For an absurd moment I thought Mr. Braithwaite was going to ask my permission to marry the pig.

"My proposition is: Let Me Have Your Pig."

"He belongs to himself," Maeve asserted.

"Ah, I see," he said, turning ceremoniously, and addressed the child. "Miss Maeve, I would very much, very much, like the company of the Pig."

"Will you eat him?" Maeve asked apprehensively. "Everybody wants to."

"Eat him!" Mr. Josiah Braithwaite was clearly shocked. "Eat him!" he repeated, as if it were unspeakable heresy. "Indeed not, miss. I will have him breed a magnificent stock, a great and notable line." His eyes were staring into the middle distance, his nostrils flared, and his voice became dreamy, contemplating the glorious dynasty. "He will be the first, the Paterfamilias of an illustrious breed."

Maeve and I listened, fascinated. But Mr. Braithwaite descended abruptly from this vision of porcine glory and spoke briskly to me. "I have a farm to the south, beside Lake Champlain.

I was going to leave today, but Mr. Alan Chisholm told me that I would meet the Great Pig if I accompanied him here. Hence . . ." he broke off and clapped his hands in joy, "my proposition is, let me, let me have the Pig. And in return, I will take you both to my farm. You said to Mr. Chisholm that you wished to find employment, Mr. McCarthaigh. Well, you can work for me on the farm or work the ledgers—for my brother Jeremiah takes care of our dairy business, which supplies the cities. As you wish, as you wish," he said, "but I'd say, try our farm life for a while, and you will see for yourself how your pig prospers there." He stopped suddenly in full flow of words. "We leave tomorrow."

"Shall we get permission to leave so soon?" I asked.

"You could break for freedom with your pig," suggested Mr. Braithwaite, his eyes shining with adventure. He snorted with glee at the idea.

"No, no," interceded Mr. Chisholm with alacrity, "I will speak to Dr. Douglas immediately. With Mr. Braithwaite's guarantee of employment, there should be no problem about your departure."

"I have little experience on a farm," I said candidly to Mr. Braithwaite, "but I can do the figures, if accounting is what you have need for."

"Can you, can you indeed?" he sang out. "The figures keep me up nights and put me off my food. Will you do *all* the accounts?"

I sat up most of the night, tense and uneasy. All this seemed almost too good to be true. But some providence had reached out and saved us from utter ruin or shipwreck. From the time the Dutch ship arrived out of the ocean's horizon to this present moment, I was amazed how much like a child—like Maeve—I had regarded the world, and not in my usual cogitative manner. The events were unfolding as if in a child's storybook, as she turns the pages and finds on them a benevolent golden-haired giant, an elf-like man bearing gifts, a deadly island sojourn ended by an absurd man's obsession with a pig. I wondered if I should rub my eyes.

I looked at the sleeping child beside me and thought how this child would grow up one day find her mate, birth children. So would they, in turn. This human pyramid, at whose apex Maeve now lay asleep, increasing with each generation would not, otherwise, come into existence—and this earth cumulatively and surely—would be a very different place. It was no country I was destined to see in its entirety, in my lifespan. But all this would not have come to pass—were it not for a series of mischance, fortunate meetings, unlikely escapes, and, for the nonce, a pig.

The next morning Mr. Braithwaite came in his carriage with all the necessary papers. We got on. The pig, hoisted in an enormous crate, followed in a cart. We rode to Quebec, took the ferry to the south bank of the St. Lawrence River, and continued south, towards Lake Champlain.

As we drove away from the river and I glanced back to look out of the window, I could see another bedraggled ship entering the final stretch to Grosse Isle, bearing its dying, the desperate, and the ill, perhaps from County Sligo itself.

# IV

*and louder sing*

*For every tatter in its mortal dress*

# Robert
## Calcutta, India
### 1911

"What do you do all day, Son?"

The day after my sixth birthday, I had wandered into his room.
I did not know what my father meant. He often looked surprised
to find me around, as if he had been jostled awake from whatever
he had been reading. But he never forgot my birthday. That year
I got a set of storybooks with pictures, for I already loved to read,
and a Hornby train set with its tracks, bogeys, and caboose, and
a small station with signals, red and green. Baba and I shared my
birthday cake.

Even after all these decades, I remember its taste—chocolate
with flecks of toffee—my favourite. I have time now for memories,
an old man alone in an old house.

I had grown up under the silence of large portraits which hung
over me, looking down from the high walls. Most of the windows
were kept shuttered, for the sun was often fierce. I would walk and
play by myself under the eyes of my dead ancestors.

My grandfather Padraig Aherne's hair was thick and coppery.

He had a dark moustache, and his jaw looked like it was made of stone. His bright blue eyes under thick eyebrows seemed to follow me as I moved about the room. I used to think he missed not being able to stride about. I was certain that his laughter emerged like a boom. His long hair was tied with a black ribbon. His hand on the back of a carved chair looked powerful, while the other rested gently on my grandmother's shoulder. I wished he could place it on mine.

Once I got up on a chair to look closer, peeping into my grand-mother's face. She had a hovering smile which made me certain that she would have loved me. Whenever I entered this room, I felt she had just finished speaking to me, and in a moment might say something again. I stood at the edge of that silence, under my grandfather's blue gaze.

"What do you do all day?" asked my father again.

"I don't know," I said. I had grown used to playing by myself in our backyard garden, climbing trees to scare the squirrels, or throwing the ball against the walls.

"You're six," he had said, looking thoughtfully at me, very like our tailor, Suleiman, who had come to our house two weeks ago to measure me for my suit, a birthday present from my fa-ther. "Joe Belletty's boy also turned six, he told me the other day," he said to himself. "Anthony." He put his hand on my shoulder and added, "Would you like to go and play with him?" Yes, I nodded.

●  ●  ●

I HAVE OFTEN thought of that morning more than seven decades ago, the first time I went out to meet the world.

Sonu-amma, our maid, escorted me across Elliot Road to a

small flat on the third floor of a building, noisy as the street. It had only two rooms, both crowded with furniture and people, but no books.

Anthony had a baby brother who sat propped on a chair, banging his spoon on the spattered dining table, while his dad sat beside him next to an open window, scratching his chin and reading the sports page of the newspaper. Mr. Belletty looked far younger than my father. "Hello, Robert," he greeted me. Anthony's mother stood at the stove, frying eggs that smelt wonderful. She had not combed her hair yet. "Tony, look, your friend is here," she called out to him.

Tony was on the floor, playing with a train that was not shiny like mine, but I felt lucky to be here. "Hello, Robert," he said, as if a new boy to play with was no surprise for him. He tossed me a wooden block, and I caught it easily.

"Hello, Anthony," I said.

"I'm Tony," he said emphatically. "My mom calls me Anthony when she's mad."

His mother laughed and said, "Here are your eggs, Robbie and Tony—go sit down there beside Ned, you two." She pointed at the chairs across from Mr. Belletty. I was dazzled. This is what it must mean to have a mother who is alive. I wondered if my mother had combed her hair right away when she got up in the morning. I hoped not. And nobody had ever called me Robbie before, but that is what she did ever after.

After eggs and fried bread, while we played on the floor, Tony told me that he wanted to be a soldier when he grew up. I immediately told him that so did I. By the time I left, we had decided to play together everyday until we could join the same regiment.

TWO WEEKS LATER my father told me that I was to go to St. Xavier's School on Park Street. But Tony's father had attended La Martiniere for Boys, farther from home, and that is where Tony would go. I set my will against my father's and discovered it not very difficult to get my way.

In the classroom, Mr. Pantaky seated us in alphabetical order, and thus we—Aherne and Belletty—found ourselves next to each other. And outside the classroom, Tony and I explored our neighbourhood and discovered a world of children who lived across the street and in the lanes surrounding us. One of them was plump Krikor Aratoon, whose father was the largest man I ever saw, with ears like pieces of pink sponge. They had tons of relatives and went to their own Armenian church and celebrated Christmas in January.

We played cops and robbers, and wrestled with the Zachariah boys, Ben, Solly, and Mordy, who used to walk to their synagogue wearing little caps on their heads, like tea saucers, on Saturdays, and they were not allowed to come out to play. Their synagogue on Pollock Street had vivid yellow and green tiles from Spain, and pillars that looked like shepherd's hooks. I went once to look around. All the adults there had beards, including one old lady.

Some days Tony and I played *golli-danda* and marbles with the twins Majid and Wajid Baghdadi, whose father, Muhammad, owned a cut-piece fabric store in Hogg Market—and who had to fast like good Muslims with the rest of their family during the summer month of Ramadan. Their great-grandfather had come from Syria. Rukhsana, their sister, had the best aim among us at marbles. But she had to sneak away to play with us, because their burka-clad mother said that she was almost a woman; Rukhsana was eight.

No one could beat the Tsang brothers, Ki Tieh and Liang, with the slingshot. Their father, who had a wispy goatee and sported a long pigtail, had come from Sichuan in China and ran a shoestore on Bentinck Street. The brothers, especially Ki Tieh, had unbelievable aim and shot down flying pigeons at will, which they took home to be cooked. But they never used their slings when Violet Stoneham was around, for it made her cry. We all liked Violet.

The Parsee brothers, Bahram, Feroze, and Jamshed, taught me chess and checkers. Their Aunt Perizaad was born blind, but noticed everything, cooked for them, and beat everybody at chess! They went to their Zoroastrian temple and worshipped fire. Their ancestors had come from Persia centuries ago. Tony told me that when Parsees died they were not cremated or buried, but left on a tower to be picked clean by vultures. I did not believe him and asked my father, who said that Tony Belletty was right, for once.

I asked Tony, "So what happens to their bones?"

"I expect they boil them to make glue for postage stamps," he said. I have never licked a stamp since then. Although I did not entirely believe Tony, I did not want to accidentally taste any of Jamshed's old relatives.

• • •

ONE PARTICULAR AFTERNOON stands out in my mind, clear as a shard of glass, even today. I liked sometimes to be driven to the Strand by the Ganges on our brougham, accompanied by Sonu-amma. I was dressed in my blue and white sailor-suit, my dark brown hair cut in bangs. I still have a picture taken around that time.

When we reached the gardens on the Strand, I noticed an ornamental gate with marigolds all over it, decorated for some special occasion. I heard a military band playing for British soldiers in regimental uniforms and their ladies, some under hats with wagging feathers. Inside the gate, children ran about among streamers and coloured-paper decorations, some sucking on candy canes. Before the brougham came to a complete halt, I remember dodging out of Sonu-amma's reach and racing through the gate towards the far counter with all the candy in the world. I tripped and fell, which did not bother me in the least bit, though my sailor-suit had a grass-stain on it. A regimental officer reached out and picked me up with ease. I took in with great admiration his navy-blue uniform, his red sash and stripes, and the splendid sword at his waist.

"Did you hurt yourself, child?" asked a young lady in a white dress.

"What's your name?" asked another woman, with blond hair and a lined face. Her fingers glittered with stone rings.

"I am Robert Patrick Aherne, sir, and I am not hurt at all." I wanted to blurt out right then that I planned to be a soldier.

"Where is your father, Robert Patrick Aherne?" The old lady frowned. "Here?"

"No, ma'am," I said, feeling very grown-up. "My father is Brendan Aherne. He is at home." I added, "We live on Elliot Road."

"Elliot Road, did you say?" snorted the old lady, glaring at the army officer. "Lieutenant Harrison, am I to understand that Anglo-Indians are coming here today?" The lady in white began to move away. The army man looked discomfited and absently put his palm on my head as I looked up at them.

"He's just a child," he began.

Her eyes blazed as she shook her shiny yellow head, and I watched fascinated as she licked her grey teeth with a slippery pink tongue. Her neck was mottled, and her cheeks splotchy with rage. *Chee Chee*, she hissed at me. *"Chaalo idhaar se."* Get away from here, it meant in Hindustani. I knew that.

"Harrison!" she said.

The army man picked me up under my arms and swung me back into my father's brougham. Sonu-amma was staring open-mouthed in fright, her hands clutching me. The army man would not meet my eyes, but pressed a coin in my palm, without saying a word. His Adam's apple bobbed up and down above his regimental collar with its gold fretwork.

"It's for Europeans only," he muttered. I don't know if he said this to me, to Sonu-amma, or to himself. Even before the brougham moved off, I flung away the coin in anger. A number of brown beggar children appeared from nowhere and began a screaming fight over the coin, right in front of the flower-decked entrance. The last I saw of them was the army man kicking about in a frenzy, trying to get the nimble, laughing children of the streets away from the grand gate.

After all these years, I still remember the sting.

Then I saw the soldiers marching in formation. Our brougham had to stand aside to let them pass. I did not know then that the Great War of 1914 had just been declared and this was its celebration. The bagpipes were strident.

I have often thought since then of the numberless columns of Indian soldiers in formation behind their British officers, many of them Irish, who died of bullets, poison gas, or despair, in soggy trenches and bomb-cratered fields, in places with unfamiliar names like Ypres, Passchaendale, and Verdun, beginning their first march towards death here in Calcutta. Those who survived would return to a different world, both changed irretrievably.

At home that evening, when Sonu-amma told my father what had happened, he called me into his study. I could see he was upset.

"It is their army. It is their war, Son," he said.

"I want to be a soldier," I wailed.

He looked completely taken aback. After a while he asked, "Why?"

"I want to be a soldier so I can wear a uniform," I said. It seemed impossible that he could not understand.

"Why would you want to kill anybody?" he asked quietly.

"I don't know," I mumbled. I remembered feeling my anger turn against him for making me feel foolish. Young as I was, I wanted to have authority, power over others. This was what I felt in the playing fields of my school, even in our boyish games and scuffles.

But this was the moment, seven decades ago, when I began to understand not just my place as an Anglo-Indian, but also that my father and I were different. I stood sullen and silent in his study, a baffled boy, not yet ten.

• • •

THE NEXT DAY he surprised me with a full set of illustrated books of Robert Louis Stevenson. I decided to read deep into the night, and my father let me. I knew this was my father's way to comfort me. I called him Baba, in the Bengali manner, rather than Daddy or Papa as most Anglo-Indians did. It was what my father had wanted.

After what had happened to me at the Strand, Baba began to explain that when the English, and especially the Irish, had first come to India in the eighteenth and earlier parts of the nineteenth centuries as soldiers or clerks of the East India Company with little hope of bringing their women, the church encouraged marriage with native converts, preferring that to concubinage and unprovided children. Many, including English aristocrats, married Indian women.

"What is concubinage?" I asked him.

I remember how he stumbled about to explain, then decided to recite the roster of famous Anglo-Indian names: Sir Eyre Coote, Clive's assistant at the Battle of Plassey, loved and honoured his Indian wife; General Hearsey, who was Scottish and Indian—as was the great James Skinner, founder of India's best cavalry regiment; and Anglo-Indian Lord Roberts, who later became supreme Commander of the British Forces in Africa.

"Then there was Lord Liverpool, Britain's Prime Minister, whose maternal grandmother was an Indian woman from right here in Calcutta—just as yours was! We Anglo-Indians," concluded my father, "well, we used to think ourselves pillars of the Queen's Indian empire."

"We don't now?" I asked. "What happened?"

"History," he said, fiddling with his pipe. I waited for him to explain.

"When Creoles in the West Indies revolted and slaughtered English colonists sixty years ago, there spread distrust for people with mixed blood." He stopped briefly. "Half-castes and half-breeds they were called now, synonymous with treachery. English officials from those islands brought their views here."

"But didn't the English know better?" I asked indignantly.

"There were now other factors too, Robert. Cheap and fast steamers through the new Suez Canal," said my father, putting down his pipe. "Missionaries came in droves. Widows and daughters from England began arriving at the ports—Calcutta, Madras, Bombay. The 'Fishing Fleet' they were called, and received an official allowance for a year, after which the unwed were shipped back, now called 'Returned Empty.' The army arranged balls, and it became a great social falling-off now if the English married, not a white woman from Oxney or Ealing, but a native bride. Missionaries openly said that marrying us would sully Anglo-Saxon purity."

"But doesn't the Bible say all people are equal in God's eyes? You said that too."

"No matter, Son. The English rail against Hindu idolatry and its caste system in the churches, and then set up their own pantheon of gods. They have their own caste system, as full of taboos as any to be found in the remotest Indian village."

"But what about the Irish?" I protested.

"They have perched their own place on that caste ladder. You see, the Irish joined the army and the police in such numbers that they were a social force to reckon with. They are discreetly sneered at by the English, but they all close ranks and hold themselves aloof from boxwallahs."

I had heard of boxwallahs. "Do boxwallahs carry boxes on their back? I have never seen any of them."

My father laughed aloud. "No, no, Son, they are in business, you know, tradespeople from the likes of Brixton or Camberwell, or Jewish merchants from Europe and Syria, or Armenian traders."

"But they are all hardworking people!"

"It's all snobbery and snootery, Robert. These are people who daily have to haggle and rub shoulders with Indians in the rough and tumble of local markets. And here's another funny thing, Robert, if you think this sort of thing funny: You know that Calcutta is lighted with electricity supplied by Mr. Ezra, the Jewish merchant? Indians in one neighbourhood named a street after him."

"Oh yes, and we've been to Ezra Street, I remember."

"Mr. Ezra wasn't allowed inside the British clubs."

"Is that why you gave up on your father's business?" I interrupted him. "Grandpa traded with the Indians, but not you, because you do not want to be called a boxwallah?"

My father looked stricken. He shook his head slowly, as if to clear it. I felt for a second that I had slapped him.

He looked directly into my eyes, "I have no head for business, Son. I did try. My father was a big enough man not to hold it against me. I am sorry I disappoint you, Robert. My father had never a word of disrespect for his mother, who kept a small shop. Parents owe their children no more than they can afford."

I felt quarrelsome and small. My father was right, but I resented his being so.

• • •

MY SEVENTY-NINE-YEAR-OLD GRANDFATHER Padraig Aherne had died in his sleep in 1907 when I was only two, but he was ever-present in my father's stories.

He married my Bengali grandmother Kalidasi late, many years after he had built this house on Elliot Road where I lived with my father, Brendan. She had been born into an orthodox Brahmin family. Married at seven, widowed at nine, she did not much remember her marriage or the groom—since a bride is sent to her husband's home only at puberty, my father recounted. She was in her twenties and my grandfather Padraig almost fifty when he heard her singing voice behind a courtyard wall. How they managed to meet is one of our family mysteries, but they fell in love and she eloped.

Grandfather Padraig, who seemed to like breaking rules, offered to convert to Hinduism. That caused a furor among the British, and he was told severely by Hindu priests that nobody becomes a Hindu: You can only be born one. Besides, Hindus did not allow widow remarriage. Padraig had managed to offend both Christians and Hindus with his usual panache. My grandmother became a Christian instead, in a private ceremony conducted by Reverend Bandopadhyay. So the conversion and marriage ceremonies were solemnized and celebrated by outcasts, which must have suited my fiery Irish grandfather perfectly.

Kalidasi's Hindu family cut her off—as if she were dead. Patrick gave her the Christian name Euphonia when she insisted upon one at her conversion. I do not know what he called her at home, Kalidasi or Euphonia. He adored her, said my father.

Years after her conversion, Kalidasi used to go under veils to a temple during the Puja festival and take my father along and offer flowers and *laddoos*; her pet name for her son was Brindaban. "One god or many gods," Padraig would chuckle, "let them sort it out among themselves without getting us humans involved, or have us kill each other on their behalf. The more powerful some people think their god is, the more they have to do the killing for that particular almighty."

My grandfather kept fine horses which were stabled nearby, at Chitpur, but my father told me that my grandmother did not enjoy taking our brougham along the Esplanade or next to Fort William, where the English walked stiffly with their ladies and raised their hats like wind-up toys when they passed their compatriots. No one raised his hat to my grandmother Kalidasi's carriage, which was far grander than most of theirs, because she was a black Hindu woman. The English went to take the air, trying to decide whom they might acknowledge and who was beyond the pale, but Kalidasi went to the Strand when she felt the need to look at the sacred Ganges. She died of influenza when my father was twenty-four.

The following year Grandpa Padraig sent my father to Bombay, presumably to learn about business from his friend, the Parsee businessman Cowasjee, out from under his long shadow. There, my father met and married my mother, Susannah Estelle O'Reilly, the daughter of Michael Edward O'Reilly, an elderly Anglo-Indian violin teacher. He returned to Calcutta with a great reverence for Mozart, Telemann, and Purcell, loads of sheet music, and his young wife, but with little sense of how businesses are run. Apparently my grandfather Padraig doted on his young daughter-in-law, and the house was a happy place again, until my mother Susannah died of something called puerperal fever four years later, soon after my birth.

Sometimes I used to say her full name to myself when I played alone in our backyard, a private chant: "Susannah Estelle O'Reilly Aherne." I used to peer into my mother's portrait, her complexion lit by some gentle lamp within her, fascinated by her long eyelashes and perfect eyebrows.

I also had a maternal uncle, Raphael Iain O'Reilly, but I remember seeing him only twice in my life. He had a freckled bald head and enormous ginger eyebrows and whiskers. He ran a business exporting grain and fruits from the Punjab through the port of Karachi to Mombasa, Aden, and other places. With no reference to my birthdays, which he generally forgot, Uncle Rafe would send me strange gifts: a mechanical clown with terrifying eyes; an elaborate Arabian maze puzzle inlaid with ebony and pearls; and a razor-sharp Afghan dagger with an agate-encrusted sheath—an odd gift for a seven-year-old.

My father had my grandmother Kalidasi's serene face, delicate hands, and large brown eyes. His hair was greying prematurely, and he wore thick glasses and spoke, everyone said, with a lilt in my grandfather's Irish manner. He was very attentive to his fine Darjeeling and Oolong teas, his briar and meerschaum pipes, his Burleigh or Latakia tobaccos, his sheet music and books, especially the ones of painting reproductions and photography of land-scapes. He loved music, and played his violin—quite beautifully, I thought—or read scores, and immersed himself in his books while he settled into a contemplative middle age as I was growing up.

When the Great War of 1914 came, many people like my friend Krikor's father, Mr. Aratoon, made quick fortunes in war-time trade, but our family business of timber and grain export went from the brisk gallop of my grandfather Padraig's days to a limp, and soon was knackered. Mr. Aratoon bought our horses and the brougham. My father seemed indifferent to the losses. I missed our horses, George and Eddie.

Now Krikor, who lived around the corner, was driven to school in our old brougham, while I walked there. On the first day Krikor offered me a ride back home, and I hit him on the nose, making it bleed, as if my father's business ineptitude had been compensated by that blow. Krikor did not complain at school or to his father. The next day, after Krikor was driven to school, I made up a jingle:

*Fatty-fatty Kriko-bloaty*
*Ate up all the ghee chapatti*

*His trousers split as he ate*
*Everything on his heaping plate!*

All our friends knew it by afternoon, when Krikor left in tears in his brougham. He walked to school starting the next day. But the whole matter tormented me. The following week I sought Krikor out and shook his hand, but for a long time it was not like it had been before.

One morning over breakfast on our verandah, I asked my father, "Are we poor now?" He looked up from his newspaper, and considered my question.

"Poverty means different things to different people," he said.

"What does it mean to us?" I persisted.

"We have this house and there is enough for your education, unless when you finish school you want to go to, say, Oxford. Well, if you wanted to," he said worriedly, "if you did, I'd have to talk to Lahey and find out what we could raise from a mortgage." Old Lahey had been Grandfather Padraig's lawyer.

"So we are not poor?" I wanted a clear answer.

"Son, we have enough left to live on, comfortably. Just enough." Then he added, "I am sorry about our horses, Son. You loved them."

After a pause I told him of my jingle about Krikor. He listened gravely. But when I told him about my apology, he surprised me with an impulsive hug. It was not unusual for him to do so, but I knew this was special.

"I am proud of what you did," he said simply. "I love you, Son."

• • •

MY FATHER SPENT the Great War reading stacks of newspapers.

At school, we started each day now, not just with announcements and a perfunctory prayer, but with something new. Our principal was an Englishman, Mr. W. H. Arden-Wood MA, CIE—an improbable name, my father had first claimed, until he checked for himself. Mr. Arden-Wood kicked off each morning with news of the war, followed by a sonorous prayer for our gallant boys—and a couple of former teachers—who were fighting against the Forces of Evil. When any of the boys brought in letters written by relatives from the war front, he read parts of it to the entire assembly, huffing with emotion, elocuting every precious syllable. Teddy Richard and Timmy Doyle, whose dads had joined up, brought in letters. They were even invited up on stage!

Soon senior boys like Dan Surita and the two older O'Brien boys enlisted. So did Tony's dad the day after Tony's tenth birthday. They came to our school in their uniforms, and everyone clapped. I wished I were old enough to enlist in the war—any war! But I knew how my father would view such enthusiasm for the British uniform. I dreamed of distant battles, holding actual guns, marching to the kettle-drums, cheered by crowds.

"Anybody who doesn't join is a coward and a rotten egg," said Tony, beaming. I picked a fight with him, knocking him flat behind the school gym. I felt no better for it. His dad had gone off in his new uniform, while mine sat at home reading about it. I wanted him to *do* things. "Someday soon I will grow up and be that kind of man," I decided fiercely.

One late April morning, almost a fortnight after my eleventh birthday, my father rushed into my bedroom and woke me. I rose eagerly, expecting him to hold out some unexpected gift—probably from Uncle Rafe. But what he was holding in his hand was the early newspaper. It was a Bengali paper, not *The Englishman* or *The Statesman*. His hands were shaking in excitement.

"It's beginning to happen," he said, hoarse with emotion. "It has begun to happen in Ireland! None of the English papers mentions this. On Easter morning, there was an uprising in Dublin. The most important buildings in that city have been taken over."

"Is Ireland free now?" I asked, caught up in his unexpected excitement.

"The leaders were rounded up and imprisoned by the British soldiery," my father conceded, "but the Uprising has begun."

"But Baba," I was confused, "didn't you say that all the British soldiers were fighting Germany?"

"Aye," he said, "but it must be the Protestants and the Constabulary." I waited for him to explain.

"Among the leaders are Pearse, Connolly, MacDonagh, and McBride," he recited from the Bengali newspaper. "One of them is a schoolteacher. Another is a poet."

"Is that a good thing?" I asked doubtfully. "Don't you need soldiers for a fight?"

"It is the common people," chuckled my father in a transport of delight. "Oh, Son, what a grand time it is for Ireland!"

In the following days, my father waited eagerly for news of the uprising, which remained stubbornly absent from the English papers. Then, two weeks later, we came to know from the Bengali papers that McDonagh and McBride, Connolly and Pearse had been executed by the English after hasty courts-martial. I remember my father reading those names out to me. Here in Calcutta, my father wept for his Irish dead. I did not know how to comfort him.

● ● ●

I WAS GETTING used to my father's unexpected reactions as he read the morning papers. He insisted I eat a good breakfast—though he would only drink cup after cup of fragrant Darjeeling tea. I remember how I relished puffy luchis or parathas with aloo and subzi greens, while in the summer I ate mulled oats with cool homemade curd and honey.

This morning at the end of October 1917, he could barely wait to tell me the news, reading out bits from the papers, his tea growing cold in his cup. He exclaimed that one of our allies, Russia—I knew it by its pale blue spread on our schoolroom map—had withdrawn from the war and was caught up in a Revolution.

"Will we have a revolution?" I asked hopefully, "At least an uprising like Ireland?"

"Ahh," he said, as if that was an answer.

In the last few months, he had talked to me of many battles. The grown-ups had been certain it would be over by the first Christmas. Even the papers said so. From my school history texts, I thought that battles happened quickly and decisively: Hastings, the battles at Plassey, Waterloo, Lepanto, Philippi . . . But this war was going on and on.

Three days before that Christmas, Tony Belletty's dad returned without a leg but with an army pension, which he complained was smaller because he was an Anglo-Indian. "Same size as his brain," commented his sister Mrs. Mildred Noney. Two weeks later, Dan Surita came back. He never left home now, wheezing around in his bedroom. His cousin Teddy Richard told us that he had been gassed.

Some months later, when the Great War did finally end, I had turned thirteen. We heard the boom of the ceremonial cannons at Fort William barracks. Anglo-Indians like Mrs. Lahey and old Mr. Noney, whose sons had joined the forces in great numbers, fought and died, were not invited to the great ball.

"Almost one and a half million Indians have served in the British armed forces," said my father, "in every grim theatre of the war. All of India provided food, money, munitions. Forty-three thousand soldiers died on the battlefields. Many more returned without limbs or with permanent injuries, and limped back to their homes, mainly in the Punjab, or Rajputana, or Coorg, some witless, shambling and shell-shocked."

"So what did *we* get from the war?" I asked him, puzzled. "Didn't we think of this before?"

"Well," he began, "the Indians now know they fought white men. They also know the British Crown would have tumbled without the colonial gift of their lives and limbs."

"That's all?"

"It's a lot, Robert. We learn slowly." He sounded rueful. "But now our Indian Congress leaders, who had been regularly thanked throughout the war for their support of the British, are asking for something. Like Ireland"—he smiled—"Home Rule."

"Will the English give it to us?"

"Shouldn't there be a difference between giving and taking, Son?"

We were interrupted by a knocking at the door, and I knew that Tony and Krikor had come by for our afternoon game of cricket. But what happened then remains with me even to this day, for I was struck by what my father said, and the power of stories became suddenly clear to me. There we were, three boys with their bat and ball, when my father began to tell us the oddest story of give-and-take, and how an entire regiment of the finest Irish soldiers disappeared from India. We stood rooted to the spot, all thoughts of cricket gone for the moment.

Tony and I were avid collectors of cards from cigarette boxes depicting soldiers of all the British regiments. We knew that the Connaught Rangers from Ireland had fought in all the wars for two hundred years, and right after the Great War had been posted in Punjab.

"They heard from their relatives and comrades returning from furlough about the goons called Blacks and Tans perpetrating atrocities against their families. Now that Free Ireland was about to become fact, these soldiers laid down arms. They considered themselves Irish, not British! At the local bazaar, they bought three swaths of coloured cloth, and local women sewed them into the Irish tricolours. They refused payment, for their sympathy lay with the young Irish."

My father paused, relishing the moment. "That very day, the first Irish flag was raised on Indian soil." The authorities tried to gag the English papers, my father had told me later, but he had gathered the news from the small vernacular papers which dodged under the fence, reporting the story at the risk of closure.

"But what about the English? What did they have to say?" Krikor wondered aloud. "Yes, what did they do?" Tony burst out.

"Plenty, boys. Two battalions of Seaforth Highlanders were sent in full battle gear."

"Were the Irish killed?"

My father shook his head. "A bloodbath was avoided because Father Livens, a Catholic priest, stood before them, ready to be slaughtered with them. Jim Daly, a young Connaught Ranger, averted certain massacre by pacifying his comrades and negotiating with English generals. He was given word that no soldiers would be executed."

Baba sat back and added with satisfaction, "News had reached the provisional government in Dublin, which insisted on the return of the soldiers."

"And the English agreed?" asked Tony incredulously.

"It was a case of give-and-take, Anthony," said my father, "well, give-and-take of a certain kind."

"What do you mean, sir?" Krikor broke in.

"The British authorities disbanded the regiment. Its colours were sent off to a great house in Boyle . . ." My father paused. "Close to Sligo from where my father came."

"Then it all ended well," I was relieved, "the English gave the Irish troops their freedom."

"Give-and-take!" said my father, "True, that is what they gave. What they took was Jim Daly's life. He helped keep the peace— and the only Irishman executed."

"No!" we cried out.

"Yes," said my father. "He led the negotiations and obeyed English law—and was punished like Daniel O'Connell eighty years ago. Jim Daly was only twenty-two."

"Who's Daniel O'Connell?" asked Krikor.

"That I'll tell you another day, I promise," added my father. "Jim Daly defiantly whistled 'It's a Long Way to Tipperary,' his regimental tune, on the way to execution, then was buried in a corner of the prison."

But even that was not the end of the story!

"Jim Daly had been shot—but he lived on, in a manner of speaking," said Baba. "Odd stories have percolated through India: A scrawled writing appeared high above human height on the prison wall: *Seamus Dailigh*, the Irish spelling of his name. Local farmers swear that late at night someone wanders the perimeter of the jail whistling that tune."

The stories of England, Ireland, and India keep getting tangled up, I observed. My friends could not wait to repeat the story at school. Krikor made a fortune buying up all the available Connaught Ranger cards, which the cigarette companies stopped printing. He let Tony and me choose the two best ones as keepsakes. I still have them. The rest he sold to the highest bidders at school and on Elliot Road.

I had realized that no one else's dad told stories like my father. And it turned into a strange moment in my head, as if I was outside myself, observing us, and the picture became a permanent sepia memory of a growing boy sitting with his friends and his father in a book-lined room with old comfortable chairs, talking in a room redolent with the aroma of tea and tobacco and old papers.

It was a picture that was to return unbidden to my mind, again and again, in my unquiet years, an anchor in troubled waters.

• • •

I WAS BEGINNING to enjoy my jousts with my father about politics and history, learning to argue with him and weigh his words. Although we Anglo-Indians lived where few Englishmen set foot, jealously keeping to their own enclaves, they were ever-present in our conversation.

"Tony's dad says that the English with very little education and no experience get salaries many times more than Anglo-Indians. Is that fair?" I wanted to know

"It isn't," countered my father, "but Indians make even less for the same work, and they hate *us* for that."

As I digested this, my father added, "You do know, Robert, the English in India—especially those who were born here—first called themselves 'Anglo-Indian,' but dropped the term when we of part-Indian blood began to lay claim to that name? By 1910 or so, they switched to calling themselves 'European.' "

"But weren't all the Europeans soon at each other's throats, using their new inventions like machine guns and poison gas?" I was discovering the pleasures of irony.

Many Anglo-Indians—our next-door neighbor Mr. Theodore "Badbreath" Nolan, for example—tried so hard to be English that they pretended not to understand Bengali or Hindi, affecting the pidgin which Europeans condescended to use with servants.

I had noted disdainfully that there was a flourishing business in skin bleachers among Anglo-Indian ladies like Mrs. Rosie Demeder, who never dared to come out under the sun. And I remember one baptismal party, after Tony's cousin Emily was born. The venerable biddies were craning their heads into the cradle, breathing together over the tiny mite. There was a lot of anxious checking behind the ears—for that's how they guessed at the future complexion of the babies.

"Not as fair as their Rosemary, now, is she?" whinnied old Mrs. Sadie Lahey, the lawyer's wife.

Her friend Mrs. Bella Murphy, who sported a yellow hide, preened and said smugly, "Nooo, but then *she's* the one with my grandfather's looovely Irish skin."

Widow Maher, their neighbor, chimed in dolefully, "But look at poor Derek and Joanie Dorsey . . . neither of their children got Joanie's pearly skin . . . they just had to be as brown as Derek."

"Oh, but they change so, the peachy darlings. There's hope," consoled Mrs. Lahey.

"Noooo, not with those two, there ain't no chance, looove," pronounced Mrs. Murphy.

Smothered under generous rouge, Tony's deaf great-aunt Mrs. Mildred Noney, clutching her mended leather bag, now blared to the cement floor in what she thought was a thoughtful whisper, "Think 'bout Georgina Flynn, *baba*! Brown as a muddy boat she is, and her Mervyn's no lighter, but their daughter— Esther, *not* Liz—oooh, she's got looovely brown hair, and such a complexion, white as seashells."

And here old Mrs. Noney reverently raised her milky eyes at the ceiling and bellowed, "And *blueblue* eyes."

Her voice rose at this dramatic moment. "Very next year Georgina has Liz, the spitting image of her Mervyn. Thick black hair a tangle of corkscrews and skin brown as a Burma cheroot. Poor Georgina!" She delivered her final line with tragic satisfaction, "Such hopes she had after pretty Esther."

"But," I broke in, unmindful of my manners, "does all this matter, Mrs. Noney?"

"Oh shoosh, boy, shoosh yourself"—she glared—"you with yer whitey skin and hazel eyes!"

Soon after that came the news that Pam, Badbreath Nolan's daughter, had been asked for marriage by an English clerk known to everybody, for some reason, as "Jelly" Carberry, and he was taking her away to that land of fantasy—England—to live in some suburb of Manchester. They spoke as if Pam had been beatified. The letter and photographs she sent some months later were studied like autographed copies of the Ten Commandments, with sighs about how beautiful "Home" looked in the dim black-and-white background. Sammy Brent's parents talked wistfully of saving and going there some day.

Yet what Home was it they spoke of, I have wondered for years now—generations away from a land that would not claim us as its own—while we spurned that other inseparable darker-pigmented part of ourselves, an undeniable sepia? All the while we were continually aware of the subject soil we trod on. We were marooned on islands of our making, discussing fairness of skin, but never reaching for the awesome idea of fairness—Justice and Freedom—my father would say wryly, for that would surely bring us face-to-face with our own darker brothers, the Indians, who were also without liberty.

I remember how, even in my childhood, I had begun to understand that there was one more liberty that we had taken away from ourselves, every time we comforted ourselves that we were by the merest, but unmistakable, shade of paleness separated from our masters. All of us, except for rare exceptions like my father, prided ourselves on being irretrievably separate from our native Indian kin, especially our first Indian mothers, naming all our babies after long-dead European antecedents, but never *ever* giving them names chosen from the darker side of our ancestral beds.

What would we Anglo-Indians do, I began to ask myself, if a time came when the world forgot to scrutinize the exact text of our skin? Would we go Home, wherever that home might be? Would we remain here in India? And if that time came when the world did not care a whit about our hue, nor whisper comparisons about it, would our children in their innocence and unblemished courage seek out and mend our truncated identities, connecting the brown and the white, seeing equal worth and sweetness in both?

We did have one secret reason to rejoice; perhaps it was Nature's way to celebrate hybrid splendour that made our Anglo-Indian women the most striking, with the most comely features, and almost without exception the most graceful dancers. Europeans always prowled about them, but seldom for marriage.

Oh, but no one was like the girl I was to meet when I turned eighteen. She was a fatherless student, come recently from Bombay, supported by a foundation scholarship at La Martiniere for Girls, our sister school. Her name was Estelle O'Brien Thompson.

I will someday be able to speak about her. Not yet, not yet.

• • •

AFTER MATHUR CLEARED the dinner plates, my father would light his pipe and linger over coffee, wanting to chat into the night. Sometimes he spoke of Grandfather Padraig and his time. During one such evening and another story about Padraig, I interrupted him, unable to hold back a question that had long troubled me. How was it was that my grandfather, who succeeded in so short a time—enough to acquire a fine brougham and horses in Calcutta, a grand house east of the Esplanade on Elliot Road, and who had given a princely sum for the starving of Ireland—never revisited the land of his birth?

"I doubt he ever went back to visit Ireland," my father offered tentatively. "If he did, he never mentioned it to me."

"You'd tell me if you went on a long journey, wouldn't you?"

"Yes," conceded my father, "but if he went, it would have been long before I was born," adding something that he had never told me before. "He did disappear from Calcutta for a few months once. Exactly when or where he went—to Burma or Ceylon for trade, or whether he visited Ireland—Declan never did say."

"Who?" I asked, completely puzzled.

"Declan Clooney, the sailor-man," explained my father.

"Why would Grandpa Padraig tell *him*?" I could barely contain my disbelief, for I had once seen the man: old toothless Declan who wandered in his head, scratched his sorry shrunken body all day long, gibbering that the Loreto nuns were trying to poison him in the sailors' sanctuary near the Kidderpore docks where he had made final port with other codgers. Until Declan died, a few years ago, my father used to visit him, usually before Christmas. A charity case, I had always thought. Why would the great Padraig have paid any heed to that rambling footling fool, drooling with the drink and dropsy and three degrees north of senile?

"But he was barking mad!" I protested.

"He was all that at the end, poor fellow," my father said gently, "but Robert, he brought me clever Chinese toys from the Moluccas. He also talked to me about my grandmother Maire Aherne. A great beauty, he said. He also mentioned my father's best friend Brendan McCarthaigh. I told you all those stories, Robert, remember?" I nodded.

Then he added, "My father never talked about all that to me. He also remained hardfaced to the English till his dying day. He even seemed to have resented the English tongue itself."

"That's an impossible quarrel," I declared.

"That's very Irish," he chuckled. "He spoke Bengali, Hindustani, Farsi fluently, and he never used the English language if he could help it."

"But *you*—you don't hate the language?" I asked in confusion.

"That's because I fell in love with all the books. My father would buy them in great numbers. It was as if English reading and English speaking were at odds in his head."

"He was broken in half inside himself?" A strange picture was beginning to paint itself in my head. "Do we all get broken inside?"

"Sooner or later," he said, pausing momentarily, "in different ways, perhaps. But we need to keep the pieces from destroying each other."

"And Grandmother Kalidasi? She spoke English?"

"She never learnt. She never needed to."

"Why do you not speak of her as much—when we are these two parts—Irish and Indian."

"Not that broken, I hope, Robert," said my father. "We call ourselves Irish just as we call ourselves by my Irish father's surname. Your grandmother Kalidasi melted like sugar in our lives. Her life is a part of us. She even made angry Padraig love this world again."

"Speaking Bengali?"

*"Haan,"* he said, changing over to Bengali as easily as drawing breath.

"May I look at that book, please?" I asked in Bengali.

Handing me his large folio book of Irish landscapes which he had purchased recently, he said, *"Robert baba, dekho ki shobuj desh.* See how green that land is." Then turning to a page, he murmured wistfully, "I have often wondered if my father had walked just here, or had ever passed by any of these places, if any of these rocks and trees were part of what he missed sorely."

• • •

IT WAS THE fifth of April 1919, and my fourteenth birthday just around the corner. In this season the *kaal baisakhi* storms, with their thunderclaps and forked tongues of lightning, descend suddenly in the afternoons and cooled everything down, but that particular year the air had grown heavier and hotter each day. My father and I, like many others in our city, were trying to sleep on our bare terrace, tossing fitfully on camp-cots under a great staring moon, when we heard a rattling at our gate.

"Telegraph man, sir!" the man in khaki bellowed from below,

shaking the chain and padlock on our gate. When my father padded back to the terrace, his face was somber.

"Your Uncle Rafe has died suddenly," he said, "in Punjab. His lawyer writes that he has already been buried, according to his instructions."

"He has left me his house in Amritsar," he muttered, and then, as if announcing a calamity, "and he has gone and left his motorcar to you."

"Oh yes!" I cried, springing up in excitement.

"Robert," chided my father, who thought my excitement unseemly. But no one else I knew owned a motorcar.

"I will go to Niall Lahey's law office on Waterloo Street tomorrow. He will write up something lawyerly to send back so that the house can be sold off," said my father, already sounding burdened by details.

"Will this make us rich again?" I wondered aloud.

"I doubt it. Rafe spent pretty freely on his luxuries and wom—" He broke off, then added, "The house is modest, in the old part of the city. And what else can we do but sell off that absurd machine? You will have that money on your eighteenth birthday."

"Oh Baba, no . . . please, please," I pleaded desperately, "I want to keep it."

"Well, it is like you are asking for a pet, Robert," countered my father, a smile breaking over his face. That smile gave me hope, and I decided to play my trump card.

"It is the last gift from the only other blood relative I knew in my life," I said.

"Eh?" My father seemed completely stumped.

"Please, Baba," I added gravely.

"Oh dear," he said, relenting, "but it is at the other end of

India. I'll need to take the train. Then I can get that house sold more quickly."

"Take me with you, Baba. The Easter break is almost here anyway," I said.

"But if we are unable to get someone who can drive back that contraption . . ." he demurred, weighed down by the enormity of the venture.

I knew what would appeal to him. "We will drive down the Grand Trunk Road back to Calcutta. No other father and son that I know have done this. We will see India together. Remember you told me how Sher Shah had built that historic road in the sixteenth century, and showed it to me on the map. Kipling's *Kim* traveled on it!"

"Ah yes," he said, brightening at that memory.

•  •  •

A few days later, legal papers in hand, and having secured permission from my school to add a week's leave to the upcoming Easter break, we were on our way, clip-clopping in a rented carriage over the pontoon bridge across the river to Howrah Station's red terminal.

We had to press through the milling crowd to the waiting train. Spying the First Class coach for Europeans, I pressed my face against a window to peek inside. Between the green tasseled curtains parted at the middle, I took in the dark wood paneling on the walls and the velvet cushions lying on the creamy leather seats.

"Come, Robert," my father called out, leading me to the Second Class compartment where the red-shirted coolie slid our suitcase under our seat. Two wide wooden benches faced each other, while two others could be hinged down to sleep another two, but so far only a portly Bengali had joined us, and he promptly occupied an upper bunk and went to sleep.

The train lurched as the engine tugged, and I insisted on sitting by the barred window, unwilling to miss anything in my excitement. My hair was gritty with specks of soot by evening. Our compartment had a small enamel washbasin, and I rinsed my face in it.

The express train raced through the green valley. After a few hours the Ganges receded from view, and the earth turned brown and dry. We rattled past small stations, towns and villages with their little temples and the occasional mosque with its quaint green dome, and sometimes, ruined forts on distant hills. Railway attendants brought us our food in covered trays, but outside, flies moved like motes. I understood why the European carriages had curtains and glass panes.

"Try the chicken," Baba insisted, and it was delicious: This was the famous Railway Curry. The vegetarian Hindu stared balefully at what we were eating and did not come down, but noisily ate puffed rice and yogurt in his perch from a small tin and went back into hibernation. I went reluctantly to sleep when it grew dark and there was nothing more to see.

By the end of the second day, I wished I could take a cool bath. I had never slept so heavily or so long, possibly because of the swaying carriage. My father shook me awake the following morning. The train was at a station. Next to him stood a dapper Sikh gentleman in an elegant linen suit, a red tie, and turban.

"*Sat sri akaal,*" he greeted me.

"Son, this is Mr. Amrik Singh, Uncle Rafe's lawyer," my father said, making introductions. "Amrik-ji, this is my son, Robert."

We had arrived: Amritsar, where my car was waiting for me!

● ● ●

"THE CITY IS *badaa* tense, Aherne sahib," commented Amrik-ji as we made our way out of the station, which was crowded with troops bristling with guns. "Let's get away from here *ek-dum*," he added.

"What—" began my father as the lawyer led us briskly to a horse-drawn tonga. *Later,* the lawyer gestured as we bundled into it. I had impulsively climbed in front with our bag beside me, next to the syce who flicked his whip on the scrawny horse, while my father sat with Mr. Singh in the seat which faced backwards. I immediately regretted my decision, for the sorry nag farted viciously as it attempted to speed. The syce turned towards me, shaking in soundless mirth at my discomfiture.

We trundled past where the English lived in white-walled bungalows with perpendicular lanes bordered by feeble beds of daisies and wilting lilies. Here and there on whitewashed trunks of trees I noticed pasted signs in English, forbidding assembly.

Away from this part of town, we moved slowly now, into the serpentine lanes of the old quarter which seemed to pacify the animal enough to stop its relentless rear fusillade. Local shops spilt into the pavement full of morning crowds amid a cacophony of haggling. Here, in the heart of Amritsar, amid pungent whiffs of pepper and frying parathas, odours of asafoetida and ginger, the recently seen imitation of England felt impossibly distant.

"What happened," my father asked, "what do those posted signs mean, Amrik-ji?"

"You know the recent Rowlatt Act curbs the vernacular press and gives the government the power to arrest Indians at will, without warrants. So, there was a demonstration here, and the police fired *fatafat* on the crowd."

"Peaceful demonstrators?" pursued my father.

"*Arre* Brendan-ji, would our Gandhi-ji have it otherwise? But it did get a bit out of hand at the end. Some *badmaash* threw bricks at a government office. The police arrested two respected persons, Saif Kitchlu and Satya Pal, one Muslim and one Hindu, who had nothing to do with the rowdiness. The government chaps have managed to upset both communities." The Sikh grimaced and added, "But what takes the slice of cake is the latest event. Would you believe it was precipitated by a little *bacchhi*, yes. Right near Rafe Sahib's house."

"By a child?" I was surprised. "And the English have brought out troops?" The lawyer twisted around to face me, and nodded. "Okay, I will tell you the whole story."

• • •

"A MIDDLE-AGED SCHOOLTEACHER, Miss Marcella Sherwood, was bicycling home, taking a shortcut through some lanes," began Amrik-ji. "She is known to be high-strung and given to tirades about idol worshippers. *Bahoot strict-sa*, she regularly canes her pupils—especially if their little palms are decorated with henna— as they often are after a wedding or a Puja worship ceremony. On this afternoon, Memsahib Sherwood turned a corner and ran smack into a naked toddler on its way to its aunt's home across the narrow lane. I know this *bacchhi* Binni and her mother, Anju. So did *hamara* Rafe-sahib, your uncle. The little *ladli* was a great favourite of his, as it happens." Amrik-ji smoothed his beard.

"Little Binni was more frightened than hurt, but the outraged Miss Sherwood screamed at the top of her lungs at the feckless behavior of heathen parents and their heedless infant. Showing a flagrant disregard for her British presence and Christian authority, Binni's mother pounced upon Marcella Mem-sahib, boxed her ears, trampled on her solar topee, and spat on her. *Whaak-thhoo!* She concluded the exercise by picking up the bicycle and, *fataak,* flung it to the side of the lane."

I burst out laughing. "And that's all?"

"No, not quite, Master Aherne," he said.

"Call me Robert," I said.

"All right, Robert. By this time the sleeping menfolk emerged, and sensing that trouble could be on its way, tried to pick up the Englishwoman from the dirt. In hysterics, she cried out at their sight, snatched her battered bicycle and sped off as fast as she could, howling in panic, her face *ek-dum* scraped by maternal fury. Our furious Anju Kaur is a sight to behold, believe me, my *dost.* Her mild-mannered *chooha* husband, Chakra Singh, just goes into hiding." I laughed again, but noticed that my father was listening seriously.

"She lurched into the English section of town and collapsed in hysterics. The police were informed that an English lady, a teacher, a person of impeccable virtue, had been set upon by a stealthily gathered Indian mob. By the grace of Christ she fought them off, escaping with her life. I got that all these details from Harpal Chand, a constable who lives next door to me. The English authorities wanted to know immediately if her virtue had been molested, but thank Heavens again, she had escaped that specific harm," said Amrik, "although according to them, that surely was the intention of the native *junglee* mob."

"Harpal told me the English officers concluded that she had probably been assaulted by demobilized soldiers who had been around white women during furloughs in France and thereabouts," the lawyer added.

"That's what they believe of the soldiers with whom the British fought side by side just last year?" My father's voice sounded hoarse. "So they called out the troops we saw at the station?"

Amrik nodded. "Those posters you saw were issued by order of Mr. O'Dwyer, the lieutenant governor. But these are in English, and few villagers arriving here can read Gurmukhi—let alone *salaa* English."

"But why are these villagers coming now?" I broke in.

"*Dekho* Robert *bete*, around this time, give or take a few days on the lunar calendar, we hold our festival of Baisakhi, bringing in the New Year," explained Amrik-ji. "It's the only festival in Punjab and most of North India for a while—for hard summer follows and then the monsoon rains descend. So Baisakhi is our last *akhri* festival for months when family members can visit their wedded daughters, grandchildren, and kin, and congregate at our Golden Temple here in Amritsar."

My father looked troubled. "These villagers know nothing about the news here!"

"No, they don't," said Amrik with a grimace. "Many families, taking their old and even their youngest *bacchhi*, started their travel as much as a week ago and have already begun to arrive."

• • •

THROUGH THE LANES, we had finally reached Uncle Rafe's house in the heart of old Amritsar. It was old, with steep stairs and dusty rattan furniture, the rooms below dark and stacked with a medley of boxes and chests, odd bits of machinery, large numbers of empty bottles. In the upstairs living room stood a hookah and an old Victrola with its enormous silver horn, and stacks of records. I found among them the arias of Caruso, orchestra pieces by "Pryor's Symphony," and assorted records of popular songs. I immediately set out to play a scratchy rendering of the comic song "The Monkeys Have No Tails in Zamboanga." As the jaunty music filled the room, I went to a small window that overlooked a narrow lane below, then leant out of the bay window on the adjacent wall, which opened onto an enclosed piece of ground. Houses backed into it on all sides, effectively making an unbroken wall all around. The space below was treeless, no more than a huge backyard.

"That's the Bagh—the garden," said Amrik-ji, stroking his beard.

"What garden?" I protested. "It's just a piece of bare ground."

"Ah, the clear eyes of youth," he quipped. "Nonetheless it is what we in Amritsar call the Bagh, Robert."

I went to the window and watched the rural families making themselves comfortable under the sky. Amrik-ji came and stood by me. "These villagers . . . they have been coming here for decades," he reminisced.

"When can I see the car, Amrik-ji?" I asked, unable to contain my eagerness.

"Oh yes, the car. Nathwa, the driver, has put it away in its garage a few streets away. This *galli* is too narrow for it."

"Please, can I go see it now?" I asked eagerly. My father was incurious, standing beside the lawyer, far more interested in looking at the gathering below. I knew that they still had to discuss the sale of the house. I would just have to wait.

● ● ●

THE NEXT MORNING we finally went to see my car in its garage on a wider street some four lanes away, escorted by Amrik Singh's office boy. The automobile had been taken out and parked outside, but the driver was nowhere in sight.

"It's an Armstrong-Whitworth!" I burst out, breathless with joy.

The elegant black machine, with wide running boards, a spare tyre in a metal circle at the rear, gleamed in the sunlight. My heart sang. I wanted to have the driver summoned and have a ride right away, but my father had to go to the lawyer's office nearby to sign papers and affidavits to finalise the immediate sale of the house.

"Oh yes, Robert," he added, "Amrik Singh sent word that Uncle Rafe's chauffeur has offered to work for us. He will drive the car down to Calcutta." My father had forgotten to give me this momentous bit of news.

"Nathwa Singh Isser," he added.

"What?" I said completely at a loss.

"That's his name, Robert. Retired army man, decorated and all that. And he understands engines—or at least this one. He'll teach you to drive in Calcutta."

"But couldn't I just learn here—then I could share the driving. Is his salary high?" I wanted to anticipate any future problems.

"Apparently Nathwa made some kind of promise to Rafe when he was hired. I'll get all the details from Amrik. And his salary can come from the sale of the house," my father said, adding, "so don't fret, Robert."

I nodded my head in relief. "May I stay back and just look?"

He smiled indulgently. "Oh, Robert, of course It's your car after all."

I crossed the street to admire it, then got in and gripped the steering wheel with both hands, shutting my eyes in bliss. *My car.* Then I heard the cough. Startled, I sprang up and saw the top of a head. The man sat stooped on the running board on the other side. As he stood up and turned, I took in his enormous height, his luxuriant beard, and across his chest a leather band in which was sheathed a ceremonial Sikh dagger. He wore a khaki turban.

"Nathwa Singh Isser reporting for duty," his voice rumbled.

"I . . . I'm Robert Aherne," I managed.

"You call me Nathwa," he said gravely, and I nodded. One eye was a scarred hole, and a folded seam of skin ran from his right temple to the thatch on his cheek. "My uncle hired a one-eyed chauffeur!" I thought.

Nathwa looked steadily at me, his left eye unblinking, and simply said, "Ver Doon," which sounded like the nearby Doon foothills of the Himalayas.

He saw my confusion and repeated, "Ver Doon. The battle in Sahib-land."

*Verdun*. I nodded.

"I drove Rafe Sahib's car before I became a *fauji* in the army." His Hindustani had a strong Punjab accent, but I understood him well enough. "When I was wounded, the army let me go. No other job. Rafe Sahib gave me back my job of driver. I have no family, just the car. I promised Rafe sahib, I look after the car, no matter what. My word, my *jabaan*. That I gave him. So I go now to Kalkaatta." That's how he pronounced Calcutta.

"Could I—" I began, but he anticipated me, holding up his enormous palm.

"Of course, Robert Sahib, but not here. We need open ground, for this is like a great horse. You need to get used to each other first. If you press something without knowing, this horse might trample everything in its way. Very powerful," he added, caressing the side-mirror as if it were an ear.

"I think we leave tomorrow," I said.

"I am ready for your command. It is your car, no?"

"Yes"—I was grinning from ear to ear—"yes, it is my car."

• • •

I RETURNED HOME, and waiting for my father to finish, listened to a number of Caruso songs until I tired of them, and stood at the window, watching the lane below. A few older women squatted around their doors, chatting, and I could hear the tinkling of their bracelets punctuating their words as they gestured. I went over to the other window that overlooked the park.

The villagers had spread out their pots and pans. I could see the glint of some of their utensils. On little fires, the women prepared their meals of chapati and lentils whose aroma sharpened my appetite. I watched their poise, the rhythm of their accustomed actions. Leaning over their fires, they held the chapatis with tongs, turning them into round flour balloons over the flame, removing them one by one, perfectly done. Infants sat about, being fed slices of mango and guava. Some older children were throwing a red rubber ball with cries of triumph, while their mothers called out, reminding them to be careful of the fires and the well, for there was a deep one at the centre of the Bagh. A few toddlers moved about sucking their fingers and ogling each other. All the mothers had remembered to put smudges of kohl on their babies, on the side of their foreheads—to ward off the evil eye.

The children tossing the ball happened to come under my window, and when they noticed me looking at them, they waved gaily and shouted, "Hullo, sahib," adding their greeting, *"Sat sri-akaal, Ingrez sahib!"* Some of the families looked up curiously and waved at me. *Ingrez sahib! They think I am English, these village folk,* I thought in amusement, simply because I was fair and wore a shirt and trousers.

Some Sikh men had taken off their turbans and oiled their long hair, combing it out in the cooling air. A colourful group of women were drawing water and filling their pots by the well, chatting as each waited her turn. I could also hear the strains of a woman singing a devotional *bhajan* in an adjacent house.

Suddenly I heard rhythmic footfalls in the lane, almost like the beginning of a folk dance, where the group stamps before the elaborate moves begin. Not wanting to miss any part of the performance, I rushed across to the window overlooking the lane, and leaning out, saw a narrow column of marching soldiers. They were stocky men I recognized as Gurkhas—mountain troops from faraway Nepal—noticeably shorter than the local Punjabis. They were now marching quickly up the narrow lane, two abreast, clutching Enfield rifles, which I recognized, used recently in the Great War. They were led by a single English officer who held a slim baton, hardly larger than a conductor's.

A couple of faces peeped out of the windows to see the abrupt entry of the troops into the Bagh. Below us, under a bristle of guns, about a hundred soldiers were marching purposefully, emerging into the last rays of sunshine inside the enclosed Jallianwala Bagh.

I dashed back to the bay window overlooking the Bagh. Once inside, the Gurkhas split and quick-marched along the two near walls adjoining the entrance and stood facing the open ground. I thought the families would now be ejected, and worried about their interrupted meal. But then I heard the officer call out an order. The soldiers knelt and pointed their weapons. The villagers in the Bagh turned slowly, curiously, while some of the children pointed excitedly, paused in their games. I felt my breath rush out of me as I heard the single word.

"Fire."

The sharp volley startled a flurry of pigeons which scattered overhead in the evening air. A row of the villagers crumpled to the ground. An eerie cry broke out within the crowd. Mothers were throwing themselves down, covering their children. Some ran towards the far wall, which looked insuperably high. I saw a mother gather her baby and grab for her older child just beyond her reach, stumbling to the ground in the effort. Everything was moving slowly, as in a dread dance.

Next I saw the officer pointing directly where the crowd was thickest. I heard his command to fire again, shrill and clear. And time snapped out of its slow dance into a frenzy. The second fusillade echoed and bounced off the high walls. I saw the crop of falling bodies, heard the rising howls of women and men, the shrieking children, and suddenly realized that I too was screaming as loudly as I could, unable to stop myself. Blood was pounding in my skull as I watched some mothers began hurling themselves headlong into the well, their babies in their arms. The order to fire came again and again. The Gurkhas were having trouble holding their rifles, which had overheated from the dozen or so times they had been fired.

I felt at once drained of blood, and strangely sharp-eyed, as if I were both the dead and the perpetrator, implicated in the act and its consequence, by the fact of having witnessed it. The children's earlier greeting kept hammering inside my head, the greeting and the misreading: *"Sat sri-akaal, Ingrez sahib!"* I almost expected to find the floor under my feet as soaked as the bare earth of the Bagh which was now covered with blood and bodies, still and writhing.

At a sharp final command, the troops turned and marched out, in perfect formation.

Dizzy and breathless, I clung to the window. It was hard to

tell the men from the women, for many of the men had their hair undone, turbans forgotten. Cries rose around us, *Paani, Paani,* and people were running in with whatever pots and basins they could find, pouring out water to the wounded among the numerous dead.

And then I heard Amrik Singh and my father behind me. As he came to the casement for air, my father looked down at the killing ground and leant for support at the sill. He was bent double, wheezing in distress. I held him up to stop him from falling to the floor. Some men down below in the Bagh looked up and saw his pale face framed in the window as he fumbled to loosen his tie.

*"Ingrez saala, oye ingrez bhaaynchot!"* rose the angry cries from below.

Amrik was tugging at my sleeve. "They think you are English, come away this instant," he hissed. He manhandled my father down the dark stairs, as I followed stumbling after them.

My father was struggling, for he was carrying a heavy canvas bag. I took it from him. "The house-sale money, Robert. Be careful with it," he said urgently. I asked him if I should get the rest of our things together.

*"Abbhi chaalo!* No time for that," said Amrik sharply, and we followed him.

At the bottom of the stairs, he headed us away from the main door, leading us instead under the dusty stairwell and along a small corridor and out into the back of the house. It was a lane so narrow that our shoulders scraped the wall as we scrambled through utter darkness. I was completely disoriented, but Amrik knew this maze well.

We burst into the street near the garage. Amrik darted into a side lane, gesturing us to hide within a doorway. In the minute or so he was gone, I could hear little above my father's laboured breathing and my own thumping heart. As I regained my breath, I thought I heard running footsteps in the lanes all around, the sounds echoing through their narrow channels.

Amrik appeared with Nathwa, who had emerged wild-haired without his turban. He snapped me a salute, then simply said in Hindustani, "I will get your car, sahib." He took a few loping steps, but then abruptly jogged back to the lane he had emerged from. Amrik, Baba, and I looked at each other in confusion. But Nathwa was back in a trice, carrying something. "Follow me after a minute," he rumbled.

By the time we reached the garage, Nathwa had pushed the car out into the street. He started to crank the engine, which grumbled briefly and fell silent. I tossed the bag my father had entrusted to me under the car seat and turned to Nathwa.

"Let me help!" I begged, but Nathwa shook his head. "*Naahin*, sahib. I will get it started. You get in as soon as it does, *turaant*! Then I'll put that petrol jerry can in the carrier." He pointed to where it stood beside the car. "To refill the car after a hundred miles. It will be rural there. No chance of getting petrol."

"But what if it doesn't start, Nathwa?" I whispered. I could hear running footsteps.

"*Arre*, it starts first shot every time. Maybe it's sleepy." He grinned nonchalantly, flashing his gigantic teeth. "I try once more, *bas*. If it doesn't start right now, we push it to a safe place. Father-sahib can sit inside and steer, no?"

As he cranked, the engine burst into life, a tremendous roar at first, subsiding into a powerful thrum. I was so intent, looking at Nathwa and the growling car, that I was astounded to find us surrounded by a crowd of silhouettes lit from behind. Someone came running through the lane with a lighted torch.

"Ha ha ha, *chaalo* Sahib," roared Nathwa, oblivious of them, urging us to get in. He turned to retrieve the petrol, when he noticed that the jerry can had been picked up by a shadow from the night crowd.

Then I heard the cries, *"Maaro saale Ingrez-ko,* kill the English, *haan tod de gaaddi,* yes smash the car!" Nathwa leapt into the vehicle. *"Yeh Rafe-Sahib da gaddi, saale,"* he bellowed, releasing the brake and revving the engine, shouting and making a sweeping gesture. *"Haat ja, haat ja tusi,"* making it clear he would run over anyone standing in the way. "Move move, *chaal chaal!"* he yelled in his army camp manner.

We stared, momentarily forgotten by the crowd, while Nathwa stood in the open car as if it were his war chariot, a hero from an older age, defiant and peremptory.

Time slowed as that shadow from the muttering crowd flung the contents of the jerry can, a ragged opal shawl of petrol, turning into a fishnet over the motorcar. The figure with the torch threw his fiery missile after it, which turned end over end in an aerial race. Nathwa was swirling in a surge of light. His hair ignited, and then his clothes, and in an instant he was the bare warrior in flames. A terrible cry rose, from the crowd, from me, from Nathwa, whose great height buckled as the boat-like interior of the car swayed in a wave of fire. I heard the glass windshield crack sharply. Nathwa crashed down, lying over the gleaming bonnet of my car, its paint curdling and bubbling. Then came an eruption from within the engine, and shards of metal and glass flew about. The crowd ran helter-skelter, some lingering at the mouths of various lanes, peeping, before slipping away.

Nathwa lay supine on his raging pyre.

Amrik, holding my arm in a violent grip, urged, "You need to hurry. *Jaldi-jaldi* to the station, now, come away. There is a midnight train. It is not safe here for outsiders, especially you. There will be more reprisals, so hurry." We ran into the night, my father and I, following the Sikh lawyer.

"They thought us English!" I panted.

"Look at what was done to Nathwa *sipahi*," groaned Amrik-ji. "We are all English, we are all Indians. You just happen to be born of both."

"Irish and Indian," wheezed my father, his years of pipe and cigar smoking telling now, as he lumbered along the dark lane.

The Sikh cut him off. "Brendan-ji, our Gurus say, we are all brothers: *bhai-bhai*. Are we? The Ingrez have forgotten that. So have we. There is no forgiveness after such forgetting." We ran, struggling for breath, until we stood by the iron gates of the railway station.

"Well, Brendan, goodbye," said Amrik, pointing. "That night train to Delhi will leave soon. Go buy the tickets, Brendan. Do not take out too much money at once," he cautioned, and left.

"My bag," said my father, turning to me, stretching out his hand.

With a shiver I realized that I had left it in the car, the bag which my father had entrusted me, containing the money from the sale of Uncle Rafe's house. It was now all ashes. I was numb with guilt.

"It could easily have been me, Son," my father said simply, emptying out his pockets. He had just enough money for our journey back, if nothing else went wrong.

"Oh Nathwa," he muttered, shaking his head as he walked into the station, "poor brave Nathwa."

• • •

THE TICKET BOOTH was shut, and we looked about, unsure where to go.

"Let's get into any compartment for now," decided my father, and we made our way down the dark platform towards the train, noticing how few bogeys there were, compared to when we had arrived. All the Second and Third Class compartments were packed beyond belief, as if limbs had been twined and stuffed in the spaces. The doors were locked from within. We could not possibly push our way through the windows, as these were barred. Hostile brown faces stared at us. What struck me was their stubborn silence, so uncharacteristic in India. There would be no help from them, I knew.

We moved farther down the platform, close to the engine, but it was no use. My father shook his head in frustration. The guard on the other end of the platform was blowing a whistle. I saw him mount his caboose at the tail of the train, swaying his green lantern back and forth. The train lurched to life, and as it did so, we heard a shout.

Someone had opened the door of the First Class compartment and was leaning out, calling us urgently, "Come, hurry, there's time yet!" A short round man in a clerical collar, he had the stoop of a far taller man, and an old, wrinkled face.

"It's the First Class," muttered my father under his breath. "Come Robert, there's no help for it. We have the fare, damn and blast it." I had never heard my father swear before.

"No lights yet," the clergymen was saying, "I am sorry," as if he was in his rectory, and this an ordinary night.

"No matter, sir," replied my father, loosening his tie, "but when the light returns, you will find that we are not Europeans, my son and I. We are Brendan and Robert Aherne, Anglo-Indians."

The clergyman leant forward, as if genially interested in our genealogy. "Excellent, excellent," he gushed, "I am the Reverend Dominic Kelly, born in Ireland. County Mayo."

I wondered if the old man realized that we could be ejected at the next station if some other European were to board and object to our presence. But I was ready to doze off for now, my heart heavy in this bewildering night; my car, Nathwa, the falling bodies in the Bagh—all flickering pictures in my head. But I became aware of another man beside the heavily curtained window. He took out a small candle, lighting it with a match and setting it on a saucer on the table. A man in his prime, hair neatly combed, his actions minimal and decisive. His eyes were amused. "Aherne?" he said. "An Irish name?"

"Do you object to our presence, sir?" asked my father testily.

"Not a bit, Mr. Aherne," said the man, leaning to light his cigarette from the candle, "as far as I am concerned, you are part European, occupying a part of a European carriage." He was smiling, and added, "I'm Tegart, Charles Tegart. I too am descended from Irish clergymen, Reverend Kelly—the son of one, and the grandson of another." And with that, the three adults began speaking of Ireland while I kept dipping in and out of a troubled torpor.

"Ah, I might have known your father, Mr. Tegart, or your grandfather, but I left the Irish shores over fifty years ago," the old man was saying. Now he would proceed to tell us about his life and times, I thought, but the clergyman surprised me, turning to my father courteously. My father needed no further encouragement to speak of my grandfather Padraig and his mother's small shop in County Sligo.

"The western coast of Ireland," said the clergyman, breaking into a delighted smile. "My parents took my sisters and me to the Donegal coast and Horn Head that last summer before I left the dear island," he lamented. "But India too has changed since I first came here. The chaos, the sudden violence. Even after fifty-four years here, I do not know what to expect. Look what happened here!"

"With a firm hand and a cool head," said Tegart, "we can pacify the locals."

"And would that firm hand be holding a rifle?" My father was truculent. "Have you got any idea what happened in the Bagh just a few hours ago, Tegart? It was a massacre. Do you not think it shames the Empire in the world's eyes?"

"You know about the incident?" asked Tegart, his voice low.

"Know? Know?" repeated my father, his voice rising, "Why, Mr. Tegart, my boy saw what happened before his eyes."

"It was bad policy. Foolish decision making. Monumental incompetence," said Tegart. "It should never have happened. I arrived too late."

"Bad decision, foolishness?" My father was choking on his words. "Mr. Tegart, do you know what happened there, do you have the faintest idea?" he challenged.

"I do, sir," Tegart shot back. "I have gathered the basic facts. Do you want to hear them? Over fifteen hundred bullets spent, more than a dozen per soldier, about four hundred dead of multiple bullet wounds, of which more than forty were children, including a one-month-old. They haven't yet retrieved the bodies of the women who chose to jump into the well with their children. Yes, Mr. Aherne, I know the facts better than anyone else. That is why this train has left for Delhi at all. To take *me* there. To report the facts."

"And Christ wept," murmured Reverend Kelly, but my father continued to stare angrily at Tegart. "How," he fumed, "how do you know such exact numbers, Mr. Tegart?"

"Because I am the Deputy Inspector General of Police in charge of Intelligence. I rushed up here as soon as I could, but too late apparently, for O'Dwyer and the army idiot Dyer had already gone ahead."

"And what would you have done, Mr. Tegart? Have the police commit the massacre, not the army idiot, as you call him?"

"I would have done no such thing, Mr. Aherne," said Tegart calmly, without any apparent emotion, "for I had intelligence of the actual situation. Those villagers had nothing to do with it, the poor fools."

After a moment's pause he added, "Yes, there had been some disturbances following the Rowlatt Act, suspending press freedom, letting us arrest troublemakers without legal fuss. It certainly helps us make the locals behave. We had a couple of troublemakers picked up—a Muslim and a Hindu—fair warning to both communities. Some native hotheads threw brickbats at government offices. Fine by us—for it makes that Gandhi fellow with his blather of nonviolence look a liar. After that it was going to be routine police action—what we call 'Watch and Ward.' But that incompetent O'Dwyer had to grab the limelight by sending the nincompoop Dyer with guns and Gurkhas," seethed Tegart.

"It could all have been avoided?" Reverend Kelly seemed to have trouble breathing.

"Of course," crisply rejoined Tegart. "We remove just one or two troublemakers—and everything settles down."

"Remove?" My father's angry eyes seemed to bulge behind his thick lenses.

"Yes." Tegart was unperturbed. "Easy as pulling teeth. You just need to know which ones to remove."

"From this life?" challenged my father.

"Ah," said Tegart, as if losing interest in the conversation, looking outside at the landscape under first light. "We should be just outside Ludhiana now."

The train had come to a halt, although no station was in sight. In the distance stood a cluster of huts and a couple of houses with tin roofs. Before us stretched a small cornfield and a shallow pond in which a number of water buffaloes wallowed in mud with their calves.

"When they crucified Christ . . ." began the clergyman, gathering energy, but Tegart had closed his eyes pretending slumber, avoiding the theological debate.

That was the moment the first rock struck our compartment.

Startled, we involuntarily covered our faces. Tegart alone sat calmly, looking at an angle through the window. "There is just a cart blocking the tracks. The fool engine driver should have driven through." But the train did not move. Two more rocks thudded against our coach.

"Wh-why?" wavered the Reverend Kelly, face blanched with fear.

"The local hacks must have used the telegraph before the authorities got to them. Now everyone in North India knows," said Tegart. "A spot of bother."

We saw more men emerge through the cornfield, screaming incoherently. Then we understood their words. *O Ingrez, Jallianwala ke badlaa, ya firanghee badmaash* . . . More rocks flew at us. They were attacking only the First Class compartment. We could hear the people on the roofs of other compartments clambering down and joining the mob, ready for mayhem. Reverend Kelly began to recite the Paternoster in a quavery voice.

"Let me out," said my father, getting up, "I will talk to them." Before I could say anything, he had unbolted the heavy door and stood at the entrance of our railroad carriage. The cries ceased abruptly as my father stood erect, his hand raised. He loosened his tie. I heard him clear his voice, and then begin speaking.

"Brothers, *bhai*," he called out in Hindustani, "Stop. We are all grief-stricken. What happened in Amritsar is a matter of anger and sorrow. I-I am filled with sorrow." A mutter spread across the crowd. Through the window, I saw the men turning to each other.

"A day of mourning for all of us," said my father, his voice faltering with emotion, struggling to find the right words in Hindustani. The men's faces were red in the sputtering fire of the torches.

"*Oye firanghi sahib*, sorry now? Talking of sorrow—after Jallianwala, *saala*?"

"I am no sahib," said my father, "I have Indian blood in me, Indian blood."

The crowd had drawn nearer. One man from the rear called out a question. "What is that *bhaynchot firanghi* saying about Indian blood, *kyaa*?" The voice sounded incredulous. "You want Indian blood? *Kyaa bola!*"

"No, no, *nehi nehi*," my father shouted, "listen to me, *baat suno mera . . .*"

The crowd hushed, and for a heart-thumping moment I thought they would turn away, but it was an ominous moment like still water on a stove just before it breaks into a boil. A large stone came flying out from inside the crowd and struck my father on his temple, and he staggered back into the doorway. I lunged and held him so he would not fall to the ground. Blood was running down one side of his face, seeping into his collar, his eyeglasses shattered. With surprising force, he shook himself free of me and stood blinking at the crowd.

"I am your *bhai*, your brother. Here I am. If you think it right to hurt me, *maaro mujhe*, kill me." The crowd seemed poised to do something—what, I could not imagine. I pulled my father inside with all my strength and slammed the door shut. I was certain that his nonviolent protest was going to get him killed. My father's reckless bravery had halted them momentarily, but its spell was broken.

Larger rocks were being hurled now, and one crashed against the window, smashing the pane, and bounced off the metal bars. "*Nikaal aur galey kaat de*, drag them out and slit their throats!" The ragged cries could be heard clearly now through the shattered pane.

"Well, that's enough," said Tegart, getting up. He had been sitting silently, watching as I held my father down on the seat, trying to stanch the blood. I turned around and saw Tegart fling open the carriage door. He was silhouetted against the growing light. The crowd was roaring, as if it knew that the only thing it would encounter was fear.

"*Tafaat jaao*, get away," Tegart called out in a loud peremptory voice. In his raised hand was a pistol. The crowd stopped, like a horse pawing the ground, uncertain whether to stand still or to break loose.

"If you don't withdraw, I will shoot your *bhains*," he said, pointing towards the water buffaloes.

Someone threw a rock, which thudded off the roof of the railway car. Tegart turned and shot. The crowd swiveled around in disbelief, following the direction of the pistol, and saw a buffalo buckle and fall.

"*Jaao,*" he shouted, "leave. *Abbhi chaalo*, right now!" He raised his pistol and shot again. A second buffalo sank to its knees, mooing in distress.

I was certain the villagers would stampede the train and, pistol or not, overwhelm us by their sheer numbers. I saw a second pistol lying on the seat behind Tegart. I immediately picked it up and pointed it through the smashed window pane, thrusting my hand out and aiming at the crowd. "Let them see there is another man with a gun," I thought between clenched teeth.

But Tegart knew his India. These were farmers, and for more than two millennia, their primal instinct, which overrode all other impulses, was to preserve their cattle. There were a dozen water buffaloes, not counting their calves, in danger. They stood in bovine confusion, staring at their dead. The crowd began to chivvy the livestock, coaxing them until the phlegmatic black cattle began to move out from the luxury of mud. The process robbed the moment of its tension, dissipating the mob's murderous intent; they had become farmers again.

Even so, a straggler picked up a rock, and Tegart moved his arm, aiming the gun directly at the man's head. The villager dropped the stone, and Tegart lowered his gun. The man stood irresolutely for a moment. Tegart motioned him to go away, almost a polite gesture of farewell. He stood watching the man leave, as the train started to move and gain speed.

"Thank you, Master Aherne," he said, turning and taking back the gun from me. "Your father is a very brave man."

"So are you, sir!" I burst out, unable to contain my admiration. This was like being in a storybook, better than Tony's dad's war stories.

"I am a copper with a gun. His is another kind of courage," he said, adding, "You kept your head like a fine policeman. You'd be a good man to have in a tight spot. Next time, I'll show you how to take off the safety catch." He winked at me. "You are too young yet."

• • •

TEN MINUTES LATER, the train lumbered into Ludhiana station, where we heard that the mob had indeed put a cart across the tracks to make the train halt. Mr. Tegart got a railway doctor to sit with my father on a platform bench and stitch up and bandage his aching head. A carriage with armed policemen had been added to the train by the time we were ready to start.

In a few hours we had raced into Delhi station, where Tegart conferred with a number of officials and left abruptly in a government car. I did not get a chance to say goodbye. We would meet up someday, I promised myself, and pushed through the crowd to return to my father's side. The Reverend Kelly told me that Mr. Tegart had arranged for the railway officials to put us on another train headed for Calcutta. We were led to a First Class compartment, but my father refused to enter.

"I shall happily ride First Class when all Indians can," he said simply.

The Reverend Kelly decided to travel with us. We ordered Railway Chicken, for the old Irishman and I were very hungry. Together, we took care of Baba. His face was swollen, and he had developed a fever. I slept fitfully, starting awake, unable to rid my head of the images of Amritsar. Neither could I shake off the picture of the policeman sitting in our railroad car, his pistol full of bullets, surveying the world as it hurtled past, daring it to misbehave.

When we reached Howrah station the next night, the Reverend Kelly insisted on dropping us home in his barouche.

"I think I shall return to Ireland soon," said the clergyman to my father, who was in the midst of thanking him.

• • •

THE NEWS FROM Jallianwala Bagh broke over the land like a thunderclap.

"The Butcher of Amritsar: That's what the vernacular newspapers are calling General Dyer," my father said. "Our Nobel Laureate Sir Rabindranath Tagore has renounced his knighthood. You know, Robert, he is a friend of the Irish poet William Yeats. And Gandhi-ji has asked the British to quit India." My father was reading and gathering all the news he could.

Upon his return from the Bagh, Reginald Dyer reported his complete victory when "confronted by a revolutionary army." He was immediately congratulated by Sir Michael O'Dwyer in an official telegram, which read: *Your action is correct. Lieutenant Governor approves.* Martial law was clamped down on Amritsar. Reginald Dyer closed off the stretch of the lane where Miss Sherwood had been assaulted, forcing Indians on that stretch to crawl on all fours, heads hung low. On the scaffold he erected at the bottom of that lane, six local youths were whipped. There had been no trials.

"Reginald Dyer was born to rich Irish parents, local brewers in India," my father told me what he had garnered from the papers. "He was raised in the lovely hill resort of Murree and their opulent bungalow in Simla, but soon packed off to a school in Ireland. He squeaked into Sandhurst, the great military academy, after which he was sent to control the obstinate Irish in Belfast."

"And O'Dwyer?"

"O'Dwyer is Irish-born, from County Tipperary. His family gathered their resources and sent him to Oxford. Failing to find a good job in England, he took colonial service in India. He spoke ceaselessly of Oxford to any who would listen, but was shunted off to provincial Punjab, far from the Delhi galaxy around the Viceroy. Well, now he is being invited to the right tables and clubs— once and for all beyond Tipperary. Dyer and O'Dwyer," agonized my father over his tea, burdened by his own Irishness, as if distant members of the family had been found to be murderers, "how could they?"

"Tegart would have stopped them if he got there in time," I commented.

"Son, did you not see that Tegart is a similar bird of a different shade? Well, I pray you never have to," he sounded somber. I did not agree.

• • •

AFTER WHAT IT called the "incident" at Jallianwala, the *Morning Post* had started a public subscription as a reward for Reginald Dyer: They raised the mighty sum of 26,000 pounds sterling, publishing the names of prominent donors, among them Rudyard Kipling, who made a generous and exemplary contribution.

"Oh, but I love his story of Kim! Remember, you bought me that book?"

The two men were scrambling to the zenith of the colonial social ladder. O'Dwyer promptly favoured the world by publishing *India As I Know It*. The book sold extremely well. He was now being invited to all the right dinners. His protégé Dyer solicited local English language newspapers to write for them.

I had told my friends what I had witnessed in Punjab, but Tony's dad, Tom Hart's uncle Georgie, even Tony himself, were reluctant to talk. Our Anglo-Indian community had always held the Army above reproach; they changed the topic. Besides, the House of Lords had formally congratulated Reginald Dyer, so there.

"But you drink that Dyer beer, don't you?" I pointed out to my father.

"You're right, Robert!" My father sprang up, summoning Mathur, who got all our provisions, and forthwith banned Dyer beer, popular throughout India, from our larder.

"Reginald Dyer now speaks as if he is Ireland-born; in turn, Irish-born O'Dwyer pretends to be English, and writes continually of his brilliant Oxford days and his First in Jurisprudence, of all things, from Balliol College. Tipperary O'Dwyer must be so irked by the inconvenient uprising for Irish independence!" My father raged over his morning tea, shaking his *Morning Post.* The colonial social comedy was making him ill. There was anger in the house nowadays, and a good bit of it was mine.

I wanted to grow up with certainties and hierarchy, like . . . like Tony Belletty, I thought guiltily. His dad did not rage over newspapers, turning right away to the sports pages.

A week later I found my father clutching a newspaper at arm's length, as if holding a mirror before himself. His left hand was trembling slightly. "Now he has written an article for *The Globe,*" he muttered.

"Who has?" I asked, sleep still tendriling within me.

"Damned Dyer," he said thickly. *India,* he read out, *India does not want self-government. She does not understand it. Any opposition to the British government is a perversion of good order, for British administration brings administration of justice to all men.*

Suddenly my father drove his fist through the page, his face pale with rage. He stood up abruptly, his chair falling with a clatter behind him, and without a glance he walked towards his room. "He is Irish?" he shouted, slamming the door after himself.

"Are you all right, Baba?" I asked outside his door after a while.

"Yes," he groaned. He was in bed—quite unusual for him at this time of morning. "What happens to some Irishmen in India?" I heard him muttering.

Mathur came in and asked me what I wanted for dinner that day—soup, baked fish, salad and blancmange, or Bengali food. I told him to make cream of tomato soup, followed by mutton pilaf, then mangoes with fresh English cream—my favorite dessert.

As I sipped my tea, I realized that the very menu I had designed was part Indian, part European. The problem of identity was even part of our daily meals, I thought wryly.

I looked around for the newspaper my father had flung away. In the middle of the torn page was the now familiar picture of Reginald Dyer. He was pasty pale. A thin moustache crawled carefully above a weak mouth. His eyes were puffy and feline in a face that might have been handsome once. My father's punch had torn him in two.

• • •

JUST AS I recall the spells of anger and its outbursts all these decades later, I also recollect the pains of love, lost or recalled, the people who had departed my life, my mother and grandmother who had remained pictures on walls all my life, or the one who turned into a different kind of picture altogether. I remember Estelle O'Brien Thompson.

If I do not speak of her now, it will be as if she never was. But her name rings a gong through my being, and memory plays on my mind, a violin bow wringing an unfinished phrase of a melody that lingers in the corners of my heart.

I can close my eyes and see her as she enters the auditorium of the school where she steps in, and I, just eighteen, look at her, and am impaled by her fleeting glance. It is as if she stood in an aureole of light—and yet a part of me knows she did not, that it was only the dusty auditorium, hollow and full of echoes. I breathe with the utmost difficulty even today as I recall it. Call it heartbreak, soul-struck, what you will. But nobody in all human history has seen Estelle Thompson as I did at five o'clock in the evening, reading for a part in *A Midsummer Night's Dream* for the Calcutta Amateur Dramatic Society. *Estelle Thompson, Estelle Thompson.* I knew then that it was quite possible to die of love.

Nowadays, with a magnifying glass, I often pore over books of reproductions, for this is how I make do in my little world in Calcutta, never having gone to the fabled museums of Europe or New York. I look at the great paintings, imagining myself into these precious pages. I throw myself at the mercy of that space, breath bated, one eye closed, the other peering into the bulging magnifying glass, entering perhaps a *quattrocento* world, or within a gilded medieval story held inside a rectangle of palpable script, or some Biblical moment under some vast treed space before an unwinding panorama of rivers glinting into oblivion. The world is lambent under the painters' gaze. I often imagined myself pacing over these vistas, wondering about the need for these deeply painted landscapes—for, surely, the casual eye is meant only to fix on the figures in the foreground: a grim St. Jerome holding the Book, an untrammeled virgin giving pap to a beautiful child, or a feral Baptist bowing before the Awaited One.

I slowly came to understand why the wide vistas are there. Nothing looks tawdry or mundane when viewed within a vast perspective. Even as the eye glances away from the painting, even before I turn the glossy stiffness of the page, I think how the miraculous and the mundane must exist side by side to make possible these ageless moments—these loci of inward radiance—surrounded by the everyday earth and light. They become a pentimento in my memories, so that the unforgettable can be held in the palm of memory.

What would happen if we remembered everything? What would our world become under the terror of such accumulation? Every sunrise blessedly dries the damp spots of some previous unbearable rain, and the smudges take the place of the shocked midnight foot coming down upon a floor terrifyingly afloat in water. We need the vistas, I decided. The Old Masters knew the reasons of the heart and what it can bear in this world of ours.

I take stock at this far end of my life, sitting in my shuttered study in this crumbling monsoon-tormented house on Elliot Road. And if anyone should scoff—what does a half-breed policeman from a dead empire know about any of these matters?—I can only turn my cheek for other insults to follow. Half-caste I am. Who is not? There is enough difference between any man and any woman that their offspring will be just that, a hybrid. And as a policeman, I indulged my curiosity under the aegis of a bullying empire. What I had learnt about life and the subterfuges of the human heart would be grist for many a raconteur.

But one thing I cannot explain, and look for explanations in the great paintings, in my readings, in the everydayness of existence as years go by: What is the cause of love? I seem doomed never to know the answer, just as I do not understand the mystery of breath or sight. I think of Estelle Thompson and try to put my life into a vast perspective to make that memory bearable. I do not know if I succeed, all these years later. I am alive. That has to mean something.

• • •

So MANY ANGLO-INDIANS attempted all our waking hours to be English, yet at some turn in the street, the glance of some Englishman coming out of a shop or a carriage clearly meant *"Chhee-chhee,"* or local Hindus sneering *"Anglo,"* making us aware by that half-word what we were not, fully. But onstage, I could let myself be reinvented. Tony had talked me into auditioning for *A Midsummer Night's Dream.* Inside the yawning school auditorium, with its cobweb-ridden rafters, we shed our own identities, our tongue-tied selves. I was chosen to play Bottom, and wore my ass's head and turned into another half-creature: half man, half ass. I became English in a stage-land that was and was not England—a Greece that was not Greece—no country.

I could not take my eyes off Estelle, looking away with a sudden awkwardness if she glanced at me. But from behind my unwieldy mask, I could look at her, unobserved. My Titania, when she spoke, made my ass's head swoon. She spoke what she thought was a queenly English, a drawl imitated from the wives of English clerks shopping among the warrens of Hogg Market. But when Estelle spoke, the accent became unlike the tawdry original, for there was that in her voice that made it a little outlandish, something hard to place, mysterious.

I learnt my lines and had no problem saying them to my fellow actors, but time and time again, when I had to speak them to Estelle, I would look into her violet eyes and begin to fumble. I could feel blood rush to my face and words becoming a blur, until one day, as I ground my teeth at the *heh heh* braying of Tony Belletty and was about to spin around to face him angrily, I felt a cool palm on my arm.

"Robert," Estelle said in a whisper, leading me away to a corner of the stage, "we'll say our lines alone."

Mr. O'Brien, the Anglo-Indian director, nodded. She sat at the very edge, while I sat on the scuffed stairs, at her feet. I looked up at her, lost in a way I had not thought possible, unaware what my eyes gave away.

Then, on a Tuesday exactly nine days later, after a long rehearsal, I went behind the front curtain and struggled to take off my mask. Titania came and helped me. When I had the head off, maskless, naked, my awkwardness returned to me. Estelle picked up the mask from my hands, and kissed it on its ridiculous mouth—as she had done during the rehearsal. What came over me I will never know. Leaning forward, blood pounding at my temples, I kissed her mouth and felt her tongue move on mine. The mask dropped to the ground as she held my face between her palms and kissed me deeply. Then she pulled away, looking at me, and chuckled. "First kiss?"

I wanted to boast that I was much-kissed, experienced in the ways of the world, but I was tongue-tied, and the truth was out. "Sweet boy," she said, as if she were far older. I towered over her, but was a small bird in her hands.

"You may call me Queenie," she said.

All these years later I can still remember that moment perfectly, the down on her arms, her tongue on mine, my palm on the swell of her breast, the dizzy spin of the universe called Estelle behind my closed eyes. A kiss was never like this, ever before, ever after.

By the time I had replaced the ass-head in the props closet, she had left. Tony came in and slapped me heartily on my back, but I shrugged him off irritably.

"Our football captain's in a daze, Mr. O'Brien, heh-heh." The director, checking his notes, glanced at us absently. "Terrible, you know," continued Tony, "how her dad was killed." I stared at Tony, who prattled on. Estelle told Cheryl Demeder that he died in a hunting accident. Shot."

"Really?" Mr. O'Brien said in surprise. "She told me he died climbing the Alps."

"He was pure pukka English," Tony said reverently.

"Her mother?" I could not help myself.

"Estelle came as a poor student supported by the Foundation from Bombay."

"Her mother?" I asked again.

Mr. O'Brien shook his head. I could not quite fathom what I felt, or why it was of any importance to me. Was I drawn to her because she was English? A part of me brusquely rejected the thought. But I realized also that it was only a part of me.

• • •

ALL THROUGH THE next ten weeks during and after the rehearsals, I spent time with Queenie. She did not talk about herself. She had an odd power of turning the flow of words so that others spoke of themselves. I told her of my father, of Uncle Rafe, and then with greater difficulty about Nathwa and my car, and what had happened at the Bagh. She was the first person in whom I confided everything, even about my motherless, womanless home. But I sensed that she held a vital part of herself secret, as if to tell would mean the end of what made her live.

After the rehearsals, Queenie had permitted me to walk with her, back to the street where she lived. After the play was staged, we had no more official reason to see each other.

Now it became a secret treasure map of my own within my native city. I would walk along the familiar pavements of Park Street, wander beyond the Albion Cinema House, turn at the Grand Opera House, go past Firpo's restaurant to 15 Lindsay Street, where I had seen her enter, hoping to run into her.

I would stand for hours, leaning against the street-lamp at the corner of Queenie's street. Perhaps she would look out her window and see me. Would she guess that I kept my vigil, afternoon after blazing afternoon, under the Calcutta sun? I could never bring myself to take the few steps to her doorstep.

And then one evening, at the end of a week's vigil, just as I was about to turn back wearily to go home, head humming with the thought of Queenie—imagining her in bed, turning carelessly in her afternoon siesta, hair rumpled, a little sweat on her parted upper lip—I was startled to see her front door open. I stood, heart-stopped. She came right up to me, smiling, and held my hand between her palms, showing no surprise at all.

She was dressed in a floral print, her splendid dark hair setting off her delicate face. I could see the coral of her lips, and her eyes were luminous, as if it were one of the happiest days of her life. I barely noticed the maid who held the door open for her. Something about her tugged at my attention, but I only had eyes for Queenie.

"Dear Robert." Queenie smiled. She let my hands go, and turned about, her skirt swirling. "Take me to the bioscope."

I nodded, though I had not a *paisa* with me. The Elphinstone Picture Palace was a little farther down the street, and Queenie put her arm through mine. I held her palm as it lay on the cradle of my elbow. I worried that she would hear the pounding in my chest as we walked. Beyond the potted plants of the elegant Elphinstone lobby, the blue spread of the carpet was spangled with stars, and the elongated motif of a bouquet stretched up the stairs and into the bioscope hall. I also saw Mr. Edward Dorsey, its Anglo-Indian manager, with his neatly brushed hair parted in the middle, a maroon kerchief folded in his breast pocket. His nickname, I knew, was Tiddly.

A balding Englishman, escorting a thin Englishwoman with a brown mole on her neck, walked past me, flicking away his cigarette stub as he strode into the lobby. He turned to the manager, saying casually, "I'll have my office boy bring you the rupees tomorrow, Dorsey," and sauntered in. The manager bowed deeply, his grey teeth a perfect match with his face. "Of course, *heh heh*, of course, Mr. Forbes-Morton, most certainly, sir! Good evening, Miss Tippit. You-all will be needing a private box, no?" He straightened up and adjusted the kerchief in his coat pocket.

I excused myself from Queenie and bounded up the stairs to him.

"My name is Robert Aherne, sir. I am the son of Brendan Aherne of Elliot Road. I'll bring the money, and more, for the lady and me—tomorrow, first thing, I promise," I said hurriedly, as quietly as my agitation would allow.

"Ah, Aherne," said the manager, smiling broadly.

"Oh yes, please, Tid—I mean, Mr. Dorsey," I said, relieved that I had saved the situation.

"You better pay it right now, mun," Tiddly said, his sneer hanging askew on his face, his incisors out. "That there is for Europeans, ain't it? Am I the Eurasian Bank?"

"But I promise . . ." I began, in absolute misery.

"Robert," Queenie whispered, suddenly beside me. She took me by the elbow and turned me around. "Robert, come with me," she said, and led me to the end of the lobby. A large flowering plant stood between us and the others. We were in a narrow corner which was not covered by the great blue carpet. She put a couple of small rupee notes in my palm and closed her fingers over them. I looked miserably at her, feeling my humiliation churn within my stomach.

She brought her face close to mine. Her eyebrows were perfect. Her breath was cool and fragrant. "Remember, I'm Queen Titania," she whispered. "Go get our tickets, Bottom."

I looked down at the crumpled rupee notes in my palm, barely enough for the cheapest tickets in the house. I bought them like a sleepwalker and returned. She was admiring the large posters in the lobby, serenely ignoring the speculative look on the manager's narrow face. We walked in together, past the plush red velvet seats at the back, to the bare wooden chairs of the section closest to the screen. But it was as if all the things around us were simply stage sets, and the person for whom it was all arranged was Queenie, who sat beside a tall, awkward boy. Estelle Thompson was the radiant being who could not be smudged.

The lights dimmed and a piano thrummed. The world of the cinema took over, its pellucid grays, blues, and blacks merging with the piano music which pulsed around us. Some other universe unfolded before our eyes. Castles, turrets, prancing horses, swordplay. I looked at Queenie, and thought that she was lost, drawn into that flickering world, among the painted faces of a magical reality.

I was watching her in this velvet dimness when she turned her face, eyes still on the screen. I bent my head to her, and she whispered, "Will you come and see me here, Robert?"

"Here, at the Elphinstone?" I asked, uncomprehending.

"Of course, silly Robert. Or at the Corinthian Theatre, or the Albion Cinema, or the Electric Theatre—or the Alfred, if you like," she murmured.

"Oh?" I breathed, waiting for her to explain.

"I will go away, you know," she said, as if reminding me of a story I already knew. "But I will always remember my Calcutta beau, sweet Robert Aherne of Elliot Road. My awkward, angry Robert."

All I could think of, at that moment, was what she heard the manager remark to me. In my hurt pride, I did not comprehend that Queenie was telling me about her whole life, even as she was beginning to live it. I sensed a gulf between us, as if I were just a boy whose gawky innocence had drawn her to me. But the moment passed. I reached out and held her hand. As she put her head on my shoulder, I wondered if she even noticed when I kissed her hair.

Through the next weeks I began to take Queenie to bioscope shows and sometimes for afternoon walks to the Strand by the river, to the Eden Gardens. We would kiss behind the pagoda there. But she never wanted to go to Elliot Road, or to meet my father, nor did she once invite me to her home.

Instead, I took her to meet my mother and grandmother at the far end of Park Street among the marble and stone mausoleums and headstones of the cemetery. I felt the need to connect Queenie to the absent women of my life.

We walked past the grave of young Rose Aylmer, about whom Walter Savage Landor had written a lament, and beyond it, the obelisk for Sir William Jones, the linguist. The trees were high and graceful above us, as we noted the place where Dickens's son Walter lay buried. Queenie paused often among the headstones, reading the names.

**Alice Agnes**
**Beloved daughter of Augustus and Joan Fairbrother**
**1847–1864**

"She was only seventeen," Queenie said, as if she had known her years ago.

Then I showed her my mother's gravestone, a simple marker with her name and dates. Queenie held my hand. We stepped away to another tombstone near it:

*Kalidasi Euphonia*
*Mourned by Her Loving Husband*
*"She Sings Among the Angels Now"*

"Did you know her?" asked Queenie.

"She was my grandmother, my father's mother. She died before I was born."

"Did she sing?"

"My grandfather Padraig fell in love with my grandmother when he heard her."

"She was Bengali?" Queenie traced her name with her fingers.

"She was. Beautiful and dark, with a voice my father says was deep and lovely."

"Beautiful and dark," she mused. "The English would not likely think that." She was standing still, her light eyes thoughtful, the last rays of the sun catching the brown glints in her hair, her complexion lit from within as if by a golden glow. Her eyelashes were long and made her eyes even more beautiful, and reminded me of someone whom I had known, or perhaps had dreamt of.

"Do you," she said in a whisper, "do you know what you want, Robert?"

I looked at her, puzzled by her seriousness. She reached out and touched my cheek tenderly. "My beautiful boy," she murmured, "I so love your innocence." Her eyes were full of regret.

She held my face between her palms. "I cannot help what I want, Robert, all the things that I want to be, and where. Even if I must give up something precious."

"What things, Queenie?" I asked, wondering what she could mean. I waited for her answer, but she had moved away.

"I have never seen my father's grave. He was born in England," she said, "near Durham."

"Where is he buried?" I wanted to know more. "You came here from Bombay, didn't you?"

"He died . . . a hero . . . yes, at the Somme in the Great War," she said as if to herself, "my mother once said."

"Your mother . . ." I began.

"It is late, Robert," she interjected abruptly. "It is time for me to return."

"Don't you want to see the moonrise?" I asked, longing to have her stay longer.

"No," she said, uncharacteristically sharp, "I am late as it is. My maid will worry." I was certain she had been on the point of telling me something important, something that would change her life, and mine, but had drawn away from the brink.

"Queenie . . ." I pleaded, wanting to restore that moment, but she had walked away, half a step ahead of me. Not wanting to discomfit her, I followed at my normal pace, but she stayed ahead, which discouraged talk. She turned and stopped on the threshold, her hand on the great teak door of the building.

"Goodbye, Robert," she whispered. I smiled, expecting her to smile back.

But she looked gravely at me. "Goodbye," she said again quietly, and turning, shut the door after herself.

The entire next week, Queenie kept out of sight and sent no messages. Determined to spend the whole day and evening—if that was what it took—waiting for Queenie, I paced up and down Lindsay Street. I ached to see her, just once, even from across the street. It occurred to me a million times that I might just walk into Lindsay Chambers and knock on every door in that building to find out where she lived. But, mindful of her dignity, as carefully as she had protected me in my moment of discomfiture at the Elphinstone, I refrained. I would wait, I told myself.

I leant wearily at the streetlamp by the corner curb. The *bhistis* came by, toting their swollen leather bags, sprinkling the roadways with water. Evening fell. At street corners, and all along Chowringhee Road, lamplighters with their ladders lit the amber gas-lamps one by one. Footsore, but feeling no hunger, I decided to saunter down to the corner of Chowringhee, near the stately Grand Hotel where I bought cigarettes, Woodbines, which I had seen English soldiers smoke. As I plodded up and down the length of the arcade under the Grand Hotel, all the way up to Firpo's, I lit my first cigarette, holding it like a stage prop, getting used to its feel between my index and middle fingers. I puffed at it cautiously and headed back to the street corner across from her door.

My heart bounded when I finally caught sight of her from

under the awning of a closed shop. Her maid opened the door, but just inside the fold of the door—on the threshold—she hugged Queenie, who let herself be held, impatiently, and then stepped onto the street. *A hugging servant?* I thought, puzzled. Perhaps an old retainer, her childhood nursery maid.

Only then did I notice the sleek bulk of the car as it hove into view, its interior lit low, the seats soft leather.

Queenie stepped smartly into the car, as if on cue. Its door shut with quiet authority, and as the car pulled away from the curb, soundless as an ocean liner edging into deep water, I saw Queenie smiling up at the man beside her. His arm was wrapped around her shoulder, his palm draped over it. On one of the fingers was a signet ring that sent a diamond prickle as it swept by, and the tip of that finger lay casually on her right nipple.

I felt a sharp pain. The cigarette had burnt down to a stub, scorching my fingers. I flung it away. I had recognized the man in the car: Sir Victor Sassoon, the immensely rich, moustached, corpulent owner of ships, spender of money in matters of pleasure, the man of business from Bombay, Hong Kong, Macau, and beyond.

I glanced back at Queenie's door.

The truth struck me then. This mud-coloured maidservant had clearly once been a beautiful woman, before the crow's-feet, the greying hair, the slight stoop of age. This was no employee. She was Queenie's mother.

I dragged myself home, but did not enter. The spreading bougainvillea and the looming deodar trees subjected the house to a deeper darkness. Only one light burned in the house where, through the ground-floor window, the top of my father's grey head was visible, coils of tobacco smoke rising above it.

The women of our house were long gone, my mother, grandmother—all turned into stories—even my childhood ayah, Sonu-amma, pensioned off years ago. My father and I lived side by side, as if under separate laws of gravity on this common earth. Were I to reach out, I felt I would encounter, not him, but the worn leather of his chair. I was growing up, but nobody had told me what manners of heartache would beset me.

I did not know where she had gone. I never saw Estelle O'Brien Thompson again.

• • •

AT HOME, THE large familiar rooms felt constricting, and I knew each corner as a prisoner knows his cell. The portrait of my grandfather stared right back at me, a hard glint in his eye, a kindred unquiet spirit. When I went up to the terrace, I found it windless, full of washing hung out to dry in the gritty air.

I was not older, rich, or powerful, which impelled me to reject what I did possess. I gave up reading for I found it impossible to sit still. Music I renounced, for it touched places that bled. I considered asking some girl out, any girl, then felt an inarticulate hostility towards all of them.

One sleepless night, I switched on my bathroom light and stood holding my razor, unable to decide why I was doing it, then drew a line across my chest and watched the beads form, red drops on an electric wire.

My father began to notice the changes, but I found his concern irksome. Tony's good humour grated on me; whenever he tried to include me in an outing with other friends and his new girlfriend, Cheryl Demeder, I brusquely turned them down. They began to leave me to my incoherent anger and silences. I could barely tolerate myself and listlessly attended lectures, but as often as not, found myself turning away from the droning classes, sometimes from the very gate of the college. Taking up boxing at a local club, I pummeled my opponents. Although I had always played centre forward for my football team, I now relished being a full-back, making bruising tackles.

Whenever my father played his violin or turned on the phonograph, I would leave home irritably, wandering the hot pavements, pacing the flagstones of the indifferent city, returning home breathless. I took to lying on the cool stone floor of my room, curtains drawn, then doing push-ups until my body screamed with pain, and dropping on my bed to sleep fitfully.

I missed meals with my father, often skipping them altogether, sometimes bursting into the kitchen at odd hours to devour anything I could find, while our cook, Mathur, stared in disquiet. Shaving one morning, I could find in the mirror no trace of the boy who used to hang on his father's words.

Loitering past the domed post office at Dalhousie Square one incandescent summer afternoon, I chanced to see notices announcing openings in the police service when the idea struck me. I remembered being excited to hear that Sir Charles Tegart had been named Commissioner of Police in Calcutta, and wondered if he would remember me.

Ready to reinvent myself, I thought with contempt of my attempts to do so onstage. Those had been futile, with pathetic consequences. I decided on the spot to apply for the police force.

Growing heady with the prospect of action and the exercise of authority, I spent the following weeks in fevered anticipation, refusing to consider the chance of another rejection. The day I received the official letter of acceptance, I returned home with my hair cut very short. My father seemed surprised, but said nothing. I had not told him anything yet, savouring my secret for the time being.

Two months after my nineteenth birthday, on the morning I was to show up for work for the first time, I went to his study and declared that I had signed on.

"After Jallianwala Bagh, how could you think of joining British service!" My father was peering at me, incredulous, an angry flush spreading over his face.

"That was almost five years ago," I said dismissively.

"Ah, so it is different in five years?" There was a ragged edge in his voice.

I repeated doggedly what I had been rehearsing in my head. "Because, let's just say, all British governance is not bad. I want to be a part of those who govern." I found myself trying to stare down my father. "I don't forever want to be part of the ruled."

All these years later, I remember vividly how my father had stood before me, bespectacled, housebound, as usual holding a half-read newspaper in his hand. *I do not want to be like you*, I had said to myself: but stopped myself from saying it aloud.

"You'll quit college?" he asked.

"I don't see the point in staying on at St. Xavier's College."

"And business is not where your talent lies? You have made up your mind, Son?" He seemed to be pleading. For a moment I felt I was being importuned by a stranger.

"Well, in this matter of business, there is a family resemblance," he added with a rueful smile, reaching over to touch my hand, but I stood too far away.

He sat down heavily, shaking his head. Old business ledgers lay ignored in a heap on the floor beside him. On his desk, numerous bits of paper sticking out between the leaves, lay his books of history, bound moss-green volumes of *The Studio*, assorted music scores. The slanted ray from the high window behind him made an untidy halo of his hair, the pouches under his eyes lending him a sleepy and child-like air. What could I have explained to him when I understood so little of my life?

"So you feel you need to hide a part of yourself?" he asked me. I was a little taken aback.

"What would I hide?" I retorted. I wondered how much he knew or had heard from others about me, or if he guessed anything of my mourning Estelle Thompson's loss. "A uniform always hides some part of the wearer," he said. "It takes away something precious, and gives you a kind of armour. But tell me if I'm wrong."

"I don't know what you are talking about, Dad," I shot back, though I did know I wanted to choose a life as far removed from his as possible, one where I would be in control of things, where I could flex and use my muscles. I wanted to fall into bed and sleep the slumber of the exhausted. But all I could say was to repeat myself: "I don't."

"You used to call me Baba," he said ruefully, "It is odd how we are made to choose sides. We are Irish and we are Indians. We don't have to choose as the world would have us do."

"I like to ride," I said, wanting my words to remind him of the comforts we had lost. "I will get to ride the police horses." But he seemed not to notice my jibe. "I am to meet the Commissioner of Police himself later today. You know him—Sir Charles Tegart."

"I had read he had been recalled to Europe. So, he has returned. No matter. It is a strange thing surely," my father mulled, "how so many of the Irish become policemen for the English Crown."

"Sir Charles Tegart was knighted," I blurted out. "Everyone knows his courage. You should remember."

"Courage," said my father, "courage," as if he were turning over a pebble he had found on the ground. "The Indian boys keep trying to kill him for all the things he has done. 'And he is in blood stepp'd so far . . .' " His voice was low, as if he were speaking entirely to himself. "You wish to polish and shine your courage too?" he asked me curiously, raising his head.

"I wish to have breakfast and go keep my appointment."

"It is early, but I shall have breakfast with my courageous son." He wanted to try to reason with me, I could see. Mathur hovered around us, and the smell of ghee-chapati and fried eggs and frittered aloos filled the air.

I felt the familiar anger rise in me. Unobservantly he reached out again, this time touching me lightly on my shoulder. He was shorter, so that when he spoke he had to look up at me like a supplicant.

"You know who you are?" he said softly, as he led me to the table. I decided to treat it as a non sequitur. My father seemed to be flanked constantly by our Indian ancestors on one side and Irish ones on the other. Why could he not be uncomplicated, like Tony Belletty's or Tim Doyle's dad?

"What you are going to become," suggested my father, "may have something to do with being Irish and being Indian," and then he added, almost to himself, "and seeking yourself."

I shook my head, trying to ignore his words, and ate hurriedly. I longed to get away in my crisp new uniform, to be salaamed to, and to snap my own salutes to senior officers, to find myself in a place where rank and order were organised, obvious, and defined.

As I gulped the last of my tea, my father intoned, *"Inty Minty Papa Tinty."*

It was the first line of a nonsense rhyme my friends and I used to chant as children as we stood in a circle, marking one of us off with every word, before starting our game of cops and robbers. The one with the last word pronounced over him became the cop. My father chanted,

> *Inty Minty Papa Tinty,*
> *Taan Toon Tessa*
> *Ugly Bugly Boo . . .*

Then, with a flourish, he pointed his finger at me, saying, *Out go YOU!*

*I was the cop.* In spite of my father's odd attempt at comedy, he looked flushed, a vein throbbing at his temple. I rose and went to my room to get dressed in my uniform. I read my name tag: *Aherne.* Yes, I knew who I wanted to be.

• • •

I ARRIVED WELL before time at the gate of Lalbazar, the vast red edifice which housed the police headquarters in the heart of Calcutta. My uniform fit me well—I had had a tailor tuck it in here and there—my face was scrubbed, not a hair out of place. I could well have been at my first communion. The officer at the front gate came out with a sheet in his hand. His name tag said Hartley. One of the fair-skinned Anglo-Indian Hartleys of Beckbagan.

"In uniform, eh, Aherne?"

"Yes, sir," I said, saluting him stiffly.

"You're one of the Special Branch boys, I see." He was check-ing his clipboard. "Sir will see lucky you at his office. You know where that is, man?"

"Isn't it here?" I looked at the three huge rectangular blocks of the large red building stretched like a vise. "I mean, where is it?"

"Aherne," said Hartley knowingly, "you won't be wearing a uni-form much, man, if you are chosen for Tegart's Special Branch. You are going to be lurking about." He gave me directions to Ely-sium Row, a quiet lane not far from the spired St. Paul's Cathedral.

I walked past the marble wedding-cake memorial to Queen Victoria that Lord Curzon had erected, in front of which sat a big black statue of her on ample haunches, jowls imperial, holding a globe, with what looked like a metallic doily draped over her bronze head. I was on my way to serve the empire she had left behind.

I came to a nondescript lane which branched off from Theatre Road, under shady deodar and neem trees, a dim, almost sleepy, path to an unremarkable building with just a number on it. As I closed the gate behind me and walked into the front hall, two men—clearly policemen in plainclothes—appeared at once from two doors on either side

"Aherne," I said to them, "to see the Commissioner."

"You're expected. Go straight up to the top floor. It's the door marked 'Private.' No need to knock, Aherne."

I climbed the wooden staircase while the policemen disap-peared as if I had imagined them. Pushing the door which swung open silently, I stepped inside the room, bare except for a few arm-less chairs and a huge bureau with a green felt top. On it lay two pistols.

The room appeared empty until, through the leg-space of the desk, I spied a tangle of arms and naked thighs, a strained neck, and two heads—red with exertion. With an abrupt heave the bodies lurched up, and one of them pinned the other down over the green felt, his hand in a painful twist-hold behind his back, the veins of his neck clear as cords. The man behind forced his adversary forward until his forehead touched the tabletop, then, leaning down, took the tip of a blood-red earlobe between his teeth, while his adversary uttered a sound, as much a growl as a moan. Who made the sound I could not tell, but the pinned man's palm thumped the desktop twice, and the wiry man holding him down released him and straightened up, and I saw that he was Tegart! The two men stood side by side, virtually naked, glistening with sweat, gazing at each other, chests heaving with exertion.

Tegart barked a word, and on that abrupt cue, both pounced on the guns and raised them at me. I had no time whatsoever to react. By some trick of mind, everything moved as if underwater, slowly, ponderously. In another part of my brain, I knew it was all lightning fast, that I would surely die. I watched the two dark holes pointing at me, the flex of the fingers on the triggers, the clicks of their hammers, the sharp report.

I closed my eyes involuntarily.

When I opened them, I saw wisps of smoke drifting from the muzzles as the men ran over. Beside me on the wall was a canvas stretched over a very thick wad of felt and cork on which was painted a likeness of a Hindu, black hair parted in the middle, thick eyebrows above dark eyes. On the left side of his chest were two holes.

Tegart, the stockier of the two men, touched the bullet holes with his index and middle fingers. When he withdrew them, they were smudged black, and he rubbed them over the painted face.

"More life-like now, eh, Colson?" he said. Colson chuckled. Then Tegart turned and seemed to notice me for the first time.

"Aherne," he said ruminatively, as if deciding on my name. Something stopped me from referring to Amritsar and the nightmare ride on the train, but I was sure he remembered and had selected me to work directly under him in the Special Branch.

"No uniform from tomorrow. Dress as you people normally would," he added. I could not place which word held the sting, if it were there at all, or if it was simply an instruction. I kept my face impassive.

"Yes, sir," I said.

"This is Assistant Commissioner Colson."

I saluted while Colson nodded and, stripping down completely, began to wipe himself with a towel.

I looked back at Sir Charles Tegart, also naked now, beginning to put on his socks. He had a few gray hairs. I also noticed that he shaved his armpits, and his nails were perfectly manicured. This was the man whom the Indian nationalists wanted dead, and indeed had tried to kill several times. Tegart had always managed to escape, and in a couple of instances, killed *them*.

"Will that be all, sir?" I asked.

"I'll tell you when we're done, Aherne," he said, not turning. Tegart and Colson finished dressing in a leisurely way, talking as if I were not there at all.

"Done," he finally announced. As I turned to open the door, Sir Charles called me back.

"Oh yes, Aherne, there are two dossiers waiting to be signed by me. Leary downstairs will be done with the paperwork in an hour. Walk them over to me. I am off to the Bengal Club," he said, tying his cravat. I knew the looming building of the Bengal Club on Chowringhee Road, facing the Maidan. Only Europeans allowed there. I would have to wait outside its back gate on Russell Street until Tegart sent some peon, when he remembered.

I shut the door after myself.

These men ruled India. *This is what I had wanted, wasn't it?* I remembered the words that my father had said this morning.

*Out go you.*

• • •

IN OUR TIGHT-KNIT group of Tegart's Special Branch, he was not Sir Charles Tegart. Just *Sir*. There was no other sir but Sir. I began to understand why I had been chosen. I was athletic, eager, and unformed. Tegart was moulding me to his purpose. I wondered what would be left of my father's son.

The Bengalis, like burly Biswas or sly Majumdar, he recruited carefully, almost warily, because he knew he could not operate as effectively without them; but he knew we Anglo-Indians would give our lives for the smallest sign of approval from this white man who seemed indifferent to their shade of skin. Some newspapers had written about Tegart's Irish nature, but I comprehended that it was nothing of the sort. Sir was colour-blind in the execution of the Empire's power. And there was some other kind of blindness in him, but I did not quite know the word for it then.

We grew into a shadowy family and kept as many secrets from each other as any other. But there were few secrets from Tegart.

• • •

I THOUGHT OFTEN of leaving the Elliot Road house and moving into accommodations for the police force, debating whether there was a disadvantage in being seen to go in and out of these, especially given the nature of our clandestine work.

Our cook, Mathur, who was getting old, would potter into my room, sometimes to have a letter written or read to him, and occasionally for desultory talk. He was lonely ever since his cat died. It must have been Mathur who saw my valise in a corner where I had piled my things that day. When I returned from work, I noticed an envelope with my name scrawled on it lying on top of my pile of clothes. I tore it open and saw, not my father's usual firm handwriting, but a wavering script:

> This is not a whit more my house than it is yours, Son. My father built it for us, his family. A home, like the sky itself, can no more be mine than yours. Robert, dearest son, by forsaking it you make me an exile too. This is the place for your family, present and future.
>
> I have no other claim to it, now or ever.

I put the letter away among my papers, but felt an intangible umbilical cord tied me to the house and could not bring myself to cut it, although more and more I threw myself vehemently into my job, giving all my waking hours to the Special Branch, returning home long past midnight most nights. I made no exception on my birthday, though I confess to feeling a pang in the small hours when I came home to find my uncut homemade chocolate-and-toffee birthday cake growing stale in the unforgiving April heat of Calcutta. By my twenty-fifth birthday, my father finally stopped having them baked. It had taken him six years to give up.

In my new life, I had fallen into the routine of walking early along deserted streets on Sunday mornings, to the wide-open green of the Maidan across Chowringhee Road, to ride one of the

Police Brigade horses. Quite often, I would see Mr. Tegart's huge Packard cruising down the Chowringhee. That was his Sunday habit, driving around the city at dawn with his Alsatian dog beside him. I would salute him, and Sir would casually raise one finger, holding his mobile court.

I remember that particular summer morning which marked the great fork in my life, though I had no inkling of it as I neared the Maidan. I noticed beautiful frangipani blossoms on the pavement. Overhead, the tree was covered with the pale ivory and yellow flowers, and the entire lane beside the museum was fragrant. Just as I bent to pick one, I was startled by the unmistakable sound of gunfire. I had faced away from Chowringhee Road. I have returned to this moment so many times later in my memory that I am certain of that. I had not seen my shadow, although it was morning: I must have been facing east. The sound echoed off the walls of the Indian Museum and the verandahs and arcades of the commercial building on the corner and the red bulk of Lloyd's Bank, making it difficult to locate its exact source. I looked quickly towards the end of the lane. Before I could turn around, someone crashed into me, and I hit my head sharply on a cast-iron railing and fell on the pavement, momentarily dazed.

A young Bengali, his dhoti bunched at the knees, was running hard. He made straight for a shoulder-high boundary wall. I drew my gun, calling out to him to stop, but before I could take aim, the thin youth dropped something and, scrambling over the wall, disappeared from sight. Broken pieces of glass embedded in the cement along the top of the wall revealed a smear of blood on one of them. The object he had dropped on the pavement was a book.

Dashing back towards the Chowringhee, pistol still in hand, I turned the corner and saw Tegart's car halfway up the sidewalk, its windshield shattered. At the corner of the pavement, his dog lay dead. Tegart sprang out from the narrow passage between adjacent buildings, pointing his gun, his face pale but his manner impassive as he looked about him. There was a cut on Tegart's cheek, bleeding from a shard of the windshield, which he wiped absently with a clenched fist.

The early morning street was completely deserted; besides, no one wanted to be questioned as a witness. This was as expected, for the miscreants made a habit of shooting informers—or witnesses—and our interrogation methods were not exactly gentle.

"Well, Aherne?" Sir said under his breath, and I told him what I had seen, adding "There's blood on him. Also, he dropped this." I gave him the book.

Sir opened the flyleaf, on which was inscribed in fancy green ink:

"Well done," said Tegart. The book was a university text of English essays. He shook it, and an unmailed postcard fell out. Tegart examined it closely.

"It's written to an address in Abdulpur in the Barisal postal district," he said. "East Bengal Province." He tucked it back into the book and handed it to me. "The killer reads English essays," he said softly, "Charles Lamb's 'Dream Children' has margin notes in royal blue ink."

I glanced at the notes. *Same handwriting*, I noted.

"Aherne?" Tegart's voice cut through my thoughts.

"Duff Hostel, Sir?"

"Yes, Aherne, students with initials SM. That hostel is for Hindu boys from outside the city, and likely he'll be running to familiar territory." He added, "The rooms are shared."

"I'll look for the table that holds bottles of royal blue and green ink," I told him. "That's the color of the writing on the flyleaf."

Sir looked pleased. "By the time we get there, he will have escaped," said Sir.

"I'll pick up all his mail—and books. I'll see if the handwriting matches any other documents." He nodded. "Shall I go to Headquarters after that to check for a list of accomplices, Sir?"

"Not you, Aherne. I'll have Lumsden do the paperwork," said Sir, adding, "You had a good look at him, didn't you?"

"Yes, Sir."

"You didn't see anyone else?" I shook my head.

"If he is from Barisal," continued Tegart, "I'll need you to go to the docks. You started the chase, Robert. I'll let you finish it." He flashed me one of his rare smiles. He was a hunter at heart.

"Robert," he whispered, "no reason to discuss this matter, now or later, with anybody else." I wondered why he was calling me by my first name now.

"But why did he have a book with him?" Sir whispered to himself.

• • •

FEW STUDENTS WERE left at the hostel and only four SMs: Satyendra Mutsuddi, Santimoy Mitra, Somenath Mookerjee, and Sibapada Mohanty. Mutsuddi and Mohanty were fat, thus clearly not suspect. Motilal had malarial fever and could barely stir. Mitra was missing. And he was the only student who had a half-empty bottle of green ink, besides the more common royal blue fountain-pen ink beside his desk. I rapidly checked his books, and the handwriting on the flyleaves and notes matched.

Inside the box under his bed, I found no letters—just clothes, a tin of puffed rice, and an unfinished jar of mango chutney. The shirts were for a thin youth. I flung off the mattress from the bed, revealing a good number of envelopes and postcards: family letters, all from a village called Abdulpur near Barisal.

I remembered reasoning that if Tegart was right, Santimoy Mitra would probably have fled home to Barisal, and the only quick way to do it was by boat. It would be too late for that very night, for I knew that the tide would have gone.

When I returned right away to Tegart's private office, Sir showed me the exact location of Abdulpur. He did not give me any official orders on paper, but sent me home for the night, instructing me where to meet him very early next morning. I was to arrive dressed as a North Indian merchant and plan to be absent from Calcutta for a week or so: *On vacation*, Sir decreed.

A covered carriage picked me up near the Esplanade. The gas street lights were beginning to pale under the first hazy glimmer, but I could make out Tegart's form in the black interior of the carriage.

"A young man with a bandaged hand and no luggage left by boat yesterday," he said. "About ten years ago, exactly at that spot, there had been an attempt. An Englishman, Ernest Day, was killed. Shot through the head. He was wearing a white shirt and khaki pants." That was Sir's usual attire, and Ernest Day had been about Tegart's build. I knew the case.

"Take as long as you need, but report only to me when you return. Only me."

I nodded, taking it in.

"I wish I could go myself," added Tegart, "but the Viceroy might be visiting Calcutta and I need to be present here. I'd have taken this vacation." He smiled bleakly. "Wouldn't be the first time," he added, putting his hand on my shoulder. "Robert, *enjoy* it."

He did not speak again until we reached the river. I understood that I was to get down there. From his corner of the carriage, Tegart handed me a bundle. It held a small compass that looked like a watch, a folded map, and a black pistol.

"Untraceable," he said, looking at me. "Get rid of it after. You'll get yours back when you return." He held out his hand for my service revolver, which I handed over wordlessly.

"No trial, Robert," he whispered, his arm on my shoulder, "no trial."

I nodded in the darkness. "Good luck," he added. "Irishman to Irishman." He had never thought me Irish before, I mused, unsure whether he was playing a private game with my head. His carriage rolled quickly away.

The sailboat, the least conspicuous of vessels, eased into the shadowy river. I knew little of Barisal, of boats, or the watery, muddy delta of riverine Bengal. We sailed downstream with the wide pull of the current, towards the mouth of the nocturnal sea.

• • •

HUGGING THE COAST, which seemed nothing more than a low green hedge under enormous skies, we followed the river south and then east for two days. We passed delta islands verging on the sea, covered with mangroves, and every now and then numbers of egrets and parrots would rise, the egrets like wedges of paper, the parrots hurtling out like green projectiles, squawking and separating and coalescing into a mass again, seeking thicker tree cover after their short, clamorous flights. On the afternoon of the third day I saw an enormous blue snake, its speckled back glistening in the falling sun. It wove its way, undulating along with the boat for a while, and then, just as silently, slid from sight. Between stretches of mangrove, crocodiles resembling charred driftwood lay on sparse bits of sand.

Now the boat was headed north, upriver and away from the sea. We could not see the far bank, as if we were still sailing up another corner of the sea. Then it narrowed, although that simply meant that the distant other bank hove into view. On the near bank I could see some signs of habitation: the occasional mosque; a clutch of huts; saris hung out to dry; a temple or two, with small slices of green or saffron flags hanging limp in the still air.

On the fourth day, we neared Barisal just as the sun began its rapid tropical descent. I got off alone at a landing where I would easily pass for a North Indian in my *kurta-pyjama* and a bania-merchant's low skullcap, which hid my hair.

Compass in hand, I knew exactly where to go along the darkening river.

● ● ●

I WARILY APPROACHED the dilapidated mansion close to the riverbank, having passed swamp-like fields and a straggle of miserable huts. When I came upon a deep and wide lake, a *deeghi*, behind this house of the Mitras, I became aware of a searing thirst. Crouching at the edge, I took a deep draught of water which smelt of moss and the rain of old monsoons, quite unlike the water I was used to in the city.

I bided my time. Like that silent feathered hunter—the horned owl of night, neither white nor black, but a stubborn brown—I would strike with surprise and resolve. It had clearly been a grand house once, with a row of stately painted pillars in blues and scarlet, peeling and faded now, and adding to the air of desolation, banyan saplings grew out of cracks that ran all over the building. The front of the mansion sank within shadows cast by a vast peepul tree, a cracked dome looming above. A feeble moon appeared in the eastern sky. A jackal yowled, and some nocturnal creatures made their urgent way. A lamp appeared at a broken window, but the rest of the house lay dark.

As I hid under the trailing dreadlocks of a banyan, I was chilled by a premonition that something was watching me. Was it Death's raptor eye measuring the distance for its swoop? I could not shake the awareness of that presence.

In the stillness of early night, as the crickets were beginning their chorus, I was startled by a howl of lamentation which turned into a wail, a long sob, making my hair stand on end.

Pistol in hand, I slipped through the open door that stood ajar and found myself standing in a long hallway with a chessboard pattern of black and white marble, facing two louvered doors of wood encrusted with dust, no footmarks on the dusty floor, or clean patches on the grimy knobs to indicate that they had been in recent use.

A kerosene lamp shed smudged light on a flat platform at the end of the hall, upon which lay the rigid figure of a man, draped to his waist in a length of marmoreal cotton. Creeping closer, even in this dimness I instantly recognized the high cheekbones, pointed jaw, and arched eyebrows of the fugitive.

Aiming my gun at the centre of his chest, I tried to shake him awake with my other hand. I noticed his eyes were half open, the pupils dull. He was stone cold.

A terrible cry rose in the desolate room, and so startled was

I—who had thought myself surprised already—that I hit my hand hard against the edge of a table as I whirled around, dropping the gun, which clattered on the dirty marble and slid across a couple of black and white squares.

From where I stood, I spied an old man kneeling in a far corner, his frail shoulders shaking. Struggling to get up, his skeletal arms stretching, twig-like fingers scraping the wall, he paid no attention to me. I could hear his laboured breath, and coming close, smelt the peculiar odour of age and misery. His frail rib cage and thin shanks confirmed that I had nothing to fear from such unarmed decrepitude. He looked at me, taking in my North Indian dress, and said in halting Urdu, "There is nothing to rob here." He said it without ire or disgust, as if commenting that there was dust on the floor, or that it was night.

"I came for him," I replied in Bengali, pointing at the draped figure.

"My grandson has been taken," said the old man, "already."

His thin face, though lined and very aged, was intelligent and his eyes calmly studied me. His simple dhoti, wrapped in the rural Bengali style, grazed his bony ankles as he moved slowly to the taktaposh, just a plank on four legs, and knelt beside the dead young man, caressing him.

"They grow up so fast," he said to himself ruminatively. "He was to join the provincial judiciary. Such dreams in a country without independence."

I let him ramble on, wondering if I had come all this way for nothing and whether I should walk back now to the boat dock, or stay in this broken mansion until dawn.

"Will you light the other lamp for me?" asked the old man.

I fished matches from my pocket and lit the lamp, rotating the knob to raise the wick. Sitting cross-legged on the floor by its glow, I lit a Woodbine and, taking a long drag, choked. Staring in disbelief, I saw Santimoy Mitra pointing my gun straight at my chest. I might have pounced upon him, but seeing his finger fidgeting on the trigger, I stayed still.

"I . . . I . . ." stammered Santimoy, "I had . . . n-nothing to . . . to d-do with . . . with th-the shooting. . . ." His voice quivered with the effort to finish his sentence. What kind of terrorist was this? The gun jerked up in his hand, and then tilted down uncertainly. "I . . . am-m innocent, Mr. T-Tegart," he sounded frantic, "b-believe me."

I looked sharply at him. How could a Bengali terrorist *not* know his quarry? Nonetheless, here we were in a remote East Bengal village. All he had to do was aim true, and I was done for. Then he could simply fling my body in the river, and it would disappear, tugged by the powerful current to the sea.

The old man was still on the edge of the taktaposh, paying no heed to either of us, tending to the identical body.

What mystery is this? I thought, but I dared not move yet. The hands of the dead man lay by his side, unscarred, skin unbroken. I looked back at the figure holding the pistol.

"I was p-passing the m-museum a-and was t-turning b-back," he said, trying to master his stutter, "and s-sorry . . . I was u-urinating in the corner. Then I heard the pistols f-firing. I r-ran into the s-sidestreet, and then I saw y-you had a g-gun and were ch-chasing me. I j-just ran. What c-could I do?"

The palm he had held out in appeal bore deep gashes. This was the corpse's double, his living twin! What mattered, I thought bitterly, if one Mitra is dead—if the other shot me to keep him company? Abruptly, a wave of nausea swept through me, a bilious taste filling my mouth. A shimmer of lightheadedness troubled my eyes. *This black-and-white marbled floor is playing tricks with my sight*, I thought desperately, as a cold sweat broke all over me.

The old man stood up now. "Santimoy, tell me," he asked sternly, "was everything you said the plain truth?"

"Yes, all true," Santimoy said rapidly in his East Bengali accent, without a trace of his stammer. "All true, I swear by Devi Annapurna's name, in the name of sacred Shiva."

"I believe you," said the old man, as if that was the end of the matter. Then a querulous tone came into his voice. "But you said that you squatted by the railing to urinate? In a public place, by the Indian Museum itself! Oh-ho, can you, can you imagine what people will say about us who are from Barisal District?"

I did not know if I should lunge and wrest the gun away at this moment or laugh out loud at the complete absurdity of this exchange.

While the two of them talked earnestly, I reached out and slapped the gun from Santimoy's hand. Gasping, he fumbled after it. I pushed him hard, and as he stumbled to the floor, I lunged for the gun, retrieving it. Let me shoot the young man first, I decided.

But an unearthly dizziness overwhelmed me, a spout of vomit erupted from within, and I realized that detritus and mucous were seeping down my quivering legs, which refused to support me. I felt the metal of the pistol at my temple. The old man held the gun. In spite of the bob and reel inside my head, I could tell his hand was steady.

"Are you Tegart?" he asked me, as if he had all the time in this strange world.

Some poison was curdling my life's blood. *Who am I?* I thought helplessly. *Amar naam Aherne*, I mumbled thickly in Bengali, hanging by this one certain thread.

"Aherne!" exclaimed the old man. "Did you say Aherne?"

I nodded feebly on the floor.

"Lie still. Do not move, Mr. Aherne," he added, his East Bengali accent elongating my name.

"Shoot me. Get it over with," I groaned.

"I shall do no such thing, Mr. Aherne. You have the cholera and will need your strength and my skill to live."

Drifting like a leaf down a monsoon of darkness, gasping and vomiting a rancid fluid, I felt my life beginning to drain out of me. My mind stirred, a blind manatee in a river of pain. As I struggled to keep conscious, my head reeled, and my eyelids trembled in spite of my effort to stay alert. The flame of the hurricane lamp inside the sooty curve of the glass cylinder seemed to whisper to me, then faded into black before the sheet over me turned into a current of radiance—rippling and rising—growing lucent into something green and fluid. I was afloat in pain.

I lost sense of time, forgot what day meant, and what was night. Words drifted into my head. *Talon:* A curved word with a feathered leg that clawed my naked skull; *Eyes:* Two peepholes squinting on each side of a bulbous nose; *Honour:* A word with two charred holes, convoluted and curved into itself. *I:* A stick moving from place to place in a small streak of blood, a painting-brush jabbed unspeakably deep within an eye-socket.

What strange visions I had! My grandfather, whose features I knew well, leant whispering over me. Sensing a tender palm on my brow, I called out for my mother. I dreamt repeatedly of a woman with flaming red hair, who kept pointing directly at me, as if I needed to regard myself for some lost message.

Each time I came to the brink of waking, crack-lipped and hoarse, the old man gave me a small drink which tasted of crushed basil and some other herbs I cannot name, but would know instantly by the merest whiff for the rest of my life. In my confusion, I kept looking for my pistol, but found that I could barely move my finger on the pillow.

The world smelt of wild lime and milkwort. A bumblebee strayed into the room and hovered, buzzing and suspended, punctuating its flight, revising it in a mindful way. A trio of jackdaws stopped between a broken windowpane and a peeling scarlet pillar to peck at something they found on the patterned floor. Above the sheet, I was startled to find my hands pale and thin, my nails translucent, not bitten to the quick as they usually were. I was emerging pulp-like, embryonic, from a chrysalis.

The very old man and the thin youth had taken turns caring for me: Washing my body, swathing it in white dhotis, changing soiled sheets. I was no more capable of helping than of levitating. The old man fed me from a small curved silver vessel, tongue-shaped, called a jhinook, which villagers use to feed newborns.

I was still too feeble to call out, unable to explain that my nostrils were full of phlegm, that I was forced to breathe largely through my mouth, leaving my tongue dry as a wooden spatula, unable to move my head if an obstinate fly perched on my lip, rubbing its insect forearms in some disgusting ablution, drinking with its hairy proboscis.

But slowly my ease of breath was returning to me. I understood the simple fact that this old man had saved me—no less surely than if he had hauled me from the roiling river nearby. I had no idea why he had done so.

"You have been abed for five days," he said. "Will you eat a little rice today?"

I sensed that I had turned slowly, a lost planet in the void, from night to the first glimmer of day.

• • •

THERE WERE BOOKS on the small table by my taktaposh. Margaret Noble's book on her Indian experience, pamphlets of Annie Besant, speeches of Eamon de Valera. On the very top of this small heap was Dan Breen's *My Fight for Irish Freedom*. In the last two days, I had read some pamphlets and leafed through books as my mind grew lucid. Some were books I had been given by my father, and had then flipped through and laid aside with little care.

Now, in my silent convalescence, I felt a willingness to hear those voices. As I lay there, I realized that all these books had been written by people from Ireland and marveled at the strangeness of this, in an obscure riverine village of East Bengal. Some of these books and papers would be enough to lodge the Indian owner in a British jail. Dan Breen's book was considered downright seditious. All news about Irish antipathy to English domination of India was routinely, carefully, and ruthlessly censored. The Irish I knew—or knew of—here in India, did not seem like these Irish in Ireland. Dyer, O'Dwyer, and their like were feared and despised. The Irish whose words I had been reading were from a different, greener world.

I believe it had been almost a week when finally I felt able to sit up in bed. Thinking I was alone, I made the effort to turn and felt my feet on the cool marble underfoot. As I did so, I heard the old man whisper my name, and realized he had been keeping a watchful eye on me, out of sight, at the head of the taktaposh.

"Aherne," he whispered, as if the days and nights of my illness and convalescence had been no more than a small interruption.

"Yes, that's my name," I said, "Robert Padraig Aherne." I paused for breath. "I don't know yours."

"Did you know Padraig Aherne?"

"Please tell me who you are," I asked him humbly, for I needed to know the name of the man who had nursed me back to life.

"Do we, any of us, truly know who we are, or become?" he replied. His sparse hair was white, his face the parchment of great age, but there was no vagueness in his sharp black pupils, no filaments of tired red in his eyes. "My parents named me Ramkumar Mitra," he said, "ninety-two years ago."

"I came from the Calcutta Police, to apprehend Santimoy Mitra," I confessed.

"You came without escort, without informing the local police *thana* in Barisal? Why is it that when you lay ill, no one came to look for you?" he said evenly. "You are a Tegart man? Everyone in our wretched land knows about your Mr. Tegart." I could not avert my eyes from his steady gaze.

"We can speak plainly," he said quietly. "You came here to kill Monimoy, did you not?"

"What?" I said in confusion. "Who is Monimoy?"

"My grandson Monimoy was my pride. He was the one who collected and read those books next to your bed. He came home to see me one last time, before going from Dacca to Calcutta on a mission, but died suddenly. That is how the cholera kills, sometimes within hours, too late for my skills. I had him cleaned for his funeral pyre, when you came. But you . . ." he said quietly, "I was able to save you."

"You can kill me now," I echoed. I knew I was still as weak as a kitten.

"Tegart must have found out," whispered the old man to himself, "that Monimoy would visit me one last time."

"I know nothing about this Monimoy," I said.

The old man shook his head slowly. "Twins they were born, but Monimoy was air and fire, and Santimoy water and patient earth. All Monimoy thought about was our poor land and the humiliations of being subject." He paused for breath. "Monimoy finished school and went to Dacca. He discovered books by Parnell and Dan Breen. Breen became his hero. Most of Ireland has now become free. Impatient and patriotic, Monimoy wanted the same for India." We sat in momentary silence.

"To throw off police suspicion, Monimoy sat for the Civil Service examination for the minor judicial order which tries cases about stolen goats and cows, and petty bribery. Pathetic imitations of power for subject Indians. In time, he received the Imperial Letter of Appointment to join the judiciary branch of the Empire's Civil Service, so the police left him alone." The old man paused for breath. "Monimoy was expected to go to Dacca. Before that he planned to go to Calcutta and pay his respects to Tegart. There he would shoot him, my impetuous grandson told me on his deathbed, for Irish Dan Breen had taught him how to deal with turncoats. Tegart is a turncoat, he said. An Irishman serving the English."

"There are many Irishmen serving in India," I demurred.

"No one can resist the temptation to grind those under their power. That is human nature. And I doubt not, Robert Aherne, if ever we Indians were to have power over others, we too would do the same. Power is that heady drink." He paused momentarily for breath. "Robert Aherne, who was Padraig Aherne to you?"

"My grandfather," I responded slowly. "He died when I was an infant."

"It was Padraig Aherne from Ireland who first spoke to me of all this. He was a remarkable man, Mr. Aherne." Ramkumar sat quietly for a while, then handed me an object wrapped in a length of faded silk, a long envelope, yellow with age.

"It belonged to my father," he said.

The name on it read *Doorgadass Mitra, Esquire,* addressed to a business house near Pathuriaghata in Calcutta, in the manner of penmanship common in the last century, dated *October 25, 1848.* A red wax seal once held the letter together.

As I read the sender's name, my breath stilled:

*Padraig Aherne, Merchant*
*Old Courthouse Lane, Esplanade*
*Calcutta, East India Company Territory of Bengal*
*East Indies*

# Padraig
## Calcutta, India
### 1848

*To my Respected Mentor and Dear Friend,*

*Doorgadass-Babu,*

*I send my greetings to you, almost a year after my last letter bidding you goodbye. It was with great trepidation of mind that I left India, and you and yours, to find if a dreadful rumour about my family in Ireland was true. I found, contrary to my hope, that the direct appearance of disaster was harsher than my abstract dread of it. I had thought that I had seen and understood enough of life's strange stratagems. Now those seemed mere caprices.*

*You, sir, had stood between me and the East India Company's soldiers, when I believed that my life hung by a thread. It is only now that we can smile, remembering how they had come to your palace to have me hanged. But you did tell them that I was not Alexander Blackburn, the escaped English clerk, but your employee Padraig Aherne, come by your private boat from Calcutta. Do you recall how that officer McMillan and I spoke on, he about County Down, while I expanded fluently on how I'd taken ship from Sligo Harbour to Liverpool, and thence to Calcutta to seek my fortune?*

*"And do you like your job as clerk with this brown merchant?" the captain asked me with casual insolence.*

*"Better than serving the English," I had thought to myself, but Doorgadass-babu, I needed to save my skin, so I pretended nonchalance. Had he known the truth, he would have hoisted me on my petard—an expression my old schoolmaster favoured. McMillan could not think why an Indian merchant of Calcutta with a great country-house would risk a lie to the great East India Company itself. And I was finally rid of Alexander Blackburn.*

*You, kind sir, believed that I rescued your only son, Ramkumar, from certain death. True it is that you were away when he took so sorely ill, but what strange custom of your religious kin to convey him in his last moments to the riverside! The end of life, its length, is a mystery to man, and it is troublesome for me to think of anyone aiding Fate. It needs no human help, I say. Fate it was that directed me, so I could succor Ramkumar, put him by my fire, and give him watchful comfort and the simple nourishment of coconut water. That alone revived him—and his fate—no skill of mine.*

*You befriended me, became my generous mentor; more indeed, for you proved a father to me, I say without let or hindrance, for my father was dead before I was born.*

*But in my own filial duty, I have been sore amiss, and in my common sense to boot. Therefore I must confess to you and relieve my torment.*

*I do not expect anyone else to understand or condone my stupidity and arrogance. I can scarcely believe it myself. It is a damnable thing that I did not write home when I arrived in India. At first I thought I would earn enough, rapidly, for my passage back home—in about the same time it would take a letter to reach my family.*

*Yet at the end of those six months, I thought to save enough for a fine shop and a small house in Sligo itself, so I waited. I confess that never having earned, my ability to make money had become a heady draught, sending my good sense a-slumber. In the second year, you will recall, I accompanied you on my first venture into the interior of Burma, so far from civilization, where you and I acquired those great stretches along the Irrawaddy River for the timber trade. Before I knew it, the third year had ended. Now my Elliot Road house was being built. I was prosperous, thanks to your counsel.*

*Each month I promised myself I would write, and each month passed with a new addition to the house, or some luxury within it. I would picture my mother, a grand lady at last, and my sweetheart here with me. What cupidity overtook my mind, as if the rapidly passing time was of no consequence, and things at home exactly as I had left it! How I ever imagined that luxuries could outweigh the solace of my news, I cannot fathom now. Mea culpa, Doorgadass Babu. I am heartsick with guilt for breaking their hearts, and now my own.*

*I had already made arrangements: In the spring of 1848, I was certainly going to fetch my mother, and bring back my wedded wife. In my obdurate pride, I dreamed of the astonishment I would cause when I finally burst upon Sligo unannounced, after more than a four-year absence, making my grand way to Mullaghmore, with my gold-headed cane, my full sea-chests carried behind me, a great man come home.*

*I had paid small heed to the earlier gossip around the ports of troubles in Ireland, for I had thought like a fool that these were the usual travails. But on Christmas morning in Calcutta, at the sailor's publican house near Jaan bazaar, I ran into Declan Clooney, a Sligo sailor of my own age. He had heard tell that my mother had fallen afoul of tax collectors and her house lay abandoned. That was all he knew. I scoffed at him, knowing that my mother's cottage and lot was, by some means, exempt. But Declan swore by our Lady of Benada and everything else besides. Now the world crumbled around me, and I would not, could not, stay.*

*Also, there was a girl I loved. Brigid, her name was, and in all ways, except for the church, I was her true husband. I knew she would wait for me to the end of her days, as would my mother. Declan, when I met him in Calcutta, was in the drinks and a-sobbing for Ireland, so full of bad news and old songs he was. You, my good friend, had returned to set up the Burma teak depot in Rangoon. Thus I had no one from whom to seek good counsel.*

*I took the very next ship to Liverpool, on the day after Christmas itself, carrying a mere satchel and my ample purse. With fair winds, it took only four and a half months, far shorter than it usually does to go there in this season. Yet, for me, it was months too slow.*

*From Liverpool, I immediately took another ship, the first that would take me to Sligo Harbour. It made stops along the way, at Wicklow and Wexford, Cork and Tralee. I thought I would go mad, driven by impatience and my anguish. By the time we sighted the shores of Connacht, I was near tearing my hair out. But the wind grew favourable—a gentle easterly one. The ship sailed sweetly past the mouths of Killala, and into Sligo Harbour.*

*I believe I was the first off the ship, on the seventeenth of May, and I ran towards my village. Alas, Doorgadass-Babu, something had utterly changed, changed terribly. The grass and the golden gorse were the same as ever, like the thriving rhododendrons. I could see piles of Donegal stone for a great building going up near Classiebawn—some wasteful folly of Lord Palmerston, who owns everything here.*

*I raced past roofless huts, grass and weeds choking the holes which had been smashed into the miserable walls. I could see all that, and yet perceived nothing. I met no one I knew. The only people I saw appeared huddled and bent, looking suspiciously as I ran on recklessly as if some demon, perhaps Time itself, was pursuing me. They took a look at me, and such I appeared to them that they crossed themselves and hid away.*

*When finally I turned the familiar curve of the path to my home, I stopped abruptly as if I had been gut-hit. My mother's cottage stood doorless, its roof buckled above its cracked walls. There wafted a faint aroma of honeysuckle, and creepers had grown right over it. Ample cobwebs stretched over the lintel. Her well-tended garden was gone as if it had never existed. I ran inside, and stood there thunderstruck, for here was not a stick of furniture, nothing but filthy straw and the unmistakable stench of human ordure, as if beasts and vagabonds had ill-used it for long. My home-proud mother! She must be dead, I knew for a certainty now.*

*Declan was right, although he had been drunk with misery. I wept and cried aloud in torment, nothing holding me back now in my mad grief. When I looked up, I saw a grotesque face regarding me. I thought I was imagining the creature through my tears. So I turned away, trying to come to terms with what I had found. Damn Daniel O'Connell, I cursed, damn Alexander Blackburn. Then the thought struck me that I was now paying for what I had done to Blackburn. What Lord above—or lord below, I thought in my misery—had decided that I was to pay such a harsh price for something I had not intended. I wept aloud. I composed myself before emerging from the broken shell of my childhood home, the proud cottage of my mother, her neat shop where everything was so tidy like. I felt a tug on my sleeve.*

*I looked down and saw beside me a short gnome-like creature. Its hair was matted and it scratched at its filthy dugs with its other hand, an unsightly mad thing. But it was smiling, and wriggling its body about, as a puppy would. I stared in consternation—and then I recognized her: Odd Madgy Finn!*

*She was the poor demented daughter of a drunk about Sligo who had drowned years ago. Her scalp appeared patchy as if some vicious person had, on a whim, pulled off clumps of her hair, leaving skin like a dried ripple of silt on a riverbed. A vivid scar marked her face which was a simpleton's, a broken mirror ever ready to reflect a smile. She kept tugging my hand. I wanted to free myself, for I was disgusted. Her nostrils brimmed with green phlegm, her skin was riven with open sores, her mouth agape and the few teeth she had left, yellow with filth. I had come these thousands of leagues, and this the only familiar person destined to greet me!*

*"Get away from me," I gestured, for the creature could not speak.*

*But that served no purpose. She kept pointing up the hill. I shook my head. I was in no mood to humour anyone. My world had collapsed. But she clung about my knees now, and kept pointing. I understood suddenly that she knew something. She had been living in my mother's broken hut, and wanted to show me something—or someone—my heart shouted.*

*I made as if to follow her. The moment she realized what I was doing, she released me and ran ahead. One of her legs was shorter than the other—and she looked as if she were lolloping, gambolling— trying, in her eagerness, to run ahead of herself. I found myself panting, keeping up with her absurd flipflop speed.*

*As she climbed upward, my mind had been utterly focused on simply following her. Now, in an instant, I knew where I was headed. It was to Mr. O'Flaherty's school. Had my family sought sanctuary there in the hard times?*

*My mind soared. I ran along with her, who seemed now no idiot—for a great smile broke upon her stained face. How could I have thought this misshapen creature a dolt, for she could read my heart's language. I took her soiled hand—and she gave it to me as readily as a lady—and the two of us ran like children to the schoolmaster's house. As we came up to it, I saw that it had been added upon. More people had come here to live! The tree still stood in front of the house—I recalled that Madgy Finn would sit under it for all the length of our schooldays. That tree had split, but both parts had survived. I knocked on the door, then banged on it, but no one ansered. Everything looked as if it had been well tended until a few months ago. Nothing was dilapidated, but now the wild creepers were beginning to take over. Climbing roses and morning glory had spread over parts of the window. There were even a few twigs and furze that could have been gathered to be used for the fire; these may have been lying by the door since winter.*

*I would break open the door. For a second, I stood stock-still. What would I find behind the door? The dead? Skeletons? No one?*

*I gathered all my courage, all my strength, and pushed. The door cracked open, and in the bursting, took me with it and I fell to the floor. I could see nothing but the shaft of light that speared into the empty schoolroom. The room was clean, with a few things lying about. Then I noticed dusty books—a number of familiar tomes which my old schoolmaster used in the classroom. Also a broken armless doll, lying discarded under a table. On it sat a dry inkpot, a child's pen, and next to it a sheet of paper, all over which was written in a childish hand, over and over again: MAEVE. Then I noticed the wall. Using charcoal, someone had written hurriedly—I would have known that hand anywhere in this wide world:*

Padraig, we are starving to death, so the only way to survive is to leave Ireland. Your mother is dead. I am sorry indeed. So is Brigid in childbirth. But your little Maeve lives. She is but four years old and looks your twin. Mr. O and we are going to the ship *Rose of Erin* for Canada. If you read this, you are alive, bless God. Come and find us there.

*The creepers snaking through the window had swallowed up his name after that. But there was no need—no need in the world—for me to stay and read that name. O Brendan, Brendan, I thought. I wept like a child when I thought I would never see my ma again. Then I roused myself and raced down the hill towards Sligo Harbour, my mind a tumult. My Brigid dead, and I—a father! Breathless, I sat momentarily on the ground, my heart pounding. I wish I could tell you, Doorgadass-babu, what sensation coursed in my heart. I thought of the creature upon earth now who had, without my setting eyes on her, changed the meaning of my life itself. Nothing was going to be the same anymore. Now Brendan and Mr. O'Flaherty were with her in Canada. O my Brigid, O my Ma, my heart wept and sighed. My Ireland is full of death, I thought. I must find life, and now I knew where to seek it—in the new land of hope—no country I had thought of before this instant. I would cross the Atlantic.*

*But first, I must go to the shipping office and find when the* Rose of Erin *sailed and where it ported in Canada. It must have made many trips in the meantime—so I must be sure to find on which voyage my old schoolmaster, with a young man named Brendan McCarthaigh, and the child Maeve had sailed.*

*My lungs were fit to burst as I ran, but I needed to reach Sligo port and find the Portmaster to study the shipping records before the sun set. I went with all the haste I could muster, but found that the office had shut its doors for the day. I would have to cool my heels till it opened in the morning*

*I took myself to the tavern at the edge of the harbour and gave a whole loaf to Madgy, who would not come in and curled up on the pavement stones like a puppy. When the tavern was about to close, I asked the innkeeper, Jim Gwynne, if I might stretch out by the fireplace for the night and offered to pay him generously.*

"Nay, no need for that. You are a Sligo boy looking for his kin. Is't not? So be my guest for one night."

I was moved to tears, but all I could say was, "Thank you, Mr. Gwynne."

I lay down by the fire, but Doorgadass-babu, sleep would not come to me. Jim Gwynne sat with me over a bottle.

"Can you tell me about the last few years, Mr. Gwynne?"

"You'll have to call me Jim," he said, "for we can't call each other mister and talk of things that'll make both of us cry over the whiskey."

"Padraig," I said.

"Aye, Padraig," said he. "I knew your mother, Maire Finnegan, by sight. A beauty she was, Padraig—such beauty as none of us ever saw, I say with respect."

"Aye, Jim, she was that," and I raised my glass.

"I know she died some years ago, God give her peace. More, I do not know."

And beside that fireplace, watching the embers, Jim Gwynne talked about those years of suffering.

"During the Great Hunger, I survived by the custom the sailors brought here, but saw so much misery that I began to get terrible sick headaches. No swig of the bottle could rid me of it, no bruising fist-icuffs, not even the occasional rut, I beg yer pardon—but that's the whole truth. Then, I don't know what came over me, I started to scribble and draw what I saw about me. I drew as I saw them—as they stayed in my head and would not be shook away. The trudging folk with their bundles, sitting by the roadside like wing-broke birds, the children bent over, bloated with the hunger, the women with their falling-off hair and filthy helpless feet. The sleeping children slowly dying around their mothers, the dogs watchful, the lowering looks of the boys that had lost their play and had taken to the stony paths. The *only way to keep all these sights from bursting my head itself, see, was to catch them on paper."*

By that inn's fireplace I looked at sheet after sheet of pen and charcoal drawings. I had heard in India about the Irish Hunger, but only now was I was face-to-face with our starving Ireland. I asked to keep a couple of them.

"Take them, Padraig, take them," he said without hesitation. I was bent over in tears, and the two pictures grew dim as I held them in my hands.

In the morning, Madgy reappeared, and I had another loaf for her, which she munched on with a right good will. I made for the Portmaster's office and sensed Madgy Finn stop as I strode inside. The man looked up and saw that I was dressed prosperously.

"I am a County Sligo man who has been in India," I said.

"India?" he exclaimed. "Bless me! They raised a good sum in that worst year."

"I came to enquire of the ship Rose of Erin, which sailed with the schoolmaster Mr. Malachi O'Flaherty, my friend Brendan McCarthaigh, and a small girl child. Will it please you, sir, to look up your records and tell me which port in Canada they sailed for?"

"Ahhh," he said, drawing a long breath, "you'd want to know that, would you?" He drew in his breath again and asked, "And sir, who are you to want to know that, if I may ask?"

"Is it privy information I ask, sir?" I said with some heat. But then, as I have learnt from you, Doorgadass-Babu, I cooled my tone. You taught me that when I need information, and fast, I should never raise my voice. I took out a sovereign—aye, a full gold one—and fingering it, said, "I have an interest in that ship, sir."

I have noticed the British crown stamped on round yellow metal arouses respect and piety in the beholder, but unaccountably, Mr. Scul-

*ly's face grew bleak. A shadow had fallen across the open doorway. I turned around and saw Father Conlon.*

*"So it is Padraig Aherne I see, is it?" he asked as if in great dudgeon.*

*"What is that to you?" I countered, too bitter even to say his name. My impatience had the better of me, Doorgadass-babu. This interfering bullyman was responsible for my Brigid being spirited away by her feckless da, that last time I had seen her upon this earth. This priest had foiled my hopes of happiness. My anger had found an object on which to place my burden of pain.*

*"I will tell you all you need to know," he began. "You will not need Seamus Scully for that. Keep your coin away, man," he barked.*

*"You had gone off without a word, Padraig, and left your mother mourning till the day she died," he thundered at me. I had no answer. I had. I did. I lowered my head now, struck anew by guilt.*

*"You whored a child on Brigid Shaughnessy, and she died in the agony of that childbirth," he declared as if it were a verdict, a tone of satisfaction in his voice.*

*"I was going to marry her, Father, for I did love her truly."*

*"Aye, love her you did," he said, making it sound sordid.*

*I felt the surge of my rage, could feel my fists ball up, the sudden fire in my blood. He was a coward, using his collar to browbeat me in my shame and grief.*

*"I mean to go to find my child, my friend, and my old teacher. I shall take care of them, so help me God. They shall not want for anything."*

*"They shall not want, eh, Aherne?" the priest sneered. "You take the tone of God Himself to ensure that wee bastard's future and fortune, do ye?"*

*Try as I might to control my rage, I caught him by his throat and hurled him upon the door. His head rebounded off the thick oak, and he slumped on his knees. It was unthinkable that I had struck a priest, but Madgy chortled with glee. I watched him get up and climb down the stairs unsteadily. He walked a dozen steps away, then turned and glared at me, a stain of blood marking where his cheek had struck the metal bolt. His eyes were steady now, and he looked at me with malevolence.*

*"Go to your damnation, Padraig Aherne," he spat.*

*"And you to yours, priest," I shot back.*

*"The* Rose of Erin *never reached Canada. It struck an iceberg and sank. The know-it-all schoolmaster, his pupil Brendan McCarthaigh, and your bastard drowned in the ocean." With that, he turned and walked away, as my world turned black. I stumbled up the stairs and banged on the door.*

*"Tell me, tell me, Mr. Scully," I cried, "Open up or I will break down this door."*

*" 'Tis true, 'tis true," Scully screamed from within, "the* Rose of Erin *was lost at sea."*

*I hammered blows upon the door until he opened it an inch. As I barged in, pushing with my shoulder, the man fell back shivering in fright. He skulked behind his desk, on which lay thick ledgers. I pointed at them. "Yes," he said hastily, "the Harbourmaster's records." He scurried to look for the relevant one. I could scarcely breathe. The news is false—it is just Father Conlon's malice, I told myself, forcing myself to hold still.*

*Scully opened a large volume. There it was: the entry record of the sinking of the* Rose of Erin*. I forced myself to read it, uncomprehending at first, letters coiling inextricably into each other, until they finally settled, firm and final as gravestones.*

*Scully picked at my sleeve. He was holding a torn page from an old newspaper which had been kept as a memento between the pages. I snatched it from him and read: The captain and some crew of the* Rose of Erin *had been found on a drifting lifeboat by an English merchant ship a few days sail from Canada. They had all perished of cold and thirst. The newspaper did not mention any other survivors.*

I stumbled away towards the quay where last they had touched land, this Ireland. A fishing boat was getting ready to leave.

"Where do you head, friends?" I asked in as calm a voice as I could muster.

"To Galway, sir, if you're for it."

"Aye, 'twill do," I said, throwing my satchel on deck.

They pushed off directly. As we went into the early-morning glimmer, floating on this murderous sea, I saw on the beach Poor Madgy Finn, dancing round and round, her voice singing a cracked song, the burden of which I could not catch over the water. It sounded like "Moo—ma—gy, Moo—maa—gy!" in a mad ecstasy, over and over again.

From Galway, I caught a ship to Liverpool, where after a single night of drinking at a portside tavern, I took a ship straight back to Calcutta.

The voyages I had undertaken are my testaments of loss, I have thought in my grief during these months on the seas. I would see the blue around me and wonder if my child had the blue of her mother's eyes. I could barely watch the reds of sunsets without recalling the texture of my mother's hair, its flaming abundance. I was sure that my daughter would inherit that. At other times I wondered if she had her mother's sweet nature or my mother's bold irrepressible heart. And when night came, my soul was seeped in its colours of despond, bitterly awake to the injustice of it all. I would have exchanged my years of life with Brendan's short one, for he had known my child, cradled her, *stood where I should have been. I would exchange my joyless life for that death.*

*On the bleak endless water, I had no one to mourn with, only the ones to mourn for.*

*After ten months and twenty-seven days I have returned to Calcutta, which I mean to make my home now, not knowing any other. Your people are mine, Doorgadass-Babu, for you had saved my desperate life once and soothed my heart—but that such knowledge and sorrow awaited me, I would not have known.*

*Come soon to my house when next you are in Calcutta. I await you eagerly, sir. You will see, I promise, I shall forthwith learn to speak Bengali, not with the disdainful accent of the English, but as a native Bengali does. For the nonce, as you have taught me, I am working at my business, which grows apace. I have received good counsel from your friend Prince Dwarkanath Tagore. He is a grand man indeed. I am learning my way.*

*I have no pity for the Englishman in my trade, though I deal in his territory. I exact my price with no let or mercy. I have discovered that the English have great respect for money, but then it is a rare man who does not. I keep my wary distance from them. What I feel most amazed by is how many of my landsmen work willingly for them. What magic do these English have? Or is it the headiness of power over others that corrupts us, even in our innocent sleep—and the English are no different from any of us, but for chance or history or happenstance. In that case, why is it that the Irish have suffered so much, for so many centuries?*

*Will a time come when the Irish will raise their sudden hands, holding whatever poor improvised weapons they can find? And what will the English call them then? Heroes of their own destiny, or brigands, merchants of terror—besmirching their desperate courage and* lack of standing armies for chivalric battles which always favour the great powers and their sciences of war?

The English have their cannons, their ships, and their factories. But I feel that the Irish will not forever be the followers of the likes of Daniel O'Connell, who sought Irish freedom under English laws. He called off the Great Meeting of Clontarf—and was hauled to a British jail. We shall rise, Doorgadass-Babu. I hope to see that day. We shall be irrepressible brothers in that struggle—Irish and Indian. But I also know that our peoples will need to find themselves—in their own proud, rightful angers.

I remain,
Your most loyal and respectful friend,
Padraig Robert Aherne

# Robert Aherne
## Barisal, East Bengal
### 1931


I thought of the anguish Padraig had endured, and what a balm my grandmother Kalidasi must have been to him. With her, Padraig took back what he could from Death, naming his only son after his lost friend.

I held out the papers, and noticed Santimoy looking at me, eyes full of compassion. In him, I had seen only a fleeing figure, a frightened subject to be chased and shot dead. Now I looked at him, truly for the first time. He smiled shyly at me.

"When did Doorgadass-babu receive this letter from my grandfather?"

"He didn't," said the old man. "My father died in Burma not long after Padraig Aherne wrote him. This was among his papers brought back to me. I never returned to Calcutta, never cared for cities. We had all we needed here. I kept the letter, meaning to send it back to Mr. Aherne, who had urged me many times to come to Calcutta where business was thriving, but I never did. Years later I heard that Mr. Aherne had died. I had not yet returned the letter."

"May Mr. Aherne have his g-grandfather's letter?" asked Santimoy. Ramkumar put it in my hands as I held them open. I bowed my head. I was to give my father the news of his half sister's birth and death.

"Please call me Robert," I said.

• • •

"WHAT WILL YOU d-do now, Robert?" asked Santimoy. I knew that he was asking the question for both of them, grandfather and grandson.

"I'll catch a boat from Barisal dock and tell Tegart, man to man."

"That's your plan, Robert?" Ramkumar was bitter. "Simply talk to Tegart, and he will be converted? You will read him your grandfather Padraig's letter—and Tegart will understand, because he is an Irishman. Is that it? You told us that he is from the North, and his kind suppressed his fellow Irish before they won their freedom in the South. There's Tegart, and then there's Dan Breen. Don't you see the difference?"

"Ramkumar-babu," I said firmly, "do not take me for a child."

"What, th-then?" asked Santimoy.

"I tracked down Santimoy and shot him dead in the night. I threw the body in the river, so no evidence remains. On the way back, I fell sick."

"Tegart is too clever to fall for this lie," said old Ramkumar.

"I have not finished." My voice silenced them both. "Monimoy will take up his job in the minor judiciary service in Dacca. There he will work for the British government, a civil servant, and refuse to discuss the tragic death of his brother. In a few years, he can retire—if he pleases."

Ramkumar flashed me a quick comprehending smile. Santimoy nodded as he too began to understand my stratagem.

"It is not the first time my b-brother and I used to trick our friends and t-teachers, by pretending to b-be the other. It was usually my b-brother's idea," he began, then grew thoughtful. "I shall b-become my brother Monimoy for the r-rest of my life! Each t-time someone speaks my n-name, I will become my b-brother again and again. My n-name is gone. Which p-part of me will live?"

The old man left the room in silence.

"I will give you something," I said to the young man, unwrapping my bundle. "This is your pistol now. Use it if you have to defend yourself. I am done using guns."

I lay down to sleep for one more night in this grand and doomed house, thinking of the rows of pillars along the graceful verandah outside, their colours flaking, ochre and blue, all of which would soon fall to ruin and be reclaimed by the tropical grasp of vegetation in this land where houses stand as long as people live in them.

• • •

FROM THE DOCKS I went directly home to see my father; I had been away for over three weeks, leaving no explanation. Here I was, touched by mortality, gaunt from that encounter. Yet I had retrieved Padraig Aherne's letter from its grim domain and oblivion, although it bore Death's finger-smudge in every line. I would need to explain to my father how I came by it—and Tegart's murderous subterfuge would unravel.

*So let it happen*, I decided.

I came upon my father sitting in his study, peering in the afternoon light at me through the open door. With a gasp he stood up, reaching for me.

"Robert?" he whispered uncertainly. "Oh is that you, Son?" I could not tell if I was holding him up, or he sustaining me, clasping hands, as if to be sure of each other's proximity.

"I have something for you," I told him, "from Grandpa Padraig."

As he looked up in confusion, I gave him the letter and watched him unwrap the silk swath and gaze transfixed at the name and address and the postal seal. He read as if the world around us on Elliot Road had ceased to exist. When he laid down the final page and looked up, I saw tears streaming down his face.

"I had a sister," he said. "Maeve."

He was mourning his dead. I had pored over the letter on the way back, and could easily recall the creak of the mast, the occasional snap of the sail, as if my sailing from Barisal had merged somehow with Padraig's voyage.

"My father could never bring himself to speak of his grievous visit to Ireland. He must have thought of it every day of his life. What must he have felt, each time he called my name! Yet he needed to remember."

"Do you think he ever discussed all this with Grandmother Kalidasi?" I asked doubtfully.

"I am sure he did," said my father simply. "If you had known your grandmother, you would understand how soothing she was. Otherwise my restless father would never have retrieved what peace of mind he did. He learned to love again."

"Then why did she not tell you about Maeve and Brigid?"

"I cannot tell, Son. I think she did not know how, and thought my father should do it, and then the time never came. That is how stories are lost in all families."

"But sometimes," my father added in the silence, "our stories come looking for us."

Mathur brought in the lamps.

"I need to get something else done," I told my father.

"You will be back, won't you, Son?" he asked anxiously.

"Yes," I told him firmly. "Yes, I will come back to you, Baba."

• • •

TEGART WAS NOT in his office. As I walked downstairs, Colson saw me and gestured towards the basement. "He's expected there," he said, surprised that I had not snapped him the customary salute.

I went to the basement interrogation room, where a snared suspect was being interviewed, but Tegart had not arrived yet. There was a strong smell of urine on the floor where the suspect was hog-tied, the soles of his feet crisscrossed with welts. A naked electric bulb dangled overhead, and a pasty-white gecko on the ceiling made a clicking sound, its blue organs pulsing within its translucent skin. Biswas and Lumsden walked in, nodded at me, and sat down sipping tea, oblivious of the others. The men I had worked with for seven years seemed different to me, feral and predatory.

"How much like them have I become in these years?" I wondered, gritting my teeth, smoking Woodbine after Woodbine as I waited.

I felt Tegart's pale eyes on me the moment he walked in. "Has he said anything useful yet, Lundy?" he barked at Monty Lundy, who was holding a cane.

"He keeps repeating that his name is Sharma and he came from Chhapra by train three days ago looking for work and knows nobody." Monty, a recent recruit, was sallow from exhaustion.

"Tch, tch," Tegart commented, "but observe." Effortlessly he kicked Sharma's kidney. The man made no noise, but began twitching, teeth biting down in involuntary jitters on his bleeding tongue.

"Does he know where the post office is?" asked Tegart. "Other details? If he's really come from Chhapra, he's written home. When did his train arrive? Was that time checked with the railway boys? Did he come through Howrah or Sealdah station?"

"Er, no, Sir," conceded Lundy, overwhelmed.

"Information, Lundy. Everything else is unimportant," said Sir. "Everyone out of here." He slammed the door behind us.

The door opened after just twenty minutes. I could hear Sharma moaning inside.

"We have the place and person—*we* pick the time to raid their nest: Just after midnight," Sir announced as he turned to leave with the group. He opened his palm, looking absently at a couple of dice, then tossed them aside.

"Come up to my office, Aherne," he said, starting for the stairs.

Standing in the stairwell to collect my thoughts, I lit another cigarette. In the brief flare of the match, I saw that the dice were, in fact, human teeth.

● ● ●

"You got ill." Tegart stared keenly at me. The light in his office was harsh.

"Yes, but I completed my job first. I got sick. I recovered."

"Ah . . . I was wondering if . . . if I needed to send Biswas to clean up after you."

"It is done."

"*Consummatum est*, eh? We do not need to think of Santimoy anymore?"

I looked him steadily in the eye. "No, Sir, no need."

"And the gun?"

"There is no gun. I tossed it in the river. But I need to talk—" Tegart cut me off. "Well, Aherne, just so you know. We found the actual scoundrel who tried to do me in. But there was no way to let you know at the time. That Santimoy was just a student. Too bad about him, eh?"

I stood aghast, yet knew that this kind of thing would happen again. I almost missed the import of what he said next.

"I'm finished with India, Aherne," he announced. *This is a trick*, I thought.

"No, it's not what you think" Tegart was trying to read my face. "London needs me in Palestine. I'm asking you to come with me."

"The Holy Land! Why?"

"Jerusalem, first. I'll be rebuilding the police stations in Palestine into better strongholds, with the best interrogation facilities. They are calling them Tegart Forts! I also think a high wall through the entire country makes sound sense. The locals don't understand, so we must persuade them to tell us what they are thinking."

"So you are not going to retire in England—or was it Northern Ireland—and keep a dog or two?"

"Oh, there will be plenty of dogs." He laughed. "I've already sent for trained Doberman and Alsatian dogs from South Africa. They're most effective in controlling the locals there. Why not in Palestine? Man's best friends, eh?"

"Sir," I said, "I want to leave the police force."

"Excellent, excellent. Great things to be done in Palestine, Robert!" He bent to show me some maps, unaware of my grimace.

"Sir," I began. *It's like tearing off skin,* I thought, *I will need to do it at one go.* "I want to leave you. I resign."

"Think it over, son." Tegart was watching my face carefully. "There's time—and a whole world out there. Palestine!"

"No." I refused to look away from his eyes. "No. I have no quarrel in Palestine. I am Indian." I felt I had finally earned the right to say this word.

• • •

I WALKED FOR a long time in no particular direction, and in a sweaty daze found myself at the gates of the cemetery, where a boy was selling tuberoses and a single astounding bouquet of red roses. Buying the slender white flowers, I walked in. The trees overhead made it a private evening as I stood before the graves of my grandfather and grandmother.

I put the tuberoses on Padraig's grave. Then I thought, how ungallant of me. I went right back and returned with the bouquet of roses for my grandmother. Red for the dark beauty of Kalidasi Euphonia Aherne. I stood there, absurdly and unexpectedly happy.

In this mood, as I walked along Park Street, then took a by-lane to return home, I glimpsed the shining marquee of the Elphinstone Picture Palace. On an impulse, I bought a ticket for the cinema and sat near the front on a cheap wooden seat. I had not even cared to find out the name of the show which had already started. I settled down under the great screen above me. And then I saw Queenie.

Through the long crepuscule of the theatre, smoky fingers

emerged from a hole in the back wall, and conjured before my astounded eyes my first love, whom I had lost to an incomprehensible world. When the show ended, the credits rolled, and I read the name she had christened herself: *Merle Oberon*.

I came outside to the brightly lit lobby where a counter sold candy, sodas, and glossy picture magazines. I picked up a magazine with her picture on its cover. In it I read, incredulously, that she had been born to English parents in Tasmania. Merle Oberon, the Hollywood star, would have to lie to Estelle O'Brien Thompson all her life. There they were, twinned, on the shiny page: beautiful and unblemished to the eye.

Instead of making her real, the blue-grey pencils of light had transformed her into a being unreal and remote. The pain of her memory had long been a part of me, as if her shadow had replaced mine behind me. But now I felt it move and stir on its own, and begin to inch away. As I stepped out of the theatre foyer, I felt free. *I* was not born in Tasmania. I too knew what rebirth was and had earned the right to honour my dark grandmother with roses. I wanted, simply, to return home.

On the familiar sidewalk that led back to Elliot Road, I thought how, as a policeman, I had marooned myself. I felt a longing for my father's music, my neglected books, and my lost friends. I knew Krikor now ran his father's business. Tony still lived in his parents' flat, although his father was dead now. I had not even gone to his funeral, I thought with shame. I resolved to visit Tony and his mother.

*Will my lost friends forgive and accept me?* I wondered. *Can they find it in themselves to take and bind me into their circle of affection again?* I felt tears I could not control. Through the familiar lanes a cool breeze stirred the trees along the street, its moist aroma presaging rain.

My father sat in his small locus of light, listening raptly to his phonograph, while I stood at the threshold watching him, letting the music possess me. When I entered and sat on the floor next to his chair, peering into the sheet music spread on his lap, the violins wove around the cello, and the piano stepped in on tiny feet, and soon I was the one turning the pages while my father rested his palm on my shoulder.

A gentle monsoon arrived upon our land, dropping slow and long. We were together, father and son, our silence sending entwining roots deep into the common ground of our old floor, while music rained above us, greening all the sere days leading up to this night.

• • •

THE IDEA CAME to me one evening when my friends Krikor Aratoon and Tony Belletty joined us for what had become our daily *adda* session, sitting around my father's study. A jaunty Artie Shaw tune played on the phonograph; Krikor lolled with his teacup in one hand and an old copy of *Punch* in the other, while Amala Martha Basu, a botanist and friend of Tony's wife, Cheryl, leant over to listen to my father discourse on his books of landscapes. Tony sat leafing through a pile of *Life* magazines. Ben Zachariah walked in with some of his friends who wanted to meet us.

As I looked around me, taking in the walls full of books, the comfortable chairs, the aroma of tea, I realized how happy I was. I thought if I could spend time in such a space every day, a place, say, like a bookstore, I would be lucky. Tentatively, I mentioned the idea, and my father sat up animatedly.

"I've just the place for rent on Free School Street," Krikor broke in. "It'll be a great place for books, and conversation and tea, and music." He added, "There's even a lovely deodar tree in front," as if that settled that.

Tony, forever the clown, sang out his rendition of Louis Armstrong:

> *Life's a cabaret, old chum,*
> *Life is a cabaret !*

• • •

AND SO THAT is how we became, father and son, sellers of used and new books, old maps and magazines, sheet music and art reproductions, piles of records which people were welcome to play on our phonograph, and fine tea always. It was as if my father's study had spawned its twin, and it had become a haven for young and old, writers and lovers of music, a meeting place, the only shop of its kind in the metropolis.

I had no idea that I could make a decent living doing all the things I was learning to love again, which my father had loved all his life. He never missed an evening, while I opened shop in the mornings, returned home for lunch and a siesta, then reopened in the late afternoon, following the rhythm of life here in our city. By early evening, the groups from the shop would take over the space on makeshift benches under the deodar tree, while people walked in and discussed and bought books, and played music.

• • •

MEANWHILE THE WORLD outside was growing darker, with the papers full of news of another groaning war, brother to the earlier Great War, which we had been told was fought to end all of them. Again countless Indian men were fighting, dying in British uniforms.

Over breakfast at home, a month before my thirty-fifth birthday, my father leant into the newspaper and let out a strange, exhilarated laugh.

"What is it, Baba?" I asked him curiously.

"It took a long time but it was done," he blurted. "Gandhi-ji will feel differently, certainly, for he always advocates nonviolence . . . but I am so glad that I . . . I must . . . rest," he trailed off, making no sense to me. He shut his bedroom door. Since I was already late to open the shop, I did not detain him with questions.

I hurried through my breakfast, glancing at the headlines before I left. There it was: a picture of Udham Singh, a boy who survived the Jallianwala Bagh massacre because he had been pinned under the bodies of his dead relatives. It had taken him almost twenty years to save money for the passage to England. He had gone to the public meeting at Caxton Hall in London where Sir Michael O'Dwyer was addressing the India Question, waited politely for the lecture to end, and then shot O'Dwyer dead. Singh's bullets had concluded the Question and Answer session.

When I returned in the afternoon, Mathur told me that my father had not yet woken up. I took a leisurely shower, thinking I would wake him up for lunch. But when I knocked on his door, I found him still in bed. By his side lay open his favourite folio-size book of pictures of Irish landscapes.

I sat beside him for a long time, holding his cold palm. My father, my *da*, my Indian-Irish Baba lay still, as if fast asleep.

As much as he loved India, he had died with a picture of Ireland, no country he had ever set foot upon—the vista of Glengesh Pass in Donegal, which he loved to look at, the last image in this world before his eyes.

# V

*fire*

*As in the gold mosaic*

# Maeve
## Lake Champlain, Vermont
### 1885

Roused by the rooster at dawn, I went out to greet the morning and discovered a bright world. We had arrived at night, and I had been carried asleep to my own room. I immediately made friends with two dogs who raced out of the barn to greet me, their breath rising in steam as they gamboled. Making a snowball, I threw it for them to fetch; the silly dogs tried to, snatching it from each other, but of course it melted in their mouths.

I could see two more cottages in the distance, their chimneys smoking. From the farther one emerged Mr. Braithwaite. "Oh, hello, Miss Aherne," he boomed. "Crisp morning, isn't it? I'm off. Tell your Papa Brendan."

"Will we be going anywhere else now?" I asked him seriously. The dogs were sitting quietly, and I could feel the sun on my cheek.

"Don't you like it here?" He sounded worried. "The great Trumbull is cosy in his sty. He has eaten well."

"I do not want to go anywhere else," I told him.

"Ah, good," he said, "of course, of course."

"Can I play with the dogs whenever I want?"

"Don and Bonbon here?" He gestured with his large head, and I nodded.

"Well, they are yours from today," he said, looking at the panting dogs. "You hear that, you two?" We laughed together, and then he was gone.

I went back in, followed by the dogs, and woke Papa Brendan, who sat up without complaint, but could not help yawning.

"They are my dogs," I told him, and then asked, "Shall we ever have to leave this farm?" He stretched but did not yet open his eyes. "Papa Brendan!"

He rubbed his eyes hurriedly. "No, dear," he said, "unless you want to."

"I do not," I said. "And you don't either," I added for emphasis.

He said nothing for a while, but smiled sadly. "Not unless I die."

• • •

PAPA BRENDAN USED to brood over the deaths and more deaths in Ireland from hunger and want, the cruelties, muttering about ships foundering, people hurting each other for small morsels, their bones sticking out sharp. The Good Lord sharpened his terrible sword on Irish bones, he would say on those bleak days, and the stench of mortality would not quit his nose, each mouthful reminding him that God held him hostage by his gut, waiting for the next black disaster.

One summer day, when I had turned ten, I just had to take him to the back of our house, where purple heads of wild bergamots and joe-pye weeds grew all about, and pitcher plants staked their stalky claims among the loosestrife.

"Sit down here," I told him peremptorily.

"Yes, Maeve dear," he said at last, hesitantly. So I told him. I certainly did not want to remember the starving dead, the drowned dead, the diseased dead, or any manner of death. Nor any ship, ocean, or anyone left on a chair at the edge of an iceberg.

As Papa Brendan listened to me, the pupils of his eyes narrowed and grew, again and again, as I raised my hand and brought down my fist for emphasis. I believe he even held his breath, and nodded—a very tiny nod—a very *very* tiny nod. Or was it that his face fell?

"Is there no part of the voyage you want to talk about ever, Maeve dear?" He looked grave. No, *nonono*, I shook my head vehemently.

"Mr. O'Flaherty?" he pleaded. I shook my head again. I had buried the Delft figure the Dutch sailorman had given me. I never told him what I had done.

Papa Brendan took a deep breath like a man getting ready to go looking for something precious, like a lost diamond, under a lake where he would have to hold his breath forever and ever, and perhaps never come back again. Then he breathed out slowly, and in my relief I caught him around his collar, holding his head against mine. He clung to me and breathed in long, and then out, as if exhaling all his stories of death.

"There is only one exception," I told him. He waited, saying nothing.

"Once a year, on my birthday, you can tell me how my father left to find the world. You can tell me how when he has finished his travels, he will come back to find me."

"I can talk about Padraig? Are you sure?"

"Of course," I told him, "for my father Padraig is not dead."

• • •

EACH MORNING AND evening but the Sabbath, I sat and read with
Papa Brendan, and wrote a tidy hand, though hastily enough, but
I was happiest on the farm, amid the mooing cows, the thistles
and cowslips, the small hills of grain put away in the silos and
barns, the earth replenished over and over. The years flowed past
us like the brook beyond our cottage, sparkling over its pebbled
bottom, the sunlight preening its sides of emerald and velvet moss.
In it swam slow wagging trout. Here the tilt of the world was just
right, and the seasons came and went like friends.

Our nearest neighbours, the Ebers and the Gabrielsens, told
me of the great towns, not just the small ones with factory stacks
like Lowell down south, but fine seaside ones like Providence, and
greater ones like Philadelphia or Boston with its busy port, but the
passage from Ireland had taken out all desire for me to stir. I did
not care to travel to any of these, nor did I brook any such talk in
Papa Brendan. We had all we needed on this farm, wanting nothing, I have told him.

I have grown attached to all the things that nest here: I love
the flicker woodpeckers, especially the clown-faced ones and their
clicking beaks, the *quueeah* of their odd notes and calls as if they
were questioning us, or the solemn nocturnal hoot of the great
owls. I know the nests of the querulous kingbirds, the purple mar-
tins which never fail to show up seasonally and delight my heart.
The bank swallows nest by the water, and I never did hear a high
pitter in all of Nature like the one from the titmouse bird with its
absurd peaked head. Nor have I seen any shade of yellow to joy
the heart as I can see on our waxwings when they come to nest
around us in the summer. In a vase beside my bed, like a bou-

quet, I keep a bunch of ringed pheasant feathers which I picked up among the furrows of our fields. I feel the kernel of the day forming as I wake and come out to greet the light as it seeps into the mist, our silence broken only by the swoop of the osprey, the shrike, the flutter of doves.

During summer afternoons, we are always visited by pearl crescent butterflies, and occasionally the red admirals, or fuzzy duskywings. And once in my own living memory a swarm of frit-illary made the vines behind our cottage appear smothered under tawny blossoms—until these butterflies rose in a vivid swarm and fluttered away to some other far meadow as through a silent day-dream. I wanted to keep my precious world left alone, unchanging, with all my ferocity of hope.

• • •

PAPA BRENDAN'S FRIEND was Richard Livesey, the postmaster, who lived a mile down the country road that bent along Lake Cham-plain. He had a taste for old books. A bachelor, he spent what money he had on his collection of pipes and fine tobacco, and made his own small stock of wine, which he refused to sell, but shared liberally with Papa Brendan. He was short and fine-boned, and sported a small grey beard, neatly combed, and a high fore-head. Mr. Livesey told me once that his brother too had migrated like him, from Yorkshire, and settled in New Zealand. He also promised to dance a lively jig at my wedding, chortling, "With nary a thought for my bad back!"

On the occasional weekend I wanted to sleep away at my best friend Amanda Eber's house, Papa Brendan would shut our cottage, walk me over, and stay at Mr. Livesey's book-crammed house. Once I came away early from Amanda's for they were going to service for Easter, and I thought to fetch Papa Brendan and Mr. Livesey to accompany me and found them sitting together, Mr. Livesey's arm around Papa Brendan's shoulder as they chatted on the bench in his tiny backyard that edged onto the lake. He beckoned me over and enfolded me in his other arm, and I told him that it reminded me of the Three Musketeers, about whom Papa Brendan had told me.

A week later, Mr. Livesey brought over for me the Dumas novel with lovely pictures in them, which he had gotten shipped over from his Boston bookseller by the fastest mail. I was sad when he died in his sleep one winter night some months before I turned fifteen. He left us all his books, and the last couple of dozen bottles of his wine and his pipe collection to Papa Brendan. Over the years, I knew how keenly Papa Brendan missed his friend and sometimes asked him to read aloud from the Dumas book.

It was Mr. Livesey who told me once that from the very first time Papa Brendan used to drop by the post office to mail his monthly accounts of the farm for Mr. Braithwaite, he would also have a personal letter to be sent at great expense. They were all written to Ireland, but in all the years he never once received a reply.

I understood that we had, over the years, kept the same vigil in our different ways.

• • •

As I GREW tall and straight, Papa Brendan would look misty-eyed at me and sigh, "Mrs. Aherne 'tis," he would murmur. "Maire Aherne to the life you are, but for the red hair."

By the time I was eighteen, I milked and cheesed with the best of them, pruned the grape arbors, cooked my soups and pies. I paid no mind to the young men who came by, awkward and gawking, especially when I made bread, and our kitchen was a celebration of the odours and aroma of life itself. For all his earlier talk of the famine, Papa Brendan grew plump with my cooking. He took care of all the farm accounts, what was spent in seed and stock, details about transport and profits from the produce and livestock, especially the piggery where our Grand Trumbull reigned and spawned numerous progeny. He had lived to a great piggy age, his lineage growing famous for our Trumbull bacon, sausage, and links. Mr. Braithwaite, in his will, had left us this portion of the farm.

• • •

I HAD ALMOST turned nineteen when Jakob Sztolberg drifted to our farm looking for work. He spoke half a dozen words of English when he first arrived, but he knew bees, honey-making, and cattle. A silent young man with flaxen hair and the most vivid blue eyes I have ever seen, he could only tell us that he came from Poland, a village called Jedwabne.

Much later, after he managed to acquire a smattering of English, he told Papa Brendan a little about himself, and we learnt that he first left home for a town called Białystok, then on to Lublin, where he worked for some traders who used to send dry goods down to Lemberg. But he had heard that the goods were all taken to the great port of Odessa, so he begged to go there. At first the merchants scoffed at his idea, but when two of them received news of illness at home and had to return to Lublin immediately, they thought to give their landsman a chance.

Odessa, its blue walls, its winding old streets, its fat stone build-ings, amazed Jakob. After work he would stroll along the beach. He loved the sea. But there were also dangers in Odessa. What that meant, he would not say. But one night, he escaped on a ship. He spoke vaguely of mobs, murderous people, and then could not explain anything more. He was happy now, back on a farm, half a world away. All this Papa Brendan understood from Jakob, bit by bit, over months. I have no idea how Papa Brendan can get everybody to talk.

Jakob was the most unobstrusive of people, quiet, whereas I was full of bustle. This trait, more than anything else, first made me notice him, a calm which I craved. He did not seek me out like the other babbling boys I had known all my life. He drew me out of myself by his silence. When I would watch him at his hives, or at any other task, like the pruning of the grape arbors, I could not help but notice the grace of his movements, his intentness, and his ease with himself. I found myself hastily looking away, pretending we had not been glancing at each other.

He had been at the farm for seven months when he made him-self a small stringed instrument, very like a mandolin, and was plucking a quiet tune one evening when I came and sat by him. He played on, smiling at me once in a while. I kept thinking of his fingers on the strings, the simple melodies he played, the woody odour of him. Then he surprised me, handing me that mandolin. I did not know how to play, so I held it, caressing its blond wood, its fine strings, as if it were he I was touching instead, and a tur-moil stirred within me. That summer night of honeysuckle and a small moon I saw him move under the horse chestnut tree, and went out to him. He took me in his arms.

"You," he said, "I need like water." We kissed and stayed up all night, watching the moon set.

I told no one of my love, did not know how to, or when. I wondered if it was because he was a wanderer, like my father. But it was clear that Papa Brendan knew it, everyone on the farm, my whole green world knew it. And soon, we were to wed.

We were Irish Catholic and Polish Jew—so no church or temple would unite us. Papa Brendan expostulated with Father Jim Bising, but to no avail. The priest sat in our kitchen, digesting my dinners and working his toothpick, but always said, "No," followed by a shake of his thick neck, much like our stud bull trying to rid himself of gnats. I knew well it was an impossible cause, but Papa Brendan said, laughing, that being Irish he could not resist it. The nearest synagogue was very far away—and I persuaded him not to waste his breath and time.

Finally Papa Brendan decided to wed us himself—under the trees—with words chosen from the Old Testament. He said that all weddings are done under the eyes of God, not priests, anyway. At the end of his reading, we made our vows, Jakob partly in Polish.

Papa Brendan spoke from memory—lines of a poem which he used to whisper to me when first I came to this farm by our Lake Champlain, on those nights when I woke weeping for my Moomagy, my grandmother Maire, or Mr. O'Flaherty. Papa Brendan would cradle me, and in the darkness say these half-understood lines which soothed me into sleep. On my wedding day, he said them again, as if he knew I had need for these words now, a benediction:

> *Therefore all seasons shall be sweet to thee,*
> *Whether the summer clothe the general earth*
> *With greenness, or the redbreast sit and sing*
> *Betwixt the tufts of snow on the bare branch*
> *Of mossy apple-tree, while the nigh thatch*

*Smokes in the sun-thaw; whether the eave-drops fall*
*Heard only in the trances of the blast*
*Or if the secret ministry of frost*
*Shall hang them up in silent icicles,*
*Quietly shining to the quiet moon.*

I wept in complete happiness now, holding Jakob's palm in one hand and clasping Papa Brendan's with my other. "I miss Mr. Livesey," I whispered, and Papa Brendan nodded.

• • •

I BECAME PREGNANT the following year. But one day, as I leant forward in my kitchen garden to pluck some basil leaves, I felt something tear in me and cried out. Jakob, who had come home from the fields for lunch, carried me inside. When he set me down, I noticed the droplets of red on my clothes. Then the pain subsided, and there was no more blood. In the middle of that night when I woke up shaken with worry, Jakob sat holding me, singing a kind of lullaby in his tongue, soothing me as he would have a fretting child. I burrowed my face in his chest, breathing him in, the smell of the outdoors, the odour of him.

But I lost our child at the end of the fifth month. I was carrying in the clean white bedsheets on a dazzling sunny day, when I felt a dull pain forming in me. The sheets on which I had sat down were wet with a spreading stain of blood that would not be stanched. I could not stop shrieking, as if that could wake me up from this nightmare. Papa Brendan heard my cries.

"I am losing my baby, Papa Brendan, help me, oh help me please!" But I knew that my poor mother's luck had followed me, and I wished, like my mother, to face death and let my child survive. But I lived, drifting from pain to pain, until I was washed up on a bank of grief. Who could understand me, I wept, I who had seen routine animal births all my life on our farm? Jakob held me, sleepless, unable to protect me.

I would lie on the rough grass, my fallow womb upon the sweet giving earth, and hug myself among the forget-me-nots and the frayed umbrellas of Queen Anne's lace, waking to the yellow surprise of the wood sorrels and the fingers of the squawroot stems. I became a part of Jakob's life in his honeybee glade, the world of tumid hives dripping honey, wandering like a bee among violet lupines, across tangles of morning glory and wild mint near the lake, or at the edges of meadows spiked by bull thistles and bergamot. Lying down at the far edge of the field, I would watch the bees skitter about and choose their flowers. But once they were heavy with honey, they would make a beeline, pencil-straight, back to the hives which teemed with life.

And though a dozen years passed, there were no more children.

● ● ●

I NEEDED TO speak of my dead. But so far had I come away from Ireland, that even when I wanted to talk to Papa Brendan about it, I could not bring myself to do so. No more could I ask Jakob of the land he left behind. One night, as I lay sleepless beside him, I heard Jakob call out in his sleep. Now and then, over the years, he would call out and mumble in his native tongue, but had subsided back into slumber. But this night, his frantic stirring, shallow breath choking, frightened me. "Tirzeh, O Tirzeh . . ." he groaned, reaching out for someone.

Next morning, I stirred his oatmeal, put an apple next to it, and said, "Tirzeh?"

He looked stricken. I was certain he was going to tell me it was his wife in Poland, then leave the oatmeal and the apple, and me, and go straight back to her. But he rose from his seat and drew near, leaning until his face was close, eye to eye. His breath stirred on my lips as it fell. "Sister," he whispered, his eyes like broken glass. "Was killed," he said, his face contorted, voice laced with pain. "In a fire . . . Pogrom in Odessa. So many dead." What was this *pogrom*? I wondered fiercely, then thought, *He is safe here.*

I held him, feeling the hammer blows of his grieving foreign heart until he had come back to this sweet world of our farm, the one I had made among the green and golden seasons, the lakes and meadows and trees, and familiar northern light.

Papa Brendan talks about the different nations. What use was this burden of nationhood, if it were no more than a bad dream trying to burgle its way in, through the sheltering leaded glass of our sleeping rooms on some unruly nights of the soul? What use was it when my father Padraig Aherne, for all his talk and dreams of nationhood, never finished his travels, and never did come back to me?

• • •

THE FIRST OF my gray hairs appeared on my temples in the fall of that year, 1884, as the world around me broke into the usual russets, reds, yellows, and brown. The leaves on the sumac that grew around the lake had turned a sharp scarlet. It was twenty-two years into my marriage.

Jakob was ill. In merely two months he had become gaunt, and his skin looked like parchment. He seemed to eye foods as if they were strange objects on his plate. I noticed the blue veins stand out more and more on his delicate hands.

In all the past autumns, he brought home honey, sometimes pieces of honeycomb. He would stand behind, and holding me, put his fingers, one by one, in my mouth, each dipped in different kinds of honey, and I would lick off the variety of ambrosia. It was as if he had worked all year just to feed me. But this year he did not do that—as if he were grown immeasurably old and had out-grown this game of nurture. Also for the past two months, I had been consumed with a dizzy nausea—which I mistook for sorrow and tears shed within.

"I am ill too," I told Jakob one morning in the kitchen. I wanted no breakfast. He reached over and held my hand. "Good," he said.

I looked at him, surprised. "Oh Jakob," I said, shaking my head, "you heard what I said?"

He nodded. "You are sick, no?"

"Yes," I said, failing to see what he was driving at.

"You missed the last two months," he said. I had thought that he did not notice, and I had thought that my meaningless cycles were winding down. "It is good. You will have baby," he said, "I know."

I stared at him, breathless for a moment. *No, no,* I shook my head. "I am too old."

"I will be dead," Jakob confided, "too soon now."

"What nonsense are you talking, Jakob," I began, when Papa Brendan knocked on our back door. But I could not get up. My legs would not stop shaking.

● ● ●

Now, AT FORTY-ONE, surrounded by the signs of my husband's mortality, I found myself nurturing a sprig planted within me that would not be denied. With my past experience, I expected to see the telltale pasty sludge of gore on my woollen night-robe that would dash my hopes; I dreaded the seismic shake in my nether belly that would reject the hold of life within me. But death was blossoming beside me, not within.

After the third month, afraid that any misstep would dislodge my baby, I lay down more and more. Jakob and I became twins on our bed, sensing that we were moving in opposite directions. He liked to put his palm on my stomach, feeling life growing there. I would hold him. When his wrist lay over my stretched hand, I could feel the ticktock of his blood, faint and lonely against my musky skin. This ebb and flow, of life coming and life leaving, made me feel like an island between contrary currents.

One morning, right after Christmas, in the beginning of my seventh month, my Jakob could not stand up anymore. Papa Brendan held vigil, sitting beside our bedside, woebegone. Two days later, Jakob died, as silently as he had lived.

We returned from the funeral on New Year's morning. Papa Brendan said he would make a marker and showed me the pattern of a star he had drawn on paper—two nesting triangles. He looked frail and brittle, but first insisted on making me a fire. Then he went straight to his shed nearby. He had said not another word. I had sworn Papa Brendan to cease speaking of death and seemed to have become a captive of my own oath.

Light streamed into my silent kitchen, filled with food from my neighbors from adjacent farms. Mrs. Gabrielsen's breads, Mrs. Eber's tray of ziti, Mrs. Henderson's covered plates lay on the counter. But I felt no need for food, and Papa Brendan did not come back for lunch. I thought he found solace in making Jakob's grave-marker in his carpentry shed with its smells of oils, lubricants, and shaved wood.

This was the table where we were sitting when Jakob told me with heartbreaking prescience about his death and my life. I sat and stared at the slate tiles of the floor which he had laid for me. I heard the distant bark of farm dogs, the lowing of cattle being herded back to the stables, the day already done, and all this time seemed just an hour, when Papa Brendan came in, carrying a newly made infant's cradle. I looked up in wonder. He said simply, "The living have more important needs."

"But Papa Brendan," I began, my heart full of misgiving.

"No, no, Maeve," he said, "no harm shall come to this child. Your child will be hale, I tell ye. You will see the child run, and I daresay you will see this child fly."

Two months later, I gave birth at dawn. After the midwife left, as I lay on the childbed, my baby in my arms, I thought of my mother. Did she have the chance, just once, to hold her infant and look into my newborn face before they put her in her coffin? The jagged thought made its way through me, and I found myself whispering, "Brigid, Maeve, Brigid," over and over under my breath. I saw my child open her eyes, blue and full upon my leaning face. "Maeve and Brigid," I said, my first words to her. "It is Brigid and Maeve again." I would protect Brigid against everything in the world. Brigid, yes, my baby named for my mother. I would take back all I could from death.

But my willful child named herself "Bibi," my restless one, forever bridling at any restraint. I wish Jakob could have seen our child, who had his flaxen hair and vivid blue eyes, running about, adored by all the dogs and piglets of the farm.

• • •

By the time Bibi was five she thought the stories of Papa Brendan magical, and through her he was reawakened into joy. He would often be found sitting on his chair, his white hair tousled, his pipe and tobacco forgotten on the small table, while around him, in a spellbound circle, sat the Ebers' granddaughter Maisie from the next farm, the Gabrielsen boys—Eric and Jared—and little Philip Chase, the pastor's son, and our Bibi, the hoyden stilled for the nonce by these stories. Bibi had turned our Papa Brendan back into the hedge-schoolmaster he used to be, by the simple magic of her childhood.

Those were our carefree years. The children grew apace, and suddenly the boys were tall with their peach fuzz, growing solicitous and awkward around Bibi. I wondered idly, enjoying the speculation which of them she would wed, which farm would become her home. She could just stay on here, and Papa Brendan and I could have a small cottage built an easy walk away.

One day, listening to the rumble of Papa Brendan's voice in the next room, weaving some story, I was drawn in towards the magic circle, a child again. I stood just outside the door, leaning under the lintel, thinking how peaceful and tranquil our lives were, when the lines of that story entered my ears like a vial of poison. I felt as if my heart was pierced, for I could sense the danger, its dreaded fin barely breaking the surface of our calm lagoon. Oh, what was I to do about unwitting Papa Brendan?

He was telling them stories of wandering and seeking, of questing and going out into the great unknown. I heard snatches of names—Magellan and Oisin, Captain Cook and the far islands. . . . How had it come to this? His stories would turn their eyes outward, to the tumultuous world out there. Little did they know about its shoals and dangers, I thought with a shiver down my spine.

I decided to break these story-tellings, misplacing Papa Brendan's glasses, asking Eric and Jared for help with chores. I worried imaginative Philip, by mentioning the dark shadows descending under the maples long before they did so. I began to draw Bibi away, making lengthy business of kitchen matters, the cleaning, and the stove. I even steered Bibi's interest towards Jakob's bee-keeping trays and hives—and tried to get Eric to help her, planning their chores, hoping that the sweet labor and youth would cleave their hearts, and they would draw together. I invited the Riegelmans' son Charles too. When all else failed, I was not loath to feign a malady, God help me.

By sixteen, Bibi had begun to rebel. She set up feuds with me, thwarting my simple insistence on small matters that she said stifled her. She would run out in the summer rain, heedless of her wet clothes clinging to her comely body, and the boys glancing. Oh, we had raging tiffs over all that nonsense. She would sulk at me for telling her not to go into the hard sun with all the boys during harvest time and set her face against me when I forbade talks about trips to Albany or Burlington, for whatever trivial foolishness was taking place there. They dreamed of a jaunt to Philadelphia to see the famous bell about which Papa Brendan had waxed eloquent, about liberty and all the great men and their doings. I did not see the point. A cracked bell was a bell with a crack. Why go all the way for that, I ask myself!

But then, a year later, he appeared, with stories of places far enough to take one's breath away. He endeared himself effortlessly, it seemed to me, to guileless Papa Brendan. I said something about this—and Papa Brendan looked at me, chiding, perturbed, in a way he has never been with me.

"Do you doubt that I know what is best for her, that I love my daughter?" I asked him with the fierceness of my maternal care. Papa Brendan looked somberly at me, and said, "If the end of loving is sorrow beyond bearing, is it not better from the first to forswear love?"

I felt he had burned my heart. I struggled to speak. "You—you say this to me?"

"Maeve dear," he said softly, "the Good Book says that. Let Bibi grow. Let her be."

I wept in hapless isolation, unheeded, the only one who really knew where my Bibi's happiness lay. What was so special about this outsider with his tales of aimless wanderings? I thought bitterly about this interloper, his handsome face burnt by the sun. I wish we had never set eyes on him. He was of the rootless tribe.

"Do I hate him?" I asked myself again and again. Yet there is something in him that I could not bring myself to hate. He reminded me of someone I loved, but never met in life.

No, no, it is far worse. I feared Frankie.

# Frankie
## Boscotrecase, Italy
### 1905

I can remember exactly when I decided to become a traveler. It was the day Padre Stefano hung up the tall maps on the three walls of our classroom. The graying blackboard with the crucifix above it occupied the fourth wall. I peered so close to the first map of the Atlantic that I could smell the glue which held the paper map to the cloth mounting. It smelt of resin and blackberries and shoe polish. For me it was the aroma of magic, and whisked my mind away from Boscotrecase with its tilted cobbled streets, the old piazza with the broken fountain, the surrounding fields and boulders, the vineyards. Oh yes, my head was in a swoon as I looked at the boot of Italy stepping into the Mediterranean, the slit of Gibraltar opening like a chink in a magic stone door, the enormous blue escape of the Atlantic.

My father, Gianni Talese, told me I had no business daydreaming. A day trip to Napoli was enough, he said emphatically, while my grandmother shook her black-shawled head and crossed herself.

Padre Stefano Antonelli's maps came all the way from America. This Jesuit priest had been born there, of Italian parents, and came to Roma as a trainee priest, then became a village priest and schoolteacher, first near Napoli, and later near the castle at Stabia on the coast before he came here. I think Padre Stefano would get homesick for America, for he began to teach English to a handful of students, including me and Pasquale, my inseparable friend, who longed to take the road beyond our village, past Sorrento, along the cliff road which led to Salerno and Messina.

Padre Stefano used to say that Pasquale Centangeli had a hundred angels in his name and two hundred naughty devils in his head. His father, Memmo, was a wiry hard man who drank, not wine, but whatever else he could get his hands on. In his pitching drunkenness, he would seek out his only son and beat him brutally. Pasquale would hide as best he could, while Memmo searched for him, beating on doors with his fist, as if he were on an urgent errand. The only one who tried to stop him was Padre Stefano. Memmo would demur, but in an hour or two would resume his stubborn search, as if beating his son into senselessness was the only anchor he had to his miserable reality.

My other friend in the schoolroom was plump, good-natured Giuseppe, already a fine carpenter, coaxing shapes out of wood even as a boy, but he found English impossible. His father insisted he join us in learning the language, for his uncles Giorgio and Armando Vesprini were already in Boston—and they planned to join them soon.

Father Stefano called me "Frankie." And I just loved it, my American name. I planned to use it for all my adventures in the world: *Frankie Talese, traveler.*

•  •  •

My OLDER BROTHER, Michele, was apprenticed to a builder in San Giuseppe Vesuviano. Phlegmatic like our father, Michele had chosen an equally stolid betrothed, Rosaria Semmilio, who lived with her family on a farm within walking distance of San Giuseppe, next to the country road to Striano. My older sister, Daniela, had got married six years ago to stoop-shouldered and balding Dario Colletti, who lived at the edge of Napoli, just off the road to Portici.

My little sister, Lucia, I loved best of all. She went about all day with a smile on her lips. Our widowed grandmother Nonna Rosa, who had doted on her, died shortly after Lucia turned ten. My increasingly asthmatic father became sad every time he looked at her, letting her do as she pleased, but Lucia absolutely refused to go outside Boscotrecase—as if the world beyond our village where everyone knew everyone else, even the dead—was as nonexistent as her voice. She had been a quiet baby and was almost a year old before anyone realized that she was stone deaf. She learnt to do most of the chores of the house.

For me, the great unknown was the world of the dead where our mother, Gabriela, had departed when I was three and Lucia was only a few months old. Sometimes I think I remember Mamma clearly, but at other times I am not really sure. Nonna Rosa told me once that I resemble my Mamma. The next day, when I was certain no one was home, I draped Mamma's shawl over my head and looked in the mirror. But I could only see myself. There were no pictures of her.

During Easter week, Christmas, and other occasional holidays, I would plead with my father to be sent to my sister Daniela. Pasquale always accompanied me. We would wander around the raucous lanes of Napoli, but it was very hard to tear ourselves away from the harbour filled with sailors from so many different lands. From them we heard of many ports: Liverpool, Aden, Caracas, Bombay. I knew what both of us were thinking: as soon as we were old enough, we would get on a ship and return years later when some distant harbour wind touched me in that one restless spot within, tugging me home.

• • •

I WAS AWAY with Pasquale at Daniela's place that winter of 1905 when our father, Gianni, died, four days after Christmas. My brother Michele arrived to take me home. Over dinner, he announced his decision, as the new head of our family, in exactly two sentences: I would be taken, not to our house in Boscotrecase, but to San Giuseppe; I was to begin an apprenticeship with his master-builder.

"But I do not want to be a builder!" I burst out.

Michele continued eating, picking out a fish bone or two. With a morsel of bread, he sopped up the last of the brodetto and, with his mouth full, said, "Tomorrow, have your things ready," as if I had remained as mute as our Lucia.

I, too, had made up my mind.

• • •

THE SHIP SAILED south from Napoli, with Pasquale and me on board. Capri sank from view as we sailed past Stromboli toward Stretto di Messina. The next evening, the lights of Reggio rose to our left and those of Messina to the right. We were kept constantly at work, helping the crew, learning about the million things to be done on board and belowdecks. A week later, we swaggered about in the port of Alexandria, where I bought a strand of garnets for Lucia and mailed it home. Next we sailed for Genoa, where on the first day of February1906 we found work on a ship that went to New Orleans, then on to Panama. We gave in to our wanderlust, deliberately choosing ships that sailed farthest away from Italy, to Recife and Rio de Janeiro, to Calcutta and Cape Town. Months slid by, and before we realized it, four years had passed.

I had grown a fine black beard; Pasquale preferred to shave, but was attempting a moustache. I treasured a photograph of the two of us on shore leave in the pretty port town of Montevideo, a stone's throw from Buenos Aires. We were leaning on a short Corinthian column, before the painted canvas backdrop of a villa. The painted sun shone above, a perfect circle with its shafts drawn in straight lines.

But the real sun was hidden for days on the voyage after as the ship headed into the grimmest of storms a little north of the Caribbean islands. The waves rose and fell eighty feet, more. I remember seeing a wall of water, black and wavering, stand over the ship's side, as if suspended. When it hit, I lost my foothold and was slammed into the metal side of the stairs to the hold. I reached out in the whirling darkness, gasping for breath. Hands—I never knew whose—pulled me into some nook of the shuddering ship. I was dizzy, choking with nausea, with a ringing in my ears when I tried to sit up. A misty rain surrounded the ship. The ocean was heaving with slow, momentous swells. So it went on for another day and night. When finally I could stagger around, I searched for Pasquale, hoarsely shouting his name again and again. The sun came up, a vivid smear on a sky of ground glass.

They told me that two men had been swept overboard. One of them was Pasquale Centangeli.

• • •

I COULD NOT bear to talk to anyone. When the ship reached New York harbour, I slipped away. I wanted hard soil underfoot.

In the city's throng, I walked without purpose or direction. I sat an entire morning on the warm marble steps of the Customs House. The park nearby was full of playing children and their families. Each blanket on the grass was a hub of activity—the fathers leaning back to enjoy the sun, smoking a cigar or pipe, some even attempting a nap, the mothers keeping an eye on the children as they frolicked, calling out in a variety of languages. As I sauntered toward the Hudson, I heard an unmistakable snort of laughter, and stood facing my old schoolmate Giuseppe, larger now, his hair receding.

"Nicolina," he whooped, turning to his wife, "it is Frankie, the pirate!" His Italian was as vividly Neapolitan as ever. "Frankie, the runaway from our Boscotrecase, come back from the dead. I almost told him how close to the truth he was, but kept silent in the face of Giuseppe's unbridled joy, as he insisted I join him, his small daughter, and Nicolina, whom I recognized from Boscotrecase.

"I'll be poor company," I said, but Giuseppe swept me along, fairly singing with joy as we walked to his home, which was not far. As I entered, I saw a picture of Mount Vesuvius on the wall. It was a familiar print, sold everywhere in Napoli, common in homes from Portici to Salerno.

"Will you be in New York long, Frankie, or off on another ship?" asked Giuseppe, handing me a glass of wine he had overfilled. *No*, I shook my head to all the queries, and lifted the glass. "To Boscotrecase," I said.

"Lucky Frankie," he continued, slurping his wine and swishing it about in his mouth. "Vesuvius erupted and took Boscotrecase and everything around it. But you and Pasquale were off seeing the world. So where is he?"

I stared at my glass of wine, but its garnet hue seemed to turn into something far darker. I sat down abruptly, spilling some of it. "Pasquale drowned," I told Giuseppe as he stood shaking his head.

"And Boscotrecase?" I asked him.

"You don't know!" he was incredulous.

The moment was a teetering droplet of rain on a sill. Then I asked him, "Lucia? Michele? Everyone?"

*Yes*, he nodded, *yes*.

I got up and left, abandoning Giuseppe, the waiting dinner, my childhood in Boscotrecase. "Stay with us," Giuseppe called after me as I stumbled downstairs. "Come back to us, Francesco, please," shouted Giuseppe from the top of the stairs. I did not know where I was headed.

I had wanted to discover the world. Frankie Talese, Traveler. I got what I wished for. Only the doors behind me had shut in ways I could not begin to comprehend.

• • •

THE TRAIN RACED upriver, its glint to the left of me, then made its way up the undulating landscape of green hills and wide valleys. When it stopped at a station, I got down on an impulse without caring to find out its name. To outdistance a burden whose phantom weight wearied me, I walked. Beyond a long meadow, I drank at a cistern which sat like an oblong cup under the sky. Dozing against a sagging fence, I watched a flock of wood doves flit from a bank of trees to sit at the edge of the same cistern to drink.

I spoke to no one for two weeks, walking without purpose or direction, resting when I wanted, an invisible visitor to this great and strange land of the living. Someday all these people would be dead and others would live, doing everyday things on these very fields and streets. Nobody noticed me, nobody spoke to me, no one needed me.

I woke under some maple trees to the first seep of dawn, and the sparrows and cardinals were stirring overhead. I lay next to a stone fence, watching for the sun. A squirrel came out twitching its tail and watching me. From a piece of bread I took from my satchel, I made a pellet, and flicked it. The creature picked it up, rolling it in its front paws for better purchase, and ate it avidly. From a crack farther down, now peeped a tiny snout from its rock hideout. The mother moved there, unafraid and in full sight of me, and nursed her baby in the growing light.

I sat there wondering what such minutiae could mean in my life, until it dawned on me that. I was being tutored about the small things on the earth, having had my eyes on the desolate vistas of water for so long.

• • •

I STRODE PAST fields of corn and wheat. It was nearing harvest season. I walked until I was footsore, and in the late afternoon I lay down and slept under a flowering tree near a farmhouse until I woke to a tickle on top of my head and then my toe. I sat up with a start, still half asleep, thinking Pasquale was teasing me, and full of longing to talk to another human being. Two piglets which had been examining me, head and toe, trotted away as fast as their plump legs could carry them. I could not help laughing out aloud, sitting on the calm green earth below the broadleaf tree.

Then I noticed a young woman, her sleeves rolled up, looking at me with curiosity. Her eyes were pale blue and her hair was unruly and flaxen.

"Where did you come from?" she said, not at all put out by my presence.

"Most recently," I said, "Buenos Aires. But I was born near Naples."

I could see that I had not made any impression at all. "You know—Buenos Aires, in South America?" I repeated.

"Sure you have!" she said, tossing her head. "If you are looking for work, you're in luck. We could use extra hands for the milking." She gestured at the barn with her head. She had picked up one of the piglets as if it were a pet.

"I'm Bibi. What's your name?"

"Frankie," I said in my best accent. *I have finally arrived in America*, I thought. "Frankie Talese."

I followed her across a meadow. The piglets pranced and circled about us as we walked down the sunlit slope. She gathered her mane of hair and, twisting it into a bun, headed toward a stone cottage. "Have you ever milked?" she asked over her shoulder.

"In our village," I confessed, "but it was our goat. Nonna made cheese."

"Nonna?"

"Grandmother," I explained.

"My Grandpa Brendan lives with us. He's old," said Bibi, adding, "Our Belinda—she is our tetchiest cow—will kick you if you try to milk her as if she were a goat. And it would serve you right too," she chortled. But before I could make a rejoinder, she had flung open the back door of the cottage and entered a large stone-flagged kitchen, cold and spartan. The only touch of color came from a few bottles of pickled beets and peppers in glass jars which caught the light at the window ledge. Above these, from the wall, depended heavy copper-lined pans. The dark bulge of a substantial stove dominated a corner. I was startled to see a woman, almost invisible in black, her hair tinged with grey, sitting still at the table near it, next to the unlit and scoured fireplace.

She was unmistakably Bibi's mother. She had been beautiful once, I thought, as I watched her sit, rigid and watchful. There was a cicatrice of severity that marked her forehead as she looked intently at her daughter, who had begun to speak excitedly. Disconcerted by the old woman's expression, I had not paid attention to Bibi's words.

"From Buenos Aires!" she concluded breathlessly.

"We need no hands," the woman said sharply, not moving her eyes from my face.

"I do not stay then, *basta!*" I retorted, stung by her manner. But Bibi was determined to ignore her mother. "Oh Frankie, you're just afraid of Belinda!" she teased, and I could not help but laugh.

"No," broke in her mother, "we need no hands, as I told you." She was standing now, her palm pressed hard against the table. I could see her work-reddened knuckles and feel the hostility in her scrubbed kitchen. I turned quickly to leave, but bumped into an old man who had just opened the door. His book fell to the floor, as did my rucksack, which lay open.

"Grandpapa Brendan," Bibi remonstrated, "we're short of milking hands, you said, but Ma won't hear of Frankie's working here." I bent to retrieve the old man's book with a murmur of apology, but as I did so, he picked up my treasured photograph from the floor: Pasquale and I under that painted studio sun. He peered intently into it, and then he looked up at me, his eyes direct and guileless as a child's.

"He's just come from South America. His name is Frankie. His folks are from Italy," said Bibi, full of news, "like Amerigo Vespucci. And they have a goat."

"Is your friend here too?" asked the old man, nodding at the photograph.

I shook my head, the loss suddenly touching me to the quick. "I lost Pasquale. On the high seas."

The old man studied my face, then reached out and touched my sleeve. "I too lost a friend," he whispered as we walked into the sunshine. Bibi followed us. The grey-haired woman stayed back in her kitchen as if she were guarding it.

"This picture," murmured the old man.

"It was taken in Montevideo," I explained, "in a studio."

"I have no picture," said Brendan, as if to himself.

"We do need more milking hands," broke in Bibi. "He can learn." I looked at Bibi in the dazzling green countryside.

"Tell us about Montevideo," said Brendan. And I did, standing under the trees. I told them over many subsequent days about all my travels, of far places. Cádiz, Recife, Calcutta, Lisbon, Cartagena.

I could make sense of all my aimless travels now, for they had brought me here to this place, to Bibi, so that I could tell her about them.

# Bibi
### Lake Champlain, Vermont
### 1909

I used to open my father's books, turning their pages. One was a fat book bound in black; another was thinner, but neither had pictures. When I was nine, years ago, I was sitting during vacation under the slow summer sun with the fat volume, my eyes on the strange script like vertical figures, imagining what it would be like to be able to read them. I had momentarily closed my eyes, when I had the strange sensation that my father held the same page, and I was sitting next to him, my hand on the very surface he had just touched.

I heard someone coming out, and turned quickly. It was Grandpa Brendan, who saw me with the book, and sat next to me. "I had asked Jakob to teach me Hebrew," he said, "but we got only as far as the alphabet. See, Bibi," he said, turning the pages to the first page, "there is a name written on it."

"That says Jakob Sztolberg, this writing?" I peered at the writing, its black coils seeping into gray on the old page.

"No, dear," he said, "it spells out Ephraim Sztolberg. Your grandfather. And this is the Hebrew Bible."

"Wait one moment, right there." I rushed off, returning with the other book. "See, I can tell the writing on this book is different."

"Yes it is, Bibi. This is a book of poems by Solomon Ibn Gabirol. And the name inscribed on the first leaf here is Jakob Sztolberg."

I kissed his name. I felt Grandpapa Brendan's palm on my hair.

"Jakob came from very far away, Bibi," he said. I nodded.

"Very far away," I repeated to myself.

• • •

EVERYBODY FELL UNDER Frankie's spell, especially Grandpapa Brendan. His tales of far places shook me loose from the earth under my feet, and I wanted to become part of all his future stories. We had begun to go fishing at the lake, just the two of us, seldom catching anything, our kisses leading us deeper and deeper into our own secret wood. And I, romping Bibi of the northern farm who had heard dread talk of the first blood, marveled at those silly tales. After our lovemaking we would speak of the world we might travel, Travancore or Trinidad, Valparaiso or Bombay. Lying by our placid lakewater, I felt transported beyond the far seas.

"Why don't we," he said, "first go to see Jedwabne, Lemberg, and Odessa from where your father sailed?" I held him close. No one else could have thought this.

"Will you take me to Burlington first?"

Frankie laughed. "I shall do better. Let me make arrangements to visit New York."

My mother watched me balefully when I returned, lips bruised with kisses, my aching body sated. I knew that battle lines were being drawn. Before she could open fire, I took the wind out of her sails by announcing that I was going to New York City for a visit. She was so furious that, at a loss for words, she sat rigid at the kitchen table, clutching her hands together. I wanted no dinner that night.

• • •

THE TRAIN WAS a swift planet, clacking and whooshing through the black night, rocking me. I dozed for a while and sat up in that somber hour when light cracks the day open, and the light turns pale as the underwing of a predatory owl, and through the window I saw the sky, still and hard as a forgotten bowl of milk left outside on a frozen morning. It was already the time when the dairy milk would be collected, and the farm astir within the barns. I laid my head on Frankie's sleeping shoulder, burrowing my face into the curve of his neck, breathing him in, and fell momentarily asleep, a bird with its head in its feathers, on a branch that moved with the urge of the wind.

• • •

WHEN I WOKE in the tumult and came out clutching Frankie's hand, dry-mouthed and wide-eyed, the ebbing crowd washed us through the channels of the platform into a vast hall. Above the marble floor on which the people surged, the roof was a sky of lights, and a huge clock ruled. Echoes moved round and round as in a vast milk churn.

I sensed the pulsing city all about me as we emerged on the street. I glanced back at the looming marble statues above the gateway. The gas streetlamps were still lit though it was light. *New York, New York,* I whispered, watching the welter of people and horse-drawn cabs. Careful of the steamy dung on the streets, we walked east, to the river. Prows of moored ships leant over the riverside road that ran along the length of this island. We could see sailors on deck, hear their occasional shouts, the creak and clatter of numerous ropes and tools. A few gulls flapped overhead, and the sun bounced off the water from the east across the sparkling loop of a great bridge in the distance as wagons inclined over its arched surface to another island.

I struggled to keep my balance as I walked with my head tilted up, staring at the great heights of the buildings, their ornamented cornices and water towers that stood like huts on stilts. Cars coughed by, bumbling one after another, like gaggles of geese past newspaper vendors, chestnut sellers, peddlers with cigarettes and candy. We walked on until the streets got narrower, the houses huddled together. Men sat on the stoops and boys played stickball or ran up and down the block. Frankie led me by the hand to a corner of a leafy park at whose center stood a white arch. Paved paths merged upon it, and people were walking about, and children ran here and there. We sat down on one of the many benches, footsore but happy, gazing all around at the imposing buildings.

In a corner a vendor stooped over a shallow metal pan, roasting sweet potatoes, a blue wisp of smoke rising from a charcoal fire under it. I realized how hungry I was. The man's face was brown and papery, like the skin of the sweet potatoes he sold. As if aroused from sleep, he swiftly withdrew two potatoes with one deft hand, and with a knife in the other, he sliced open the potatoes and insinuated a smear of butter, swaddling the smoking lumps in torn newsprint before handing them to us with the air of a man who had nothing to do with them. They were delicious.

"Where are we going? Do you know?"

Nodding his head, Frankie walked me through more crowded streets and soon arrived in a short block, lined with shops and houses, busy as anthills with people going up and down. While Frankie dashed into a store momentarily, I waited on the sidewalk. Peddlers went by calling out their wares while carts and wagons trundled past, and kids roistered in noisy groups.

Frankie led me up a stairwell, and I wondered where we were headed. Nobody paid us any attention. I could smell the cooking on each floor. Finally Frankie stopped and fished out a key which shone like a talisman.

"Who lives here, Frankie?" I whispered. No one was inside. In a corner stood a fine wooden wardrobe full of clothes and some women's dresses. Beyond, it opened into another dim room without any windows but with a bed covered with a flowered sheet, everything clean, though worn with much use. On a coverlet, I found a child's toy, a carved wooden horse. A framed print of some smoking mountain hung on one of the walls, on another a picture of Jesus holding his own golden heart which sent out a beam. One other room lay beyond it: the kitchen. At its center sat an enamel bathtub, glowing like a receptacle made for the finest cream. Above it glinted a tin ceiling, spangled with its private map of rust.

"My friend Giuseppe is away to Boston to visit his wife Nicolina's folks. They had planned it for weeks. That's when I got the idea to show you the city. When we leave, we'll return the key to Mr. Lepore at his photographic studio," said Frankie. I lay down, exhausted after the heady sights. The only light came from the smudged front window, in front of which I saw a rusty platform, a metal ladder extending above and below.

"What's that?" I asked sleepily.

"That?" said Frankie, holding me. "That is a fire escape."

• • •

"WAKE UP, WAKE up, Bibi!" Frankie was shaking me.

"What is it?" I asked, startled. "Is there a fire?"

"No, *cara*." Frankie hurried about. "I almost forgot about the ships."

"But we've seen the ships," I reminded him.

"No, no, we must hurry, Bibi." He was pulling on his shoes. "This is special. That's why we chose this week."

"I thought it was because Giuseppe and his family would be away."

"Oh come on," he said, tugging at my hand playfully.

In the sunny afternoon all the world had gathered on the narrow park at the bottom of the island which they called the Battery. Countless peddlers were selling colored balloons, crushed ice with gem-like syrups, steamed corn, and roasted peanuts. We passed a building with wide stairs, and marble statues in front. "The New York Customs House," Frankie explained. We held hands, making our way through the merry crowd to the edge of the water. Then I saw the lady I knew well from her pictures, smaller, across this shining stretch of water, than I had expected. The afternoon sun etched her bronze against the sky as she stood with her torch on her island. I knew I would talk of this moment to my children in the years to come.

Frankie bought me something I'd never seen before: ice cream in a cone of crunchy wafer—which I ate with gusto, while he drank a bottle of sarsaparilla soda. And now the great ships sailed into view, covered with the most splendid flags, fluttering in the warm breeze. Frankie showed me the one from Italy, its tri-color flag flapping in the wind, and shouted loudly in Italian while everyone cheered, our voices part of a great chorus, with people everywhere—at all the windows of the buildings, on the trees, even on the statues in the park, and all along the Hudson riverfront. What a city was this New York! Great hurrahs went up as each stately ship passed. Oh, Grandpapa Brendan would have known all the flags, and for the first time I wondered what kind of ship Mama had sailed on.

On the ships, brass bands blared, drums booming. Some ships—those from England, France, and Germany—set off their cannons to salute the crowds. The first ones startled everyone into a hush, but soon we got used to all of it: the music, the booming cannons, the clatter of drums, the waving flags as more ships hove royally into view.

Like a small black cloud my thought troubled me: Why was it that every ship from all the nations mounted their cannons, and none without armory? What if these boats turned their guns on each other rather than play their gay music? I whispered this to Frankie, who at first seemed startled by the thought. Then he broke into a laugh.

"This is 1909, the first decade of the twentieth century, Bibi," he chortled, "and we are done with all wars, forever. We will have better ships, better cars, better flying balloons, and better everything." He was without a worry in the world. Indeed, the world was floating with joy at this September festival to honor Henry Hudson, after whom the river was named.

As evening fell, the fireworks started. Searchlights moved across the night sky like luminous fingers. A band struck up, and all around, people rolled up their picnic blankets and danced. Behind us, the city appeared jeweled with lights. All the windows, nooks, high gables and corniches of the noble buildings twinkled. We danced—Frankie and Bibi—with all the rest of the merry world.

Past midnight, we walked back arm in arm. Frankie had bought walnuts, and fed me, piece after piece, touching my tongue with his fingers.

I was melting with happiness when we reached home, hand in hand.

Frankie put little candles in the walnut shells, and they floated all about me as we lay in the tub. It was our bay, and the candles a private grove of lights. I felt him enter me as easily as a boat slips into a cove and clung to him, united, entwined, heartbeat to heartbeat, through the magical night, not knowing which part of our bodies belonged to whom.

Throughout the next ten days, I walked with Frankie all over the city, watching the astounding parade of city life. One evening, before we returned to our loaned apartment, Frankie ushered me into the small shop where he had picked up the key and told the man to make a photograph portrait of the two of us. Frankie examined the different backgrounds the man had, rolled up like curtains. Finally he made his choice, a painted scene with Roman ruins, colonnades, and distant hills.

On the last day it rained, and the lights of the streetlamps looked slick, reflected off the black streets as we went over to pick up the finished portrait. I studied it for a long time before Mr. Lepore packed it for us. I thought we looked formal and grown-up, Frankie's arm draped over mine. Behind the cardboard of the photograph was engraved,

*Torquato Lepore, Photographer*

and below that, in smaller letters, the date: October 8, 1909. I had expected our names there. How would anyone know who we were, a hundred years from now; who would look at this picture and know what this time in our lives meant?

"Where are we going from here, Frankie?" I asked.

"Home?"

I shook my head. "I don't want to go back to the farm. Can we stay in the city?"

"If you married me right away!" chortled Frankie. Then, in a serious tone, he said, "I like the farm, but if you want, we can live in the city."

"I want to live here," I said decisively. "We can set up home here. Like Giuseppe."

"Marry me, Bibi," urged Frankie. "We could get married at the farm."

"No, Frankie," I said, digging my heels in, "let's set up home here. I too can get some kind of job. Maybe in a store?"

"Your mother, your Grandpa Brendan, they will worry, Bibi." Frankie sounded hesitant. "Giuseppe is coming back with his family. Where will we both stay—I have no money left—" He broke off, seeing the keenness of my disappointment. "Okay," he said, making up his mind, "you go back, tell them at the farm, and I will stay back and find a job."

"I just wish I could stay and help," I suggested.

"We want everyone to be happy, Bibi."

"Do we?" I retorted, then added reluctantly, "All right, I'll go back to the farm, as you say, and tell them."

"So when do we get married?" insisted Frankie.

"Only after we have a kitchen to put our own bathtub in," I said, smiling.

We emerged from the doorway of the shop. The covered wagons trundled on the glisten of tar, like hearses in the night, as the sturdy horses drew them up and down the endless avenues.

● ● ●

BUT FROM THE very first day back on the farm, my mother and I were at war. Her weapon was her love for me, for the farm. Mine was for Frankie and the world out there. I had not known that love could be so corrosive.

As the weeks passed, my serene joy turned to bafflement. There was no news at all from Frankie, as if he had never existed. But he had touched me to the quick, leaving me swelling, navel distended, breasts changing, belly nurturing our child. I did not feel sick at all, but healthy and rosy with good health. Yet I could never keep my tears at bay after the sun set, another day in this universe without Frankie. My ma took care of me wordlessly, yet she irked me, even while I depended on her. I grew heavy and slow, until on a glorious late-May morning, I gave birth to a boy. It was an easy birth.

She cleaned the baby and gave him to me for suckle. He did so noisily, manfully, I thought, and remembered my Frankie at the same breast a lifetime ago in that candlelit room. I peered into my child's face, ruddy with its exertions of birth, and felt that my heart would melt away. *Our boy*, I whispered as if to Frankie, and held my baby. I kissed his small face and noticed that he had a birthmark on his left cheek, like a red pea, which I had earlier taken for a drop of birthblood. I counted his toes, nuzzling his curled pale feet. His tiny fists were tight shut, like rhododendron buds. Then I saw another birthmark, like a tiny red map, on the back of his right hand. I thought I had never seen anything so beautiful. *You are mine forever*, I whispered to him again.

I gazed at my baby, the damp tendrils of his hair, his suckling mouth. I inhaled his baby smell, his small sweet breath the odour of my own first clear milk. I felt faint with love for Frankie and our child. I looked at the birthmark again. It was as if one of my father's bees had left a drop of tawny honey on my son's face.

Everyone who sees him would notice that sweet spot on his bonny face; it was no blemish at all.

"I'll call him Frankie," I said to my mother, speaking to her for the first time in months.

"You will do no such thing," Maeve said, daring me to contradict her. "We shall call him Padraig," she said, her eyes suddenly full of tears. "He is ours. He is home."

"Padraig," I said tentatively, and we held each other, mother and daughter, yet knowing that nothing was the same as before.

● ● ●

I HAD MADE up my mind. For nine months I had borne my child in my womb. I would stay for nine more months, amid my mother's disapproval of my hope, awaiting news of Frankie. I could not bring myself to think of him as a smooth-tongued trickster. By gesture or look, by glance or touch, that poisonous knowledge would have made itself known to me; I was sure my mother was wrong.

*Her father, Padraig, had fallen off the face of the earth, but my Frankie will be found,* I thought, and I waited. By the eighth month, I had managed to wean my boy. But I was also weaning myself from my old life on the farm. I squirreled away money, doing sewing and making quilts, preparing for the great flying leap that would take me to Frankie. Grudgingly I knew that I could not have done this without Mama, who loved my son with all her broken heart! He would lie ever contented and safe in her arms. I could not fend off the knowledge that once I had too. I thought of this a hundred times and sensed her thinking the same, but whatever ice stood in our way would not thaw. Unlike her, I trusted Frankie.

On a chilly Friday in early February, I set off with a small bag.

It held a few of my clothes. I had sewn my money into its seam. I wrote a note and kissed my boy, and took a train, sleeping and dozing, as it trundled its way over bridges, and finally down the great stretch along the Hudson. It was dark when the train pulled into New York.

A quiver of panic passed through me as I stood under the huge domed hall with the clock. For a wistful instant I hoped Frankie would magically appear and take my bags from me, as if this had all been planned, but I walked down the entire smooth length alone.

The shadows between the looming buildings seemed deeper now, the roads narrow and bleak. Filthy snow lay piled underfoot. The few people around were muffled against the cold, hurrying home, as if the streets needed to be emptied before some unspeakable darkness would tide into the city, drowning those left in its empty canals.

Before I knew it, I was lost. I had been certain I remembered my way to Giuseppe's home. Surely they would take me in for the night. Or Frankie himself might open the door with a whoop of delight! But I found myself in an unfamiliar night, all the doors of the buildings around me shut.

Just then I noticed a woman ahead of me, head bent against the wintry river wind, quick steps echoing on the pavement. In the alleyway that branched off, a man lurked in the shadow. All of a sudden, the woman moved rapidly toward one of the buildings and tried the shut door. I caught sight of her face, pale and frantic, as she broke into an awkward run. The figure emerged and loped after her. He pitched her into the half shadow of a doorway. I heard the double thud of his fist hitting her, and her head against the immense door of the office building.

The woman fell to the pavement, bent double, for the man had kicked her midriff. Now he aimed a blow at her head, fist drawn back from his shoulder. I ran and hurled myself at him. There were few on the farm who did not know my strength. I toppled with him in my grip, pinning him down. With a great wrench, he got me off him, but I grabbed at him and his cap fell off, revealing the rusty hair on the fringe of his hard bald skull. The man struck my hands aside and punched me on the cheek with such force that I fell back in a swoon. What happened in the next moment or two, I am not sure, but as I sat up, I heard the lady next to me raising a shrill alarm. As I staggered up, preparing to throw myself at him again, he ran away and quickly turned the corner.

In his hand, he had my small bag with all my money.

• • •

THE WOMAN'S NOSE was bleeding, her hair disheveled, and one of her shoes, its heel broken, lay a few feet away. Clutching my torn dress, I felt lightheaded with pain, my left knuckle and cheek bleeding.

"I bit him," said the woman with satisfaction, "My name is Grunwald, Josephine."

"He stole my bag," I said, close to tears.

"Sometimes this happens, neh?" she said dismissively, "This is New York."

"Sometimes?" I mumbled as the dullness of pain settled into one part of my head.

"Okay, maybe once in a long while," conceded Josephine, "but it's no coincidence."

"He robbed me," I said stubbornly, unable to understand what sense the woman was trying to make of this assault and robbery.

"I recognized him," said Josephine Grunwald. "Malouf. A hired thug."

"Hired?" Now I was confused. They hired thugs in this town to rob farm girls? Who were these people!

"They are paid to beat up union organizers. I'll bet that Mr. Blanck hired Ijjybijjy Malouf."

I could not shake him from my mind, that balding coppery head, his too-large tongue lolling in a sloppy mouthful of saliva, his predatory slink. "What a strange name. Ijjybijjy?"

"My friend Clara Lemlich at the Leisersohn's strike pointed him out to me. Was a boxer once. Mouth full of broken teeth. They call him Ijjybijjy, for that's how he sounds."

"You know all this—so why don't you go to the cops?"

Josephine laughed heartily as if I had told her a great joke. "And who else would I complain to? The President, God, Tammany Hall, Mr. Hearst?" Then she saw me holding my aching head. "You know where you are going, yes?"

"No," I said briefly. There was not much to say. "I am lost."

"You have the address, neh?"

I tried to explain about Giuseppe's place and made a complete muddle. "I am looking for my . . . my . . . husband."

"My . . . my . . . husband," Josephine repeated after me. "Do you have children?"

Yes, I nodded. "My mother is caring for my Padraig," I added. "I will find Frankie. I will recognize his friend's place when I . . . find the park, the one with the white arch."

"Washington Square Park," said Josephine. "And how long since you saw him?"

I stood in silence.

"More than a year?"

I did not answer.

"You better come home with me."

I nodded. My head hurt. Josephine reached out and held my hand.

"What is your name?" asked Josephine.

• • •

A LARGE MARMALADE cat rubbed against a tall pile of books until it fell over. Then it sat on a tome, slowly moving the tip of its tail, regular as a metronome.

"He is Gideon. He likes to knock down things," Josephine chuckled. Two elderly men sat on chairs at each end of the table: one plump, with a green eyeshade, smoking a short pipe; the other, with a carefully tended greying moustache, holding a book only a few inches from his face. He rested his cheek on a frail bony fist, utterly unsurprised that Josephine's face was flushed, her hair in disarray, and I a complete stranger in a torn dress with a bruised cheek.

"Shalom," said the man with the pipe. "I'm Julius, Josephine's father, and this is my brother Arthur." I half nodded, half bowed, unsure how to respond. My head hurt with every move.

Books, pamphlets, and newspapers had taken over the entire household. They covered the cramped dining table, chairs, the floor, the windowsills, every surface available. They were mostly in English, but some in another alphabet which I instantly recognized from my childhood.

"These are in Hebrew!" I exclaimed.

"You read Hebrew?" asked Julius, his eyes twinkling with pleasure.

"I," I began, unaccountably drawn by the man's warmth,

"I . . . recognize the script. It's Hebrew, isn't it? My father left some books."

"Left?" said Arthur, as Julius leaned forward.

"He died before I was born," I said. "His name was Jakob Sztolberg."

"I'm sorry," he said, and reached out, gently touching my hurting wrist. His frail hand, his long tapered fingers, and the pale skin with its parchment-like wrinkles filled me with tenderness.

"He was from Poland," I said. "He went to work in Odessa." I felt like telling them all I knew about him, what he was like, everything Papa Brendan had told me. There was not even a photograph of him. He had been slender, with pale hair, blue eyes. His village was called Jedwabne. He had a small sister, Tirzeh. She had died in something called a pogrom.

My father had only been a story in my life, never entering the blood of my existence. In this home, I suddenly felt I would not be surprised if my father were to walk in here, any moment, as if from within a story. I sensed here the deep sediment of tradition on which I stood now, like a tree seeking roots to hold it in place. The old man patted my hand. "Welcome home, *kind*," he whispered. "We are all the things we have lost."

"*Kind*?" I asked, after a while.

"*Kind*: child," said the elder with the short pipe. "You'll pick up Yiddish as you stay with us."

"I have a *kind*, a boy," I said, feeling my tears rising.

"*Gut, gut,*" said both men, genially.

Josephine came up to me solicitously. She had rolled up her sleeve, and I could plainly see the welt on her arm and her cheek. I knew my own face also looked a sight. "Come through here," Josephine said, leading me through the long, narrow apartment.

"Wash first, before applying the tincture of iodine. It will sting, so use the salve, like last time," Julius called out after his daughter.

"Yes, Papa," Josephine sang out as she prepared to bathe my face from a bowl of cool water. I marveled that the old men were not in an uproar. I tried to imagine my mother, Maeve, and what a furor there would have been had I walked in bruised, leading a battered stranger home to our farm.

When we returned, the heap of papers and books had been moved to the corner, and four plates lay on the table. A deep tureen of soup sat amid various bowls, filled with beets, peas, and sour cream, and a large blue-and-white china platter with a side of roast beef on it. Next to it sat a large round loaf of bread, rather like a puffy dome without much of a building under it. I looked at it, bemused, and Josephine, catching my eye, whispered, "Babka," under her breath. I loved the sound of it. I was ravenously hungry.

• • •

THE NEXT DAY when I woke with a fever, and Josephine's father insisted I rest. Josephine went off to work, as did her uncle, Arthur, who worked in a hotel, keeping accounts. He left wearing a brown suit, carefully adjusting his homburg before the small hallway mirror, while smoking a cigarette. Old Mr. Julius Grunwald stayed home with me, shuffling about, arranging papers, then settling down to read for four straight hours, chuckling or snorting occasionally, while I slept.

The day after that was a holiday, and I had revived. My face looked better, and Josephine and I stepped out to find Frankie. I had a lurking fear of Ijjybijjy Malouf, but Josephine strode with such a brisk air that her vigor dispelled my dread. The sun shone overhead, and I felt full of hope.

We crossed Washington Square Park and turned at street corners I now recognized by day. When she smelt fresh baked bread, Josephine called out, "Wait here a moment, Bibi. I'll get a loaf of rye bread. And some markowitz for Uncle Arthur. He loves poppyseed." She ducked into Fischell's Bakery, while I stood on the sidewalk, looking about impatiently. Up and down the narrow street were signs of many shapes and sizes, even some at street level, for many shops were in the basement: Kriegel's Shoe Repairs, Bialystok Bread Shop, Rosen's Patent Medicines, Heidt's Watch Repairs, Levin & Schlossberg's Kosher Meats.

Wondering what was taking Josephine so long, I turned toward the basement-level bakery, and ran smack into a young man. The oranges he was carrying fell and began rolling away on the sidewalk. Chagrined, I picked up as many as I could to hand them over, with an apology, but I stood rooted when I looked closer at the slender young man, his unruly pale hair under his yarmulke, fringes of his prayer shawl trailing on the sidewalk as he trapped his runaway oranges. He stood up, a shy smile indicating his thanks. A ringlet of hair tendriled down the side of his face. But what riveted me were his eyes, pellucid blue, dark around the pupils. I felt an inexplicable tug within my heart. Holding his clutch of oranges as best he could, he continued down the street. I stared after him as he turned the corner, leaving my life. "I have met Jakob Sztolberg. I have met my dead father," I whispered, "and he has come, young again, from Poland." My eyes filled with tears, and I did not notice when Josephine had returned.

"Where did you get that beautiful orange," asked Josephine, "in this season?" She looked about for the peddler, seeing none. I clutched the orange, unable to reply, my heart choking with love in the midst of that busy street.

A roil of activity surrounded us. A vendor was selling hot

wieners; another, fresh fish from a wagon. Soon we stood in front of the building where Giuseppe lived. Across the street I saw the familiar sign painted on a shingle: Torquato Lepore, Photographer

We went up the flights of stairs to the apartment and knocked on the door.

• • •

To my astonishment, Giuseppe indicated that he had been expecting me.

He stood at the door he had opened, his vast bulk completely blocking it, smiling and motioning us to enter. It took a moment for him to realize that he needed to stand aside. He had the shy man's problem of not quite knowing what to do with his hands, clasping them and then letting them hang limply by his side, then gathering them together again. He looked back and forth, between Josephine and me.

With great diffidence, he chose Josephine and ventured, "Miss Bibi . . . ?" It was clear that English was not his forte. I pointed at myself, and he smiled and nodded with relief. My heart was singing.

"Is Frankie going to be here soon? Where is he? Does he know I am here? Why has he not been in touch?" The questions tumbled out of me, unruly, jostling each other, and finally the one which had troubled me most: *Was he already married?*

Giuseppe looked at me helplessly. He made as if to speak, then stopped and rubbed his forehead, straightened up, and then slumped again. "Miss Bibi," he started, and then his voice petered out. I did not know what to make of this, but Josephine took over. She reached out her hand and touched Giuseppe's clenched palms.

"*Giuseppe, mi chiamo Josephine,*" she said, a little hesitant about the unfamiliar language. "*Dov'è Frankie?*" It was as if a cloud lifted from Giuseppe's face. He smiled hugely and broke into a rapid torrent of Italian.

"*Piano . . . rallentate, prego, Giuseppe,*" soothed Josephine, slowing him down. "*Può ripetere, per favore?*" I was impressed that my new friend understood Italian, but she caught my look of surprise and casually explained, "Union work is mostly with immigrants—at least half of them Italians." Then she turned to Giuseppe and asked him in Italian if he knew Nino Tancredi, whose pamphlets I had seen at her home.

"Everybody, they know Nino," laughed Giuseppe, now very much at ease, and continued to tell the news. Once in a while, she would stop him, and ask, "*Che?*" or "*Quale?*" Giuseppe would explain, sometimes pointing animatedly.

I could tell that many of the things he related were sad, even grim. He faltered at one point, overcome by emotion. He had a lot to tell. Then he got up and went to a bureau against the wall, bringing back an envelope on which were pasted several colorful stamps. He took out the pages and read something from one of them. Josephine listened intently, her head slightly cocked as if to indicate full attention.

When he stopped speaking, she asked him a number of other questions, which he answered, some in detail, a few in monosyllables. Then she asked him a final question, which he answered, pointing at me, saying what sounded like "*sua mama,*" and "*lettera.*" Josephine's brow was knitted, while Giuseppe kept pointing emphatically at his letter.

*"Addio, Signore Giuseppe. Mille grazie."* Josephine said, getting up. I stood up too, and looked first at Giuseppe, who beamed at me, and then at Josephine.

"I will tell you in detail on our way," Josephine said. "It's not all bad news."

I climbed down the familiar stairs with Josephine, oblivious of the children who dodged up and down, between us. We walked past the men sitting on the stoop, soaking the late sun as it slanted between the buildings.

We entered a small shop around the corner that sold blintzes, pierogies, bread, and black tea. Its damp air smelt strongly of food. A woman in a soiled apron brought hot tea and placed a plate of sugar cubes before us. Josephine put one between her teeth and sipped her tea, a frown on her face, focusing her thoughts.

"You said it was not all bad news," I whispered, unable to keep still.

"Yes," Josephine said, as if I had suddenly switched on a light in a room where she had been sitting alone. "Yes, in a way, it is not completely bad news.

"In the April of 1906, the weather was beautiful," she began, "and people were out, as usual, working in the vineyards around Boscotrecase, which produced white grapes for the wine, a local specialty. Wildflowers and broom bloomed in vivid patches by the side of the mountain, which began to shudder, and a devastating eruption began. The top of the mountain crumpled, and swift river of lava poured in a torrent down the slope as if emptied from a vast ladle toward the village of Boscotrecase."

Grandpapa Brendan had given me a childhood full of stories when my head filled with images rising beyond the words themselves. "Vesuvius!" I blurted, remembering the picture on Giuseppe's wall.

Apparently it had been so unexpected, so eerily swift, that as the sharp smell of sulphur and the drizzle of ash descended on the startled village, it was virtually surrounded by streams of lava, widening, joining up, squeezing shut. Dead tree stumps and live trees erupted into flame as the incandescent streams reached them. Few people got a chance to escape. Those who did were out in the fields, for one reason or another, and had a chance to run for their lives.

"Everyone in Frankie's family perished," I told her. "I know. Frankie told me."

"No, there is more," Josephine interrupted me. "Giuseppe said that Frankie's brother, Michele, was with this man Italo Spinelli, a vineyard owner, and he was taking Michele Talese on his horse-drawn cart to Terzigo when they heard the mountain explode. They saw the smoke, the flying boulders, and felt the earth shaking violently. The horse panicked, upsetting the cart and ripping the traces, and bolted. Both men were thrown clear, but unhurt. They saw an enormous fist of cloud opening out over Boscotrecase, its fingers erasing the light, turning into a black wave. Almost blinded by a fine mist of ash, they glimpsed Michele's little sister, Lucia, running beyond the olive trees, outside the village for the first time in her life, her feet bleeding, her mouth foaming like a colt's. She was shrieking. They had never heard her voice before. The earth underfoot seemed to undulate like a shaken blanket. The broken carriage jerked back and forth, as if startled into life."

Michele swept up his sister as if she were an infant, with Spinelli hobbling after them, as they ran from Boscotrecase in the direction of San Giuseppe. He shouted to Italo that his sister Daniela was visiting Boscotrecase with her family, but they both realized there was now no way to reach them. They could see the mountain slope on fire, the lowering clouds of ash, the orange explosions and the volleys of boulders, and off in the far distance the smoke and rubble of what had been the villages of Striano and Boscotrecase. A few trees with smoking leaves lay uprooted by the tumult, like women with their hair on fire.

Michele ran with his sister in his arms, terrified by the thrumming of the earth, until they reached the village of San Giuseppe, with Italo gasping and lagging after them. Michele managed to drag his sister into the courtyard of his master, the builder Giacomo Miale, while Italo collapsed there, wheezing.

A steady patter of small, porous lava stones and soft ash winnowed down from the sky which now had the look of a collapsed cloud. A sulphurous stench hung in the air.

Michele, seeking shelter, spied the church at the end of the small piazza, beckoned to Lucia to follow him, but she refused to move, crouching, her eyes dilated in fright. *I'll come back soon,* he gestured to his sister and Italo before limping across the small piazza. As Michele pushed open the heavy wooden door of the church, Italo sat near Lucia, catching his breath. From where he stood, he could see that the vaulted darkness of the church was full of little flames, for it was packed with villagers who were on their knees, holding candles.

As Italo continued to peer at the church, he was startled to see that a filament web of embers flew off the neighboring roofs and coalesced, a fiery Milky Way. As the wind rose and fell, the net of fire descended—as if cast by an invisible celestial fisherman— over the roof of the church. It was followed by a terrible patter of hard, smoking stones. With a wrenching sound, the roof began to buckle. People stampeded into the piazza, trampling over the fallen. But once outside, many were struck down by the new onslaught of stones from the sky. Flying ash continued to swirl above the traces of the church, collapsed under the hail of death.

Italo Spinelli fully regained consciousness a couple of days later. He had been taken by cart, he did not know by whom, to Napoli. He returned to a devastated Boscotrecase a month later. He heard that Michele was dead, as were Daniela and her family. So, he had been certain, was Lucia.

A widower who had lost his home, vineyard, everything, Italo finally decided to come to Boston, with the small number of surviving Boscotrecase neighbors who were migrating here.

• • •

THERE HAD BEEN a surprise for Giuseppe at Boston, recounted Josephine. Nicolina's grandfather Enzo had stubbornly stayed on after the loss of his house in Boscotrecase. He had escaped because he had gone to Napoli to see a notary, and watched the disaster from across the bay, awestruck. His wife's brothers told Giuseppe that their grandfather Enzo had been persuaded to come to America from Napoli. Italo Spinelli had sailed with him.

They were greeted by Enzo's extended family at the port in Boston, and headed for a family celebration. Armando and Giorgio sat on either side of the old man at the head of the long table. The youngest men, made their greetings, but hovered around their cousin Mariaelena Vesprini, a dark-haired beauty.

The usual topics were discussed around the dinner table by the elders: The mozzarella and the pasta in America—and definitely the available olive oil—were nowhere like what you could get anywhere in Campania, even farther inland, at Basilicata; the savour of local prosciutto . . . ahh, the less said the better; and the wine . . . Did they all remember the old country's Lachryma Christi? They shook their heads in sorrow and remembrance.

Only after these immigrant rituals, familiar and much respected, did everyone exchange recent news. Giuseppe told everyone how he had found Frankie Talese in New York. At the end of the feast, when their favorite people were being toasted, Giuseppe raised his glass for Padre Stefano Antonelli, who, he had by now heard from Enzo, had died in Napoli a few months after the disaster. Something stirred in old Enzo's memory, and he sat up excitedly.

"Your friend Francesco!" Enzo exclaimed. He reached over and grasped Giuseppe's sleeve, spilling his wine. "The padre found his sister, the mute one." But try as he might, old Enzo could not remember where she was now.

"Lucia!" exclaimed Giuseppe.

It was then that Italo Spinelli spoke up and recounted in detail his tale of Michele and his fate. Giuseppe wept openly, and the table had fallen completely silent. The tragic reality of Italy sat occupying the small, overcrowded apartment in Boston, as if the present did not exist, except in relation to what had happened in the old country.

"Francesco must go as soon as possible," Enzo whispered urgently to Giuseppe, who sat wide-eyed about what he would have to tell Frankie the moment he returned to New York. "Frankie will find his sister. He will find Lucia," he told everyone.

• • •

"Lucia is alive," I said, feeling my breath constrict, "but where is she?" She was part of my family now, an aunt for my son.

"The news comes eventually, sometimes randomly, neh?" Josephine patted my arm. "She will be okay, Bibi. You will see," Josephine said gently, "Frankie will find her and return to you and his baby. It will only take time."

"The hardest thing is to wait," I said, thinking of my mother. "But did Giuseppe tell you why he hasn't written?"

• • •

WHEN HE HEARD the news, Frankie had clung to Giuseppe, as if he were back on the storm-tossed Caribbean. He had not given much thought to Italy on his voyages, with the young man's certainty that everything would remain exactly as he had left it.

"Frankie got a job on a ship to Genoa," continued Josephine, "but there was a catch: the ship was sailing the very next day. With luck, he would be able to work his way back from Napoli, and afford passage on the same ship for Lucia." She looked directly at me now. "According to Giuseppe, the hardest thing for Frankie was not being able to tell you in person."

"He said that?" I asked, smiling now for the first time.

"Frankie wanted to explain things to Maeve and you, Giuseppe told me," Josephine said. "But there was too little time." She held her finger up and added, "It was a Sunday, so Giuseppe could be with Frankie the entire day. On that one day Frankie he had before sailing off, he wrote this letter to your mother, Mrs. Maeve Sztolberg," Josephine said, "that's what Giuseppe told me."

"What!" I did not understand at all. Frankie knew how Mama resented him. "No, Josephine," I asserted, certain that she had misunderstood, "he must be mistaken."

"But that is precisely what he did, Bibi, believe me," Josephine insisted. "Maybe I understand immigrants better, neh?" she added. "He had done this to show respect to your mother: The first hopeful step to honor her in his new family."

"And he didn't write to me!" I was not sure I was hearing right.

"No, Bibi, listen," said Josephine, with quiet emphasis, "he *did* write to you, asking Giuseppe and Nicolina for advice as a married couple, telling them exactly what he had put in his letter."

Giuseppe had said that Frankie's letter to me was short, because he felt sure that I would understand, without preamble or argument. I was his soul, his *alma*, he had written, and if life on the farm was what I wanted, he would stay there; he wrote that Lucia would love that too. "This is going to be my final voyage, I swear," Giuseppe said Frankie had written. Then he put both letters in a single envelope, inscribing both the names, *Mrs. Maeve Sztolberg and Miss Bibi Sztolberg*, above the address of the farm. Giuseppe had mailed it for him the very next day.

I was thunderstruck by what my mother had done.

• • •

OUR TEA HAD long been finished.

"How much time does it take to go to Italy, find someone, and bring her back?" I asked Josephine. I moved my empty cup beside the saucer, then put it back restlessly.

"That is not what is most important," said Josephine softly, almost in a whisper.

"What can you mean?" I said so loudly that I startled myself. "I'm sorry," I said, lowering my voice, "I don't understand."

"Bibi, think hard. Italy is a long way away. You never know what might have happened on the way, or over there. How Papa and Uncle Arthur came from Slovakia . . . you cannot begin to imagine the ordeals, Bibi. They could not tell from day to day where they were going, or if they would even survive."

"But Frankie has only to go by sea and back."

"Look, Bibi. Think of what Frankie said to Giuseppe. He loves you, neh? But he needs to do this thing before he comes to you. Can you understand, yes?"

"Well, there is one thing I can understand only a little, but another thing I don't understand at all. Okay, maybe it is harder than he expected to find Lucia."

"Yes," said Josephine, firmly. "Wouldn't your own father have gone back to find his sister Tirzeh, if he had the chance?"

"Yes, yes, of course," I said, "Maybe Lucia is sick. Maybe he ran out of money. Perhaps he could not easily find her. But why does he not write to me? He owes me that much." I stopped momentarily, adding bitterly, "Maybe he does not want our baby."

"Wait, Bibi," said Josephine, "how do you know he has not written? And he does not know about the baby, no?"

I agreed feebly. "But why doesn't he return?"

"I don't know, Bibi," said Josephine almost to herself. "But he loves you. You are lucky to have that, neh?"

Josephine stared at the empty cups. I noticed her capable hands, unadorned by any trinkets, and began to sense the core of loneliness that Josephine Grunwald guarded. She was a union worker, a secret organizer, the target of hired thugs like Ijjybijjy Malouf, a staunch friend of her coworkers, a much-loved daughter and niece, and nothing else. She was generous and thought nothing of sharing her room with a virtual stranger, a room full of books and pamphlets and a narrow bed. I understood that it would be somehow hurtful to Josephine if I were to apologize now, at this moment. Josephine's clear intelligent eyes exuded an unsettling honesty. Few men would ever attempt flirtation with Josephine Grunwald, never getting to her deep reserve of strength and real humor that I already understood and loved.

"You know what I would be lucky to have?" I said impulsively, rushing on. "A job, like you do, making enough for a small place of my own. I would be doing something besides just waiting for Frankie to come back. I would save every penny," I said wistfully.

"The baby? Who would take care of him?" asked Josephine levelly.

"My mother can take care of him. She already does. That is all she likes to do. More than anything else." My bitterness spilt out of me. "If she could nurse him, she would, till he is twenty."

"And is that all you can say about her?"

I made myself face Josephine's direct gaze, but could not quite meet it. "She loves us . . . me," I conceded in bitterness, "very much. Too much."

Josephine did not answer immediately. I could not stop my tears now. "I miss my baby, but what else can I do?"

"And what is the other thing you do not understand at all, Bibi?" said Josephine, already knowing the question which I had not been able to ask.

"Why did my mother never mention the letters?"

Josephine's smile was ironic, but her words were gentle. "Surely you know the answer yourself, neh? You told me how she does not allow anyone, including the old man—Brendan?—ever to speak of leaving. She has waited all these years for her father to come to her. She never realized she had all the father she could have asked for. Your mother—she did not want another woman, her own daughter, in the same household, waiting, waiting like her."

"So, should I not wait, if my truth is to wait?" I asked defiantly. "Why can't I choose for myself? She always has."

"Yes, Bibi," said Josephine, "but you are alike in too many ways to agree with each other—yet. Mothers and daughters often walk a hard path." She stood up. "Come, let us go. It's getting late."

The thought of Ijjybijjy Malouf came to my mind suddenly, and I looked anxiously at the shadows on the afternoon street.

"Don't live in fear, Bibi," said Josephine, as if she could read my mind. "Besides, I have my weapon, neh?" she added, patting her small umbrella, which, I noticed only now, had a hideous point.

"Are you good at sewing?" she asked as we strode briskly.

"I am indeed," I replied proudly.

"We shall see how good, yes?" Josephine said, "I'll teach you some tricks of the trade in the next couple of days. Then I'll explain where to go for an interview. I'll tell you what pay to expect. Don't accept anything less."

"Oh yes." I was brightening immediately. "Yes!"

"And don't mention you know me," said Josephine pragmatically. "They know I'm a union girl. Then they wouldn't hire you."

I nodded happily. Linking our arms, Josephine walked to her own beat. "We bargain for our wages together. If the owners are unfair to us, we quit work together. When they want us, we go together to work—if we agree—on our terms, fair and square. We are human beings, neh? Well, some of the owners are not." She chuckled at her own joke. "I'll give you some pamphlets by and by. But first, the sewing tips. I need to see not only how good you are—but how fast and accurate. And for how long. We work many hours, see."

I said yes to all this. A question was forming in my mind. Josephine read my look and simply said, "Of course, you'll stay with me and Papa and Uncle Arthur until you've saved enough. They have already grown so fond of you, I should be jealous, neh?" She chuckled and asked, "Shall we go visit Uncle Arthur at his hotel now and tell him? Shall we go right now? Are you tired? Can you walk?"

"Of course," I agreed, and we headed uptown.

We amused ourselves by watching the fine shops as we walked up Madison Avenue. I admired the mannequins, spangly bags, and hats with feathers, and longed to pause and gawk, but did not want to hold back Josephine, who never broke her stride. As we turned right to go toward Park Avenue and the big hotel where Uncle Arthur worked, Josephine asked me, "Will you write to your mother before or after you find your job?"

"After," I replied firmly.

"How long after?"

"As soon as I can show her I can survive on my own."

"She will worry. So will the old man Brendan. See, Frankie is not the only one to worry others."

"Yes," I demurred. "Okay, a month after I get my job."

And then we were in front of the grand hotel.

"Let's go down and see Uncle Arthur," said Josephine.

"Down?" I wondered. We peeked in through the grand entrance where uniformed doormen stood like deposed kings in mufti. They just ignored us, as if they had been trained to see from a long distance the amount of money anyone carried. Smooth marble columns and huge potted palms rose from the most gleaming floor I'd ever seen. Tall floor lamps glittered amid plush sofas. I felt even the air was different, balmy and warm, without noise, just a hush with a few sounds of the tinkly kind, of fine china and wineglasses, rippling bars at the piano. One of the uninformed bellboys glided up to Josephine.

"Come to see your uncle, Miss Grunwald?" he said with a quick smile.

"Yes, Moishe," she said.

"It's Morris here," he reminded her.

I followed Josephine through a discreet side door, clattered down some steep iron stairs, until she pushed open a great big door with the painted sign that read BOILER ROOM. Off to one side of the very warm cavernous room were a few partitioned spaces, waist-high, with a foot or so of framed glazed glass above. In one of these, under a lamp that was suspended from a very high ceiling with flaking paint, I spied the familiar balding pink head adorned with a banker's green shade. Uncle Arthur sat at a cheap wooden desk, his jacket draped behind his chair. A cigarette dangled from his lips, a cylinder of ash suspended precariously as he leaned over a large ledger, looking intently at columns on a page, a seasoned general inspecting his troops.

He broke into a grin, his face creasing like crumpled paper, clapped his hands, and called out, "Seymour, Seymour." Uncle Arthur whispered something to the nearsighted young man who appeared, adding as he left, "Tell Maxie Shapiro in the kitchen."

In a few minutes, Seymour reappeared, carrying a tray laid with the most immaculate white linen, and on it, two splendid desserts. The spoons were monogrammed, as were the serviettes. For Uncle Arthur he had brought pale tea in an old porcelain mug.

"Peach Melba," Arthur said with a flourish, "meet Miss Bibi Sztolberg and Miss Josephine Grunwald!"

● ● ●

"You'll be just fine, Bibi," Josephine told me at the packed elevator door, giving my cold hand an encouraging squeeze. "You sew far better than most beginners here." She went up the stairs one more floor where they worked on special orders.

I felt breathless as I walked through the heavy door into what seemed to my eyes like a world unto itself. So this was the clothes factory. I can barely remember who directed me to my seat amid the hectic *clackety-clack* of machines, smell of cloth, chirpy or sharp talk among the girls, the sudden quiet when the two owners came by. The girl next to me pointed them out: short, dark Mr. Harris, and then the broody, pale Mr. Blanck with his stiff black hair. The quips that followed after a safe interval, between her and the older woman next to her, were funny and bitter at once.

"I'm Annie," the girl spoke a thick brogue, "Annie Starr. And this is Julia Rosen." But Julia went on working, barely acknowledging me.

I felt a little apprehensive around the stolid middle-aged women, or the bent older ones who fretted about getting slow or their tired eyes. The cutters were all men and, being better paid, thought the world of themselves, Annie told me. I noticed too, how the boys in the cutting and shipping sections made eyes at pretty girls, some of whom giggled or snapped back pert answers.

Oh, there was plenty to watch, but little time, as I focused on my job, sewing linings on a pile of coats dumped beside me. Twice that afternoon, our supervisors, Anna Gullo and Lucy Wesselofsky, came up to me, pointing out this or that wrong stitch or bent seam. *Oh bother those two!*

As we walked home that evening, Josephine noticed I had my head bent, eyes fixed on the sidewalk underfoot. "Bibi?" she said, "it is that bad, yes?"

"No, no, it is not," I said, gritting my teeth, and then conceded, "I just have to keep thinking of my first pay, and it gets easier."

Josephine laughed. "The workers of the world are all united on that one issue, neh?"

• • •

BUT THE SECOND and third days were easier. Crowded together, sharing tools and materials, I made new friends among my co-workers, even some who spoke little English but chattered among themselves in Yiddish, Italian, or Polish, but they all tried their English on me. On the second day, Rebecca Feibisch gave me two pierogies from her lunch and said something nice to me in Yiddish. Although I did not comprehend what all her words meant, I had already begun to pick up words and phrases from Josephine and her family, feeling a deep connection to the language, touching my father through it.

Rebecca spoke often to me, as did Sarah Sabasowitz, a thin girl with bright, mismatched eyes. Poor Julia Rosen was bent and aged before her time, although she was probably thirty and seldom talked or smiled, unlike Sarah Kupla—young Sarah never could stop giggling—and plump Ida Kenowitz almost always got her started. Sarah and Ida were inseparable and shared everything: tools, scissors, lunch, and confidences. Ida joked that they would end up marrying the same man!

By the end of the week, I had begun to learn a lot about rapid stitching from Julia Rosen, although she had a temper, and also from plucky little Vincenza Bellota, who, though only sixteen, had to take the ferry early each morning all the way from Hoboken, where she lived with her gruff uncle Ignazio. Vincenza's high Neapolitan laugh was unmistakable, and she made me her friend, offering to teach me Italian words once she came to know that my Frankie was from Boscotrecase.

My back and eyes hurt by the end of each day, but I already knew better than to complain. Josephine had told me that for each one of us—almost a hundred and fifty who worked here, on the ninth floor—there were dozens of others working the same or worse hours in basement sweatshops, damp back rooms, often the prey of violent employers. Here, at least, that did not happen.

Mr. Blanck did the ledgers, grinding us for each penny, while his partner Mr. Harris knew about the actual cutting and sewing. "He is always cutting corners," I whispered to Vincenza, who loved my joke. What he liked best was to come up with ways to dock our pay. He was so fearful of anyone taking the smallest scrap that he had the doors to the roof locked, so no one—even on a break—could take a breath of fresh air.

Huge open windows to the east and south opened to a fine view of Washington Square Park for those who worked on the tables around those windows. But even for beginners like me who sat far inside, there was enough natural light, for which I thanked God ten times a day.

The day I walked back with my first pay, I was elated, but then it hit me that this would go on, without the novelty, week after week, for months, and then years. In the street, for an instant, I felt a momentary revulsion for the already familiar mixture of the smells of fresh starch, new cotton and wool.

How Josephine managed tirelessly to do all she did, I marveled. Apart from the grind of daily work, she went to the Alliance, a stone's throw from the Bialystoker Synagogue, to take classes in history and learn to play the piano. She had already taken me to the Cooper Union to hear a free lecture on workers' rights. Afterward, she walked up and talked to a man she said I must meet: It was Mr. Abraham Cahan, the editor of the *Forward*. Josephine felt she could talk to everybody in the world. And she went to union meetings with her friends Clara Lemlich and Yetta Ruth, and brought back bundles of pamphlets, some of which she secretly gave to fellow workers.

On my third week at work, one of the supervisors slapped stoop-shouldered Julius Roth, who had protested loudly that he had been docked part of his pay for a mistake someone else had made. He left by the stairs after being fired.

We rode up, packed tight on the freight elevator, only when we reported for work. Mr. Zito, the operator, always hummed some show tune or other under his breath.

> *Every little movement has a meaning*
> *all its own—unh-ha*

His hands were known to wander in the crowded elevator. After each trip, he wiped his palms on either side of his Brilliantined head, as if coaxing that chinless balloon to stay glued on his round shoulders. He chewed mint all the time. But everybody knew another story about him: how he had taken a half day off, without pay, to help a sick seamstress, supporting her down all nine flights of stairs—the elevator was out of bounds to employees except for going up at the beginning of the shift—then propped her home to her mother.

Each week, a man called Max Schlansky came by and went away with a packet. This Schlansky wore a black homburg and spoke to no one, but there was about him an air of malicious power.

"What does he do?" I asked Josephine at home.

"Schlansky? He breaks strikes. He breaks people," she replied, making a face.

One day, another man came by—for a smaller packet. A shiver ran through my frame, but I kept quiet. He was not treated with the same wary respect by Mr. Harris or by his assistant, who gave him the packet. This man also did what Mr. Schlansky never did. He counted the money. Then he spat on the floor, conveying his dissatisfaction before leaving.

It was Ijjybijjy Malouf.

• • •

WE BENT OVER our work, twelve hours a day, surrounded by the sounds of our trade, but found ways to chatter, bantering and gossiping, while our fingers were flying, scissors snicking, steam hissing and rising like local clouds where the girls did the pressing. Some, like Sarah Sabasowitz, struggled to keep pace with the seasoned ones like Annie Starr, who could finish lining a suit jacket every six minutes. I had been at my job about two months now, and could already finish eight in an hour. Fifteen-year-old Bessie Viviano with her nimble fingers finished eleven, but because she had no head for figures, she got short-changed each time. I told her to keep count by putting a small colored string in her pocket for every ten she finished, a trick I had thought up for myself.

When my neck hurt, I would close my eyes momentarily, clench my tired palms, and think intently of our new home: Josephine had helped me find a tiny apartment with a kitchen—and a bathtub in it!—close to Water Slip off the East River. It would be available in a week or so. In that same building lived Hepzibah Schiffman, a plump smiling widow whom Josephine knew well. She would look after my boy while I worked. That is why I did not mind how much Anna Gullo the sour-faced supervisor scowled, sticking her head through lines of hanging patterns that hung like paper ghosts.

I did not want to acknowledge it even to myself, but I thought often of the sweet life on the farm. I longed for Grandpa Brendan and his simple affection. Most of all, I longed for Frankie's arms around me, but what I missed most keenly was his zest for life. It fed mine. I yearned for my little boy, how he smelt, his minute perfect fingers, his chortles when I would pretend to hide behind my palms and then go peek-a-boo. He never did tire of that game. I felt our lives, Frankie's, Padraig's, and mine, were a grim version of that hide-and-seek game, where we were each trying to come find each other. Had my baby forgotten me, did he miss me? I thought with anguish if now he loved Mama more than me.

Not daring to ask for a couple of days off to go to the farm, I wrote to Mama with the news of my job and asked her to bring my son the next weekend, adding the news about Frankie and his quest in Naples.

I had so wanted to prove to my mother that I could manage on my own, but felt no great triumph now. A month ago I had felt the need to stand squarely before her and ask why she had not given my letter, *my* letter by rights, from Frankie. But the sharp edge of my anger had blunted. I thought of my little boy safe with her and missed the uncrowded rhythms of the farm. Oh, I knew that she loved me too; it was its insistence and grip that galled me. Yet the days away from her had taken away its sharp vinegar. My heart was torn over my proud, obdurate mother who was silent about too many things, while I need to talk.

*Why do I always need to set my will against hers, Grandpapa Brendan?* I thought, *Will Mama see things my way now, stand by me, and say, "No need for Mrs. Schiffman, for I am right here for you"?*

• • •

377

JOSEPHINE HAD GOT up early this particular Saturday morning. It was the first time in years that she had taken a day off work, for Uncle Arthur was turning sixty years old. Shy as a schoolboy, he beamed about all the fuss Josephine made. He too had taken the day off. But I would be paid today and hand over much of that money to my landlord. I would be given the key to my own place right away, or a day later, if the landlord did not want to work on his Sabbath. I would miss Josephine, and the two old men, but felt a deep pleasure that I would have a home of my own.

I expected my mother to arrive either today or on Sunday at Josephine's, but I was certain she would come this weekend. Josephine insisted that it would be no problem for all of us to share her room for the day or so until I had my apartment ready.

Josephine appeared happy, joyous as a child on her own birthday. She made Uncle Arthur his favorite breakfast, then went about the apartment busily arranging for the birthday dinner and also the probable arrival of my mother and son. Before I left, she said, "I thought of something else, Bibi. I met Nino Tancredi at a union meeting, and he said that he was working with Italian immigrant groups from Naples and the church there. I just thought to send word through him for news of Lucia and Frankie."

I felt my tears gathering. "But I wrote dozens of those letters," I began.

"Hush," she said, touching my arm, "this is different. You know how the mails are. Nino is going himself next week. He is such a close friend, a good union man. He will do this personally for me. He promised. I wanted to wait until I had some news, but today I thought you should have some joy too." I smiled, my heart aching to gain faith.

I left reluctantly, for the apartment was full of cheer. I stood at the door, watching Uncle Arthur and Uncle Julius shake hands, chuckling as they sat down for a leisurely cup of coffee and quiet smoke, while Josephine bustled behind them.

When I stepped out into the street, I felt amazed by the beautiful day. Twenty-fifth of March, and already glorious weather, the sky a deep blue lake. Out of the corner of my eye, I caught sight of that receding figure: the shy young man with the fair hair, vivid blue eyes, yarmulke on his head, crossing the street away from me. For a moment I thought I'd call out after the stranger, "Jakob Sztolberg, oh stop for me, Jakob. It's me, Bibi. Don't you know me, Papa?" But he had gone from my life again. I looked up at the sky and saw the glide of a pale hawk as it soared above the sparkling city and watched until it disappeared from sight.

"I am happy," I told myself. "Someday I will meet my papa, I know, in no country where time exists. Won't that be something!"

• • •

MY BACK HURT by late afternoon as I labored on, absorbed in the frenzy of the closing work week. The operators worked their stuttering machines, and the runners scampered up and down with fabric lengths, putting them into wicker baskets by our side, and picking up the finished pieces: sleeves and tucked collars and such. Everything around me screamed *hurry, hurry!* The machines were clicking at a gallop. The foremen bellowed the number of pieces needed, checking various piles, in a complicated race. I wondered if I could ever fit back into the farm again.

I raised my head briefly to ease my aching shoulders, staring into the distance, not really focusing on anything. With a jolt, I recognized the receding coppery head of Ijjybijjy Malouf. A cigarette hung from the corner of his mouth. He walked through the busy room, pushing his way with his muscular shoulders, looking neither left nor right. He slipped into Mr. Blanck's glassed-in office and kicked the door shut behind him. The green glow of the banker's lamp on Mr. Blanck's desk made them look submerged and mossy. I watched, fascinated, hands on my lap—the only person on the work floor not caught up just now in the frenetic pace of the closing hour.

"Nine more sleeves, double quick!" bellowed Mr. Bernstein to one of the runners.

Just beyond Mr. Abramowitz at his cutter's table, I could still see Malouf and Mr. Blanck but could not hear a thing. They seemed to be quarreling. Mr. Blanck's mouth opened and closed, his face livid, and he kept pointing his index finger, whether to make a point or to show Malouf the door, I was not sure. I watched Ijjybijjy clenching his jaw, smoke curling up from the cigarette in his mouth. Suddenly he pushed Mr. Blanck with his open palm, making him stagger against his desk. Malouf turned around, as if on a mechanical device, and slid out.

He flicked something into Mr. Abramowitz's bin of scrap cuttings of cotton and lawn before he slunk off toward the main door. There Ijjybijjy swiveled around to stare at the room, as if he were a curious passerby. A small smile played on his lips. Mr. Blanck seemed relieved to be rid of the man and bent down to make a phone call.

By the time I glanced back, Ijjybijjy Malouf had gone.

Ten more minutes to closing time, so I settled down to work, although I longed to go to one of the tall windows and look upon the greening heads of the trees. I wondered where my boy was, and found myself wishing my mother had an easy trip down to this unfamiliar city. I felt a sharp twinge that I had made an adversary of her. In the last year, her face often looked tired, her back a little stooped. When I was a child, she would bring johnnie-cakes and cookies made from mulled oats and honey out to us—Grandpapa Brendan and me—with glasses of milk at this time of day. The simple memory comforted me.

A dancing light played just beyond my range of vision as I leaned down to finish the last of the needlework. An odor of burning leaves and their crinkling sound as they curled in the fire?

In a trice, something jolted me upright. I saw the sudden palms of fire, vivid and ochre, reaching out from the bin by Mr. Abramowitz's table. The fire danced in reflection on Mr. Blanck's glass office, where he stood screaming soundlessly. The tables that lay side by side, the tissue and lawn, the heaped layers of cotton ignited. Dangling from the network of wires overhead, the paper patterns in translucent tissue fluttered aflame. A whoosh of smoke gamboled and rolled toward the windows like a gray wave. The window beams crackled and the sound of breaking glass tinkled in the air. A tongue of fire licked along the wall and out a tall window, seeking the balmy air outside. The smoke lowered in the ululating room.

The door on the far side was locked. Rebecca Feibisch and Sarah Sabasowitz were among those hurling themselves against it, and in a terrible pantomime of bewilderment, crumpling down, clothes afire, on the smoking floor. I whirled around and saw the inseparable Ida Kenowitz and Sarah Kupla standing against the flaming wall, wide-eyed in terror, holding hands, their skirts swirling about them.

The smoke unfurled itself lower and lower, making it impossible to breathe. People were now running into and over each other, with a dreadful creaking underfoot as if the floor were splitting. Cinders clattered in clumps from the roof. Wisps of cotton and lengths of lawn caught fire, rising like crazy magic carpets into the smoke. I heard the wailing of Julia Rosen, the piercing shrieks of Vincenza, while all about me flickered light, but not of a kind I had ever seen before. And beyond them, I could see the slow pirouette of Annie Starr, her eyes shut as if she had heard some dread music. In front of me I saw the pale, silent face of little Bessie Viviano.

I stood as still as ever I stood on this earth, before I knew what I had to do.

# Maeve
New York City
March 25, 1911

I had that dream again.

In the first months after my Jakob died, I had a recurrent nightmare: My grief had turned into a box with a complicated latch I was too weak to shut. It was so densely packed that, once opened, sunlight and air had swollen the contents, making it impossible to grapple the lid down to close it. I struggled with the box until I would heave awake, choking, in a night thick as smoke.

Bibi had written from New York; she knows about the letters. I needed to speak to Papa Brendan urgently, stranded as I was on my island of woe, the black waters rising. When he came into the kitchen that morning, still sleepy, I spoke directly.

"I want to die, Papa Brendan. I wish it were all over. I want to walk into that lake with rocks in my fists and never come out."

He looked gravely at me, his eyebrows white, his cheeks like pink fabric wrinkled.

"Is that so, my girl?" he said, as if I were a wee child who had taken a bad fall.

My withholding the letters was past explaining now. I handed him Frankie's letters, which he read, saying nothing, while I sat as if it were the dead end of time.

"You did wrong, Maeve," he said simply. His eyes were keen, watching my face, aware of my plight. "But you can turn it about, you know?" I sat looking back at him, entirely confused by his manner.

"Come, dear," he urged, "come away from this dim kitchen, for 'tis a grand morning outside." He led me, my palm in his, to the wooden bench under the horse chestnut.

"You can bring all the happiness back into your world, and your girl's love to boot. Do you know that?"

"And how am I to do that, Papa Brendan?" I retorted.

"Take a ship to Italy," he said. "Take Bibi and the child. Help them find Frankie."

"What?" I was completely dumbfounded. "Papa Brendan . . ." I wavered.

"You need to right the wrong you did Bibi." He was looking sternly at me now. I hung my head. "Nay, nay, Maeve," he said, "look up, look at me. Think who you are: Padraig's daughter, dauntless Maire Aherne's blood. Take that ship to Naples. You can take on the Atlantic. You did once."

I took a deep breath. "And you, Papa Brendan?"

"Ach," he said, blinking in the growing light, "I need to hold the fort here. Besides, I have to do the ledgers each month, don't I? You'll be back before you know it. And don't you worry about the money. We have enough and more, saved over all these years, eh, my tightfisted girl?" He was grinning at me.

"Will you be all right by yourself in that while?" A great weight was lifting off me.

"Aye, certainly," he said, "although, I must say, girleen, I will have to fend off Mrs. Gabrielsen's endless baking!"

"She likes you," I teased him, amazed to find myself in a jocular mood so easily.

"Nay, nay," he chortled, "the widow has made eyes at all the men here, young and old. The lady cannot help herself any more than a sneeze in pollen time."

• • •

I HAVE GIRDED myself, for my hapless love has outweighed the sum of all my fears. I ask nothing in return but my daughter's trust back. Aye, I am the wanderer's daughter, but I know why I am setting out. Yes, oh yes! With Bibi under my wing, I shall sail that dread Atlantic again.

That is the first thing I will tell Bibi when I see her.

I woke with a jolt on the hard railway bench, holding my sleeping grandson. The gum of uneasy sleep was still on my eyes as the train grated into the station. Standing within the doorway of a looming building, like the mouth of a cave, I reread the sheet on which Bibi had sent her address.

It was almost noon by the time I found it, reluctant to ask help from strangers. Bibi had already left for work. The apartment felt cramped, its sepia light burdened with the smell of tobacco and old paper, the wallpaper close and constricting, and the family's oddly pronounced English unfamiliar. I did not know what to say to the two elderly men and the busy young woman, Josephine. Both men spoke with an old-fashioned courtesy. Papa Brendan would have thoroughly enjoyed their company, but I retreated into silence.

How is it that Jakob never felt alien to me? These Grunwalds are from that part of the world, but I felt ill at ease. They kept talking of my daughter as if Bibi was theirs. Then the two men continued talking about people they thought I would know about. But these names, McClellan, Hearst, and Charles Murphy meant nothing to me. They discussed Tammany Hall. *Was that a person or a place?*

Josephine Grunwald was solicitous to me and made baby Padraig comfortable and served us lunch. The food was strange, the shape of the bread unfamiliar. I did recognize the seeds of rye and thought the taste not unpleasant. The soup had bits of bread and meat in it, and I made myself eat a small portion out of politeness. Little Padraig had woken up and tried to haul himself unsteadily up by the chair, but flopped down on the carpeted floor. The old man with the pink bald head seemed delighted with the child and had him stand again. Padraig, without a trace of unease, firmly held the man's thumbs, propelling himself a few steps before the old man planted him on his lap and offered him a piece of bread. The child gummed it with gusto, while a large cat watched gravely from a corner.

Josephine was preparing quantities of food for the evening, dishes I did not know. Nonetheless I went into the crammed kitchen to help with the chopping and cutting. I could see plainly that Josephine cooked with speed and efficiency, but no talent. I did notice that Josephine's kitchen had some oranges, sugar, butter, flour—ingredients for Irish Burnt Orange Cake. When the young woman had quite finished and was about to untie her apron, I asked her, "Could I use your kitchen, please?" Josephine seemed surprised, thinking in confusion that I was intending to cook my own meal. She held out her hands and said, "But I cooked everything for all of us. You will eat, of course, with us, neh?"

"Thank you for that," I told her. "I will bake for your family."

"Of course, yes, please use anything you like," said Josephine.

"Bibi tells me what wonders you can cook, but only if you want to make something. The kitchen is yours." Then she earnestly added, "This home too, as long as you wish."

So I baked. I felt calmer now.

The aroma of my cake soon made the two gentlemen sit up in anticipation. When I returned to the kitchen to take it out of the oven, Josephine followed me.

"Bibi will be so glad to see you," said Josephine.

I could not help a shadow passing over my face in spite of myself.

"She must miss your cooking," Josephine said, trying to put me at ease. I was silent, for I could never bring myself to speak of my heart's ache to a stranger, kind to Bibi as she was. All the troubles that I have had with Bibi made me slow to answer.

"For certain she loves you," added Josephine. "The letters are no matter."

I stood stricken. The words had been so unexpected, it was as if the young woman had taken a plate and smashed it. *So Bibi has told this stranger what I have done*, I thought, bitterness curdling within me. What could this woman from no country I knew, from a strange city, begin to know of our safe garden where I wanted to protect my willful daughter? My heart was a slab of stone. Yes, heavy misery it was made of—and guilt—and also my helpless love.

I barely managed to speak. "Write me down, kindly, the address where my Bibi works," I said as evenly as I could manage. "I have a mind to take the child there and meet my daughter when she is done for the day."

"You will?" said Josephine, breaking into a smile. She wrote down the address and began to explain how to get there. "It is not far."

What does this young woman know how far I have traveled, and how could she even begin to comprehend how turbulent the world could be for the likes of us, torn and uprooted as we had been from our Ireland, leaving us lost on some sea or on some unsure ice beneath us, until we found our own piece of earth?

Padraig had crawled over to me, struggling to stand up, clinging to my skirt. I picked him up and held him close. I would change him, take my small bag, and walk down to meet Bibi. I would wait on the street as long as I needed to. It was already afternoon.

In the park just across the narrow street from where Bibi worked, I found a bench under a tall elm, its bare branches showing traces of incipient green buds. Padraig sat wide-eyed on my lap, watching a flock of pigeons picking amid the sparse city grass. I had not slept much on the train, reading and rereading Frankie's letters.

I do not believe wanderers come back. "We belong to places," I thought wearily. "Those who think the whole world their home never find their place in it. That is why we have different countries, as surely as we need walls to our homes. Papa Brendan has begun to talk of Ireland again. Yet what is Ireland to him, or he to Ireland, once he left?"

By late afternoon, almost five, I picked up Padraig, tired and sleepy now and content to lie quietly in my arms. I wiped his face clean and kissed him on the little birthmark on his cheek. Then I carried him out of the park and stood across the street. There it was—the door through which Bibi went in and out of work.

• • •

HOW OFTEN WHEN she was a child, Bibi would storm in from play and for no reason at all, call out, "O Mamma!" and throw her small arms about my neck and cover me with kisses. Where is that child gone, I asked myself, heartsore. "Where are you hiding, Bibi?" I whispered, as if we were playing hide and seek again. This wait seemed endless. *Please God, let her come to me with a smile. Please sweet God, give me a sign.*

At first, it seemed a trick of the eye. A blue filament, like a whisper, blew out of one of the high windows. What could that be, I wondered. The street below looked just as it had a moment before. Carriages clattered by, people sauntered past, the shop-signs and billboards looked crowded and dusty. I looked up again and saw an unmistakable smudge of smoke defiling the sky. With a sharp crack and tinkle, shards of glass crashed to the pavement where the startled people ran out into the street to avoid the spars.

Standing in front of the main door was a driverless delivery-cart. The blinkered horse shook its head, flanks quivering under the rain of glass, then with a startled flinch took off. The wagon trundled after it. Its wheels caught against the curbside and over-turned, but the horse dragged it on, breaking into a wide-nostriled gallop. People up and down the street gesticulated, screaming and pointing excitedly at the upper floors of the building where a bil-low of smoke surged out of one window, and then another next to it. A palm of fire darted out from within and began to scorch the outer wall, turning it black.

Then I heard it, the chorus of cries and wails from above. Within the cave-like windows, I saw a thicket of limbs. From this strange bush came an ululation that made my hair stand on end. A body emerged from the cave of smoke and came flying out, suspended momentarily, and then plunged. I was certain it would happen—something miraculous—anything that would prove God's existence.

I heard the sudden thud, a hollow sound of body smiting

metal. Moving forward, I saw a broken body, twitching, a dense liquid seeping out of it, across a ribbed iron sheet stretched on the sidewalk. The body was bent oddly, but all too human. The middle-aged woman's hair, which had been pinned carefully, had come undone. The metal had buckled where she had hit it in one mortal impact. The odour of char rose from the smoldering shoulder of her coat. And as I stood, there fell another body, and then another. I felt a great thud upon my heart as if someone had landed directly on it. I lurched back, knocking into people, holding my grandson in a convulsive force. He clung to my neck, suddenly awakened, frightened by the shouts of the people around them. A voice rang out above all others, *Look, look, see there.*

Some people had managed to escape to the roof, and my heart leapt with hope. They were standing at the parapet. They seemed to be swaying, but they were certainly safe. I searched frantically for Bibi.

Then I saw my daughter.

The pounding in my heart made me choke. I sank to my knees and put the child on the ground, for all strength was draining out of me. A lowering blackness troubled my sight. My daughter, my headstrong Bibi, stood at the high open window, swathed in a luminous shawl.

She stepped out into the wide air and flew down to meet the earth.

We lay together in a strange country now, a few feet apart. My hands moved blindly over the gritty earth, reaching for her. "Bibi," I called, "oh my Bibi," groping for her in the sudden darkness. There seemed to be pebbles all around, pebbles that were wet and familiar.

"Where is my child?" I thought, wondering what dreadful

weight on my chest made it impossible for me to breathe or cry out. A cracked voice rang in my ears, keening above me, a voice I recognized: *Moo-maa-gy*, it cried, *Moo-maa-gy*, again and again. And I knew these pebbles now. They were from the sea-edge at Sligo, where I had played by myself one last time in Ireland, before Papa Brendan carried me carefully in his arms over a swaying gangplank onto a ship, about to enter an ocean.

But this time I had fallen through, into an impenetrable darkness.

● ● ●

A CHILD WAILED, his palms soiled, cheek smudged by dirt, his nose runny.

An ambulance driver careened his wagon on to the sidewalk, honking furiously. It ran over a limb or two and parked under the cascade of bodies, so that its roof would break the falls. Firemen had arrived in a swarm. They spread out a tarpaulin and stretched it out, but the next body fell with such force that the fabric was ripped from their grasp. They hurriedly rigged a ladder, but it reached only halfway up the tall building. The last of the bodies fell past it.

The child watched a car at the curb across the street; its gleaming wheels caught his eye. Bibi's son clutched his grandmother's lifeless body, stood up, then lost his balance, and sat abruptly on the grimy sidewalk.

Carefully picking himself up, without aid, he toddled unsteadily, taking his first steps on earth, away from all his relatives, into the swarming and deadly city.

# VI

*singing-masters of my soul*

# Kush
## Jessore, East Bengal Province
## 1947

"Will you take me to that great house?" I asked my father on the morning of my seventh birthday.

"That old house is n-no more," Baba told me sadly.

"Do houses die?" I asked him.

"Yes," he said sadly, "Everything d-dies." I thought about that carefully.

"But we should know where we belong," he continued, "and who we are," as if he was speaking to himself.

Baba was born by a roaring river near Barisal in a great house with pillars. He lived with his old grandfather, whose name was Ramkumar Mitra. *His* father's name was Doorgadass, and he was a famous merchant. He traded with the English and the Dutch. He even had a timber business in Burma.

"We must remember the names of our ancestors," Baba told me as he took me on the horse-drawn gharry to show me his office, where I read what was written on a wooden board outside:

Monimoy Mitra, MA
Civil Court, Jessore District
Bengal Province, India

It told you where he was and who, but I told him there was a big mistake here. I don't understand how Baba had MA after his name. He is my *Baba*, not Ma.

Ma was different, in a way I did not understand. I do not remember my mother ever caressing me. She could not bear to be touched.

So I asked Baba how I was related to Ma. He took a minute to understand what I meant and mulled it over, blinking, then blurted out, "Good God, Kush, b-because you grew inside her. She is your *mother*!" He made a vague gesture with his spread hands, as if that explained everything. It did not.

"Who decided that I would go into her?" I persisted. "Why *her*?" He began to stammer a long answer, as if he had been involved in some kind of mistake, but was honestly trying not to blame anyone. "Besides," he said, finally, "I have to start work now. Qadir will drive you home."

When I returned home, my mother's maid Sushma had told me that I had been born that day. I laughed at her. "No, *nonono*, I don't remember being born this morning."

Sushma set my breakfast down with a clatter, chapatis, and a soft runny egg. Then she told me it was exactly seven years ago and there had been another brother who had tried to be born, *the same day*. The firstborn, the one who did not breathe.

"Ask your ma," she glared, daring me, "ask her. She wanted *him*."

"And me?" I began angrily, but I knew the answer.

"Your poor ma refused to nurse you, and can you blame her! And you, bawling and screeching from that first hour, such a bother in a sad house! Your father had to go off and buy a milch goat. What with its bleating and your yowling, she needed to rest from that day," concluded Sushma with satisfaction. I knew the rest well enough.

Ma went into perpetual mourning for my brother and lived alone on her great bed. Baba slept in his study.

I decided to talk to my mother about my birth when she woke up and explain that I had not meant any mischief and none of what happened was my fault. Under her bed, thinking it a good playspace, I smuggled my favorite picture book. Lying on my stomach, I turned a page. The leaf fluttered. My mother called out, "Laub, oh Laub, is that you, Laub?" Sushma hurried in. I could see her shadow growing larger on the wall behind her.

"No, no, *bahu*," she said, "it is only Kush under the bed."

I heard my mother's voice choking, stiffening, "Take him away." Sushma dragged me out before I could say anything. Before shutting the door on me, she whispered, "He did not live because you had taken up all his blood inside your mother. Stay away from here."

I went out into the backyard, walking on until I reached the dense trees where I was not supposed to go. "Snakes and scorpions and *petni*-witches live there," Sushma had warned me once. Today I wanted to see for myself if anything she said was true. And before I knew it, I was lost. The tendrils of the banyan trailed around me, creating an early evening. A part of the bark moved, and suddenly I was aware of speckled wings and the round eyes of an owl, a perfect match with the branch it sat on. We regarded each other carefully until its gaze shifted, and I became aware of someone else beside me. And I knew immediately who it was—I just knew without having to look!

From that moment I began to sense him around me, my twin— pale Laub—because I had taken away his birthright blood: pale in the darkness of corners, under the broadleaf trees, in all the hidden places of my life.

*It's not your fault,* he whispered that same night when I drifted into sleep. He was lying next to me in the darkness where no one else could see him. *Is that you, Laub?* I would think—and he always let me know where he was.

I knew I could not share him with anyone else at home.

• • •

NO MATTER WHERE I explored in the afternoons, I had to be home by sunset, because Baba had appointed his retired clerk, Binod-babu, to come and tutor me. I would watch him in the twilight as he ambled past hedges of *hetaal* and *akondo*, carefully picking his way lit under the oscillations of his handheld lantern.

As I intoned the scales of the multiplication tables, swinging my legs in rhythm, the night outside would be nudged awake by the hum of insects. Some of the winged ones flew and whirred into the study, the carapace of their moth wings touching the smeared heat of the kerosene lamp. As I sang out the numbers, I could feel my mind sharpen in wonder—how they stayed the same in meaning, while everything else—like leaves, or the sky, or day and night—changed so much and so soon.

Baba took up the task to teach me English, a small teaspoon at a time. At first I thought he was teaching me a secret language that nobody else spoke, in which I could think my secret thoughts.

As I learnt, my brother Laub learnt too, in twin measure. Some words tasted heavy and metallic, like *lead* and *iron*, and some phrases made small pictures behind our closed eyes. We repeated "a school of fish," "a gaggle of geese" to ourselves. Numberless fish, gliding and flickering under the waters. The silly waddle of geese headed for the ponds edged with waterweeds. We decided to make up new phrases: *a slink of foxes*—for we had seen them in the bamboo groves behind our bungalow, in the direction of the wide river where I was forbidden to explore; *a jamboree of bees*, when the hive became a swarm. Together we would think up phrases: *a melody of cuckoos, a rattle of woodpeckers, a squirm of earthworms*—and then, I would whisper, *"Laub?"* And my brother would be there, just out of sight, invisible to everyone else.

I never told Baba, or Qadir his servant, and certainly not sour Sushma, about my brother Laub. I was afraid that if I told them, my brother would be made to go away. Then I would surely lose him, and he would be unhoused, again through my fault—and then if I called out, *Laub, is that you?*—there would be no answer.

• • •

BABA WENT TO his office every day on his horse-drawn gharry, which Qadir Chacha drove. Often in the mornings, I rode beside him on the gharry to drop Baba at his office in the red courthouse building with its red-blue-black British flag. To me it looked as if they had decided to firmly cross out the crucifix at the centre.

Qadir Chacha lived in a small hut off to one side of our bungalow, under a guava tree, next to his nag Burak's stable. Old Burak liked to have his bony ribs scratched, whinnying and snorting with pleasure.

Qadir also ran errands for Baba. He would come in to clean our front verandah, but he would never come any farther inside, nor was he allowed to touch our food—not because Baba himself cared at all, but because Sushma was fierce about it: Qadir was Muslim. Baba told me to call him Chacha—uncle—because it was the custom with older servants. Qadir Chacha said his prayer on a tiny roll-up rug in front of his house, facing west. He would wash his hands and feet, sit with his ankles tucked under him, and raise both palms, looking up as if someone invisible was standing in front of him.

He told me about a pir who used to live near the river. Qadir Chacha whispered that djinns had built a tiny mosque overnight for that holy man, Ali Suleiman al-Badr Khurasani, a mosque as lovely as a pearl. Many years ago, when the old pir died, he was buried there. About the pir's mazhar, the cloth-covered mound of his tomb, Chacha told me many stories: Young men given up for dead after snakebite and left there after prayers would rise and wander around, alive but listless; women, barren after years of marriage, would eat a mango from the trees that grew wild around the mosque, go home, and find themselves pregnant, although the children were usually mischievous. When the girls grew up, they sang beautifully, said Qadir Chacha, nodding his head. Some years after the old pir's death, there was a terrible scourge of cholera. Most people in the nearby villages died. Now, no one lived in that great bend of the river. Cane vines, wild jarul, and hetal trees took over, along with dreadful sheora trees, where *shaakchunni*-witches were known to set up their nasal caterwauling, demanding fish, unnerving travellers at night.

Qadir Chacha said it was only a half hour's walk from my father's bungalow, by the wide river. Desperate people went looking for it when grief or despair drove them to thoughts of drowning or poison. Poor farmers or simple fisherfolk would speak to the walls of the small mosque and come back comforted.

The pir never made any distinction between Muslims and Hindus, for God the Merciful, he said, distributes His store of grief equally among his creatures, whether they were followers of the Book or no. That is why the old pir was hated by the full-bearded mullahs in their town mosques and the angry madrassah maulvis in skullcaps. Pir-baba was invoked by the poor—of both religions—for whom hardship had no separate names. Qadir Chacha insisted that the holy pir had known the ninety-nine names of God, and was blessed with the knowledge of His secret hundredth name.

The dead pir was loved by all, even those who had merely heard of him. Some even whispered—here Qadir Chacha dropped his voice to a whisper, for it was a grave matter—the holy pir's tomb, the mazhar, moved about, from one new moon to another, even as a river shifts its course in the great alluvial valley which we all shared, the living and the dead.

Qadir Chacha muttered mysteriously that some poor villagers had recently seen unknown beings flit around the riverbend, that djinns had been known to hover about and congregate, talking to someone there. Their voices, Qadir Chacha whispered, were unearthly and metallic, and their wings like moths' were adamantine black, folded one over the other.

When I felt Laub growing afraid, I asked Qadir Chacha defiantly, "How do you know? Have you ever seen any djinn, white or black?" And he tilted his eyes, sputtering, "*Tauba, tauba!* Oh, how can you say that, little Baba? I just heard tell, that is all."

Sushma screamed for me from the verandah: *Time for dinner,*

*Time for lessons, Time to take a bath, Time to just come inside.* Sushma did not like Qadir. She did not like him telling me anything. But Laub loved to go and listen to him.

What thrilled us most in the nighttime was to wonder if the djinns were beginning to arrive secretly at the courtyard of the pir's lost mosque to sing. Those evenings when the old private tutor was racked by cough, or his gouty frame not equal to the walk from his cottage a furlong away, I would skitter out quietly so Sushma would not know that I had gone to Qadir Chacha's mud hut for more stories.

Inside, Qadir Chacha's hut smelt like the cool earth, but woody too, for he puffed his hookah here. The small lamp in his room would bounce off the single picture on its special ledge, so that it became a luminous mirror. One afternoon, I took it down to peer at the square building draped in soft black fabric on which was flowing calligraphy. Around it appeared swirls of light. Looking closer, I realized that these were not waves of light, but a flow of people—so small next to the vast dark cube of the building that they were like innumerable bright spots.

Qadir Chacha took the picture carefully from my hands, even before Laub finished looking at it. He kissed the glass pane before putting the picture back.

"That's the Ka'aba," he said to me, "the house built by Ibrahim and his first son, Ishmail."

"First son?" I asked.

"Yes," he nodded, the shadow of his short beard wagging on the wall behind him. "Ibrahim, God's beloved, had another son, Ishaaq. But these two hated each other, all their lives." I could sense that Laub was troubled.

"Why?" I said, preparing myself for whatever was to come.

"Kush, where are you, naughty boy?" I could hear Sushma screeching from the verandah, peering, with an ineffectual hurricane lamp raised at face level, "Kush?"

"Why?" I urged Qadir, ignoring Sushma's calls. "Why did they hate?"

"I do not know," fumbled Qadir. Then he said, "Run along today. I will tell you other stories tomorrow." I nodded. Qadir Chacha's stories were fine, but he never knew *why* the stories were the way they were.

I knew I would have to go elsewhere for answers.

• • •

Soon Laub and I ventured far beyond the backyard, past the hedges of dhundul, past brambly woods thick with fireflies, into the edgy tangles of bamboos. You couldn't run through bamboo-woods. I discovered why. One afternoon when I was running in it, a twig almost entered my eye, hitting me just under my eyebrow. Blood dripped into my left eyeball. When I looked up, one eye smeared and the other just startled, everything appeared disjointed. My brother Laub was frightened, saying, *Sit down, sit down, shut your eyes*, and I did. I heard the words in my head where my brother speaks.

When I blinked open my eyes, to my astonishment, I spied the broken walls and the low, moss-ravaged dome of the lost mosque under dreadlocked banyans. Right behind it whispered the powerful river. Thrilled, I called Laub, "Let us go in!" Indigo shadows were drifting down like birds. Laub was scared. Under the sagging roof was a cloth-covered mazhar-shrine where the miracle-working holy man had lain, for years and years, dead in his tomb. I peeped in through the cobwebbed window. In the corner, in a great heart-thumping moment, I saw someone. He raised his hand. In it, he held a pair of black tongs. He clicked it twice, in greeting.

Then he said, "Come in, enter, both of you.

In the shadow that hung around him like his rags, the only things visible were his forehead, his eyes, and his hands. The tongs he held in his left hand were now pointing at his heart. He was tall, we could tell, even though he was squatting on the far side of the mazhar For an anguished instant, the thought that *he* was the dead pir himself crossed my mind. Was he sitting out here because he was tired of lying in his tomb-bed?

Under the green spread of wild vines, the ruined mosque lay in shadow. If ever darkness had echoes, they moved here. The man tapped the tongs on the ground and pointed. We sat down, Laub and I.

"Is it true what they say about you?" I asked. I could sense that Laub was pulling back, still afraid.

"You can tell what is truth?" He had two teeth missing. His beard was straggly and his hair lay matted below bony shoulders. His black djellaba was torn in places where his ribbed chest showed through, behind beads and amulets wrapped in black and brown rags.

*"Tomago ki naam?"* he asked in a strong East Bengali accent.

"Kush. My brother is Laub."

"Yes," he said simply, but he did not tell me his own name. In my head, I made up a name for him. *Kalo Pir*, the black faqir.

"You can call me that," he said, "although the one who lies buried here, my Ustad, was the real pir, blessed by the Nabi, may his name be praised."

*How does he know what I have named him?* I thought indignantly. How can he read my thoughts? I was defiant, but curious. I wanted to learn what others thought: Then I could get home before Baba returned from his office; I would know what my mother thinks all day; I could even try to figure out if Laub has thoughts that are hidden from me.

"Do not be alarmed," he said, sensing Laub retreat. The man seemed to shift about on the broken floor. His eyes were like two pieces of glass. "Maybe the djinns tell me."

*"Djinns!"* I said, taken aback.

• • •

I COULD NOT wait to get back to the lost mosque, and would slip away every other day, whenever I could evade Sushma's beady eyes. I had so many questions for Kalo Pir, because there seemed to be so many stories.

The shadows cast by the swaying trees overhead made the broken tiles of the courtyard seem to move. My brother and I drank in stories of other worlds. With his tongs, Kalo Pir would stir the embers, tossing in shining pieces of some substance that smoked and sputtered blue perfumed wisps.

"Tell me the real truth about Ishmail," I said bravely to Kalo Pir a week after our first visit. I knew Laub did not like me to poke around the story which Qadir Chacha had started, but I had to know. Besides, it was just a story.

"You think it is just a story?" chuckled Kalo Pir. "Aaah," he breathed out long and slow. "But you also want the real truth, eh? Not just the truth, no?"

Why did grown-ups always end up teasing us, sooner or later?

Is it because they knew more stories? Did they think they knew what everything means?

"No, no," said Kalo Pir, clicking his tongs. "Only Allah knows the meaning of all the stories."

"Tell me about Ishmail," I insisted.

"God summoned the boy's father, Ibrahim, and wanted proof of his love."

"Whether he loved Ishmail?"

"No," said Kalo Pir. He was no longer smiling. There was an odd glitter in his eye. "Allah wanted to know if Ibrahim loved God."

"You said He knows everything."

"He does. But He wanted Ibrahim to discover it for himself."

"How?"

"He asked Ibrahim to prove his love by slashing his son Ishmail's throat."

"That would prove his love?"

"Allah thought so," said Kalo Pir. I held my breath, unable to ask the next question.

"Ibrahim took his knife and was about to do the qurbani, but Allah had his proof now. He is merciful." My chest hurt from holding my breath.

"Allah had turned Ibrahim's knife blunt. He had his proof. An angel stayed Ibrahim's hand."

"What happened then?" I knew Laub was restless too.

"Nothing. There is nothing else in the story."

"No, no, Kalo Pir, *no*," I said. "Did the knife become sharp again after the test was over? Tell me. Was the knife safely taken away?"

"The story ends there," said Kalo Pir.

"It cannot end there!" I said in frustration. "If the knife remained, if it became sharp again, what could stop someone else from coming, using the knife to slash Ishmail's throat? To prove something else?"

Kalo Pir stirred the last embers with his tongs. "The Christian padres—and also Jews, the sons of Ishaaq, tell an earlier story."

"That is different?" I asked hopefully.

"Yes and no."

"What do you mean?" I was confused.

"In their story, it is Ishaaq whose neck is under Ibrahim's knife."

"That's no better."

"You think so?"

"Yes, yes, Kalo Pir," I said, for it was obvious to me. "The knife remains. It is one brother or another."

"Yes, Kush, it is always one brother or another," whispered Kalo Pir, "and the knife is sharp when finally it is time." His face had an inky tint. After a while, he brightened. "But there are other stories."

*I don't like his stories*, Laub was whispering in my ear, but I pretended I did not hear him. "Yes, tell me," I said to Kalo Pir.

• • •

"THERE HAVE BEEN all kinds of troubles," Qadir Chacha told me after Baba came back from work the next day. Someone had derailed a train by tampering with the track. Hindus were blaming Muslims, and the Muslims were furious and blamed the infidels.

"So who do you think did this?" I asked Qadir Chacha.

"Bad people."

"Hindu bad people or Muslim bad people?" I persisted.

"What does good or bad have to do with religion?" he said, genuinely puzzled.

While Sushma kept a vigilant eye on me, I could not get away to see Kalo Pir, but I needed to talk to him about good and bad people.

The next day there was more trouble in town, Qadir Chacha was stuck waiting for Baba, and Sushma was tending to Ma's headache and demanded absolute silence. I reasoned that I could not be quieter than when I was away, and slipped away immediately to ask Kalo Pir my question. And he told me, in a very roundabout way, which I was beginning to see was the way of grown-ups.

● ● ●

KALO PIR TOLD us about the Abdal, the one godly man, whose identity is known only to God. "That person is crucially important," said Kalo Pir, "because it is only for him that God perpetuates this world."

"And when he dies?" I asked, anxious but skeptical.

"Why then, God chooses another in his place."

"And what happens in between his death and the next Abdal?" I persisted.

"Even if there were an instant," smiled Kalo Pir, rearranging his ragged djellaba, "it is an instant when God makes Time stand still, while He chooses the next Abdal. The smoke above the embers remains motionless; the clouds, the birds in flight, even the gills of the breathing fish stop; the falling fruit is suspended in air, its shadow unmoving in its spot. Then God's choice is made: the fruit can fall, the fish breathes, the wisp of smoke and the rest of the universe moves."

"How do you know?" I whisper urgently.

"I don't have to know, as long as He does," chuckled Kalo Pir. Then Kalo Pir told us about paradise, which he called Firdaus, of the unspoilt trees of the Garden of Adn before Adham sinned and Haiwa our common mother erred, when their hearts were pure, and they had been full of *ilham* of the soul. And he went on to tell us of the celestial mosque called the Zurah, where seventy thousand newly created angels prayed. He spoke dreamily of the four rivers of Firdaus and of Sidrat-al-Muntaaha, one of the many celestial trees, a great one bearing innumerable leaves. Each leaf has a person's name written on it. The leaves fall, new leaves grow. When a leaf falls, before it touches the soil of Firdaus, an angel of death catches it and races towards the earth to do his errand.

My brother, Laub, listens intently.

"The angel puts on the face of the person to be taken, so that he will not be terrified. The Almighty is merciful."

"How do these angels come?" I ask.

"Angels come to this earth all the time. On the night of Al Qadr during the month of Ramadan, angels in untold numbers descend, jostling and laughing in silent merriment. The paths of their comings and goings are similar to Al Sirat."

"Which is?" we ask impatiently.

"Al Sirat? That is the path, narrower than a spider's thread, sharper than the sharpest sword. The good pass unharmed over it."

"And the bad?"

"They have their own ways. They always do. There is Iblis himself, of course. Then there is Dasim, the son of Shaitan Iblis, who causes quarrels between husbands and wives. There are many others. To keep all of them at bay, one can simply say, *'Audhu Bil-*

*lah,*' or the sura of al-Baqarah—and all the evil ones will flee one horizon away, at least."

"Is it true?" I ask.

"Will your not believing make it untrue?" Kalo Pir smiles. "Or my saying it make it more true?"

"Why do you always answer with a question?" I snap.

"Why not?" he replies, clicking his tongs.

The evening breeze smells of the river. It is time to go home. Did Laub's angel come inside the womb, or meet him at its door? Did the angel know I was just a span away? *Could the angel tell Laub and me apart?*

"When it is that time for you, Kush," whispered Kalo Pir from the darkness, "will *you* be able to tell the angel of death from your brother Laub? Even in the night?" His eyes were glittering.

I did not know what to say and went out of the mosque and waited for my brother. *Laub,* I whispered, *Is that you, Laub?* I felt a shiver down my spine, afraid of my brother for the first time.

He must have slipped away, unnoticed.

$$\bullet \ \bullet \ \bullet$$

MY FATHER WAS waiting for me, pacing the courtyard when I returned very late.

By this time in the evening, he would usually be in his study, in his slippers, picking absently at his court wig and poring over long dossiers he brought back from work. But today, he was pacing outside, his boots very muddy. I could tell he had just walked home, not come by the rickety gharry Qadir took such absurd pride in.

"There you are, b-boy!" he said in relief. "Where d-did you go?"

I had no intention of telling him about my adventures and thought to use Kalo Pir's method of talk. "Why did you walk back? Where is Qadir Chacha?" I asked.

"Oh, you know about th-that?" he said, easily distracted. "P-poor Qadir is upset. His horse has b-bolted. He th-thinks that it will c-come back by itself for its evening feed." He sounded distressed. "They've b-been setting fires and f-fighting in town." I knew he must be nervous, because that's when he stuttered most. The town with its court was just fifteen minutes by the gharry, a different world of dusty offices, a red post office with betel-juice spit-marks on the walls, and a market full of angry people pushing one another. Qadir Chacha had told me of different groups of people waving green, red, or saffron flags and fighting each other—and the police. It did not make sense to me and I had not paid attention.

"The c-country is to be split," my father muttered, speaking half to himself, "split between Hindus and M-muslims."

"Like the mud alley-paths between paddy fields?" I asked. I could imagine the whole land like a quilt, split into innumerable countries. "Will we have our own country? Will Qadir Chacha's hut be a different country?"

"Eh?" Then he patted my head, "No, no, not q-quite like that. There's just going to be t-two countries now, I suppose. I wonder what this p-part of the land is going to be."

"You don't know?"

"They have asked an Englishman in a g-great British university to d-draw a line on the map," my father said, appearing close to tears. "If he d-draws the line along the river to the east, then we will b-be in India," he muttered as he shook his head disconsolately, "but if he draws that l-line along the other river to the west, t-twenty miles away, then we will end up in P-pakistan."

"The Englishman knows where we should live?" I was incredulous. "How?"

"How d-do I know if this E-Englishman knows anything at all?" he shouted with sudden vehemence and strode off. "Mind you, you are not to go into t-town at all. You are t-to stay home."

I ran after him. "India or Pakistan—what is the difference?"

My father stopped at the door and slowly turned around. He bent to look me in the eye. "The M-muslims want their own country. They want us g-gone. In other places, Hindus are d-driving away M-muslims. Some people set fire to the c-court building today. No one knows what is g-going to happen. Your m-mother is c-crying. Try not t-to upset her even more."

"After they have their lands, will the Muslims and Hindus become friends again?"

He looked at me without answering immediately. Transferring his court wig to his left hand, he walked through the door. I noticed a bloodstained bandage across his wrist.

"Stay home," he said, and left me.

I could feel my brother's terror. I really needed to go to Kalo Pir and have him explain everything, I decided. My father had no answers that made sense to me.

• • •

QADIR CHACHA HAD not yet returned, though it was well past my bedtime. I dozed off, then sprang up because a light had appeared outside my window. Opening my door, I saw it was the red moon looming over Qadir's hut, and him crouched by the threshold. I ran across the backyard.

"Burak is gone," he said. He had named the knock-kneed creature after the Prophet's flying horse, and gave it lumps of molasses. He wiped his face, twice, as if that would help. When he felt my palm on his shoulder, he wept openly.

*I must see Kalo Pir*, I thought again. The grown-ups at home were either worried or weeping.

"Both sides were shouting and throwing stones," Qadir muttered. "That's how it started. They began to break into shops. I was looking for your baba when someone set fire to the gharry. Poor Burak was still harnessed. He started running in fright, really galloping—which I never thought I'd see. One burning wheel was wobbling from the axle," panted Qadir. "I ran after him, but he was just gone. Oh, where could he be?" He blew his nose. "It is my disgrace that Munsef-babu, your father, came back walking, feet muddy . . . I was waiting in the fields at the edge of town . . . for Burak. Some people torched the courthouse," Qadir said, expecting me to be shocked.

"When did you come back, Qadir Chacha?" I asked.

"An hour ago. I thought Burak might have wandered back to the stable." Qadir's voice was failing. He still held a lump of dry molasses.

"He'll come back. *He*'s not mad," I said.

"Everyone else is," said Qadir, dolefully shaking his head. "There were people with knives and machetes, saying they'd purify this country. It's going to be free of infidels, Hindus, they said. They want to clean the country—and make it *Pak*."

"What is *Pak*?" I said

"*Pak*? It means pure," said Qadir, "They want to make this The Land of the Pure, Pakistan! This will be East Pakistan."

"There is a West one also?" I wished adults could explain better. "Are those for two different kinds of pure people?"

Qadir Chacha, who was chewing on his beard, said miserably, "One-Eyed Rafiq-ud-din the mullah is now in town, threatening that his people were going to make this land so pure that they would even clean the land of unworthy Muslims. What is happening to us, little Baba?" he said, patting my head absentmindedly, "and Burak is gone . . ."

"Who did One-Eyed Rafiq mean when he said unworthy Muslims?" I insisted.

"He says, anyone not a Sunni Muslim—or those who use holy places to speak to everybody, including Hindus." Qadir Chacha spat on the ground. "That Rafiq and his followers harm people, then slander them. They burnt the ricks and rice granaries last autumn, then blamed the Hindus. Now they've joined Rahmat-ul-lah, the Wahhabi."

"What's Wahhabi?" There seemed to be so many groups among grown-ups.

"A Wahhabi is a pure Muslim—he sticks only to the old Arabic teachings, whatever they are—and hates anyone who does not, for they will all go to Jahannam, where all infidels will burn forever, even those who revere tombs of the saints of Islam—everybody except the mullahs and their followers. They were shouting they would confront the pir's disciple by the river and ask him if he is on *their* side. If he is not . . ." Qadir broke off.

"But Qadir Chacha," I said, suddenly fearful, "you said that djinns protect Allah's beloved ones. You said that the pir by the river comforts all human beings, didn't you? *Didn't you?*" He was holding me tight to calm me.

"Qadir Chacha, let's go."

"No, no, no," he whispered, "It is so dark!"

"I know the way," I assured him, adding, "You can ask him about Burak. He's sure to know."

"Your father . . . would not like that . . ." Qadir muttered, ". . . and I . . . I forbid it absolutely," his voice quivering with indecision.

•  •  •

As WE RAN together under the huge red moon, the trees seemed to move about behind us, but we did not dare look back. Qadir Chacha held my palm in a sweaty grip, until I was unsure whether it was to comfort me or to be comforted. "Burak used to be afraid of the full moon," he panted beside me.

I rushed on until I was at the wall crusted with dry creepers. A brick dislodged and fell with a clatter, setting off an indignant nightbird, which cackled and swooped above us. I spied the low doorway to the left. Leaving Qadir Chacha, his hands clapped on his ears under the flying cacophony, followed me as I ducked through the courtyard into the mosque's sanctuary.

Kalo Pir's candles were unlit, but the cloth that covered the old pir's grave was iridescent with curling and dying embers. One or two sparks flew up and were lost in the gloom of the chamber.

*The djinns must be here*, I thought inside my thrumming head.

A charred odour hung in the air. I stepped out of the door and saw a djinn resting on broken cobbles at the far end of the mosque. Under the smudged red moon, the carapace of its wings appeared folded, one over the other. A metallic gleam rose from its midriff like some upright ornament. I moved closer, careful not to wake the still djinn. Overhead, the bird wheeled in a crazy gyre.

"They burned the mazhar," panted Qadir, emerging from the sanctuary behind me. "The Wahhabis desecrated the shrine."

Hands folded over his chest, feet at an impossible angle, eyes open and opaque, his djellaba caked with dry blood, slashed fingers curled around the impacted blade in his chest, lay Kalo Pir.

• • •

THROUGH THE SOILED shadows below the trees we rushed back, Qadir Chacha and I. The grass was heavy with dew, and the old red moon had set. I emerged through the hedges of wild sheora and dhundul behind our bungalow, surprised to see my father sitting beside piles of clothes and books. I thought he would be angry, but a cleft of uncertainty had worked its way onto his forehead, giving him a puzzled look, devoid of authority.

"Kush . . ." he whispered, as if verifying my presence.

"Yes, Baba," I said, longing to tell him where I had been and what I had seen, but he appeared distraught and absentminded.

"Kush," he said again. "Go to your mother. See that she gets everything together, but in just one box."

I had no idea what he was talking about. The first time in my life I was being sent to my mother, and not a word about my nocturnal adventure: Was she worried too? Sushma must have complained about my absence. And what *everything* needed to be packed into one box? Was I being sent away for my truancy? I entered my mother's bedroom and smelt its close odour of mourning, and saw a box, open and half-full. All over the floor lay items of clothing, old photos, smaller boxes. On the bed crouched my mother on all fours while Sushma hovered over her, wringing her hands.

"We have an hour, less," Sushma croaked at me, as if all this were my fault. I glared back at her.

"Why?" I asked my mother. All she did was bury her face in the bedclothes and wail.

"All right, I promise . . ." I began. All this because of a night out without telling her! *What did she care?* Resentment welled in me.

"Son, you need to take a few clothes." My father had come in and stood behind me.

"Why? Why should I go anywhere?" I burst out.

"None of us thought it would c-come to this," he said softly.

If I had to leave, I would! Would they send Qadir Chacha away too? Fine—I thought angrily—I would go with him to his village in Bihar which he had told me about: yellow wheatfields, lychee trees, the small hills nearby. I would leave with him if my father did not want me either. I looked Baba squarely in the eye. "I don't need either of you," I said. "In two more months I will be eight years old."

My father blinked. "What do you m-mean?" he muttered, his palms pointing upward. One of them had a scar, long since healed, though he never told me how he had cut himself, no matter how many times I asked.

"Kush," he said, now kneeling in front of me, face-to-face. "The c-country is broken. There are k-killings everywhere. We have to get to the city, to C-calcutta." He stopped, tentatively reaching for my shoulder.

"A long way? Across the river?"

"Yes," he said. "To the west."

"When will we come back?"

He shook his head in silence.

• • •

IT RAINED ALL night. The bullock cart on which we sat crowded together swayed and squelched in the mud. The plaited bamboo awning above us held in place a piece of tarred canvas, a ragged sari ineffectually draping the back. It was gloomy inside. I could feel the lurch and pull of the wet, muscular beast, wheezing and trundling us over the unfriendly suck of mud below. The rain fell, lulling us under its drone. Ma sat propped with pillows, her back to the wet driver, who had not spoken a word, while Sushma perched beside her, cramped in an angular crouch, snuffling and moaning. Baba and I huddled together where the mattress sloped outside and grew increasingly soggy.

In a trench by the night road, I spied a number of bodies piled over each other. Their stretched limbs looked like firewood, pale and stiff. At the lip of that trench lay a dismembered hand, its index finger stiff and pointing.

I leant out of our cart to see, but Baba pulled me back, roughly for once, drawing the sari closed across the back so Ma would notice nothing. "Hush!" he whispered to me, his hand shaking, his back tense, each time I started to ask him something. He winced everytime he heard the smallest noise, although the dripping rain, the hum of monsoon insects, and the shifting curtains of night hid us as we left our home far behind.

Every couple of hours the bullock would abruptly stop, impervious to the clicking sound the driver made or the blow or two of his switch, while the reek of manure filled our nostrils. Then the beast would choose a green patch and graze, dumb and insistent. The driver sat resigned, quiet as a stork, while the bullock fed. Finally it would urinate copiously, its sulphurous whiff drifting in the wet breeze, and with great reluctance, would pull us out of the placid space and move unhurriedly on, past village after deserted village. If we were fleeing, we were doing so very slowly indeed.

The rain stopped near dawn. When I poked my head out from behind the drying sari curtain, I was greeted by a faint aroma of flowers. Looking up, I saw the last white scattered stars, like jasmine overhead. The bullock stopped yet again, and I waited for the familiar whiff of the beast's offal. But it simply stood. Then I heard the sound of the moving river. Across that was safety. Ma curled asleep, holding close the small box containing all her jewels.

I stood by our belongings stacked under a peepul tree, its branches heavy with the rains that had swept through the land. A hawk flew high, wheeling in slow circles in the clear sky. I wondered if it could tell the difference between where we were headed—which Baba now called "our country"—from the land we were leaving behind, because someone had drawn a line on a map in a far country where it was day when here it was night.

My mother sat on the only suitcase we had, Sushma beside her on the ground, cross-legged. Baba had gone to the hut at the edge of the river. Fishermen lived there, he told us, who could ferry us across the river.

"Will there be a cart to take us from there?" asked Sushma, querulously. I could see a scowl on my father's face, and then he looked sideways and said, "Yes, of course." Mother looked reassured. I realized, for the first time in my life, that he was lying.

My father came back with a brown whip of a man, and between us, we carried everything except Ma's mattress, swollen to twice its girth in the rain.

The fisherman was taciturn. He said his name was Jadab when Baba asked him. "A Hindu name," my father muttered, as if comforted.

The boat was just a dugout with a single oar and a ragged sail, its bottom slippery with mud which gave off a fishy stench. Ma began to complain, but at the sight of the groaning river on which torn branches swept along by the slap and tug of water, she fell silent. Sushma looked with great disapproval at the boat, but kept her own counsel.

My father steadied Sushma into the boat. I scrambled up the side and almost lost my foothold, but Jadab caught me in a sure grip and hoisted me in. Baba cradled my mother carefully in his arms and sat her on the side of the boat, quickly clambering in behind her. My mother had swaddled her small box in a shawl and clung to it.

"Do not lean over the water," Baba said anxiously to me, as Jadab shoved off from the shore, but I leant over the swift cobalt water anyway, drawn by its forbidding depth. The fisherman stood at the stern, grasping the shoulder-high oar, his muscles taut and slippery over his hard bones, as he propelled and guided the boat, his eyes slits as he faced the salty wind. The bank, with its large peepul tree beneath which we had sat, receded fast.

"Calcutta?" Jadab asked.

"Yes," nodded my father.

Jadab paused at his oar and towelled his face with his gamccha, which he then tied about his waist. "Two days' walk," he said, pointing at the approaching shore. "One, if you have a cart."

"Where can I get one?"

"You want a cart?"

Father nodded again.

"I'll get someone," said Jadab, pausing to scratch his neck, "but he will not take money. A piece of jewellery." My mother clutched the box under her shawl. Jadab turned his head, as if checking the horizon.

Some trees which grew at the edge of the shore perched on

spidery legs. "Mangroves," my father pointed out. "That means the sea is not very far away."

"An hour," said Jadab, pointing downriver.

As the boat nosed into the muddy headland, I jumped down with the large suitcase, sprawling in the gum-like mud of what was to become India. I struggled quite ineffectually to stand up.

Sushma hunched at the back of the boat, her nose wrinkled with distaste at the mud on the shore. Baba climbed down and held out his hands for Ma, but my mother, hugging her shawl-swaddled box, looked around for some other way.

Swiftly, with one hand, Jadab snatched at the box. Ma cried out as her shawl unraveled, and the box clattered onto the deck. As she leant to retrieve it, Jadab lifted his oar and hit her sidewise, and she plunged screaming into the shallow water. With practiced speed, Jadab thrust the length of the oar into the bank and pushed. The boat rocked and teetered.

I was stuck in the mud, the suitcase beside me, while Baba was stranded, up to his knees in the same muddy bank. Sushma screeched, perched on the boat, trying to retrieve the jewel box from its stinking bottom. As the lurching boat angled away from the shore, Jadab raised his oar and thrust it again in the water. One more heave and he would catch the swift current, and the boat would be away. I watched as he dipped the oar and rose with it, his rope-like muscles glistening in the early sun.

My father raised something he had fished out from under the waistfold of his kurta. He held it out slowly, like a sleepwalker, less than a man's length from the swerving boat. At the sharp report, birds on the mangroves squawked and rose in a body. Jadab's head snapped back as he fell in a heap, his oar falling on the deck with a *clunk*, next to the jewel box.

The current caught the boat in its powerful tug, pulling it sharply downstream, where it rotated out of reach, gathering speed. My father tried to wade out, but by the time he had struggled up, the boat was out of reach. In his frustration, he threw what he held in his hand after it, slipping and falling to his knees in the mud. Sushma was standing now, balanced precariously on the boat, clutching the jewel box she had retrieved, her mouth distended in a scream. We could not hear her over the howls of my mother, thrashing in the water, crying out for her jewels as the boat spun downstream towards the ocean.

I thought I saw my brother Laub's arm raised helplessly above the lip of the lost boat.

• • •

WE WALKED NUMBLY through the countryside. All I remember was my father plodding ahead, his muddy shoes in front of me. More and more feet joined ours on that hypnotic march, a great and growing stream of the ragged and exhausted, flowing towards Calcutta. We walked doggedly, weighed down with fatigue and bags. We stopped when my mother would cry out in weariness, then sat or lay listlessly under the roadside banyans, tamarinds, and barren mango trees, and when evening came, we ate what little puffed rice Baba had brought. On the second day, I remember the milestones on the side of the road, little tombstones with diminishing numbers printed on them. I stared at the asphalt, fissured like unending maps, until daylight faded into black. We were going slower and slower because Ma was exhausted. We slept under a tree, our hunger turned into a hum of pain. I knew Baba could not help. On the morning of the third day, with no words but just a sip of water which Baba had saved for us, we were on the road again.

When I looked up a couple of hours later, with the sun high, my head swimming with weariness, I suddenly saw the city all around me. Underfoot, the macadam was cut open by curved tram tracks, while overhead spread spiderwebs of tram cables and electric lines. Writing covered everything: billboards, walls, shops. There had been little to read in our village landscape; but here, the insistent script named everything. Even the trams which trundled past us like small steamers were smothered in print. My mother and I followed Baba into narrow lanes until he walked into a dilapidated house and up a staircase and knocked on a door. During the interminable bargaining among grown-ups, I curled up on the dusty red of the cement landing and fell into a deep sleep.

When I woke in an unfamiliar room, I could not, for a moment, remember who I was, or where. The room was dim, airless, with a single barred window whose ledge was green with sunless moss. I lay on one of mother's old saris, in lieu of bedsheets.

"I'll g-go to Mr. Aherne," I heard my father whispering to my mother, "t-to the P-police Headquarters. I knew h-him once." He looked about for a comb, but not finding one, he used his fingers. "He'll h-help us."

He returned late in the afternoon, stooped with disappointment and fatigue. "I c-could not find him. He has long l-left the p-police," Baba mumbled, "and they are too busy for my questions." He took his shoes off. He had no socks, and his blisters were bleeding.

I realized that this rented room was where we were to stay. In the morning I ate what Baba cooked ineptly on a bucket-oven on the landing. His gold ancestral signet ring was missing from his finger.

"I will go look for work now," he said to us as we ate.

Until early afternoon, I sat in blind boredom. Then, just to test matters, I asked my mother if she wanted some water. She turned her back to me and curled up tighter. I went outside and sat on the stair landing, waiting for Baba. I was thirsty, but past caring. A cat skittered up the stairs. When I stretched out my hand, it sniffed my fingers, then went past me to a frayed mat at the bottom of the stairs and sat cleaning itself. I watched it hold its hind leg up, like the picture I had once seen of a musician holding his cello. I heard something behind me, and turned, thinking, *It is Laub!* My mother stood holding out a glass of water, and I took it from her, unable to say a word. She returned to the bed. I came and stood by her and drank half of the water.

"Are you thirsty, Ma?" I asked.

She nodded gravely. I gave her my glass to hold, and was about to fetch her a fresh one, when she lifted it to her lips and drained it. She lay down on the bed. Her face was unusually flushed, and a vein pulsed under her forehead and hid itself in her long, unkempt hair, which spooled over the pillow.

"Come to me, Laub," she said. Without a word I lay down beside her and closed my eyes. I could smell the musky odour of her hair, and realized I was lying upon it. I kept my eyes closed and felt her fold me in her arms.

I woke up to a commotion in our room. There were strangers in our small space. I came to know them later: Tewari-babu, who lived next door, and owned the stationery store at the end of our lane, and his wife, Shanta-Auntyji, were leaning over the bed, alongside Baba, who looked dazed. With them was Dr. Gupta, a local homeopath, under the sole electric bulb that hung from our ceiling.

"No pulse, no pulse," he muttered, shaking his sweating head, "Big stroke she had, Mitra-ji. Nothing to do now. All over." The bed was wet, for they had poured water on my mother's pale and bony face. The men gathered by the window, talking. I slid over to my mother, putting my mouth next to her ear.

"Laub has left," I told her, reaching to touch her face. "Ma, I am Kush." I was shocked how cold she was.

• • •

I ACCOMPANIED BABA to Nimtollah Ghat on the Ganges, where Tewari-babu, his grown sons, Manoj and Saroj, and some of their friends had carried Ma, lying on a flimsy wooden bier, upon their shoulders. Now she lay on a bed of logs, by the river, her hair hanging down to touch the ground. On her, they had heaped splinters of wood and kindling, around which circled the chanting priest swathed in an ochre shawl covered with Sanskrit writing. Baba said these were the hundred and eight sacred names of Lord Krishna.

The priest poured ghee over the wood, and on Ma, then lit a twig and handed it to me. I held it, not knowing what was expected of me. He daubed Ma with more ghee till her face glistened in the sun. Her eyes were not completely shut, as if she was about to wake.

"Hold the flame to her face," directed the priest.

I shook my head. *Nononono.*

"Do it, boy," he said, beginning to lose his patience.

"Ma spoke to me." I wanted to touch Ma's face, sure that

she was now warmed by the sun, when I felt Baba stay my hand.

"This is something a son has to d-do," he pleaded. "Can you d-do it for your m-mother?"

I flung the sputtering twig, barely missing the priest. The river-water glistened, sending a shaft of light that burned my eyes.

"I will d-do it for you, Kush," my father said, so softly that I almost imagined he had said it. "Go lie down under that t-tree there. Son, you d-do not have to see any of this."

"Are *you* supposed to do this? Are we supposed to do any of this?" I pleaded.

"I d-don't know, Kush. But these are our r-rites, given to us by our f-fathers."

I lay down under the tree, facing away from the sacred river, the burning pyre. I closed my eyes. I clasped my palms over my ears, but I could still hear the hiss and crackle of the growing fire.

• • •

MY HEAD FELT unfamiliar when I touched it the following morning. It had been shaven, according to custom, after which I had accompanied Baba into waist-deep water to consign Ma's ashes to the Ganges. We had repeated unfamiliar Sanskrit prayers after the priest. *I don't understand these words. And neither will Ma,* I thought.

With Tewari-ji's help, Baba found a job in a shop at Burra-bazaar, keeping numbers in a ledger, no longer an employee with a comfortable salary in the state judiciary, for that state was no longer a part of dismembered India. He was too tired to explain any more. We ate two meals everyday, one early in the morning before Baba left for work, and the other past nightfall, after he trudged home.

When I was enrolled in a local free school, the few boys who took any notice of me smacked my shaven head because it amused them. Then they discovered where we had come from and derisively called me Refugee, as if it were my name. I learned quickly how to remain unobtrusive, never drawing attention to myself if I could help it. I walked to school and back on my own.

In Jessore I used to be an explorer with my brother, Laub, and had found the lost mosque and Kalo Pir. I was a different boy now, in a different place.

I made friends with numbers because I could count on them. I poured my attention onto the precision, the reliability of numbers, arranging them carefully in this changeful world. Prime numbers were my favourites, for nothing and no one could divide them. After Ma, we had been reduced from three to two. Two is a divisible number, very vulnerable. I longed for us to be three; I wanted Laub to return to me, but he did not.

•  •  •

I FINISHED SCHOOL, then college, unsure what one did after studies. I wanted only to deal with numbers, mainly because I was not sure what to say to other human beings.

In the midst of general political turmoil, I completed my Master's degree in Mathematics, and though I scored among the highest marks, there were no jobs to be had. I wanted to teach at a college, but had only the prospect of keeping ledgers at the shop in Burrabazaar. My usually pliant father bitterly opposed this eventuality.

"N-no, and no a-again," he declared to our peeling ceiling.

I took up private tuitions for meager sums, training the bored and the hopeless in simple algebra and trigonometry for their exams. Baba continued to fill out application forms on my behalf, single-mindedly submitting them to various academic and government authorities. I watched him, an accomplice in futility. I would be called to the occasional and perfunctory interview, waiting for hours in forlorn corridors. Nothing came of them. After months of these, I mentioned the ledgers again, so I could ease his financial burden.

"Wh-what!" he glared, this time six inches from my startled eyes.

I continued with my tuitions. Two years later, the impossible happened. A letter appointing me junior lecturer of Mathematics to the local branch of City College arrived one afternoon; I barely remembered the long-ago interview. I was to start in seven weeks.

I asked Baba to quit his job by the end of the year, but he had a fear of change, even if it meant respite from his daily drudgery. He took down the old biscuit tin from its ledge, emptied his small rupee hoard on his bed.

"You must get new glasses, Professor Kush," he said, counting out the few notes.

"I will," I countered, "if you buy a new pair too."

Baba was accustomed to holding his newspaper close, as if he wanted to wrap his balding head in the newsprint. His eyeglasses dated from the time he was a civil court employee. Like the British Empire, his eyeglasses had come apart, but unlike the Empire, he had held the pieces together, with tape, which he occasionally replaced with his usual care.

For me too, anything more than a few yards away became vague shapes whose colours and edges melted into each other: buildings, approaching red buses, tramcars, swerving automobiles. I had serendipitously, miraculously, survived swift bicycles and the sudden rickshaws.

"We have money for only t-two lenses," he said firmly, "and we can hardly b-buy m-monocles."

"Then let me buy new glasses for both of us when I get paid."

• • •

I WENT TO look at the formidable redbrick building with its labyrinth of crowded corridors. "I am to teach here in two months' time," I marveled in the hot afternoon.

Instead of walking back, I decided to take the tram in anticipation of my elevation from penury. Its trundling gait and rhythmic clicks induced a half-sleep, and I had almost dozed off in the aisle of the packed tramcar. Suddenly we jolted to a stop. Hemmed in by the crush of bodies, I could see little, but heard angry slogans, wailing police cars, and the rumbling of Black Marias.

The crowd was hurling stones prised from the pavements. These thudded upon passing vehicles, including our tramcar, when I heard sharp reports of gunfire. A young woman next to me crumpled silently. The rest of us huddled on the shard-littered floor. Through a jagged pane, smoke stinging my eyes, I spied khaki-clad police kneeling and firing at demonstrators.

*I must get out,* I thought in panic, crowded next to the window, but was unable to move in the packed compartment. Someone threw a bottle, its mouth stoppered by a burning rag, and the rear of the tramcar whooshed into flame, singeing my face and eyelashes as I joined the stampede to escape. Momentarily blinded, I found myself at the tramcar gate, and leaping clear, fell hard on the asphalt. In a red mist, I crawled to the far end of the sidewalk, where I lay shaking in pain, watching the tramcar as raging flames climbed charred metal. The street had become preternaturally quiet. Amid the scattered pieces of paving stones stretched two young men. I could see the dark punctures of their bullet wounds.

*I need,* I urged myself, *I need to reach the Medical College Hospital.* It was a small distance away. I have no memory of when they put my arm in a cast, or who stitched my forehead. I kept passing in and out of consciousness.

My frantic father searched for me in city hospital after hospital till he found me. He brought me home on a stolen bamboo *tthela*-cart, used by small shops to deliver dry goods, for no other vehicles could be found on the streets on this day and night of chaos.

Through the deserted streets, Baba, who had never dreamt of stealing anything, transported me, weeping loudly in relief

• • •

I STAYED AT home healing in the next weeks while my father cooked me boiled barley, which he insisted was nutritious. I tried to distract him by asking him to read me the newspapers. Entire neighbourhoods of Calcutta—Kasba, Ariadaha, and slums like Phulbagan with its warren of lanes—had become free zones without police control, my father read out to me. Low-ranking policemen, like traffic constables, were often ambushed by Red Guard–style teenagers who wielded knives, iron rods, or bicycle chains, and snatched their service revolvers and guns for further guerilla-like attacks.

After six weeks my arm had healed, and the cast was taken off, but my elbow still felt stiff and tender. I did not tell Baba, for he would fret, and I just wanted to go to work.

The days and nights now changed the city into two very different places. During the frequent power cuts in the smog-ridden city, police prowled about in the dark, surrounding this or that area in "combing operations," nabbing young people indiscriminately, hauling them off in their Black Marias. Baba read out newspaper reports that after days of beatings and the occasional rape in jail, selected detainees were taken before dawn to the deserted fields of the Maidan and told to get out and run. Then they were fired upon, supposedly killed in encounters with the valiant police. This last had been the brain-child of a handsome politician who seldom failed to point out to journalists his resemblance to Gregory Peck.

Meanwhile, professing undying faith and piety in dialectical materialism, some local goons had a field day collecting protection money. Within twenty years of Independence, one student group dubbed themselves Marxist-Leninist—a name recalling marriages between Hindu deities, I thought. They had declared Mao their spiritual leader, asserting that Indian independence was a sham. They flaunted lists of their future targets on the wall, calling them class enemies, crossing off names as they were killed, but not always in the order listed, spreading further confusion. India was no country, they declared, and the parliament was a pigsty. Students fought with the police—and most vigorously—among themselves. Through all this my father and I went warily to work, never knowing when the the next rush of violence would trample us underfoot.

"I h-hope th-there are no more b-break-ups," my father mumbled apprehensively. "But then, what is a n-nation? Who d-decides?" I thought about his remark, between reading chapters in a book on the mathematics of Chaos Theory.

"Wh-where would we g-go again, Kush?" said my father, completely at a loss.

In this turmoil, starving villagers were beginning to show up in the city in bewildering numbers, cadaverous, virtually naked, swarming onto railway platforms, begging in straggling groups by roadsides and lanes. Out of our one window, for the first time, I now saw rows of beggars on the pavement, their pathetic squabbles, evening domestic fires, their routine roadside defecations. Three days before my twenty-fifth birthday, we woke to a newborn's mewling—while the crows fought and cawed over the discarded placenta.

• • •

ONE LATE AFTERNOON when I returned to our room from my day's teaching, I found my father hunched over his bed, examining something minutely.

"Bedbugs?" I asked in alarm.

"Eh?" Baba was startled. "No, n-no," he declared, regaining his bearing. "B-barisal," he said tenderly, "Our ancestral house. In Barisal. East Pakistan now. The one that is gone forever."

I saw now what he had been doing. On his frayed bedcover he had spread out a wide rectangle of paper. "Handmade paper from China Bazaar!" Baba whispered, as if it were a secret. On this creamy sheet, smooth as alabaster, he was making a sketch of a mansion. It had a semicircular driveway with a covered portico, spacious enough for a horse-drawn carriage. The graceful space was supported by pillars with an Oriental design similar to Corinthian columns. Three wide steps led up to a sweep of verandah which stretched along the entire edifice, and above these was a circular dome, on four sides of which peeped cupolas. A vast peepul tree cast a sepia shadow across the arched entrance.

I leant over the bed, my head next to his, silent in admiration.

Drawn in jet-black India ink, the walls and doorways were so vivid that I felt I could enter the palace. I had no idea he could draw so well.

"I was born here," my father recounted. "My grandfather Ramkumar Mitra raised me after my parents died very young of the influenza. It was built long ago by our ancestors. My great-grandfather Baboo Doorgadass Mitra was a merchant prince. He lived here when he was not in Calcutta or Rangoon doing business with the English, the Dutch, and the Burmese. He had been a friend of Prince Dwarkanath Tagore, the poet Rabindranath's grandfather, who had gone to Europe and was received by Queen Victoria and her nobles. There he met Charles Dickens, and even that old Irish rebel Daniel O'Connell, then out of prison, but broken by years. By the time I was born, just before the First World War, Doorgadass was long dead. The house had fallen into disrepair, and a part of the dome had been damaged by the cyclone of 1876. Cracks appeared along the roof and the walls. It was falling apart, like the country did later." My father's stutter was momentarily gone.

Over the next few weeks, my father laboured over it, forgetful of time, fading light, or mealtimes. He paused only during the frequent power cuts. Even in the gloom, he would sit beside the sketch, his hand upon it, as if it would otherwise disappear. The smudges from his palm became part of the picture, as if his presence had seeped into its texture. One day I found him using not India ink, but paint, upon the pillars, unexpected crimsons and blues that were faded and flaked. The house aged before our eyes. And then, he stopped. He put the picture away, sighing as if from the exhaustion of leaving it.

I missed seeing my father work on the picture. When I tried to raise the topic, he shook his head slowly, as if he had been asked to account for a dream he had had.

"It is over," he whispered. "N-nothing more."

With my father's permission, which he gave absentmindedly, I got a frame for it, a cheap black one, and hung it on our wall. Regretfully, I thought it looked like a black-bordered Hindu obituary notice, but it would be too expensive to try to find some other frame.

• • •

MY FATHER STILL used the old bucket-oven on which he daily boiled rice and lentils, attempting simple curries, often confusing spices, producing barely edible results. Baba himself ate little, treating the food as a matter of disputation between what was left of his teeth and what was on his plate. Out of expediency, he had begun to drink milk when hungry, supplemented with an occasional handful of puffed rice, but he still insisted on cooking for me, stubbornly refusing to allow me near the open flame.

One evening he sat across from me and confided, "Other than you, Kush, I d-depend only on c-cows." I did not quite know how to respond to his deeply felt sentiment.

But then came days when the cows let him down. More and more, he felt an acidulous rebellion in his belly. He now referred to his belly as a colonial nation where he had to send punitive taxes. "It is b-bloated and rancid," he declared, and the sour urge to vomit obsessed him.

He used to worry about his eyes, his throat, his sinuses, the first creaks of arthritis far more than he had ever fretted about his stomach; this simple pouch he filled with unremarkable supplies every day. An abstemious man, he was incapable of ill-treating that demanding cavity with spicy or oily foods. He tried to make do with less and less, but a gauziness affected his vision in spite of his new eyeglasses.

"Something is t-tap-tapping here," he said, pointing at his chest. "What if some small o-organ has c-come loose, knocking a-about to find where it belongs?" His pupils bulged behind his new glasses.

Late one night, he struggled up from his bed, crept to our one window, and flung it open. Half-awake, I saw him feeling about for the familiar bulge of the clay water pitcher with the upturned glass on its spout, but his limbs had turned disobedient. Reluctant to wake me, he waved his hands about to locate the pitcher, overturning it. The floor was soaking wet amid shattered earthenware.

Startled by the sound, I switched on the light to see him struggling up, clawing the wall with wet fingers, and reaching for the blur of the pillared house. The picture fell with a crash, and my father slid to the floor beside the broken globe of the pitcher and the shards of glass hanging off the tilted mansion.

"Wh-where is Robert Aherne?" he wheezed at me. "T-tell Mr. Aherne I threw his g-gun away." His pupils looked like enormous.

"I h-have to t-tell you s-something," he said emphatically. "I am n-not Monimoy!" I looked at him in panic.

"Just lie back, Baba. It's me—Kush," I said with as much calm as I could muster.

"I am n-not Monimoy," repeated Baba querulously, gasping for breath and trying to get up. I tried to make him lie down, pushing his shoulders, firmly and gently. "Try to rest, Baba," I pleaded.

"Don't tell T-tegart," he rasped urgently, "I am not Monimoy. D-do you understand? Only Robert Aherne knows."

He lay still for a while, then grew agitated again. "Kush," he called out, "Kush!"

"Yes, Baba?"

"I am m-my brother," said my father.

"Baba, who is Robert Aherne?" I said. "Are you having a nightmare?"

"Tell him!" said my father firmly, "G-guns are no use at all. Tell Robert."

I waited for his agitation to cease. It did. It was a few minutes before I realized that he was not breathing anymore.

● ● ●

ALONE NOW, I forgot to eat as often as I remembered. It seemed bizarre to me that I needed to repeat the action of eating each day. I did boil some rice and vegetables for myself, when absolutely necessary.

A month after my father's death, in the middle of a lecture on finite integers, I looked at my students, and chalk in hand, in mid-sentence, realized that I had completely forgotten to eat since the day before. I felt lightheaded, almost joyous. At this instant, there rose a sound of angry shouting at the end of the corridor—screaming, scuffling, and swearing—and all the students rushed out of the classroom to see what was happening.

Most outer walls of the college building had been painted over with slogans. Red handwritten posters were sloppily pasted along the entire length of the dirty corridors, on stairwells, and even on notice boards. One student group proclaimed that China's Chairman was their Chairman. Another group deemed this a betrayal of Mother India, unpatriotic and pathetic.

Just now someone had been caught tearing a Maoist poster— or had been arbitrarily accused of the act—and a fight was in progress.

As the rampaging circle of students suddenly broke formation, I saw someone flung upon the ground, crouched and shielding his head. I caught a glimpse of the man, his mouth twisted, bloody. Niren Ghosh, a senior man from the History department.

Niren-babu had been one of the few professors who noticed me in the college staff room as I entered awkwardly on my very first day.

"New?" he had said to me. "Brand-new?" He was thoroughly amused by my reticence. "Sit down, young man. You are a teacher, so you *can* sit here. You see that lazy fellow in the khaki shirt? That's Sridhar, a fourth-class employee. He can barely sign his name, but he is a great admirer of Karl Marx. He will get you a cup of tea— for money, of course. Drink only black tea. Never trust the milk. That is the most important thing I've learnt in my twenty-three years of teaching here." I ordered the black tea. Some weeks later, when Niren Ghosh was not there, I had a cup of the tea with milk. Ghosh was dead right, I decided immediately.

And here was Ghosh, on all fours, trying to escape like a beaten dog through the legs of the students who were jostling each other to land a blow or a kick. With no idea that I was about to do so, I flung myself on the circle of students. Thwarted by the heaving wall of bodies, I promptly lost my footing and fell on my back. Frantically, I tried to retrieve my new glasses before someone trampled them. I picked them up from beside the spit-smeared wall and put them on, but one of the arms was bent. On my knees in the dusty corridor, I tried to adjust it when Ghosh's sharp cry instantly brought me back to the present: A student had twisted Niren-babu's arm behind him, pushing it up while the professor screamed in distress.

The jubilant young man was chanting with religious fervour, "Chairman Mao is our Chairman!" His friends chortled with pleasure and chorused, "Smash the black hand of revisionists who tear our posters." After a final kick which had the air of an after-thought, they left the professor on the ground, their jubilant voices ringing out as they thudded down the corridor, "Red Guard Zindabad! Long Live the Red Book."

Niren Ghosh lay on the floor, his face bleeding, his shirt tattered. Gently I raised his head to my lap as I squatted on the filthy corridor.

"Shame on you," hissed Niren Ghosh. "You did not defend me," he mumbled thickly.

"Ghosh-sir," I protested, "look, my glasses . . ."

"You're here to gloat." Niren Ghosh was weeping now. "And now you will go to the staff room and tell everyone about this. Over tea." Then he spat at me.

I was aghast. "I . . ." I began, as Ghosh slowly rose to his knees. I stretched my hands to help the professor. Groaning, he twisted his body away from me and, in obvious pain, began to shuffle away. I noticed the wet stain spreading on the beige trousers of my senior colleague, the moist imprint of his torn sandal on the dusty corridor, and decided that it would be more seemly not to let the older man know that I had witnessed this last sign of humiliation.

I waited for a few minutes, and then left by the rear staircase. From the side lane, I could hear another fight in progress at the main gate of the college. I knew that the fight would spill into the neighbouring streets. Local political parties would step in with their goons; passersby would be beaten up or pelted with stones, or have exploding soda-water bottles thrown at them, and bags snatched. I stepped down the stairwell, away from the fracas, and began walking home.

I suddenly remembered how hungry I had felt in the classroom and bought some roasted peanuts from a roadside vendor, eating hurriedly, barely tasting what I chewed. On an impulse, I studied the piece of paper they were wrapped in, a scrap torn out of some book. Smoothing it, I read the only part still legible:

> *Why should not you*
> *Who know it all ring at his door, and speak?*
> *Just truth enough to show that his whole life*
> *Will scarcely find for him a broken crust*
> *Of all those truths that are your daily bread*

I looked up to scrutinize the sky, which seemed to be made of broken pieces of glass. The roar of the city bore down upon me. A tram turning in its curved track made a cutter's screech, blade meeting whirling whetstone. I walked aimlessly into smaller and smaller by-lanes, until I was exhausted, swallowed into the hushed interior of the city. The only sound came from the babble of a news report on a radio left on a windowsill and the conspiratorial cawing of local crows. *What have I to do with this place?* I thought. *Where do I belong?* I contemplated the constancy of prime integers. I yearned for some far corner of Earth that was a Republic of Mathematics.

In the oppressive midday heat, I sat down footsore and lost on the worn steps of a house that had clearly once been prosperous. The steps were marble, stained through decades of neglect, and the wide entrance revealed an inner courtyard, at the centre of which stood a broken altar. Under it, a stray dog lay curled up with a knock-kneed puppy, probably the only survivor of its brood.

On a step, still tepid from the daylong sun, I found part of another soiled page, which I picked up, expecting another inscrutable message. The rumpled once-glossy black-and-white photograph revealed a broad classical building with a round columned tower above it. I could faintly discern some writing on the frieze under a dome. I squinted to read the faint print. *Euclid, Aristotle, Pythagoras* . . . The other names were smothered under snow. I carefully deciphered the soiled text:

on the edge of Lake Ontario, one of the largest inland lakes in the northern hemisphere, this University in New York State houses distinguished departments of the Sciences and the Arts. Although one has to contend with formidable winters, the summer flower gardens and the autumn landscape are spectacular. All year round, concerts are held under the aegis of its own Eastman School of Music

I thought of the bungalow where I had lived as a child, its unkempt garden and the bamboo grove at the back, thick and green in the swaying heat. With the sharp clarity of loss, I recalled the hidden mosque, my lost brother, Baba, and the dead pir. When I came back from my reverie, I saw about myself the filthy stones of the city lane, the walls stained brown with spat betel juice. Above, in red strident letters, slogans screamed at me: THIS Is NOT Our Homeland! and This Is the Decade of Liberation.

I shut my eyes in exhaustion. I wondered if Professor Ghosh had been able to get a rickshaw, for he had been in no condition to walk. A single violin had begun to play in my head. I knew it at once, this beautiful and dreadful prelude that would sweep me into the strange country of a blinding headache, leaving me immobile for two days or three. The thin dog skittered past me, its puppy held in its mouth, back into the angry city. After a long time, I folded this second scrap of paper with the message, and put it away carefully as an idea started to seed and grow inside me.

I needed to find my way to a land lost in snow, where there was a belltower on which were carved the names of Euclid and Pythagoras and all their shining, visionary company.

Trudging home in the haze of heat, under layers of dust beginning to settle on the grimy leaves of pavement trees, peepuls, neems, and tired deodars, I climbed the broken slabs of the red cement stairs and opened the door to my room, where I smoothed the picture of the domed building and studied it. I took out a clean sheet of paper and, laying them both on the table, side by side, I cradled my head between my palms, holding my headache at bay, willing myself not to sink into bed. I peered close, reading again those famous names. Feeling tied to an enormous weight, I leant forward with effort and started my letter:

*Dear Professor . . .*

Someone, continents away, would open and read me. I slumped, the writing done, my arms stretched out on the table in submission. There was nothing more I could do now. I would post the letter when I could. My headache was a hum around me, the room dwindling away.

"I'll take this picture of the house I have never seen—to that house I have only seen in a picture," I said to myself, and fell on my bed and sank fast asleep.

# Kush
## Rochester, Upstate New York

In the middle of a seminar, someone was reading a paper, occasionally writing on the blackboard. Engrossed in the complex calculations, I had been making notes for later clarification. Drawn into the intricate logic and linking of numbers, my mind rapt in the architecture of the equations which were suspended over my consciousness like an ethereal solar system, a mobile of balanced splendours, I felt open to some revelation.

Looking up, I was amazed to see the windows white in a way I had never seen before. So this was snow! I rose like a sleepwalker, leaving my notebook open, my fountain pen forgotten, and left the room.

I found myself in front of Rush Rhees Library, which seemed to float in space. A distant violin began in my head, joined slowly by a delicately plucked santoor. But I knew this to be different—not the familiar violin which was a prelude to pain. Underfoot, the world had turned white, and all about me the light had been trimmed cerulean by a careful and mysterious brush. This world was silent, on tiptoe. What should I name it, I wondered, remembering how Laub and I would make up phrases in English, our secret language: *a slink of foxes, a stir of ants.*

I opened my eyes, my mouth, slowly. Before and during the rain, it smells of the earth. Before and during snow, I decided, it smells of the sky. *A flight of snow, Laub, we'll call it a flight of snow.* It was the first time in many years I had spoken to my brother. In all this time, his loss was a phantom pain, familiar in my chest, my missing rib.

Snow stirred and floated in the pantomime of a cataract which poured over me. I remembered that each minute snowflake was like no other: Like individual numbers, I thought, enthralled. I walked on blindly into the billow, this eternity, into the innumerable white numbers, walking on them, breathing and smelling them. The numbers possessed the great elms, the tented pines, the smothered maples, and transformed the pillared buildings into receptacles of all the numbers of infinity, as they swirled down on this new earth.

Behind me, my footsteps were smoothed under fresh snowflakes as I walked. I am *Shunya—shunya* itself, I thrilled. With a shiver of delight, I remembered that *shunyata*, the Sanskrit word for *emptiness*—the empty vessel of the mind—was also the word *shunya* used by everyone in India, too casually, to denote the Mathematical Zero. But here I was, held in this evanescent *shunyata*. I let my mind become the zero underlying the white plenitude of all the snowflakes dancing around me. I suddenly understood: Even the existence of a single snowflake—or all the snowflakes—upon the *shunyata* of my mind denoted mathematical Infinity!

$\frac{1}{0}, \frac{9}{0}, \frac{1000000000000}{0}, \frac{\infty}{0}$ were all Infinity, the supreme supine helix, a sleeping Buddha, the $\infty$ endlessly closed upon itself. In this swirl of snowflakes, I wondered how I could bear to live with the thrill of this moment for the rest of my life, through all those uncounted ordinary days that lay before me.

I closed my eyes, feeling tears down my cheeks, and in the white, blind world around me, an intimate presence. Shutting my eyes, I held out my hands, palms outstretched, and stood still, absolutely still, to hear that voice better. *Is that you, Laub?* I whispered. *Laub,* I called from behind the darkness of my closed eyes. *Laub, is that you?*

When I opened my eyes, I saw my empty palms fill with snow-flakes, ashes from some celestial heatless fire. In the middle of the quadrangle, I did not turn my head, for to do so would have been a breach of profound trust. I knew there had been a second set of footprints, twin to my own, rapidly covered and kept secret by the torrent of falling numbers.

• • •

HEADING AWAY FROM the wide quadrangle in front of Morey Hall, I took the steps past the pillared auditorium, to the river, its black water beginning to yield to the pale traces of sky. I lingered by the small interfaith chapel perched above the wintry river, turning finally towards home.

Soon I reached my tiny apartment by the canal, near the curve of the Genessee River in the blue rumour of light. At the kitchen window, hungry, I was unable to bring myself to break the perfect whiteness of an egg I held in my palm. Outside, the last edges of the world were turning white before my eyes. I felt inexplicably comforted by the soft wax and moulding of snow that fell, and fell, and fell all about and within me. Lying on my narrow bed beside my curtainless window, I noticed the immaculate ceiling.

Waking up some hours later, I looked out of the window and saw that it was still night, but it felt as if I had levitated. The low azalea bushes had turned into a row of sleeping sheep. A diaphanous glow tilted up into the room. I felt lightheaded with hunger. On the kitchen counter, I found the egg which I had not broken. There was nothing else to eat. I opened my fridge and watched a small mist wisped out from its empty lit interior.

Then I remembered. Wandering the aisles one late night at Wegman's, a vast store lit like an ocean liner, not knowing what to buy until I had been confronted by a vast number of identical tin cans on which were pictures of batter-fried chicken; I had picked one of these unnaturally heavy cans and gone to the counter.

For weeks I had been living off cardboard containers of soup. Sometimes I boiled noodles, and dumping them into the soup, ate from a large cereal bowl, draining the last of the soup by tilting the bowl with both hands. Then I would make tea, relieved that I would not have to think about hunger for another day, and sit at my bare table to immerse myself in my books.

But tonight—was it still night?—I was troubled by a strange appetite. I took the can out, picturing the meat inside. I did not own a can opener, so I got out my lone knife, braced the can on the kitchen table, and wedged the thin end of the knife into the top edge of the tin circumference. Then I hit it with my heaviest book, a hardcover Oxford University Press tome on mathematical logic. It worked. The knife cracked through the top and sank into what seemed to be Vaseline. I moved the knife, poised for the next mathematical blow. The crack widened. I was pleased with my ingenuity. After making a circular gash of a few inches, I prised open a corner. All I could see within was an oily slosh, like melted soap.

I carried the can to the sink and began shaking out the contents. I studied the side of the can again, a close-up of perfect fried chicken, breaded and toothsome. Then I read what was written on its side: *Crisco*. Vegetable shortening.

I had no idea what "shortening" was, but understood that all I had to eat in this hungry winter dawn was a can of whitish frying medium. I lit the stove, poured out some of the ooze, cracked the solitary egg, and ate it straight off the pan. But my body was still full of hunger, as if a zest for life had woken inside me and would not be denied.

So out I went, plodding through the knee-high snow, muffled in my thin anorak, mittened hands stretched out for balance. The sky had cleared, and a small bent moon hung overhead. So did a variety of floodlights over white-quilted parking lots near the hospital. I waded alone down Crittenden Boulevard. The parking lots ended; so did the lights. Apart from my plumed breath, it was silent. The houses huddled together, and the end of the road was lost in a milky darkness.

Then I saw them, a group of slender deer gathered at an intersection far beyond, their delicate brown fetlocks kicking up powdery snow. The world belonged to them as they crossed the broad white avenue, towards the large, hilly cemetery beyond it. Aureoles of light above the avenue magically changed hues, red, amber and green and back again, reflected in the drifts of snow.

Just as I reached the store, I realized I had forgotten my wallet, and began to laugh. It was a laughter that shook the plinth of all my sorrow and I felt some great weight falling off me. I shivered with pleasure and cold.

That is how my future wife first saw me.

Having finished her gruelling medical intern's shift of close to thirty-six hours, she had gone straight from the hospital's pediatrics ward on the fourth floor to the supermarket, bought groceries from her neat list, and returned to her car in the deserted parking lot. But Dr. Seetha Rathnam's temperamental car would not start. She pumped the accelerator several times in irritation. As a faint smell of gasoline seeped through the rusty Saab, she realized she would have to wait a little while before she could crank the engine again. She possessed a strong sense of the pragmatic and refused to panic, sitting quietly and biding her time, when a man appeared out of the night, clearly having walked a long way.

He stood as if in a trance under a solitary lamppost, then began to laugh by himself like a child beguiled by the sheer absurdity of some tale. He pulled back the hood of his parka, his eyes glistening brightly with tears of mirth.

Seetha could see plainly he was Indian. *Another eccentric grad student!* she thought. Then she rolled open her car window.

"Give my car a push, please," she said decisively.

• • •

I COULD NOT have been more startled if the car had spoken. I nodded and got behind the small car and pushed. It began to move, slowly at first, and then with gathering speed. Seetha turned the ignition and put her car in gear. It coughed and lurched forward. She looked in her rearview mirror, but I had disappeared from sight. Putting her car in neutral, engine idling comfortably now, Seetha stepped out.

"I think I have twisted my ankle," I mumbled in embarrassment, lying on the narrow layer of ice the car track had made.

# VII

*The young*

*In one another's arms*

# Billy Swint
## Clairmont, Upstate New York
### 1974

Mom likes to keep her special pictures on her dresser. In her wedding picture, I can make out Dad's birthmarks, one on his face, and one on the back of his right hand, with which he holds Mom close to himself. But the picture is black-and-white. His birthmark on his cheek glows red when he is angry. When he clenches his fist, I can see the other birthmark before it lands on me. No one can protect me.

She also has other pictures on the lace doily in front of her oval mirror, next to her combs. Mom had lovely long hair. Beside the combs her parents stare, unblinking, black-and-white and long dead, from inside their shiny silver frames: Grandpa and Grandma Donovan. Their permanent address was Mount Hope Cemetery. My sister Sandy's baby picture and mine are also on that doily. My dad, an orphan, had no pictures, none.

Mom had a pendant locket strung on a thick gold chain she had inherited from her father, together with our house at 166 Haddon Place. After she wore the necklace on special occasions, like

Thanksgiving, she would let me carefully open the minute clasp on the pendant. Inside, on either side, were engraved silhouettes of *her* grandfather and grandmother Donaldson.

She once said that this was the most precious thing she owned.

• • •

"WHAT A NICE accent you have, Mrs. Swint!" Mrs. Herbert, my first-grade teacher, said during the meeting, and Mom blushed. Dad hadn't come. My mom was pretty, always surprised when anyone said something nice to her. "Is it English?" I liked Mrs. Herbert although her teeth looked large when she sang.

"Yes," said Mom, "yes it is. My parents came here when I was eleven."

"Do you miss England?"

"Miss it? I miss Liverpool. We lived in Dingle, next door to my cousins. I miss them."

"Do you visit?"

Mom shook her head. "Dad couldn't leave his business. Donaldson's Garage."

"Oh, isn't that a coincidence. My dad always got his car fixed there, all the oil changes and stuff. It's such a small world." My mom and my teacher smiled together. I smiled with them.

"Is your dad still running it?"

"It's *my* dad's now," I told Mrs. Herbert.

Mom had stopped smiling. "I've got to go start supper," she said. "Archie likes it on time. Oh, come along, Billy, hurry up!"

"My grandpa died," I confided to Mrs. Herbert, but she wasn't listening, staring at my mom hauling me along, her handbag open.

• • •

I LOVED MY school and my crayons, and Mrs. Melanie Herbert, who said that my drawings and my singing were her joy. I think I love the name Melanie. It's like melody. And Herbert is sort of like sherbet, which I like, tingly and lemony on my tongue.

But then, one day, the letters arrived: twenty-six of them!

As long as I spoke words, or thought about them, they were wonderful. Then came the twenty-six letters. They were in *every* word, Mrs. Herbert said. They looked like hooks and locks, and twisty threads. *S* was a serpent sometimes turning into *g* just to spite me. Then *p*, *b* and *d*; *T* and *J*; *m* and *w* squirm about, pretending to be each other, all of them vicious. The pencil began to hurt my hand, because I was trying to remember those nasty shapes, holding it so tight that my fingers were red and aching. Sometimes I shut my eyes to squeeze all the letters out of my head. But when I opened them, they wriggled on the page.

I really hoped that letters would soon be forgotten, just another part of school we'd leave behind on our way to all the fun things, like drawing, singing, learning to name trees and flowers.

But soon EVERYTHING that we were doing in school had to do with reading and—worse—writing. Those twenty-six letters were driving me into a small corner where I could not breathe.

One day Mrs. Melody Sherbet herself picked up my sheet of paper, looked disgustedly at me, and tore it in four pieces. "Lazy," she hissed. I was sure everyone heard: my sister in her classroom, Mommy at home, and particularly Dad, in the garage. Mrs. Herbert slapped a fresh sheet of paper on my desk, held my fist—with its enemy pencil—and said, "Don't dawdle, Billy Swint! Write properly now." She squeezed her fingers over my pencil-hand.

The twenty-six little demons were going to trick me, I knew. Their shapes kept jumping up and down. Why couldn't nice Mrs. Melody Sherbet see what was wrong? I dipped my head and bit her thumb. I hadn't known I'd do that.

She cried out in surprise. Then, snatching back her hand, she pushed me away. My head twisted and hurt, and I could see her large teeth now, smeared red with lipstick, her nostrils hovering over me, one a black **O**, and the other a **D** with two hairs sticking out of it, like bits of black twine. She was ugly.

"Shit piss cock booger crap fuckfuckfuck," I shouted all the bad words I knew, trying to clear my head, shivering, clutching my pencil and twisting it about—until it broke by itself. I was squirming to get away, and hit her shin accidentally, but she didn't believe it.

The principal sent me home.

• • •

DAD PULLED OFF my belt, holding it by the buckle. The first sharp whack across my chest set a red world dancing before me. My pants, without the belt, slid down. I dribbled pee through my undies on the carpet, but my father was poised like a pitcher, red birthmark bouncing up and down with his hard head. The second swish missed and left a mark on the table. *Whick-whack*. The sixth caught me across my left arm, which I had raised. My mouth was open and I heard screaming somewhere. Air rushed out of me. I am scabby stupid slime dimwit cretin Billy Swint. I am scum.

I am hurting somewhere—where? The nineteenth swish scrapes me above my eyes, and I feel a small part of my left eyelid peel off. The red is everywhere, but I have no more pee to dribble down. I see my dad stand over me, paper-cutting knife in his hand.

"I'll cut off yer pecker now," he announced. I was quivering, my palms over my penis, sheltering my small pods underneath. Mom appeared suddenly and threw herself on him, clinging to his chest, his belly, giving me a shove toward the door, beyond which I stumbled and fell. Her dress was open all down the front.

"Oh love, ooh, love, oooh, love." I heard her struggling. At the doorway, I lay crumpled, but couldn't turn away from this fasci-nating battle. Was my mother getting revenge for my hurt? A hot breath filled my chest. I heard my father groaning. Was he hurt? She shoved her chest into his choking face, which broke free, and then was smothered by the white globe with its jiggling pink target. His bristling moustache disappeared beneath it.

"Get outta here, *shoo*," she hissed to me. But I could not stir. She straddled him, arching back, suddenly slumping over him. Another groan from him. She must have really hurt him. Suddenly his face appeared from under her. With the free hand, he flung my belt at me. The buckle missed my eye, but grazed my cheek.

*"Git, yasumuvabitch,"* he spat in agony. My penis was intact, but unaccountably tense. I slid out quickly, slamming the door shut, but still could not drag myself away. Lying there, eyeing the chink at the bottom of the door, I could see only a part of his palm. They fought while I stood covered with smelly sweat. Could it be mine?

"Oh, oooh, oh," Mom cried out, while he grunted in pain. Yes, hurt him, hurt him, *kill him killhim killhimkillhim*, I urged Mom on. Suddenly, I heard my mother cry out. Was it some deep wound inflicted inside her? I could hear her labored breath, and then him groaning and choking, slower and slower now. In the silence, my heart thudded on.

Then I heard something. He must have revived. He was trying to hurt her again. "Oooh. *IS* that you? Love?" she cried out, somehow delighted, as if he has shown her some magic trick. What do those words mean?

I wished I had a long knife to cancel and cut off the pictures in my head *slash-SLASH-slash*. I would hack them away *yesyesyesyes* and run. I wanted to cancel his face, her face too, for sounding pleased. *She is supposed to be hurting him.* But what strange game is this? I stood up uncertainly, my body smarting all over. I needed to open that door and see. I put my palm against it, but I was pulled away. There stood my sister, Sandy, grinning slyly.

"Peeking, you shit? You're a dirty little prick, Billy, aren't you?" she smirked.

As I turned to the top of the stairs, I saw the top of her head, bent, attentive, straining to listen to the last rocking groan of my parents' fight. I was dizzy and vomity. In the bathroom mirror, I saw red welts all over me, like birthmarks. I spat at myself in the mirror.

• • •

I HAD TO go back to school. Cretin stoooopid halfwit dumbass conehead. I understand these words, simple facts of everyday life. I scraped along, passed reluctantly, from grade to grade, like a lump of shit through the system.

During one meeting with my parents, my seventh-grade homeroom teacher called me "severely challenged." I sat up in surprise. This was Mr. Wofford, his wattled neck rising above his strangling tie, a few hairs floating out of his ears like probing antennae of carefully nurtured insects.

*Severely Challenged!* I imagined horses with muscles moving like cables under sweaty hides, the gleaming knights atop them, all shiny and metallic, rearing in frenzy, holding lances tipped with deadly metal. They thundered toward each other. From the melee and dust, I am the only one rising up, victorious in the last joust— *Sir Severely Challenged!* Battered but victorious.

I looked at Old Woffo. His tongue lolled pinkly, and wobbled about in his loose mouth. Bubbles appeared at both corners of his mouth, turning into a private ointment on each yellow end of his lips. His words were always moist with spit. "Severely Challenged," he burbled above me.

"Dumb as dirt, you mean?" snorted my dad. "Oh, love," Mom protested nervously. She was clutching and unclutching her handbag.

"Eh . . . ibegyerpardon?" stumbled Woffo, tripped by the interruption.

"Stoopid," offered my dad, teeth bared, the kind of smile he wears when he pulls off the belt from around my pants and flails at me, while I, eyes watering, nose running, hands clutching falling pants, stumble about, sorry ass sticking out, severely challenged, and my mother comes in bucking and snorting, joining the play of rescuing me. I wondered if it was a ritual he had invented for Mom—and I the accessory before the fact.

• • •

YEAH, I WAS dropping the occasional grade, but I had acquired some important skills like smoking pot to calm my nerves. By the time they pushed me up to tenth grade, I was older and richer than anybody else in school; I had figured out how to sell the shit rather than just buy it. I could tell the different currency notes—Jacksons, Franklins, et cetera—by instinct. They paid me, hastily, surreptitiously, the notes rolled up, scrunchy tight: I put them in my pocket. I just knew if they'd paid me enough. Shit, I was severely challenged, but my arithmetic of touch was perfection itself.

I also discovered that if someone rattled off a bunch of numbers, I could total them just like that. I can add, multiply, divide, like 9764852 divided by 1597648 is 6.1120171—see—correct to the seventh decimal, all in less than a second. Don't ask me how I do this. I just can. It ain't worth much anyway. Anyone with a five-buck calculator can do exactly the same shit. But it's the same kind of knowing that tells me what to bend and coax when fixing an engine, or makes the wood yield itself to my hands. It's a rhythm, man—a rhythm, that's all.

I can't seem to make it past the eleventh grade, although I'm amazed I've come this far. But I have no illusions. I am scrawny, sure, but I have grown my carapace. I dye my hair jet-black. I wear stomping boots. I can light my cigarettes in a rainstorm. I was the first in our school to accept Marley as my personal savior. I just understood why Peter Townshend would need to smash his guitar. Yeah, man, for sure everyone loved the Beatles. But here, upstate, the kids are still listening to Belafonte and his tired bananas, for fuck's sake, while I had discovered the Ramones.

Yeah, a certain kind of female digs me, begging for smokes and my ant-egg pills. I was sucked off long before the jocks got beyond flicking towels at each other's arse. I wear my black leather jacket, my tribal patches. My tribe of the lost valley, the church of the pissed night, sailors of the drowned boat. Oooh, Billy, she whispers in my ear, you're cool. Yeah, I know the routine. I give her what she wants. She is usually inert by the time I enter.

See, I have friends—sure—lots of them. I don't have to tell lame jokes. Any girl who wants the shit knows to come over to Billy the Kid. The ones with hollow breath, blue nostrils, begging mouths. They are broke, need grass or more, always telling me they are my best friends—*luv ya to death Billy, my billabong, my main man!* They sidle over, mumbling, numb minds, and in their own ways, severely challenged, in manners I recognize well. I dispense my little ant-egg pills, spread a little joy, dude. My kindred. They smell bad—of good intentions, old vomit, self-pity, fake affection, and crap. I smell too, of contempt, anger, and the knowledge that I am what Dad calls me: Illiterate Dogshit. How could I—and the rest of the world—possibly smell otherwise? Yeah, you tell me.

Sure, I could leave high school any day I want to, but I don't. I have nothing better to do, and after all, this is where my clientele is, where the babes are, my corridors of power and commerce. But my best friends are Jack Daniels and Tanqueray, the djinn.

When Jack or the djinn lurch me about, I hide where I can—under cemetery trees, behind the high school parking lot, against the metal bins of the PAL League—but mainly in the tiny loft built into the back of our garage at 166 Haddon Lane. This is where I hid my treasures ever since I could walk. Only our cat Russ comes and joins me there sometimes, nocturnal and golden, sharing my pulsating darkness, silently watchful through yellow slit eyes. Oh yeah, I talk to him. Russie, Russie, burning bright, as I bungle through the night; but he is a gentleman cat who disapproves of my cigarette smoke.

Here long ago I had stashed away Dad's kidney stones which he brought back from the hospital—a trophy I stole—the only time he was ever sick. I want to crush them to bits some day, to celebrate something. I don't know what, not yet.

• • •

AT THE END of the summer, on a sweaty day in August, Sandy got married. I threw up on the hood of the rented limousine that whisked Gus and Sandy off to the airport for their honeymoon in Myrtle Beach, after which they were relocating to Scranton, Pennsylvania. Just think of the name: *Scrraant-tton*. Oh yeah, like a broken engine.

I had flunked—so, eleventh grade again—and at the beginning of term, I went and sat down on the only empty seat next to some girl. Hair in two shiny pigtails, dark eyes, skin like a Hershey bar.

"Billy," I said to her, wondering where she was from. I had never noticed her before. It seemed unlikely she would become a customer. But hey, you never can tell.

"What?" she whispered back.

"Billy Swint," I said.

"Devi," she said.

"Hey, Debbie," I said, rolling the word out like a bag of wet laundry.

"No," she said, looking at me with eyes black as dominos. She reminded me of calm water, despite myself.

"What?" I said, disarmed by her smile.

"Devi," she said, "not Debbie."

"Davey?" I teased her.

"It's Devika," she said firmly, "Devi, for short." Her breath smelt lovely, spicy, a cool unfamiliar aroma. I inhaled the fragrance. She looked directly at me, and without saying anything reached into her school bag and handed me a small beige pod, seams on its skin with a tinge of green. I split its skin open and found three rows of shiny black seeds.

"Never seen anything like this," I said. Never met anyone like her either, I thought.

"Chew it," she said. I put it in my mouth, skin and all, letting it roll on my tongue, then bit down. The tiny pods burst with a lovely smell which filled my mouth.

"Cool," I agreed. Devi smiled back at me. I was grinning like an idiot. "I'll give you some free grass."

"No, thank you," she said, "I don't . . ." She shook her head. The pigtails moved from side to side. "It's good stuff. Free," I insisted, "really"—my $10 twist.

Just then Mr. Bottgriend appeared out of nowhere and grabbed me by the hand and began calling loudly for Miss Lonnie-Marge McBaggott, our assistant principal. She had creased cheeks, folded like saggy balloons on either side of her narrow nose, and pink nostrils like slits in ham. Her open mouth and pointy tongue made a perfect **Q** of surprise.

"Billy Swint!" she wheezed when she saw what was in my palm. Griendy's grip was a moist octopus.

"Mr. Bottgriend gave it to me," I said smoothly.

"What!" Miss McBaggott almost collapsed under the weight of my confession. She raised her hands up to her limp hair in despair. "Donnie, sweetie, you promised," she half-hissed, half-croaked in reproach, looking at Griendy's ample face. I see him looming over me, a large pudding with nostrils.

"Bobo darling, you believe this turd?" he snorted.

"Ask Devi," I said coolly.

"Debbie?" Griendy asks.

"Devi," I corrected him.

"What?" he said, thrown out of stride. In that moment of his inattention, I snatched my hand away and threw the maryjane out the window, where it would fall on the walkway one floor below. I was home safe. I knew that a good Billy Swint puffie had no shelf life at all—they get picked up instantly.

I was told to go down to the office, where a huge fracas ensued over my fate. Teachers milled about, and everybody—including Sammy Budds, the custodian, who was one of my business rivals—joined in. While they were all raging in there, I lolled on the chair outside. Devi walked in.

"They'll kick you out, Billy Swint," she said.

"Yeah, I know," I said, and then added, "Devika."

"That's perfect," she said, "that's exactly how to say it. Devika Rathnam Mitra," she said to me: Black eyes, dimple on left brown cheek, pigtails, sweet breath.

"That's the name of the pod?" I teased her.

"No, silly—the pod is cardamom." She smiled, gave me three more, and left.

I remembered it for years: *Devika Rathnam Mitra.* I had actually made a friend, although it was only for a day, my last day at school. So, school was over. I was relieved, actually. This was all the prom I'd get.

Newly emancipated by the school system, I began my walk back to my house in a dead end, what I called my cool-de-sack. On this beautiful September day, as the haze of summer hung in the air, and the trees were waiting to break into flaming colors of early fall, I felt ready to begin my life for real.

I remembered I had two bottles hidden in the garage. A half-full Jack Daniel's, one full perfect immaculate Gin. I would never have to spell. Goodbye Twenty-Six: Fuck ya all.

• • •

THINGS HAD BEEN changing at home. Archie had got into some kind of money mess. He didn't say what. I didn't ask. 166 would have to be foreclosed, so my cool-de-sack was gone with the wind. We would have to move across town, to an apartment. Mom had to trade in her lovely big Buick for a Ford Shit Pinto. I heard Mom crying one day, because Archie wanted her to give him her precious pendant necklace. He wanted to sell it, but Mom didn't give up, crying and moaning, keeping a firm grip on her gold jewelry.

Russ, that grand old purrer, got sick and died. In the last month he used to pad around in a circle, as if he had turned into a slow top. Fuck, it was heartbreaking to see him so sick. Sandy was long gone. Archie wasn't going to have me hanging about, getting sloshed. "You're paying by the week, you dimwit squatter." That's how Archie put it.

I have problems reading, yeah, but the writing on the fucking wall had been staring me in the face. I had expected Mom to stop him from kicking me out, but she didn't have the balls to say a word. Well, fuck all that. It was time to get out. I was the last extra guy standing. Hell, it was high time. I stole her pendant necklace—well, I had to inherit something, didn't I? I'd let Big Archie take the blame, I thought with satisfaction. She'd never dare accuse him to his face, I knew.

I left home for the big world out there. Well, that just meant that I took that job at the convenience store, working nights. With a little dealing on the side, especially at the store in the late hours, I managed okay. I moved into my own digs across town. I could now do some serious time with Mr. Jack and Miss Djinn.

The Great Swint did something typical before he had to vacate the house. He chopped down the horse chestnut tree in our backyard. My Billy Tree. It was in full bloom, with white candles all over it among broad green leaves.

But in my nightmares, I was the one doing it. Hacking him down.

• • •

THE DAYS HURTLE sideways into my mind, some sticking to a gummy part, some shearing off. For the life of me, I can't always tell the difference between what did happen and what could happen—what could not, or absolutely did not. My mind is a scarred thing in black space, spinning, bombarded by shards of memory, asteroids of words screamed at me: Hard to tell the difference.

I lost the tip of one digit somewhere when I was jacked or ginned, sliced off at a car door, or maybe someone bit it off. Was it me? Hey, *mea culpa*, whatever the fuck it was. The sharp acid churns and boggles in my throat. My fingers smell rotten from wiping vomit. My memory is a muddied quilt. I wrap myself in it. I rock, I tilt. I lie down swaddled in it, head slosh-full of memories. Where have I been, what brought me here? I sleep. I wake. I rummage about and find my Jack bottle and my Gin bottle and I go up their hill—and then all of me comes tumbling after. I bury my head in the crook of my arm and cradle myself in the darkness. Rockabye Billy, the cradle will fall . . . I wake again. I wonder how the day has passed, and it is night again.

I sit huddled, waiting for a kind of knowledge that waking brings at the end of a blind binge. There is no past or future. Just the here, the now. And the bottle is empty. Two weeks to payday. Time to report at the store.

• • •

I WAS QUIETLY transferring a couple of quarts—Jack and his identical twin—when Paulie, the manager, nabbed me.

"Jig's up, kid," he said, putting both thumbs on his pants, as if the poor shit was in a western.

"Okay, I quit," I said, taking the bottles out of my jacket.

"Ain't going to be that easy, Billy. I'm calling the police."

"Oh come on. Everyone does this, Paulie."

"No, they don't."

"Paulie, I won't come back here, okay? Don't call the cops."

"I won't, if you promise me something. I know you're not a bad sort, Billy."

I was ready to swear to any crapola to get him off my back. I just didn't want the cops checking out my digs. I had what was left of my stock taped behind the sink. Not to mention Mom's locket.

"I want you to go to a meeting."

"What! Like a parent-teacher thing? You're shitting me, right, Paulie?"

"You heard me. I'm totally serious. It'll do you a world of good. Trust me."

"What kind of meeting? Chrissake."

"It's AA. You know, Alcoholics Anonymous. Just go there three days. Go with an open mind, Billy. That's my condition. Or I pick up that phone. Your call."

"Okay, okay, yeah," I hear myself saying. The fucking comedian.

• • •

HERE I AM for my sixth meeting.

I sit in this church basement, a surveyor of cracked linoleum, sipper of tired coffee. I smoke Winston after Winston, drowning the stubs in my Styrofoam cups. We are the underground nation, friends of Dr. Bob. We do not aspire to the Ten Commandments, we have just one Thou Shalt Not, and twelve unsteady steps to get there. The first few times I sat at the back, as close to the wall as paint. I had been surprised to find Paulie there. But he made no move to recognize me. I guess I was grateful.

A bent man with a boiling cough came over to me on my third visit. He had a lined face, observant eyes. "Jerome," he said. "You are welcome here."

"I'm not Jerome," I said, "I'm Billy Swint."

"We don't have no use fer last names here, Billy," he said, stubbing out his cigarette, burbling in phlegmy camaraderie. "I'm Jerome."

"Cool," I said lamely. I wasn't looking for a wing to be taken under. Strictly for the birds. Jerome did not push. "It's okay, man," he said, giving me space. I slid into my corner and listened, because stories happened here: Disasters under high spirits, goddamn grace under pressure and shit. This was AA, two letters of the alphabet I think I can handle.

"I'm Jerome," he said at the lectern. "I'm an alcoholic."

Everyone greeted him. I am a citizen of a secret country with no last names. And one night, out of the spring rain, in walked Gillian. She sat in a huddle with her sponsor, a rail-thin woman called Rachel whose iron-gray hair was nodding as she listened to her. Finally Gillian stood up to speak. I could see the scratches and bruises on her hands, frieze-dried marks of torment, and a red welt down her cheek.

"I'm Gillian," she mumbled, tears coursing down her cheek, her nose runny. *Someone give her a tissue*, I thought, *this could be me*. She wiped her face with the back of her hand.

"My boyfriend kicked me out because I am an alcoholic." She bent her head and wept aloud. I could see her saliva dripping on the linoleum top of the table. "I was fired last week. Don was laid off seven weeks ago." She seemed to be using up all her strength to stop shaking. When she looked up, I was astonished to see how much anger shivered in her face. "It's okay for him to drink. But me, I'm an alcoholic, kicked out, sleeping in the street." Her split lip was bleeding afresh. "I'm so sick of myself I could die," she muttered. Then, she looked up defiantly. "I'm done with Don. Never again. I want another life." She faltered. "I don't know how . . ."

"Love ya, Gillian!" said a voice. It stopped her in her tracks. The anger drained out of her eyes. Her face looked pale. I realized I was the one who had spoken. We had been told not to speak out of turn, but I knew I would die to be so interrupted in this hard world. I wanted to hold her hand but did not, of course, because Rachel would have decked me. I got her coffee instead.

"I'm Billy," I mumbled.

A week later, I picked up enough of my own courage.

*I'm Billy* . . . My voice faded in the church basement, which was hazy with smoke.

"Hi, Billy!" it answered in a chorus. "Speak up, Billy," someone urged. "You can tell us, buddy." It was Paulie.

*Yeah*, I said to myself, *sure I can*. Let me tell them of my pals Jack and Gin. I am done weaving a curtain of bullshit around myself. I saw Gillian's face in the crowded basement, smiling at me, looking curious. I was curious about her being curious.

"I'm Billy," I tried again, coughing to clear my throat. "I'm an alcoholic." I want to say, *Oh, Gillian, please will you save my life and have coffee with me? I am in the basement of my heart. I cannot sink any further.* Except I can't say it. Not yet.

The cigarette smoke circled about her like a censer. "I'm going to need a cup of coffee after this," I blurted out. The room chuckled with camaraderie. Gillian looked at me, her smile dividing all my life between then and now. She fished about in her handbag, then lit her cigarette, her face aglow in that cupped light.

• • •

IN THE FOLLOWING fortnight, Gillian landed a job stacking shelves at the A&P in Oakridge, about two miles from Clairmont, and I had begun work in a lumberyard close by. We rode the same bus route to work, and I made sure I got on the same bus. In six weeks, we moved in together.

From our small apartment we could hear the percussion of the long goods trains. They soothed our sleep, touching our old building with the thrum of unseen fingers. Our one room, just off the staircase, had two large windows, side by side, which faced the shady street. The floor was old mosaic, the size of large, uneven dice. In front of one window stretched the iron geometry of the fire escape. Gillian put her pots of geraniums there. The tall windows let in the most marvelous mellow light, and our river flowed only a block away, just beyond a narrow park. Some evenings, a magical fog came from it and greeted me at our door as I returned from work, my back sore from lifting, a fine powder of wood chaff on my cap.

Our bed stood by the tall windows, Gillian's great-aunt's hope chest at its foot. On it she placed a flowering plant. We hung a small square mirror on the wall in which we could see ourselves making love, and next to it we put our carved elm chair. It had a sagging seat, its old tapestry fabric worn and smudgy. But it was an old beauty, and I never tired of caressing the subtle pitch of its broad arms. Gillian had hauled it from someone's old barn, and the wood had been grimy with dirt, which I had helped clean and polish. Beside it, made of buckled plywood, was a small desk with a hutch on it, which I had painted white for her, where she wrote in her journal. I never peeked. Besides, I never wanted to see letters again, *ever never*, as I used to say as a child.

Beyond that room was our tiny kitchen. We kept our vegetables and fruit in a large round woven tray I'd picked off the street and hung from the kitchen ceiling. Our small bathroom had tiles the color of old piano keys. A little light seeped here from the large windows way in the front, a luminous drape. This was our safe haven. I wished I could have Russ, the gentleman cat, back with me.

I did not think constantly of Mr. Jack now. Hand in hand with Gillian, I went to our smoky church basement, and found friends. What peace we found, we learned to share, like children at playschool. Cyril, who had fallen off the wagon but was now back, mysteriously minus a tooth or two, Fiona of the wild hair, flirty Alice, mumbling Tom, who always gave us a companionable wink. We were a hideaway nation, recovering, covering our tracks over the hard and bitter terrain of the world. We were kind to each other. We were each other's kind. One day at a time, for chrissake. As simple as that.

This was no country the world outside cared to know.

●  ●  ●

I HAULED TIMBER from the trucks to the yard or vice versa. Sometimes I did small carpentry for Mr. Peter Foley, who found I had a neat hand with wood. Mr. Foley whistles to himself, clear as a flute. Once I asked him if he was making up the tune, and he said, no, it was Handel. Another time I asked him if he was whistling Handel again, and he smiled and said, no, it was just pure Peter Foley. He never rushed me, and figured out never to ask me to write anything down. He took care of all that sort of stuff. I hang my coat next to his.

I offered to buy small pieces of cedar wood left over from a special job.

"You want to make something, Billy?" I nodded.

"For a lady, eh?" He grinned.

"Yeah," I said. "I'll work in my own time," I added.

"Use whatever tools you need, Billy. Anything you want." He took out a box of tools for fine detailing.

I made a small, delicate box, with a sliding top, my best piece of work. It smelled beautiful too. Mr. Foley looked at it with admiration, and turning to me, he said,

"Exquisite! Well, all I can say, Billy, is that she's one lucky lady."

*Lucky lady* . . . I thought in misery. It was for Mom. I was going to put her pendant necklace in it and find a way to return it to her.

● ● ●

ONE AFTERNOON I got off early because of some problem with the power saw.

"Take the afternoon off, Billy," Mr. Foley said, and I went straight to the supermarket to wait for Gillian to finish. But she wasn't there.

Her friend Regine with the snake tattoo on her ankle said she had had a fight with the produce manager, Gary, who picked on her if he had nothing better to do. Gary, the one with the pimpled neck, the overflowing paunch, and one shirt button popped above his bulging equator.

Worried, I went straight home to find the door bolted from inside. Gillian wouldn't open! I climbed the rainwater spout to the fire escape. I stared at Gillian on the floor, cradling a bottle of vodka, her face bruised. She must have fallen. Everything in the room was in shambles.

Driving my fist through the long pane, I scrambled across the bed and grabbed her arm. I flung the bottle out of the window and turned on Gillian in a fury. She was paper-pale, but refused to guard herself with her hands. "Okay, go ahead, hit me."

"Why?" I cried out, "Why, Gillian? It's our six-month anniversary coming up. We both have jobs." *God*, I thought suddenly, *I need a drink.* Being sober was a paper bag of flinty stones I carried inside me. I was constantly aware of their edges waiting to pierce the flimsy package in which they slid and shifted. Now, in panic, I wondered if it was about to tatter, and the deadly pebbles spill into my waiting bloodstream.

"I'm going to call Jerome. We need someone to talk to us right now! You need to call your Rachel this minute. Gillian," I screamed, "Gillian!" She turned and bit my ear. I cried out and wrestled her down. Before I knew it, I had her nipple in my mouth. "Oh Billy," she moaned, "is that you, my love?" reaching to hold me in her clenched hands.

And I lost it. Something troubled me to the core. What was it? Something in my head was echoing, gonging, *is that you-ISTHATYOUisthatyoulove?* I threw up my hands, expecting the whistling blow of a belt. I pushed Gillian aside. She reached for me again, but I hit her face with my open palm.

"Stop," I snarled, "stop talking," and I entered her hard. She cried out. I felt a deep disgust for my life, my hands, my body. But she reached for my face, moving my hair from my eyes. "Billy, oh, Billy. We need to help each other."

I sat silent, not knowing how to speak, how to tell her about those years, about Archie.

"Will you let me love you, Billy? Will you love me back?"

I nodded, unable to speak in the choke of my tears.

"Hold me now," she wept. I did. My hand bloody, my face buried in her hair. In the blackness, all night, into dawn.

# Devika
## Clairmont, Upstate New York
### 1983

I could write my full name, Devika Rathnam Mitra, by the time I was four. I also knew how to write the names of my parents: Dr. Kush Mitra and Dr. Seetha Rathnam Mitra. I used to think that *Dr.* stood for Dear, because I love them. Baba calls me "Devi," but also sometimes "Ma." He explained that in Bengal, a father calls his daughter that, because one day she will be the mother of all their descendants. I liked that.

Chitto-Uncle and his wife, Kamala Auntie—my parents' Indian friends were all uncles and aunties, even if you met them once—knew my parents from when they first moved to Clairmont, soon after my mother took up her job at the hospital and Baba began to teach at the math department in the university nearby.

Chitto Uncle, or Chitto-kaku, as he also liked to be called, in the Bengali manner, and my baba were unlikely friends. They probably would never have connected in the old country. At least, I think so. Chitto-kaku prided himself on being practical. He knew about sales at Sears and Two Guys or in malls as far away as Albany, income tax loopholes, mattress bargains, investments in strip malls, reliable car repair shops, which Indian grocery store was cheapest, and other very practical matters. He owned two Dunkin' Donuts franchises and a gas station, and planned to buy a small motel soon.

He knew answers, but they were inevitably about things I had no interest in. He never once talked about books, but would bustle into our house, full of local news and advice. He wagged his head, which had some hair around the fringe, and one outcropping of salt-and-pepper hair, like an island, just above his forehead. His ears sprouted hair, as if in compensation for the lack of it on his head, while his eyebrows were awesome, and he had one gold tooth.

Plump and comfortable, Kamala Auntie did not go out to work and wore saris all the time. She told me that in India she would swim in the local river in her sari; her family had come from a place called East Bengal, which became Bangladesh. That's the land where my father was born, although their families did not know each other. They too had been refugees after Partition, when the country broke apart like an old plate—which is why she feels a special affection for my father. She calls Baba *Kush-da*. You add *da*, to show he's an elder brother—or someone who is like one. That's funny—for I read in a book that the Irish call their fathers Da!

Kamala Auntie's family had been very poor; she only studied till the sixth grade in a Bengali medium school. But Baba and Ammu say that she is very smart. Her parents were both killed in East Pakistan before her two teenage brothers escaped with her to the outskirts of Calcutta, when she was only two. There is some kind of incomprehensible affection she feels for Baba, simply because their ancestors lived at some time on the same land.

Chitto-kaku and Kamala Auntie had no kids, but three pet cats: Bhola, Bablu, and Tuni. She got them from a shelter. Chitto-kaku is allergic to cats, so he has to take regular medication. He must adore her, Ma said. But I also feel the unquestioning affection both Kamala Auntie and Chitto-kaku give me. I mean, I got a prize for a spelling bee, and they both cried for joy. Even Baba got a little embarrassed.

Kamala Auntie speaks broken English with Ammu—because Ammu is not Bengali. Her family is from Madras, where she went to medical school before coming to America. She grew up speaking Tamil, although we speak English at home.

But Baba taught me Bangla—as if his life depended on it, Ammu says—and we have always spoken that with each other; Ammu never learned to speak it well, because she's always busy and says she has no patience with languages, although she pretty much understands what Baba and I are saying. I knew for sure the time he and I made plans to go and buy spicy *chanachur* snacks from the Indian grocery store, but Ammu said I was eating too much junk food. We had been speaking in Bangla—yet she knew what we were up to!

Ammu seldom cooks, but Baba likes to. He taught himself, with cookbooks, after he got married. But twice a year or so, during long weekends, Ammu makes elaborate preparations, soaking rice and lentils overnight, grinding spices by hand. She makes a tremendous mess in the kitchen, but at the end she produces perfect and simple dishes, like the gigantic and paper-thin crepe-like dosa which we eat with creamy coconut sauce and spiced lentil sambar.

Once I darted into the kitchen for something and, for the first time in my life, caught Baba kissing Ammu. They were very awkward about it. Baba pretended he had simply been helping her with something. I had not realized that Indian moms and dads kissed. It seemed bizarre—as bizarre as imagining our American teachers in sari, or kurta, I mean, could you even imagine Chitto-kaku and Kamala Auntie kissing! It's too weird.

Baba loves me best. He talks about our Baba-Daughter team. But we never play any games, like American kids with their dads. *They and us:* I mean, I have an American passport, just like them, but we are so different. They *do* things together—like gymnastics, camping, jogging, softball, or homework—if they are lousy at reading or math—but I am good at school stuff, always have been. Baba is usually baffled when it comes to fixing things. Their dads buy tools and stuff all the time. I doubt Baba owns a screwdriver. *They* go to church: That's usually a big deal for them. Then they go to Sunday family dinners where their parents have fights with their uncles or aunts or each other. It is all so intriguing.

It's different with us: Baba and I just talk! We talk about everything under the sun. About insects and ant colonies, the double helix, the Three Musketeers, the *Odyssey*, *Lorna Doone*, Julius Caesar, the discovery of longitude, the spirits that bothered King Vikramaditya—whether they were ghosts—if there could even be such things as ghosts, chaos theory, Charlie Brown, Christian Gauss and how he added all the numbers from 1 to 100 in a few seconds when he was a kid, whether there could be a largest number which could never be counted, the fact that Charles Darwin and Abraham Lincoln were born on the exact same day, same year—which is also my birthday, February 12.

Baba and I sometimes fried fish—which we both love. He buys frozen *ilish* from the Indian grocery store, or gets them fresh-caught in season from down near Haverstraw on the Hudson. It's called shad in America. I help Baba smear the fish with turmeric and salt before he fries them. He uses the garden hose to clean my hand, but it always stays yellowish for a whole day after. In third grade, I asked Baba why turmeric stained our hands, but not salt. So he explained about molecular structures. I loved that. We are all made of atoms and molecules. So are all things.

I was so excited I told everyone in school. It was more interesting than what we were taught in school about Creation. That story said that everything had just been created, but not *how*: That was what really interested me. Surely even the first man and woman and everything else were made of atoms and molecules. Baba also told me that there really was no "first man or woman" like in the stories. Sister Margaret and Sister Bonnie and Sister Carmelita were upset. They informed me that I was a heathen, which was okay with me. They claimed that Eve had been made from a rib. *All of her?* That sounded odd, I said, for which I was given detention, which is a waste of time.

Baba told me to ignore them. "They'll always have a bone to pick with you." I got the joke, of course, but I was the one who had to go back to Sister Margaret's class the next day.

• • •

With all this stuff about God, and saints, and the Holy Land every day at school, I once insisted on Baba taking me to the Hindu temple a few towns away, but we both got bored after the first time. It was nothing like being in India, although that is what Kamala Auntie claimed. But I should know, for every two years we would all go to India, where we stayed with Ammu's mother in Madras.

I called her Paathi. She lived in a house with red tiles and an enclosed courtyard in the middle of which grew a big tamarind tree with the dancing Shiva, daubed with vermilion, under it. A cuckoo used to sit in the branches and sing endlessly in the afternoons. Ammu became like a child herself when we were with Paathi in Madras. She is so brisk and busy here in Clairmont. I loved it when Paathi brushed our hair, and kissed both of us. Then Ammu would kiss and call me *kutty*, which means "little one," and let me lie on her lap. There, she had all the time in the world. Baba would sit contentedly on the red-tiled verandah, which runs all around the house, and smoke local cigars, sipping the southern coffee, his favorite kind.

Just last year I found Ammu crying in the kitchen one morning after a phone call. She told me that Paathi was dead. Ammu insisted on going to work even that day, because she said it was the only thing that would calm her. She let Baba drive her there, for once, though she drives far better than my absentminded father. She handled everything, even this grief, in her own way. Baba and I sat together in his study, very sad, remembering Paathi.

But once, late at night more than a full year after Paathi died, I heard her weeping alone in the kitchen downstairs. I had gone down for a glass of milk. I held her, and she let me. She was whispering for Paathi in Tamil, in words that I could not completely understand. I hugged her for a long time. It was as if Ammu's grief had no map, no calendar, a story with secret words. I have thought about this many times since.

Baba told me once that we must remember the names of our ancestors, to the seventh generation. He taught me their names. My ancestor Doorgadass Mitra used to live in a mansion now in ruins. It only survives as a picture my grandfather drew from memory; it hangs in Baba's study now.

After fourth grade, we visited Calcutta, where my father grew up and went to school, but we couldn't visit where he had been born because he was too young to remember the exact place. The only one who would have known was my grandfather Monimoy, but he died a long time ago. My grandfather never even saw America. It is kind of strange how, after all these years, Baba gets a bit quiet when I ask him about his childhood.

Chitto-kaku's brother and his family invited us over when we went to Calcutta. They just sat in a row on their sofa and smiled continually at us, after offering us huge amounts of too-sweet desserts and too-sweet tea with milk already poured into it.

Oh yeah, I also saw my first elephants in the Calcutta zoo. Sad hulking creatures, shackled at the leg, swaying back and forth, accepting peanuts with the ends of their moist-tipped trunks. I suppose that moist stuff was elephant nose-goo. I was not thrilled.

I enjoyed myself much more on trips with Ammu and Baba in the small holidays we took, just by ourselves, after visiting Paathi in Madras. Like Lake Periyar, miles long, with a half-submerged petrified forest of leafless branches stretched akimbo, like still black dancers in the water. We stayed on a small island in the middle, surrounded by gentle green hills, everything quiet here except the breeze. The only house on this solitary island used to belong to a king of Travancore; he would come there by himself to think. You had to get there by boat, which the boatman kept at a small jetty, just for us to use. He was also the cook. All around the island were forests. In the evenings we watched buffaloes and wild pigs come to drink water. The monkeys also came in groups.

One afternoon, when my parents were resting indoors, and I was wandering about the island bungalow, I saw a small herd of elephants come to the far bank. The mother elephants were teaching their babies to swim. I quickly called Ammu and Baba. I loved watching elephants this way. When we returned to Clairmont, I insisted that Ammu teach me how to swim, no excuses—no talk about being too busy, or surgery schedules and births. I put my foot down. Ammu taught me in Chitto-kaku's pool. I had never seen potbellied Chitto-kaku or Kamala Auntie in the pool. Ammu said that they liked having a pool to sit next to. I learned to swim by the third day.

• • •

NOTHING IS FOREVER, except numbers, Baba said. When I asked him on my tenth birthday whether numbers existed before God created the earth in six days, he said that if God was forever, then so were numbers. He said that there is a book called the Qur'an which says that "there is no God but God." Baba said that it is really about Zero and One, which is the basis of all things binary. Why couldn't we have a simple answer that everyone agreed about? Baba suggested that if God existed, He was in everything that we could think about and that it was especially true of mathematics. I repeated this in school, and the nuns were so confused they didn't know whether to punish me. No one told me at home that there were questions I could not ask.

Once when I asked my mother where babies came from; she simply took me with her to the hospital the next Saturday and I watched her deliver a baby. Three years later, I began to bleed one afternoon. My father in a panic called Ammu, who came home immediately and explained it to me. I was fascinated that it would suddenly happen to *me*! When I told my friends at school the next day and wanted to know about them, they reported me to the nuns. The nuns told me not to talk about such matters. These were shameful things, secret, said Sister Adolphus, and part of Eve's curse.

I pointed out that I did not care about Eve, and my mother who was a gynecologist had explained it all to me. Sister Adolphus, looking stern, asked me sarcastically if I knew everything in the world. Not everything, I conceded, but I had seen a baby born. Had she? That seemed to stump her completely. I was sent home with a letter.

Ammu laughed when she read the letter, and my parents simply transferred me to a public school. I didn't mind. I hated the uniform.

• • •

A FEW YEARS later, the spring I finished middle school, Chitto-kaku convinced my parents to buy a house in foreclosure, which he swore was a bargain. My father would never have been able to find such a house by himself, his head buried in mathematical equations, and Ammu was always busy at the hospital and perfectly happy in our three-bedroom apartment. She had little interest in houses or matching cushions and such. She agreed simply because she loved to take baths, and this house had a really large bathroom with a window that looked onto a fine garden. And I would be able to walk to my new high school.

One odd thing about the house was a freshly chopped tree in the middle of the backyard. When I asked Baba, he said nothing but just shook his head. But the day after we moved in, he insisted on taking Ammu and me to Byng's Garden Center, where he bought a sapling of horse chestnut to replace the one that had been chopped down. We planted it together. "It'll grow lovely white flowers, Devi," Ammu said, "and you'll see why they are called candles." Then she remembered a poem:

> *O chestnut tree, great-rooted blossomer*
> *Are you the leaf, the blossom or the bole?*

"Who wrote that?" I broke in. "That is so good!" Ammu smiled at me, adding,

> *O body swayed to music, O brightening glance,*
> *How can we know the dancer from the dance?*

That very afternoon, we went down to Stern's Bookstore and my parents bought me my own copy of Yeats.

• • •

WELL, I WAS glad for I had a bigger room to myself, and Baba turned one of the ground-floor rooms into his study. There he put up the family tree I had made when I was in elementary school, which he loved so much he had it framed. It hung next to the picture of the huge ancestral house in Barisal. The rest of the walls were taken over by books. I loved to curl up our comfortable old leather sofa to read or chat with him.

I liked our wide two-car garage, which had a kind of high platform, almost head-high at the very back, like a secret place. I climbed up there and found quite a number of empty bottles, mostly Jack Daniel's.

"It's like the house was Mr. Jack Daniel's," I commented, and Chitto-kaku laughed until he doubled over coughing, as if I had made a great joke.

"Did you notice Baba, our house numbers, 1 6 6, add up to 13. Is that unlucky?"

"That's just an old superstition, Devi," he said, "but prime numbers are my favorites."

• • •

SINCE WE INVARIABLY parked our cars in the driveway, the garage was the perfect spot for frying fish on a rainy day, for Ammu had banished this particular activity from inside the new house. We would eat our fried *ilish* there till the rain let up, a favorite Baba-Daughter team activity.

Baba had bought me a small ladder for the loft at its back, where I kept some of my books. There I found a small matchbox with strange roundish pebbles in it. I asked Baba what it was. He did not know. In the evening, I showed Ammu—and she said that they were somebody's kidney stones. "How do they form inside the kidneys?" I asked. And she explained. I took them to school to show our biology teacher at my new high school. But in our homeroom, Mrs. Bonnie Grounder, the English teacher, said they were icky, wrinkling her discolored nose, wagging one thick-jointed finger. No one wanted to touch them. Carol Miele, who usually wore a scowl, asked me the next day why I had saved them. She said her mom had wondered if we Indians ate them. I did not care to answer, for I know that there are no real answers to stupid questions. People who ask questions to make you seem strange or ridiculous do not really want to listen to your answers anyway.

But I made other friends, even some Indian kids, like me. Maya Chhabra told me that Ammu had delivered both her and her kid brother, Mayur. Her mom sold Avon stuff, and Maya said her dad was going to get her married off after high school to someone in

India she had never even met. Vijay Kohli's parents just wanted him to study all the time so he could become a doctor, like his uncle in Utica. Neither of them was allowed to date or receive long phone calls. My parents had no such hang-ups. I had a boyfriend, Jimmy, who was kind of dorky but cute. He was fond of horror movies. I soon got bored with him.

• • •

To my father's great delight, I chose his old university. My undergrad years breezed past faster than I could have imagined, and I stayed on for grad school. I loved books, and did not have any lucrative career in mind, so I thought that being a grad student was a perfect alibi for reading what I chose.

At a party on the University Quad during the first week of good weather, just before spring break, I first saw Neel. The students were making the most of the sun, for everyone on River Campus knew the tattered joke that Rochester has two seasons: winter and the Fourth of July.

They were playing Jefferson Airplane, then Jethro Tull. Some kids were dancing or throwing Frisbees, but Neel sat in the sun, soaking it in, and listening to the music, his hands busy, folding sheets of paper into animal shapes: giraffes, tortoises, birds. I knew the word *origami*, but had never seen anybody do this before. When passersby stopped to admire one or the other animal, he would tell them with a casual wave of his hand that they could take it. Intrigued, I walked over and sat down on the grass near him. A Frisbee wobbled and fell on the grass next to me. I ignored it.

"I am Devika," I said, smiling at the two animals in front of him. One was an alligator and the other was a squirrel.

Glancing at my hands, he wrote something on the paper he was folding and gave it to me. It was a bird with its wings poised to take off in flight, beaks apart as if emitting a call, its ruffled wings shaped like seashells.

"This is a bird that doesn't exist, Devika Mitra," he said in Bengali.

I was absolutely flabbergasted. "How did you know I was Bengali?" I asked. "And my last name?" Then I understood: It was spelt on a wristband Kamala Auntie had made for me from pieces of copper. Because I loved the shape and design of the Bengali characters on it, I wore it a lot. He had read the name easily, although it appeared upside down from where he sat.

"What's yours?" I asked, but he pointed at the bird in my hand.

"The bird will tell you," he said, getting up with a laugh. "I'm late for a seminar. Bye, Devika Mitra."

A phone number was written on one wing of the bird, which I unfolded. But I could not fold the bird back into existence. For that—and his name—I would need to call him.

• • •

OVER THE NEXT few weeks, we began to meet on campus, Neel and I, usually after my afternoon seminars. He would usually be lying on the grass in the quad outside Morey Hall, waiting for me, his head propped on his satchel. It was still mild, in the first part of October. We would stroll down to the Rathskeller where, over snacks or a beer, we chatted.

He would tell me about physics and his own research on light. And he listened with care when I spoke about the plays of Synge, for I was thinking of doing my doctoral research on him, working with George Ford, a leonine old man who was my favorite professor.

A few days after I had told Neel, I found he had read three of Synge's plays in that time. When I told Neel of my plan of going to Ireland next year to spend the summer doing research, he said, "Ah, my grandfather went there recently," but added nothing more.

• • •

"WHAT KIND OF Bengali name is Aherne?" I asked Baba when I had stopped by at home a month into the fall semester. He says you can tell a lot about someone from India, just by his name.

"Aherne! Not an Indian name . . . Aherne . . . someone once told me about that name, yes," mused Baba, "but I cannot, for the life of me . . ." He trailed off, in a reverie.

By this time, I had been seeing Neel for almost four months. I told Baba he was a graduate student from India, studying light in the physics department, almost done with his dissertation. He would probably go back to India, I confided to Baba, who asked me if we were serious.

"I'll tell you when I know," I told him. But I had avoided the topic of his plans so far, unready to read more into my diffidence to address it.

• • •

NEEL STAYED OVER some weekends in my small upstairs apartment near the university, a couple of rooms with a kitchenette and a small deck in a clapboard house overlooking a maple-treed backyard.

Lazing in bed one lazy Sunday morning in October, I could not resist my curiosity and started to ask him about his life back in India. Neel launched into a description of his favorite coffeehouse across from Presidency College, where he had been an undergrad.

"It's right across from Sanskrit College, up a broken staircase, bang in the middle of four blocks of decrepit buildings, chock-a-block with small publishing houses, their books spilling into corridors and tiny lanes, Devi, the biggest concentration of publishers in the world." Neel seemed transported, a faraway look in his eyes.

I was baffled, expecting to hear about his family and parents, but let him go on, childishly delighted to talk about the place. I had not seen this side of him before.

"Oh well," he reminisced, "actually, Devi, the coffeehouse was dim and reeked of the fumes of the Charms that we smoked."

"Charms?" I said, sitting up, "Those don't sound legal."

"Naah, it's not what you think," he grinned, "Charminar cigarettes—strong and the cheapest. Packs a mule's kick. You'd have to hold them horizontal, otherwise the tobacco drizzles down—like Orwell's Victory cigarettes. We lived on those and shots of black coffee—'infusion' is what the waiters called them. None of us had money for anything else. But yes, some of my friends, like Nondon, smoked something really heady."

"Hash?" I leaned in for more details.

"Don't knock that fine old Hindu tradition. It's the preferred whiff of Lord Shiva. They have a saying: 'Hang it—it is hemp after all!' "

"But Neel, tell me about the people important to you."

"In those coffeehouse days, they were Frantz Fanon, Gramsci, Lévi-Strauss, and even that frozen relic C. P. Snow. And dear old Hegel."

"Okay, okay, I get it," I interjected, "this coffeehouse of yours was part Plato's academy and part Haight-Ashbury. But what about home? Tell me about your family and those other things that matter." I was not letting him get away that easily.

"Well, madam," he said, affecting a solemn face, "are you referring to my displaced bourgeois origins and the confused traces of multinational bloodlines, eh?"

"I am about to pour coffee on your head," I threatened.

"Okay, I surrender," he said, rolling over on his stomach, "but I could only think of one place at a time."

"And would you take me there?"

"I would, Devi," he said, then his face fell, "but I wonder if you'd like it as much I did. During the frequent power cuts—we call these 'load-shedding'—it was hot as an elephant's armpit." I broke into helpless laughter, and he was surprised that I had found him funny. I kissed him, aroused by a new closeness, and before we knew it, we found ourselves making love.

Later, as we held each other close, I thought aloud, "Mrs. Nolan probably heard us, Neel," but he rebutted, "That pious lady is definitely in church this Sabbath morning, Devi. She's not a heathen like you, despite what the nuns tried to teach you in your tender years."

I hit him with a pillow. It was the most carefree time I had spent with him, yet we had not yet spoken of the future.

We went downstairs, took Mrs. Nolan's rake and, just for fun, swept the backyard, hanging out under the riot of colors of the maples with a couple of bottles of Genesee Cream Ale, which Neel always brought over during his weekends. Mrs. Nolan was so delighted by the sight of her neat yard as she pulled in that she insisted we take half a pecan pie she had baked the previous day.

Neel decided to stay back and drive into campus together next morning, because Mrs. Nolan's pie merited serious attention. As I heated up a frozen tray of Baba's Hyderabadi biriyani for what Neel called a real intercultural meal, Neel folded sheets of paper to make a rhinoceros and a large imaginary insect for Mrs. Nolan's two grandsons.

We turned in early, draped over each other on the saggy sofa which had come with the apartment and, turning on the TV, found that they were about to show an Aparna Sen film on PBS, the only channel that ever showed the occasional foreign film, and luckily, the only one my set received properly, without wavering; I had, by now, grown used to seeing a wraith-like Dan Rather intone the daily evening news on CBS. Tonight's film turned out to be about Anglo-Indians in Calcutta, and I noticed Neel leaning forward, rapt.

"That's just the kind of place and people among whom I grew up, Devi!" Neel said softly, as the credits rolled up. "My great great-grandfather Padraig had come from Ireland," he began, which explained the name Aherne.

His grandfather Robert Aherne had married a Bengali botanist, Amala Martha Basu, a daughter of Christian converts, who had died of malarial fever contracted when she had gone to the Kaziranga forest in Assam on a botanical survey trip when their daughter, Mary Aherne, Neel's mother, was fifteen. Neel had lived with his mother, a schoolteacher, in his grandfather's house. He had no siblings. Mr. Aherne ran a shop which sold old and new books, prints, and sheet music on Calcutta's Free School Street. "A stone's throw from where Thackeray had been born and spent his childhood," said Neel.

"William Makepeace Thackeray, the Victorian novelist! Did you also live in one of those old houses?"

"Oh, it is old and creaky enough." Neel grinned. "My Irish ancestor Padraig built it on Elliot Road, half a mile away through small lanes, if you know the way."

The family used to leave together in the mornings, his grandfather Robert to open his shop, his mother, Sarala, and he to their respective schools. After school Neel would walk to his grandfather's shop, where he would leaf through books and reproductions and listen to music, usually jazz. "We always sent for the big chicken patties from Nahoum's, a dozen everyday," he concluded.

"You must have worked up quite an appetite!" I interjected. Neel shook his head. "Some of them were for my grandfather's visitors. His friends would come by. Old Tony Belletty, who always carried his hip flask of rum, Krikor Aratoon, the retired businessman who had a special wide chair for himself—he's *th-a-a-t* wide, Devi! Often we would all listen to LPs of jazz, Bessie Smith, Thelonious Monk, you know. Young local musicians like Lew Hilt, Amyt and Anjan Dutt used to drop in all the time. So did Pam Crain, the lovely jazz singer. Nondon Bagchi used to show off his percussion on teacups with his spoon! They were beginning to get gigs at Trinca's on Park Street. Yeah, they were a lot of fun. The store is a favorite for collectors. People drop by, jazz lovers, musicians, just plain folks, everybody. They love to hang out with him. He listens, and not just to music."

Neel mentioned his father just twice, as if he was a long-dead relative. Divorced from his mother when Neel was barely one, he had left town and remarried, never once returning. By second grade, he had learned not to ask his mother about him.

I could not imagine a universe without my father. "Is that why you took your grandfather's name?" I was puzzled.

"Well, that kind of happened," mused Neel. "My mother got an affidavit reclaiming her maiden name after the divorce. When

I was enrolled in the nearby school, the clerk had automatically written my name down as Aherne. My mother did not correct him. So Aherne it remained." And so they lived together, the three Ahernes, until his mother died of breast cancer when he was in college. I knew he missed her too much to talk about her yet.

"Where is your father?" I asked.

"Australia, I think," he replied, in a tone that did not invite conversation. His usual reticence had returned. We had not spoken about his plans, but the moment was gone.

• • •

THE FOLLOWING WEDNESDAY, I arrived unannounced at his room, high up in the Valentine Tower. I liked its monastic simplicity, the odd percussion of the heating system, the high window view of the canal that led to the river. I had brought with me a cassette of an early Mozart flute sonata I knew he would like. It was just beginning to snow, glimmering evanescent lake-effect snow under a rare cloudless sky, a local phenomenon.

"I just got a letter from my grandfather," Neel announced. "He wants to see New York."

"But isn't he really old?"

"He's just over eighty, Devi, but spry and really independent. You'll like him."

"Would he like me?" I countered. "Does he know of me?

"He will be here in just a couple of weeks, Devi," he said with a teasing smile, "and you can give him the third degree."

"Why don't you bring him to my parents' for Thanksgiving? Will he be here by then?"

"He's arriving right before Thanksgiving—he knows there is a holiday in America, and says he wants to wander around New

York with me for a week, at least. He particularly wants to see Greenwich Village and has already booked rooms at the Chelsea Hotel. Don't ask—it's where his favorite poet, Dylan Thomas, stayed. He wants to see everything. The Met, the Frick. And yes— the Botanical Garden up in the Bronx. My grandmother Amala used to mention it."

"Oh," I said, my disappointment showing. "Can't you go there after Thanksgiving?"

"How can I let him down, Devi? He's been talking about this for months now. It's a big deal to come, and I didn't really think he would. All my life I knew I could count on him. He's never asked anything of me." He held my hands in his. "I'm sorry, Devi, really. You asked me about him before, and I've been meaning to share this with you, something he had sent earlier."

From his desk, Neel picked up an old envelope with several Indian stamps on it. He took out a letter whose pages were creased by many foldings and refolding, and handed it to me. Postmarked at Elliot Road Post Office, Calcutta, a year and a half ago.

"Devi, he's the only family I have."

"You want me to read it now? This old letter?"

"Yes. I need to drop off this research paper. I'll be right back, so please, please don't leave. Devi?"

I nodded. "I'll be right back," he repeated, and left.

I began to read slowly, with the flute and the waft of snow in the background.

*19 September, 1987*

*My beloved Neel,*

*I have now settled down in Elliot Road, my dear grandson, back from my trip to Ireland. It seems so strange to return to the familiar old house; I still expect your mother to walk in any minute. The memories follow me around all my waking hours, and even in my dreams.*

*I know you will probably laugh at my sentimentality and tease me about my long-planned pilgrimage, or what you will. But I did need to make this journey.*

*When your great-grandfather Brendan died (I know it was years before you were born) he had a book of Irish landscapes next to him. When I found him, the page was open on a double-page panorama of the Glengesh Pass. He had never been to Ireland. I have often opened the book to these pages and studied them, inch by inch, with my magnifying glass, wondering what it was that drew him, time and again, to that book of Irish pictures. I came to know that landscape as if I had been there, many times.*

*My grandfather Padraig had come from an Ireland racked by famine—the kind of famine that I myself saw in Calcutta and the surrounding countryside in 1942–43. Again, that was a man-made famine. All the grains were taken from Bengal's fine harvests for the war effort in Burma, leaving the Bengalis starving. Over a million people died in the streets, mothers begging feebly for a bit of rice-gruel (not even rice!) for their swollen-bellied children. These were Jim Gwynne's pictures of the Irish dead—you remember them, don't you?—brought to dreadful life again. What had the Empire learnt from the 1840s to the 1940s? Or perhaps, they learnt too well.*

*That British Army in Burma under handsome Lord Mountbatten withdrew in a panic when confronted by Japanese artillery. All that grain wasted or rotted in the rains. Poor Mountbatten, so wary of bombs, was blown up years later in his yacht by Irish militants in the harbor off Mullaghmore. But enough about blood and death. I know I am rambling, dear Neel, and in case you are wondering, let me tell you, because I miss our late afternoon chats at the store. The*

*Nahoum patties don't have the same flavour for me, with you so far away.*

*As I was saying, I was always curious about this book of Irish landscapes that my father, Brendan, pored over. Well, I decided to make this trip to Ireland and walk in the landscapes of that book. I secretly wished to judge, to see, how Irish I was, or how I felt about the land itself. My father knew himself Indian and Irish. I was at one more remove. An irresistible curiosity, a tug in my heart, drew me. I have always thought of myself as an individual, one of millions in India, far from Ireland. I think of Elliot Road when I think of home. Some day, before it is too late, I will tell you how I came to comprehend this.*

*If I think of nations, it is when they are misbehaving, or are playing sports like good boys. What does it mean to belong to a nation? Is it the accident of birth? Is it a memory, a yearning for some obscure stamp on the soul, some tune that plays in the blood? Or is it what others insist you are—painting your corner of the room around you?*

*I so wish you had come to Ireland with me, dear Neel—you, the rationalist—isn't that what you call yourself? And I, the fuzzy leftover of a colonial era. Who am I? Who are you? Who are we? We look at the lands of our ancestors and we are left with our own incomprehension, as if we are people who glance through biographies written in a recently lost language. Could I know, for instance, which sights would have brought my ancestors to tears of joy or inconsolable grief? Which cottage, which crossroad, which tree?*

*Have you ever—looking at yourself, your face in a mirror, your hands—wondered: Who is it that is looking at these hands, this face you think you know so well? What is this consciousness that is thinking all this, aware of this very instant in time? Who is this self, this I? Does this sentience have a name, a place in time? Can this deepest awareness have a national stamp? Or are all identities like layers over an unnameable core, an infinite nova that is just mind—that has no home, that cannot be housed, named or held—and has no country?*

*When I reached the Glengesh Pass, I looked with my physical eyes at the landscape I already knew so well, the dips and swells of the land. The green Irish earth was firmly and undeniably underfoot. I had the strangest of sensations. It was as if the being of my father merged into mine, as if he were looking from inside my head. In the bright cave of my skull it was his lamp that seemed to flicker and come to life. I cannot explain it any other way.*

*I woke one morning, my second day, in Sligo, the town that I had heard my father speak of. My night had been full of dreams. I stepped out alone at dawn. The curve of the path stretching out of town seemed like a message. I saw two sparrows, feathers puffed and brown. They looked no different from the ones around our house on Elliot Road.*

*What was Irish about this land? I wondered. What is my connection to it?*

*I felt like a traveler millennia ago, a hunter-gatherer, a tribesman, walking, not knowing how the earth would unspool before me, walking on until I felt the urge to stop. My naming the land came from my urge to settle down. What I named the land came also from my memory of where I had been: an Aryan tribesman from a far land, calling this land Erin in honour of his lineage and ancestors. I knew that another long-lost member of my early relatives from pre-history had taken a different path in that primeval diaspora, and the land where he settled with his kin, he named for the same reason, Iran. So many lands, so many variations of the same names.*

*I think of how our families were spread over the earth: How these names turn against each other, their languages having grown apart, their eyes only upon their own piece of ground, jealous of others, fierce and grasping. I raised my eyes from the earth and saw the expanse of the endless sea, glittering and admonitory. It was of a color no map ever showed.*

*Glengesh Pass was so inextricable from my father's dreams of it that it was no place on earth; and I was not just sprung from the blood of the Ahernes. My Irishness melted like sea-salt within this temperature of my being, making it possible for me to be Indian as well—a human being descended, who knows, from how many sources, the product of so many lineages which are unknown to us and will forever remain unknown: Erin, Iran, Aryan, human . . . maanush, the same word for "humankind" used in Bengali and by the Gypsies all over Europe! I felt sure that my father knew—in the last moments of his life, his mind's eye on the landscape of Glengesh Pass—that we all stand at the same great isthmus in the geography of time. We are all related: Our mortality is our one common nation.*

*You value the rational; I feel the limits of logic. You decided to study light; I ponder obscurity. Neel, I take comfort in the mystery of that opposition and celebrate the elusive nature of our histories.*

*You tell me about the snows and maples of America, and I rejoice in your sight of them. You have told me how the leaves change colours in variegated splendour in the weeks before winter comes. Please remember to pick many leaves this autumn. Put them in an envelope and mail them to me. Your letters are so short, dear Neel, so factual. At least that envelope will be a letter of many leaves.*

*Next year I shall definitely come visit you in America, in the autumn. I am saving every penny. I've been looking at reproductions of the great paintings in its Metropolitan Museum. I want to discover Greenwich Village together, Neel, and we must go to the Blue Note to listen to jazz and stay up all night! There is so much to do. I so look*

*forward to exploring New York together, then visit your university, and*
*go for walks in those maple woods of yellow and red. I miss you.*

*Your loving Grandpa*

Something in the letter reminded me of my own, very different, father: intent, open, and wondering, as if those two men who had never met had come together in my mind. I felt a growing tenderness, knowing that Neel had included me in this letter, although I was not its intended recipient.

When Neel returned, his anorak smelt of snow, and I held his cool hands in my warm ones.

# VIII

*For every tatter in its mortal dress*

# Billy
## Upstate New York
## Thanksgiving, 1989

Four and a half years. Shit, it's been that long. Closer to five. I wanted to marry Gillian, but she insisted that we complete our twelve steps before standing at the altar. But we went ahead and fixed the date, for a week before Christmas.

But there was still one step I needed to complete: To make peace with those I had hurt. I had to square things with Mom. I owed her that much.

"Billy, you gotta do it," my basement friends urged. It nauseates me to think of being turned into Billy the kid again, Archie's shitty son. The ghosts of all my humiliations lurked, a line of wounded soldiers from a disastrous campaign. I argued back and forth with myself, Gillian, with my sponsor Jerome. Gillian was certain that I would live through the reconciliation, as she called it. Jerome too.

"Ya'll be the stronger for it," he assured me, coughing before and after the sentence.

"He ain't got no power over ya," announced Jerome, smiling, wrinkling the greenish veins around the rheumy estuary of his eyes. Flicking away the butt, he announced, "Ya'll see, Bill. Hey, five years of sobriety, man. Yo'mum—she'll be proud o'ya. When's ya anniversary?"

"You don't know Archie Swint," I grumbled.

"Yeah," he said, his chest burbling with phlegm, "but he don't know what y'are now. Ya need to get this off ya mind. Once and fer all, Billy. Ya'll do it."

"He won't care," I said with dead certainty.

"It's for your mom, Billy," Gillian reminded me. "She'll be glad to see you for Thanksgiving. That'll be nice for her."

"He'll be nasty," I began, but Gillian just kissed me and said, "Call me when you are through, and I'll drive over and get you." She was having Thanksgiving dinner with her sponsor, Rachel. She was going to bake a pumpkin pie and a big batch of my favorite cookies, and expected me back for dessert.

"You might be having dinner, or watching the football game," I said. It was my desperate Hail Mary pass.

"I'll come when you call, Billy. I promise." We looked at each other, and I remembered the odds we had overcome and felt a surge of confidence. I am going to be fine. It's been five years, goddammit. He could even be dead. Or paralyzed.

"Why don't you let me drop you off?" Gillian persisted.

"I'll take the bus." I was sure. "I need some time by myself going there."

So it was decided. Gillian would drive our trusty blue Datsun. I would join her later, as soon as I was done.

• • •

I HAD KEPT away from my folks all this time. Three years ago, I saw Mom carrying a heavy grocery bag. I was about to cross the street to help when I saw Archie inside her car, tapping the steering wheel impatiently.

Lost in these thoughts, I got off the bus and started to walk toward our old house at Haddon Place, then had to snap myself back into the present and realized I was almost a mile away from Mom's apartment. *I am calm, I am calm*, I told myself as I walked.

*Camelot Apartments*, declared the flaked sign. I half-hoped that they had moved again. They would have had no way of letting me know. Or, he could be dead. *Oh yeah, oh yeah, sweet Baby Jesus, oh yeah.*

"Fuck this, I am going to pull myself together," I told myself. I'll see Mom and return her pendant in my gift box. I will tell her how I made this box, about the delicate tools I used, about Peter Foley and my job. And Gillian.

I turned the corners of the fake-brick apartments, laid out like a kid's building blocks on the scarred lawn. When I came to 114D, I recognized the dried flower and pinecone garland my mother used to hang on the front door of our Haddon Lane house, dusty and tatty now, with Mom's Ford Turd Pinto rust buggy, parked in front. I rang the bell.

I could not see into the dim stairway when the door opened, even under the cobwebby stairwell light. Mom stood on the mat, its gray plastic bristling around her bedroom slippers, her hair flurried with gray, as she peered at me uncertainly, her face eroding into a shy grin of recognition. Then he came.

Archie Swint loomed over her, standing squarely behind her on the first stair, his thick fingers proprietorially on her sweatered shoulder. "They said they'd taken the garbage away," he sneered, "but here it is, on our doorstep, see?"

"Oh Archie," began my mother, reaching out to me. His fingers closed on her shoulder, holding her back.

"What brings you here?" my father asked.

I held out the Saran-wrapped parcel of chocolate cookies Gillian had baked at home. "Happy Thanksgiving," I managed to say, out of breath.

• • •

I STARED AT the dull glaze of the plastic under which the patterned tablecloth lay limp and fuzzy, a far cry from my house-proud Mom's previous home. I looked surreptitiously at my father. Gaunt, hard, indestructible. His sour, masculine odor infested the apartment. Gray stubble stretched over his bony jaw. Flared nose over thin lips. The birthmark on his cheek seemed to have grown larger, a drop of clotted blood. Ropy muscles slid snake-wise under the wrinkled cover of his skin. He had been about fifty when I was born. It seemed impossible that he had ever been a boy, a child, anyone's baby. He looked more than ever made of rock and embedded metals.

Mom, only sixty, looked as if he had kept her long submerged under stagnant water. Her skin had grown loose and porous, and her nostrils drooped between puffy cheeks, filamented with tiny veins, and gray pillows under her eyes which had no light in them. She moved slowly, uncertain of her feet. I glanced at them. Toenails overgrown, ankles shapeless as undone pink socks. She smiled, at nothing, as if trying to listen to some whisper, her mouth vague and wet around the fissured edges. I wanted to hold her, but felt Archie's swiveled gaze, under tangled, complicated eyebrows, alert to every move.

A bare tree branch clawed at the fogged window pane. Mom had put zucchini and carrots into a plastic colander. Steam rose from it, and the kitchen was close with the smell of vegetables past their prime. The kitchen occupied all of my senses, pushing out everything else, taking over the recesses of my memory. As she puttered about, he sat on his chair facing the dim window. I could see his nostrils cavernous, his downturned mouth, his presence seeping into everything, like sludge-drip from under a car.

I stood next to Mom to get as far away as I could from him and his glass of whiskey, which he clutched in thick, root-like fingers. In the close botanical fug, he was speaking low, a growling generator spewing smoke. As much as I tried to block him out, his words were undoing me, bubbling up from that bitter stream, "loser, shit-head, ungrateful, illiterate," as if he were dictating my biography.

Moving to the window, I began to wipe at the pane, desperate to remind myself of the world outside, where Gillian and I lived, the lumberyard, Peter Foley's whistling, carpentry, clean cold air. I did not know when I would ever have the opportunity to speak to Ma alone.

Mom went to the living room, and I followed her. The backs of her hands, resting on the doily on top of the television, were blue and disorderly, a wriggle of earthworms breaking surface. Her rings looked like some strange stone bait, shiny and sharp. Archie had trailed after us, a buffalo on the mudflat of the carpet, his baleful eyes watching. The coffee table held four small framed pictures, all of Sandy's wedding. I urged my eyes away from them and smiled gamely into the cramped room with its sofa, hassock, bulging recliner, the defeated throw pillows.

Absently, Mom had taken out an enormous feathered hat from a closet and put it on, throwing her face into deep shade. *Was she losing it,* I worried, relieved when she, just as absentmindedly, reached up and took it off with both hands, holding it carefully, as if it were a full tureen of soup and set it down on the worn magazines on the coffee table. My father looked on, unmoved by the bizarre ritual.

"One more plate," whispered Mom escaping into the kitchen. Now it was Archie and me in the ring.

"How are you, Dad?" I said, sounding faint and diffident.

His teeth gleamed at me. "A nice question," he said, the air slipping sibilantly between his teeth, "a nice question surely."

"I'll see if I can help Mom," I muttered, panic rising in me as in a dream where you dreaded a wet basement, but your feet dipped into water at the very top of the staircase. The kitchen linoleum shimmered underfoot, reflecting the overhead fixture, a blurred sac of light that followed me like an eye every time I moved.

"Something I can do, Mom?" She kept wiping her dry hands in the towel she held, then put a number of cookies on a plate. "Have some," she said.

I chewed on one. I knew these well. The anise-flecked Christmas cookies took me back to childhood. "Merry Christmas," she said brightly.

"You mean Happy Thanksgiving?" I asked, bewildered by her mistake. After a wavering second of indecision, she righted herself. "Yes," she said, smiling brightly, "have another cookie." She had lost a tooth at the side of her mouth.

"You made them for Thanksgiving this year," I said, trying to fill the silence. Her eyes blazed at me. "These are Christmas cookies," she said sharply. I had no idea what we were arguing about. In walking up to their apartment, I had given up all rights to logic.

I looked at my fingers splayed on the kitchen counter, scabbed knuckles, nails bitten to the quick in the last few days, then fixed my eyes on the box of cereal propped in a corner, observing the letters on it begin to slip and slide, an obscene inky wriggle. I felt the gorge rise in me and turned away.

I watched Mom, my only protector, helpless, smelled the stale odor of age, saw the failing carpentry of her teeth, the pauses in her speech.

"I am so sorry, Mom," I said to her as quietly as possible. "I've brought back something that belongs to you." I felt I was a small boy again, back from school. She was holding out another cookie in her hand. Her eyes looked moist. "You went away, Billy," she said, as if betraying a secret. "Why did you come back?"

"Mom," I whispered, "Mom, did you miss me?"

I gave her the little cedar box, but she absently put it away in the sagging pocket of her apron without a glance. "Miss you?" she muttered vaguely. I reached over, wanting to touch her hand, but saw that minute flinch of her shoulder, the alarmed curling-up of her fingers.

"Mom—" I began, but she was looking away, raising her trembling veined hand, her back tense.

All this will make sense somehow, I told myself. Jerome, Gillian, my basement friends can't all be wrong. I felt my head and chest burn with words, longing to tell her about my home with Gillian, the smoky church basement from where we emerged time and again baptized into hope. I wanted to tell her that it was all right, that I was fine, inspite of . . . well, inspite of everything. I had brought back her pendant. I had made her the little box with all my skill and love. I wanted her . . . to pay attention. But all I felt was her frailty, her fear, seeping into me in the close air.

As if on cue, Dad walked back into the room. I could hear the roar of the toilet somewhere in the background. He was smiling, at my elbow, holding out a glass of whiskey before my unguarded face.

"Let's drink to Sandy and her new baby in Scranton," he ordered. I stared at the amber tilt and wink of the whiskey.

"Well?" snarled my father. The half-empty bottle sat on the counter. The old voices in my head had jolted awake. I willed them to be quiet, but could not help shivering as I glanced to see if he was wearing his belt.

"I . . . I'll have s-some soda," I faltered, sitting down.

"Whiskey and soda?" Archie Swint was looming over me. I felt his breath on me.

"Just soda," I said. *This is his space, and he commands it still.* The old tomcat spraying his pungent piss. I tried to push the glass away, hoping Mom would come to my rescue. But it was he who reached out and cupped his hand around mine, the first time his flesh had touched mine. I went limp, the intervening years erased, unable to stir in this choking nightmare.

In a surprising tilt, he poured the whiskey into my mouth. Some of it dribbled on to my collar as I tried, too late, to clamp my lips. The terrible warmth down my gullet startled me.

"Don't waste it," he chortled gleefully, filling the glass again.

I coughed and choked, but when I looked up, there was the second glassful. "To the baby," crowed my father. The world was tilting. I held on to the tabletop.

"That child won't be a Swint," he growled, "but what of it? Swint was just a name I chose."

"What do you mean?" I asked him, sitting up, dumbfounded. This was news to me.

"I'll tell you," he said, "how I chose Swint. But have another drink. He bent over me, his fingers curling down over mine around the heavy glass, its design pressing into my flesh.

"Swallow," hissed my father, sipping his own with relish, "and I'll tell you what exactly a Swint is." My mother shrank back into the corner, her hands inside potholders like amputee stubs.

*Who am I?* I drained my glass. *Tell me, tell me.* The sharp smell of whiskey clawed at the basement of my being, scratching and swatting something awake deep inside me. He reached out and poured another glass of whiskey. Full to the brim. I shook my head *no, nonono*, but there he was, one eye oozing goo, a gleam in the other one, his shrewd, goatish look making it clear what he thought of me: Scumbilly, Billy-swine.

"Where do we come from, Dad?" I pleaded with him, "we Swints?" I was reaching beyond him to ancestors I had never seen, dim shapes in my blood who would raise me up, above and beyond my father, but it was through him I had to reach out, I thought helplessly.

"Swints?" he said, turning his face about. A small ooze ran down one eye into a fissure on his cheek. "Fecked if I know. I could be part Eskimo," he said.

"I had no name when they found me. Who knows where? They weren't great note-takers those days. Packed me off to Boston, is all I was ever told, and that I'd been left in the streets . . ." His voice trailed off, then began again. "Some of the priests were always looking for nancy-boys. They're the ones had it cozy. The meaty soups, yeah—woollen socks, even handkerchiefs. For those dainty pantywaists. I got my nose broke, learned to fight, knocked out teeth as needed. Not like you," he jeered, swiveling toward me.

I looked down at my glass. He filled it.

"What about the name?" I persisted.

He ignored me. "Reckon I was fourteen when I lit out. Caught a train and sneaked off it at Rochester. When I climbed up the stairs, I saw this poster of a boxer pasted on a wall: *Archie Swint, King of the Ring.* Gloves held up, eyes that meant business. Mustache, solid legs. I liked the name. Shit, I never heard anything more about him. Maybe he croaked. Who gives a squat."

He drained his glass. "I got my first job in a car dealership. I was the doll-up man's assistant. My job was to shine up the wheels, the bumpers, running boards, headlights. My boss did the body. Old Gordie Potts. Took a shine to me." He chuckled at his own joke. "When they asked me my name I told them, 'Archie Swint.' That was that. Nobody else had heard of the damn King of the Ring but me."

"But didn't you have a name . . . at . . . at the . . . ? " I pleaded, not knowing how to name the place.

"*Orphanage*, you wimp. Having problems saying the word? Always were a softie. I don't even know how many I'd been in by the time I was old enough to understand."

"Maybe they knew the name which was really yours," I pleaded.

"Naah." He gestured dismissively. "They knew nothing about me, so they made one up. I figured I'd name myself. Why the hell not?"

"But a name's important," I grumbled.

"A rose by any other name smells as shit?" He barked with laughter, pleased with himself. He stood up to pour another drink.

"Oh Archie," said my mother, "I've forgotten the cranberry sauce."

Archie Swint turned and smacked her. It was exactly halfway between a slap and a hard pat; that was the baffling part. He always knew how to confuse us.

She turned away quickly and leaned over the open oven, as if she were checking it. She must not have remembered to turn it on, for no heat emanated from it. I could see her shoulders quivering.

I rose to my feet. But Archie was already standing over her, head swiveled sideways at me, daring me to move. With one hand he reached for her buttock and cupped it, his fingers working into the fold of her crotch. She jerked upright, her face damp and startled. He wrapped her in his other arm and swung her close. "Oh, love, is that you?" she squawked in panic.

A shudder of revulsion shook me.

"I'll get the cranberry sauce," I said, rushing out, "so I'll take your car, Mom," and picked up my gloves and the keys from the bowl on the small table at the top of the stairs. I needed to get away from the groping reach of Archie Swint. I needed to throw up in peace. "Get me some canned peaches," he called out from above. "Canned peaches!"

The Ford crap Pinto bucked uneasily under me. It had been a while since I had driven a stick shift. I lurched along until, after a block or two, it got easier. I kept thinking of taking my gloves off to drive, but the thought that Gillian had given them to me—in another, simpler life—made me keep them on. My protection, my talisman. I drove carefully, for I expected some deer to leap into my path, but none did.

The supermarket was closed, its parking lot deserted, and all the other shops around it tight shut. Sitting in the car, my shoulders hurting, I felt a bleakness I had no strength to resist. I started the car and it lurched forward, then rolled on as if by itself.

A misty rain began to fall. I had no idea how long I had been in the car, which had no clock, and I needed none; Gillian woke me in the morning and told me when to leave for work; at work, my foreman Peter Foley told me when to take my lunch and my breaks and when to go home. He wrote down my overtime hours as needed. When I got home, we were in our own universe, where all my time was ours, in that room with the hope chest at the foot of the bed.

But here, and now, a strange twilight had given way to a stranger night. I was lost. As I turned a corner, the car fishtailed over thick wet leaves so that it careened across the double line, but I righted it with effort. The trees on both sides leaned into each other, so that I felt I was driving under arched wickerwork. The headlights picked out odd objects, a discarded mailbox, the remnants of a deer run over long ago. A doll, its vacant eyes staring from the middle of the road, made me swerve in sudden terror. Then I saw a building, tiny lights twinkling all over it. I brought my car to a crunchy, pebbly stop and stood before it, shaking with cold and indecision in the bleak drizzle.

I walked in and asked for my friend Jack, straight up, as I slumped at the bar, clutching its polished wood as if it was the side of a storm-tossed ship. There was a large silent TV screen above the bar. On it drifted huge and improbable animals, floating above a mute city of lost and pointing children in a pantomime of joy. Jack and Djinn held me up and muttered into my ears in turn. I was back in my world of whispers.

I stood hugging the car, for my planet spun. Man, it was beautiful, and the road undulated like a wave in the ocean, and the soil below me rose and fell. The surge underfoot rolled far away, followed by another, but now I knew how to ride it. It was the gentlest, the friendliest of billows, and I chuckled with the pleasure of riding the next crest, carried by the purring oceanic creature under me. Water beaded the window, but I had forgotten how to use the wipers. Through the thousand beads, I could see bright stars ahead and above me. Some were big red stars, which sometimes, magically, turned green for my particular delight, transforming into incandescent fruits hung like orbs in the sky above.

I closed my eyes for just a moment and was startled by the crashing of branches all about me and a thud. The tide underneath had passed me and left me stranded. I had hit my face on a circular object in front of me.

Blood poured from my forehead. I picked wads of tissue from the box beside me and dabbed my face, wiping the blood from my eyes. I could hear something loose inside my head rattling like a dried pea. I tried the door, but it would not give. I pushed at the other door, which opened suddenly, tumbling me out. The cold air made a plume of my breath.

My head pounded. All about the car, broken branches, dry stalks of hedges impeded my sight. *Home*, I thought, *I need to get home*, feeling the weight of some terrible event, but unsure if I needed to be home to witness it, make it happen, or make it stop. I just knew I needed to get home. Setting off in a desperate half-run, turning corners, out of breath, bumping into picket fences and boulders, crossing black streets, panting past hunchbacked houses and wet lawns, I had no idea how I came to it, or whether it came to me.

A fear began to build inside me, a drumbeat, as I gripped the latch. I could feel its metallic chill even through my gloves. *If the front door is locked, I'll creep away and sleep hidden and safe in my garage loft*, I said to myself.

I stood at the main door, and turned the knob. It was open. The lair of Archie Swint. The djinns were humming in my head. I could make out very little in the room, but the walls, the fireplace, and mirror above it. The scene hung exactly like a painted sheet before me, flat and unreal as I slipped across the living room in the dark. I knew it like the back of my hand. *My home.* In the kitchen now, I could make out the familiar cabinets on the far side, the pale gleam of the counter.

*Oh what if Archie came down and found me here?* I thought, like a cornered cat, hackles rising, peeing in fear, but claws out. *Where are my claws?* I thought desperately. I saw the kitchen knives, handles protruding from the wooden block. I took the largest one.

I began to climb the stairs. My gloves that Gillian had given me were a perfect fit. I could hold the knife firmly. I had had enough of being scared. Once Archie Swint was afraid, all my terrors would go away, forever.

I pushed their bedroom door open. It opened with a familiar squeak. The bed seemed larger, and the two of them lying in bed, smaller. *Because I'm no longer afraid,* I exulted.

He stirred and rose up, looking directly at me. Mom shifted and sat up in a trance, blinking, her mouth shaping words. Why must she always put up with him? But suddenly Archie reached out with both hands.

"Love, is that you, is that you?" he whispered.

I had never heard him mention love, and he was mimicking Mom's disgusting submission. My gorge rose in an acidic slosh, for he was mocking me. Dizzy with rage, I made two slashes. I wanted to cancel them out.

The first slash made her fall back. The second evaded Archie's reaching hands and found his face.

*Love?* he whispered again.

Holding the knife with both hands, I drove it into his chest, leaving it there.

Even as I ran through the empty streets, wheezing past the railroad tracks, I felt protected by the gloves that Gillian had given me.

They were wet, with brown splotches on them. Blood, I thought, from when I hurt my head in the car. I'd clean them at home.

Archie must have been afraid, so he cannot ever catch me again. *Ever never*, like I used to say as a child. But I'm all grown up now.

# Kush
## Clairmont, Upstate New York
### November 23, 1989

I stare in consternation at my proud and lovely daughter, who is flushed, on the point of tears, her plate untouched. I wish Seetha were here with us, but she had been called away to the hospital; babies are born even on Thanksgiving. I have not cooked turkey, for neither my wife nor daughter likes it; instead I had made saffron pilaf, ginger-sautéed shrimps, and for dessert, Devi and Seetha's favourite South Indian *payasam*, with a top layer of toasted slivered almonds.

"Stay with us," I plead with Devika. I cannot help looking at her belly, though it will be months before she shows, marveling, *my grandchild!*

"Neel has no idea, Baba. He has gone down to New York to meet up with his grandfather, who is visiting from India. I don't really know his plans. He probably intends to return to India now that he's almost finished his dissertation. He may not want to get tied down. Oh, this is so tacky, Baba." Her head is bowed.

"But Devi, surely he loves you?" I venture, and know immediately I have said too much.

"What if Neel wants no part of this. I just can't imagine what he will say!" Devi moves back in her chair, holding her palms together, clenching them. She stares at her plate. There is a smear of saffron on the white china, the pilaf untouched, the curled digits of shrimp growing cold.

"Oh, such a horrible cliché," she whispers to herself, then adds defiantly, "Why should I even tell him? I may never want to see him again." Her tears are silent. She does not wipe them away. I am confused by the complexity of her reaction. *Don't young people nowadays talk to each other about love?* "Stay home with us," I whisper. "Your Ammu would want it too." My palm extended, fingers tentative, but my daughter is too far away for me to touch her.

A picture from years ago flits through my mind: Seetha at work, and me feeding Devi in her highchair, one hand pretending to fly a yellow Fisher-Price plane, the other tugging at her bib with its green clover pattern. I feed her pureed peas, opening my own mouth as she opens hers, pink gums with a little mother of pearl sliver of tooth.

"Baba-and-Daughter Team," I plead with my pregnant daughter, hoping that she will remember the old phrase. I feel undone by my love. "No," she says vehemently. She pushes back her chair, which scrapes on the hardwood floor. "I've already called and made an appointment at the hospital."

"At the hospital?" I repeat, in confusion. "It's all right then. They'll tell you everything's fine."

"No, Baba," she says, glaring at me. "Why can't you see! I'm twenty-three, I'm supposed to go off to Ireland next summer. Not this . . ."

"Didn't you discuss—" I begin, but I can see that Devi is not listening.

"It will look as if I'd planned this," she whispers to herself, tormented, "to make him stay." She twists the napkin in her hand, until it drops unnoticed to the floor. "I need," she adds to herself slowly, louder now, "I need to get rid of it."

"Get rid of it?" I could not keep the horror out of my voice.

"Don't keep echoing what I say, Baba," blurts Devika in undisguised irritation, "Yes, that's what I said. I'll get rid of it." She stands clutching the back of the chair. "You . . . you should be relieved," she weeps in accusation. "After all, you're the immigrant Indian. You're *supposed* to be dead set against unmarried pregnancy. What will the other Indian immigrants say: *Let's keep it quiet, et cetera, et cetera.* Don't tell me you suddenly turned pro-life and Republican!" She sounds hoarse. *It was as if she is teasing me,* I think dully.

In a rush of surprise, I feel words bubbling up within myself: *Is that you, Laub, is that you?* I had never thought of myself particularly as a Hindu, as someone who believes in rebirth and all that. Do I know what I actually believe in . . . Mathematics, certainly. I shake my head, as if that would help clear it.

"This is your baby," I begin slowly, trying to be as calm as I know. "I love you, for you are my daughter. Logically, therefore I love . . ."

"Cut it out, Baba," she says sharply. "You're supposed to make it easier for me. It's not a baby. It's a first-trimester embryo." She is weeping bitterly now, chest heaving as if she has run out of breath. By the time I look up from the table, my daughter has stormed out of the room, and left the house.

• • •

I PUT THE leftovers away, leaving the smeared dishes in the sink, too dispirited to do anything else. My heart sore and troubled, I went to my study and listened to music. First a little Bach, then an evening violin-raga of Pandit Jog. Devi's happiness was like a country that I needed to defend. I had always believed it was the right of a woman to decide about her body. But this was my daughter: Was she able to decide about her happiness as simply as she spoke about her right to decide?

What about my concern for the child growing within her—for whom society dictates that I feel affection *after* its birth, but gives me no right to guarantee its safe arrival? The immigrant Indian community would become a buzzing beehive of gossip. Everyone within it pretended that their daughters were, by some divine decree, virginal—or at least inviolate from premarital pregnancy. Yet I also knew from Seetha the number of deniable Indian pregnancies discreetly terminated at her hospital. She would never discuss names, but I surmised that some were girls Seetha herself had delivered years ago.

I also knew, with certainty, that if Devi gave us her baby to raise—for whatever reason—Seetha and I would joyfully do so. I had a quick vision of the two of us with the child in our backyard garden under the dappled shade of the flowering horse chestnut, and imagined myself showing the child a leafy branch, explaining how the Fibonacci series of numbers could be seen in the parting of twigs, in veins of leaves, and high above—in the formations of Canada geese flying overhead. I shook my head, to clear it of these vivid pictures.

I shut off the music and sat alone in silence. *Who am I to decide anything? Only her father—who merely brought her into this world,* I thought ruefully. I would reason with her. I could talk about . . . about what . . . I wondered. Love? Childhood? Death? *Why do we talk so often about death when we talk about love,* I wondered helplessly. *Is death a game God invented, then decided it was going to be part of everything?* I felt no wiser now than I had felt at twenty. I simply loved more helplessly, without the resilience of childhood. Almost four hours later, Seetha returned home from the hospital. I was reading in bed, unable to sleep. I could hear her tired steps on the stairs.

"Devi's left, I see. I don't want anything to eat, Kush." Seetha yawned and sat down on the bed. "Sorry it took so long, a difficult birth. A boy," she said. "But something interesting happened today."

"What?" I was always fascinated by her work.

"You'd think it would have happened earlier, in all these years of my career. But it didn't until tonight." She was smiling. I waited, for I knew she wanted to tell me her way.

"She was in labour for eleven hours, absolutely exhausted, but it all worked out well in the end." I nodded.

"She held her little boy to her chest after I had cut the umbilical cord and cleaned him off. I like to do that myself, Kush. Remember?"

*Yes, yes I did.* She had insisted on doing that even for our Devi, after her own birthing. She wouldn't let old Dr. Hennessy do it. She cut her own umbilical cord. *Is that why Seetha can be so calm today?* I fretted. *My umbilical connection with my child was invisible, thus impossible to cut; so it must remain always between me and my daughter.*

"As she was nursing him for the first time, she looked at me and said, 'Please name our baby boy.' The father—he was all smiles now—said, 'Yes, yes, please give our child a name. Your choice. Any name. We will accept. You helped him so much.' " Seetha was smiling in recollection.

"And did you?" I asked, although I knew she did.

"Yes," said my wife. There were silver glints in her hair. She was the most elegant woman I had ever known, still mysterious to me.

"I named the child Manu."

"The First Man—from our ancient texts! Where are his parents from?"

"Syria. Their son's name will be Manu al-Sadegh."

"A fine name."

We sat in companionable silence. But I still felt restless. Seetha looked at my troubled face.

"Did Devi choose to abort?" she asked me. Bluntly, I thought. The question burned through some tender part of my mind.

"How can you let her?" I asked, already knowing the answer Seetha would give me.

"We have always supported her decisions—if they are rational."

"Is this a rational one?"

"She has to decide if it is."

"How can you be so hard, Seetha?" *Am I angry? Who am I angry with?* I wondered. "You are so happy about Manu al-Sadegh. How can you let our daughter—"

"I am not letting her do or not do anything. Devi has to make up her mind, Kush, don't you see?"

"To let her child die?" I said in torment, unable to explain myself, but decided to go to my daughter tomorrow. I must get her to talk to her young man. Would she let me do that? Would her pride keep her from speaking to him? I kept thinking of all the things I wanted, needed, yearned to say.

"I'll go talk to Devi tomorrow," I said, "first thing in the morning."

"Yes, Kush," she said.

I put down the book I had been reading and watched Seetha

getting ready for bed, putting the fragrant creams on her long brown arms, her comely face that still moves me deeply. She smelt of sandalwood paste and jasmine, aromatic herbs, things she gets sent to her all the way from Kerala. I watched her in the mirror.

"I've been reading the Upanishads," I said to her. "Want to hear a bit?"

She nodded, sitting on our bed, brushing her hair rhythmically, a ritual that helped her to fall asleep.

Even as a burdened cart trundles on creaking, just so does the carriage of our mortal body, within which abides the Soul, moving on when a man gives up his vital breath of life . . . And like to the caterpillar, reaching the end of one leaf of grass, moves with ease to another and undulates itself across it, in the same manner does the Soul, abandoning the body and its burden behind, proceeds on to another body and moves onwards . . .

I closed my eyes and felt her come close and kiss me. "You're a sweet and strange man, Kush," she whispered. "I tell you good things about birth, and you tell me lovely things about death."

"That was what the ancients said, Seetha. Do we know any better?"

She lay on her side, hugging a pillow. I opened the window a tiny crack. Seetha liked a tiny trickle of fresh air, no matter the weather. I did it for her every night, and she knew I remembered. I thought of our years of marriage, our small acts of comforting each other, as I switched off the light and lay down beside her. She turned and put her arm across me. I could feel her breath on my chest. "Kush, I'm glad you will talk to Devi," she whispered before she sank into sleep.

I looked up at the milky suspension of the ceiling. Despite

the room's darkness, sleep evaded me. "When is the right time to have a baby anyway? What if Devi, my headstrong, prideful child, went and impulsively put an end to the child within her?" I asked myself. "The ancient Upanishads speak of the soul moving on, like a caterpillar from one leaf to another, with ease, with insouciant grace. But my daughter's child—this would be a soul I would never get to know—a child of my blood, my flesh," I mourned. I was in a strange half-sleep, and the thought of my brother, Laub, returned unbidden to me.

I had never been able to talk to Seetha about Laub. She knew about my dead twin, of course, but did not know about Laub's presence in my childhood. I thought with longing of that distant day at the university when I had walked into a world of swirling snow, the one magical day in adult life that Laub had made his presence known to me.

*Where are you now, Laub? Have you grown older and tired too, like me?* I had always thought him slender and pale, shy. I was drifting towards sleep when the door slowly opened with a small squeak. Seetha, a very light sleeper, had stirred—so I could not have imagined the sound.

"Devi?" she mumbled thickly in her sleep.

Layers of darkness troubled my sight. It was not Devi. My heart lurched with joy. I could make out, even in the darkness, that slender shape, his pale indistinct face.

"Devi?" murmured Seetha, sitting up.

A sudden movement as the figure waved something shiny, and Seetha fell back against her pillow, as if banished back into sleep by a spell.

"Is that you, Laub . . . *is that you?*" I whispered, tense with love and longing.

Laub came right to me. In the gloom, he looked translucent.

For a frozen instant, I remembered what Kalo Pir had once told me in that lost mosque. *Is it you, Laub,* I thought, *or is this the last angel who has come wearing our face?* Something glinted in the dark. There was a sharp sting across my face as I reached out with both hands. *"Laub . . ."* Then I felt a hand strike my chest.

Something entered, direct and shining, straight into my heart, connecting us inexorably. I fell back from where I had arisen.

# Devika
## Clairmont, New York
### November 30, 1989

For the past few nights I had fallen into ragged sleep, alone, struggling awake after one obstinate dream: I had been sleeping on a bed drenched with blood.

I had my appointment today. Lying in bed, drained of tears, I looked out the window at the bleak dawn. I put both my palms on my belly and imagined the fetus, its digits shaping, nails emerging like soft mother-of-pearl. I had a sudden clear vision of the child being formed out of my own intimate clay. Lying in my own warm bed, I thought of it growing cold later that day: the draining, the mortal cooling of its sac, its lifeblood failing.

I wrapped the blanket around myself, feeling frayed by lack of sleep, and stepped onto the deck, staring at the shadows under the rhododendron and saw the first hesitant light. Dawn was gathering, a tidal basin while a glitter of frost crinkled on the twigs and branches as I faltered, hugging myself.

The answer came to me, simple and lucid: The only blood relative I had left on this far continent was inside me, its intimate

existence like the tight-leafed protectiveness of the cold rhododendron. I made my choice that moment, for myself, with whatever
clarity love brings. I took a long bath in warm water and the Kerala
oils Ammu loved. I had a breakfast of local apples and Indian tea.

I went on a long walk along the sleepy edge of town, past the
park, through the maple and pine woods that lay beyond the town,
and turned back. Striding briskly now, my tiredness dropping away,
I thought of my child within me. I felt momentarily comforted, but
at this moment I felt full of things I needed to tell Baba, right away,
things I desperately needed to ask Ammu. I remembered those
times when Ammu and I would comb each other's hair. Her head,
with its cascade of dark hair elegantly streaked with gray, would
rest on my shoulder. Baba would sometimes, in passing, put his
hand on my hair, playfully mussing it. That had happened just two
weeks ago, on Saturday. Sounds around me grew muffled, all colors blanched, and I thought I would fall, suddenly sick with grief.
"Ammu, Baba, I've decided to keep my baby," I whispered.

I would now have to form a world around us I could bear to
live in. I had no idea when such another wave of grief would
come and try to pull me under. I could see nothing, my eyes filling
again with tears, no one in my life right now to hold me if I fell.
Chitto-kaku and Kamala Auntie were away in India for a niece's
wedding. They would grieve in their loud Indian manner, weeping
aloud, abandoning themselves to their mourning. I would have
to comfort them and felt a reprieve that they were away for now.
I needed time to myself, my grief a new wound, and I wondered
how I might nurse and shield it from others, even from well-meant
words.

As I walked back home through the deserted morning street, I
noticed a squad car parked at the head of our cul-de-sac, the officer

dozing against the fogged window, one hand limp on the bottom of the steering wheel. Sent by Sheriff Zuloff to stand guard discreetly over the house, I supposed, although the yellow police tape had been removed. I went through our gate, but as I approached the porch, I noticed two feet sticking out. I felt wary, but the sneakers looked familiar. One more step, and I saw Neel slumped over his rucksack, fast asleep, and beside him an old-fashioned leather suitcase I had never seen in his room before. I shook him by his shoulder. He blinked up at me, then scrambled up and held me. "I am so—I . . ." he began to falter. "I heard . . ." I stood stiffly in his arms, listening to his torn breath. "I . . ." he started again, and then seemed to gather himself with effort. "Are you all right, Devi?"

"Am I?" I began, then blurted, "I am pregnant, Neel." I looked at him carefully, noting his reaction.

A smile flickered and his eyes began to tear. "Oh Devi," was all he said.

"Are you staying? There's really no need to," I said over my shoulder as I walked into the house. I did not yet trust myself not to cry. Needing to do something, I filled the coffeepot and turned on the stove then, opening cabinets, pretended to look for something. This kept Neel momentarily silent. I stared at all the rows of spices Baba had bought, including the black mustard seeds for our *ilish*, and the small jars of spices Ma used for her twice-a-year sambar and dosa. Slamming the cabinets, I stood at the window, suddenly dazzled by the brilliance of the day. The coffeepot began to boil.

"Devi," Neel began, "when I heard what had happened . . ." and stopped, his voice cracking. He fell silent, for something else had distracted him.

When I turned, I saw he had seen the crumpled piece of paper I had smoothed on the kitchen island. My hospital appointment, and the name of the procedure. I could see this new shock slowly registering on his face. Neel could barely speak in his distress. I looked at him as if he were a stranger trying to convey something from an impossible distance.

"D-devi," he stammered, "we . . ."

I removed the coffeepot. "Milk, sugar, black?" I asked him briskly, although I knew he liked it black and sweet. I felt oddly detached from it all, the streaming light, the steam curling from the kettle on its trivet, the dishes in the sink. Neel's mouth opened and closed. He said something, but my world was muted. I bent to pour the coffee. He was shaking his head slowly, his eyes closed. Like a child, I thought, like a child who cannot tell if he is lost. He moved toward me, leaning on the counter, and cried out sharply in pain.

Neel held his hand up—he had leaned his open palm on the still-hot burner where the coffeepot had been. I reached quickly and turned on the cold water in the sink. "Put your hand there," I said impatiently.

"No," said Neel, his face pale, his eyes angry and stubborn. "No."

"Suit yourself, but you'll get a blister," I told him.

"No," said Neel again.

"It's your hand," I said. "Do what you want."

"It's our baby," he said. His palm was an angry red as he held it out toward me, a supplicant. I took him by his wrist and put his hand under the tap. He let me do as I pleased with his hand, as if he had given it away.

"There is already so much death," he said, his face buried in my disheveled morning hair. I could hear him draw his breath, smelling my hair. He loved to do that after we made love. He held me carefully, on a headland canting toward perilous water. "Don't you feel any love for our child?" he said. *But you don't know what I've already decided*, I wanted to blurt out. Tears were streaming down his face, while his hand, a seared red, dripped water on the kitchen tiles. "It's what I don't want you to do," he pleaded.

"What do you think I'm going to do?" I asked him, wondering if I should get him some of Ammu's calamine to put on his palm.

"I love you, Devi," Neel said simply. With a sudden force, Baba's words at the dinner table, perhaps his last words to me, hit me. I was choking.

"What?" I said, completely taken aback. He had never said this before.

"I love you," he whispered, "Does my saying the words make it more real? Don't you already know, clear as light?"

I tried to calm myself, wiping my hands on a kitchen towel. "I have already decided to keep my baby." But I said it so softly he did not hear me in his frantic search for words.

"Do you actually want me to go down on my knees?" he said awkwardly. What was he asking of me, I thought in panic. "Will you—" he started.

"Stop, Neel," I said, demanding a moment of stillness.

All the events and decisions of my life seemed to be gathering, heaped one on the other, jostling at this narrow isthmus of the present. *I want to understand, weighing each piece, part by part,* I thought, clutching the table. I looked away, outside the kitchen window, and saw a man smoking a pipe under the horse chestnut in the backyard. I would use this excuse to get away for a moment. I needed the time to collect myself.

"I'll be right back," I said to Neel, leaving him kneeling on the tiles, looking up at me as if I were losing my mind.

"I'm going to talk to that plainclothes cop. I'll have him leave now and go back to Chief Zuloff. I don't need anyone to watch over me," I rehearsed as I rushed outside.

The garden was sparkling, and the light caught a glint of red in the man's gray hair. His face, lean and lined, was clean-shaven and reminded me of the knight in my favorite film, the one in which he plays chess with cowled Death by a rocky coast. I could not remember having seen this policeman before.

"You can leave now," I said firmly as I came up to him. "There is no need for you to stay here anymore."

"I am very saddened by what happened," he said quietly. I nodded, slowed before his poise.

"You can go back," I continued. "I can call Sheriff Zuloff if you want." Up close, he looked too old to be a cop.

"Ami Neel'er Dadu," said the man, putting away his pipe.

"What?" I said in confusion, searching his face, "What are you saying?" Then I understood, in a rush. He had spoken to me in Bengali. *I am Neel's grandfather.* I leaned against the bark of the horse chestnut. I needed that firm trunk, its steady presence.

"Mr. Aherne, the letter you wrote to Neel. After Ireland," I said stiffly. "Well, I . . . I read it." He nodded, but said nothing.

"I'll tell you right now. I am pregnant," I added, leaning against the bark. "I just told Neel, who did not know." My teeth were clenched, my hands clasped tightly about myself. I interrupted him as he made to speak, "He's inside. He's free to go."

He said nothing, but held out his arms and folded me into himself. He somehow understood that I needed him to know the worst about myself. I wanted him to dislike me immediately, so that our interaction would end abruptly and soon. My defiance was my only, frail weapon.

"Neel blistered his palm," I mumbled.

"Yes," he said simply. He touched my hair with his fingers, and I sensed that he did that when Neel needed to be comforted. I clung to him, my head burrowing into his chest, trembling, and he held me, providing me that small important space to stand on.

When at last I let him go and stood at arm's length, I had stopped shaking. I led him inside to my father's shuttered study, off the living room. I curled up on the sofa, hugging my knees as I used to, while chatting with Baba. Mr. Aherne turned his head when he heard Neel in the kitchen.

"He's got off his knees. He must be making coffee," I said softly, just to him.

"Knees?" he said, "Ah, he had the good sense to propose, did he?"

"I don't think I let him get to it," I said, smiling at last.

"I don't suppose you'd let his grandfather complete his job for him?" he said, his face breaking into a grin. I was struck by how natural it looked, for his lined face in repose was full of inwardness, meditative.

"Are you surprised?" I asked him, suddenly full of confidences. "Oh—and I took you for a plainclothes cop."

"Should I be?" he tilted his head. "And incidentally, many years ago, I used to be a policeman, in plainclothes, when the British ruled India."

"I wonder what Neel is up to. Let me get us some coffee," I said.

When I went into the kitchen, I found that Neel had managed to wind a moist napkin around his palm. He had also set a pot of coffee on Ma's favorite tray from India, with three mismatched mugs on it. He had reached the limits of his efficiency.

"Devi, will you," he began again uncertainly, standing in the middle of the kitchen, "will you marry me? I can't kneel, holding this tray and all."

"Yes, Neel, I might," I said, "oh, but please don't kneel. You'll just tip the coffeepot and scald the other hand!"

We came into the study together, where Neel set down the tray, wincing as he flexed his palm. He went to raise the blinds. Light pooled into the book-lined room. As our eyes met again, I could not help smiling, our different pains set aside. *I will*, I mouthed the words. He read my lips, and came over to kiss me.

"Let me take care of that hand," I told Neel. "I'll be right back."

His grandfather had risen like a somnambulist and walked toward Baba's desk, while I went upstairs to fetch Ammu's first-aid box, which had gauze, antibiotic cream, and small scissors to tend to Neel's hand.

When I picked up the familiar box, its touch transported me to a different time of skinned knees and scraped elbows and Ammu administering to me, speaking gently while Baba hovered over us. As I listened to the wooden creak and shift of the house, I grew aware of all that would never happen now: Ammu chatting on a Sunday morning with Neel and me, coffee cups steaming, the pages of the *New York Times* divided between us, and the sound of a child's footsteps preceding Baba's as they tromp in from the deck into the kitchen, laughing together, and in that magical film, I see Ammu leaning down to speak to the child holding my father's hand. *My child*, I thought with a pang for his loss, waking abruptly from my reverie, marveling as if it were my own childhood memories, now transposed to this house.

Sinking weakly on the top step of the staircase, I leaned my head against the banister and closed my eyes to hear them again, but even as the sound of their voices and laughter faded away, the memory of their mirth fell like misty rain and soothed the ache within me, its unseen waters rising to obliterate the walls between time past and future. I felt a smile forming on my face. I heard Neel stirring in the kitchen and remembered why I had come up here.

I picked up the first-aid box from the stair beside me, wiping my wet face on my sleeve, and went down to tend to my man, the trace of my parents' presence seeping into my day, sustaining me.

Taking out the ointment, bandage, and small scissors, I finished dressing Neel's hand when it struck me that Mr. Aherne was still standing in front of the picture above Baba's desk, studying the mansion that did not exist anymore. The semicircular porch, the pillared wings, the looming dome above it, and the large peepul tree in front with its innumerable leaves meticulously sketched in India ink. I could see his rapt face reflected on the glass pane of the picture, the lines of the house rising behind it like pentimento.

"You like the picture?" I asked him. "My grandfather Monimoy Mitra sketched it from memory after he became a refugee in Calcutta. That house was somewhere else."

"I know the house well." he said quietly, "And his name was not Monimoy."

"Not Monimoy?" I looked up in surprise. "What do you mean?" I protested. "Of course I know my own grandfather's name!"

I drew him to the other part of the wall, near the bookcase.

"See?" I pointed.

Here were the seven generations of my ancestors, which I had written in fifth grade with colored pencils on kraft paper that Baba got framed. Mr. Aherne stood peering at the chart.

"There is a mistake here, Devi," Mr. Aherne said quietly, "did your father never tell you?" Then he added, almost as an afterthought, "Ah, of course. Santimoy never told anyone. After all, he was told not to."

"What?" I did not try to hide my skepticism.

"Yes, dear," he said. "Your grandfather was Santimoy. His twin, Monimoy, died young."

"No, no," I interrupted, trying to clear up the confusion. "It was my father, Kush, who had a twin. My grandfather named him Laub—you know, after one of King Rama's twin sons in the Ramayana. I don't know if my uncle Laub was identical to my Baba. He was stillborn."

"So Santimoy's children were also twins?" Mr. Aherne sounded surprised. "I did not know that, of course." Then he added, smiling at me, "Well, that does run in some families. But I do know for certain about Santimoy and Monimoy."

It was a mystery that Robert Aherne would know so much about my family. "Aherne!" I exclaimed. My Baba had kept mumbling the name Aherne after I had asked him. He kept trying to remember details. "That name meant something to my father. You might have been neighbors in Calcutta?" I suggested, but he shook his head.

The clock struck ten. This was our noisy grandfather clock Ma had bought at some antiques shop in Cold Spring Harbor after they moved to this house. It only chimed at the hours it wanted—and poor Baba, try as he might, never could get it right. Sometimes it chimed only once a day, sometimes every hour of the night. It did not help Baba's insomnia.

Mr. Aherne went on, unaware of the chimes. "Monimoy had died of cholera the very day I reached that house near Barisal. I saw his body. I was a policeman then, undercover, working for a man called Tegart. Have you ever heard of him?"

I shook my head.

"He is in the history books. For the wrong reasons." He sat silent for a moment. "I had been sent by Tegart to kill your grandfather." I felt the shiver run down me, as Neel looked up sharply at his grandfather, pained and astonished.

Mr. Aherne saw my anxious look and shook his head. "We became friends instead. And Santimoy's old grandfather, Ramkumar, nursed me back to life. I would otherwise have died of cholera. I can say I was reborn in that old house."

I glanced up. There he was on the chart, Ramkumar Mitra, my grandfather's grandfather. My head was swimming in time, and Baba's familiar study had become an unfamiliar terrain.

But what had also registered on my heart was Neel's quick rise to protect me, even from anything his grandfather uttered. I understood he did not know how to mention my parents, yet wanted to comfort me. He was mine to lean on.

"What happened?" I asked Mr. Aherne. Neel sat beside me, holding my hand, listening.

# Chief Sandor Zuloff

## Clairmont, New York

### November 30, 1989

Through the open door of my office, I watched Delahanty, our rookie officer, dealing with a codger who had walked in half an hour ago, snarling about his missing car. I was waiting for any radio dispatches that might relate to the Thanksgiving Day homicides. We were fanning out the search wider for anything unusual in the area—not a good omen, I knew from experience. The closer to the location of the crime we got the leads, the better. I needed to keep my ears to the ground, but had heard nothing yet.

The man walked over to the counter again as soon as the clock showed ten o'clock. He leaned on it, tapping on the wood impatiently, his face gray and unshaven, eyes red-rimmed. He reeked of stale liquor and impatience.

"Wait a half hour, you said, and a half hour it's been, see," he hissed. "I'll talk to your boss. See, it's ten now."

"Take a seat like I said," returned young Delahanty curtly. "Chief's busy right now."

"Yeah?" The man was unfazed. "Two days it's gone missing—I

want someone to tell me something, for feck's sake. I wanna see him right away, your Chief—whatsisname—yeah, Zulu."

"Zuloff, Chief Zuloff," said Delahanty.

"Zoo-whatever," said the man. "My name's Swint, Archie Swint. Car's missing. Son's made off with it," adding under his breath, "sumuvabitch." He scratched his cheek and examined his nails. "Heard anything yet?"

"About your son?"

"Feck my son. Just you find my car. Been two days now. I got my rights."

Delahanty ignored him, rummaging through reports I told him to bring to me. I needed to see every last thing, anything at all, that happened in the last week. He followed me into my office and gave me a sheaf of papers. The clock edged on for another twenty minutes. I emerged, having reread the reports on that double homicide on Haddon for the hundredth time, and stood at my office door marked *No Admittance*. Delahanty was speaking on the phone, while Archie Swint fidgeted in his seat, his wife dozing beside him.

"Where's it?" barked Archie Swint suddenly. His startled wife sat hugging herself, her eyes blinking uneasily under the fluorescent lamps. She flinched when her husband spoke, then slowly looked away, head lowered, clutching her bag to herself.

"Where?" rasped the man again. I turned my head to look at the man carefully.

"Car," spat the man, pronouncing *a* as in *cat*, in his Upstate accent. "Where's my damn *car*?"

"Keep a civil tongue," I suggested. The man swiveled his glare at me, then crouched back, looking away, as if he had seen a larger dog. The woman shifted uneasily in her seat, drawing her knees together.

"What's the report that just came in?" I asked Delahanty, under my breath as he rummaged through his papers.

"About the double homicide on Haddon?" he asked, looking up at me. "Nothing more so far, Chief."

"That car," I said.

"Oh yes, sir, came in this minute. Tony on patrol saw a blue car ditched pretty far into the woods—off the county road. He's getting it towed. Maybe ten more minutes."

"Here?" I asked Delahanty, and the young man nodded.

"Double-check if it's his," I told him.

"Plate numbers, sir?" Delahanty asked across the counter. The man stood up creakily, tugging at his baggy tartan shirt, adding under his breath, "About fecking time."

"Plate?" asked Delahanty again, and the man spat out the number. His wife mumbled inaudibly.

"Being towed here any minute now," Delahanty told him. "It's pretty banged up. You'll have to pay the tow truck."

"Sumavabitch, I knew it," Swint snarled at his wife and rushed for the door, leaving her behind. Delahanty called after him, "You'll have to fill out this form, and I'll need to see the registration."

"She got all that, it's in her name," said Swint, gesturing backward with his thumb, as he barreled through the door, leaving it open behind him, letting in the chilly air. The woman stayed, lost in her thoughts.

"Ma'am," the young officer called her. As she shuffled over to the counter, her handbag fell open. "Oh," she said, bewildered and stooping, her scared eyes blue with hardly any lashes. The young man came around the counter and helped her pick up her things. "Thank you," she kept muttering, "thank you, thank you . . ." A hair-snarled brush, a lidless lipstick, some soiled peppermints, hairpins, a frayed change purse. She struggled to read his nametag.

"Delahanty, ma'am, Bill Delahanty," he said to her.

"Why, Billy's my son's name too!" Her lipstick had seeped into the fissures around her smiling lips. Officer Delahanty felt protective of her. "He the one took your car?"

"Yes," she said, dropping her gaze. "He asked us, didn't he? It's not like you think."

"I'll just need you to fill out this form, Mrs. Swint," he said gently, helping her put everything back in her handbag. "And, yeah, I'll need your registration. Is it in the car?"

"What?" She looked up vaguely.

"Your car registration, ma'am," he reminded her. "You need to fill this out."

"Oh yes, yes, I have it here," she said, fishing it out after a while. "I forgot my reading glasses. I won't be able to write," she confessed humbly.

"Can you sign without them?" asked Delahanty.

"Oh yes, yes," she said eagerly, "I can also read most of it if I hold the paper like so," she added, holding it at arm's length.

"That's good," said Delahanty, smiling back. "You tell me the details and I'll fill it out, okay? Then you sign it, and we're done."

She nodded and handed him the form. Officer Delahanty noticed that her fingers were swollen, and her rings, a thin wedding band and a beautiful solitaire diamond ring, looked embedded.

"Lovely ring, ma'am," he said, companionably.

"Eh?" she said, momentarily confused, then added animatedly, "Oh yes, that's my grandmother's ring. It has her and Grandpa's names inscribed inside. I never saw Grandpa, but Grandma left me her ring when she passed on." Officer Delahanty went on filling out the form, and she answered him absently, looking at her ring.

"There's a mistake here, ma'am," said Delahanty, looking at Mrs. Swint's car registration. "The address on this doesn't match the one you gave earlier."

"What?" she repeated, "what address?" growing flustered at being brought back to the present.

"You said 166 Haddon Lane, but it says different here on your registration."

I listened, still as a hunter who has heard a rustle.

"Oh," said Mrs. Swint sadly. "I'm sorry. I got to thinking of the ring and the house Daddy left me, didn't I? We used to live there. My son, Billy, loved it. It had a tree with lovely flowers in the backyard. And rhododendrons. He's a good boy. I have his picture from high school, I do," she said, fumbling about and finding it in her bag. She handed it to Officer Delahanty. "His name is Billy too," she repeated, smiling at him.

"Where does he live, Mrs. Swint?" I asked. Officer Delahanty looked quizzically at me. He had no idea that I had been listening. She had become pensive.

"Ma'am, where is your son, Billy?" I asked again.

Mrs. Swint looked close to tears, her face pale with shame. "I—I d-don't know."

She signed the papers like a blind person and proceeded to leave. Officer Delahanty caught up with her at the door, giving her a copy of what she had signed. She put it in her bag without glancing at it. It hung open again, its clasp undone. She clutched at the banister and began to step down gingerly, one step at a time.

"One sixty-six Haddon Lane," I whispered to myself, picking

up the creased photograph from the table; I had not returned it. "Where are you right now, Billy Swint?" I thought, before I put it in my pocket.

I was in a trout stream now, knowing I was about to reel in the line.

# Devika

## Clairmont, New York
### November 30, 1989

In the study, the light from the open window caught the picture of the old mansion sideways, and reflected on it, I could see the outline of Mr. Aherne's thoughtful face over the the India-ink lines and painted pillars of that long-ago house in Barisal, in a land abandoned by my grandfather, whose real name I had now come to know.

I wondered now if my father thought often about his dead sibling, Laub, whom we had never discussed, though I knew about him. There was so much about the past, about my own parents, I did not know, about all that broke or shaped my family.

Mr. Aherne's old leather suitcase lay open at his feet. I could imagine him packing it carefully by himself in another old house, in Calcutta. I had a feeling that these were the only clothes he owned. I could see his neatly folded shirts, alongside two carefullly rolled ties, and underneath, three silver-framed pictures. One was his own wedding photograph, black-and-white, which he handed to me when he saw me looking. He had his arms around his wife.

They were both smiling into the camera, she in a sari, standing outside the marriage registrar's office, the sign visible. The second picture, in color, showed Neel's mother when she was about ten, all three sitting under a multicolored umbrella. Behind them sparkled the sea. I noticed the strong family resemblance between the father and the young daughter—and Neel—and wondered for the first time whom my child would resemble.

"Can I make a copy of this picture?" I asked impulsively.

"It's your turn to keep the original. Give me a copy when you can." He handed me the picture, frame and all.

The last picture, in black-and-white, was of some other woman, cut from an old glossy magazine—but I recognized the face immediately: Merle Oberon. I knew her from *Wuthering Heights,* Baba's favorite film—based on my favorite book. Baba had a black-and-white videocassette which we had watched many times.

"Why do you have her picture in a frame?" I asked him, unable to curb my curiosity.

He shook his head and said, "Another day."

"Actually, Grandpa, you never did tell me either," protested Neel.

"Another day," he repeated, "I will, I promise you both." Then he took out a long cloth packet, carefully wrapped in a length of faded silk.

"And what is this?" I asked.

"This I will tell you today," he said, getting to his feet. "May I put that picture on the wall on this coffee table?"

"By all means, Mr. Aherne. Bring the house down."

They smiled at my words, and I was surprised that I could smile again. I remembered how Baba and I would sit and chat about all things on earth and laugh at the silly jokes we made. It cheered me to remember those times, and that Neel was here with me now. He helped his grandfather take down the large picture and set it down carefully on the table, before they sat on either side of me, looking down at it.

Mr. Aherne unwrapped the silk and took out an old envelope which once had a red wax seal, now faded and crumbling.

"An old letter?" I said in anticipation. "Is it about my grandfathers Santimoy and Monimoy? After what you told me, I don't know what names to use to tell them apart!"

"No, Devi," explained Mr. Aherne, "it's not about them. It is from an earlier time. I brought it along because I thought it time for me to hand it over." Neel held my hand, and I sensed that reading this old letter on occasion must have been his family tradition.

"You are part of this," said Mr. Aherne, discerning my thoughts. "You and Neel and your child are very much a part of this letter written by my grandfather Padraig Aherne, who had come somehow to India, and your ancestor Doorgadass Mitra, the merchant prince, saved him from being executed by the East India Company.

"Did you know that Ramkumar had been given up for dead," said Mr. Aherne, "left by the river according to ancient custom? It used to be called *antarjali jatra*—journey into the water. No longer practiced, thank God. My grandfather Padraig revived Ramkumar. Without these two persons, there would have been none of us." He looked around the table, and continued. "Ramkumar gave me this letter, written to your ancestor Baboo Doorgadass Mitra."

*Baba should be here*, I thought, with a catch in my throat, imagining Ammu and him sitting here. Neel draped one arm over my shoulder, and he knew what I was thinking.

Mr. Aherne was laying the pages one by one on the picture of the old mansion. The sheets looked frail and aged, and the black ink of the script on the brittle paper showed edges of red: So like Mr. Robert Aherne himself and his reddish hair, I mused.

"I thought I'd bring the picture of the mansion here, and put the letter on it, for I saw it first in Barisal," he said. I nodded in agreement.

"From now on you and Neel are going to be the keepers of this letter," Grandpa Robert said. Yes, *that* was what I would call him, I decided. He sat back, looking at us, letting the stories of his life flow into ours. I imagined our families gathering in the shadows, unseen but present all around us.

I thought of the story Baba told me once, remembered from the lost land of his childhood. Someone there had told him of a great and timeless tree—the Sidrat al-Muntaha in Paradise: For each birth the tree sprouts a new leaf. When a person dies on earth, it falls, but before it reaches the ground, an angel of Life flies to gather it for a celestial book, made of innumerable leaves. Each leaf, with its parting veins of doubts and reconciliations, green forever in that great Book of Names.

We read each page together, Neel and I, our heads touching, the picture of the great house under us, revealing different parts of itself as we lifted successive pages, our reading holding us together in no country I could name. We were in India, Ireland, and America, all together.

# Afterword and Acknowledgments

My debts of gratitude are many, beginning with my grandfather, Kumud Bhushan Ray, visionary, builder of railway bridges, and avid Tibetan scholar, in whose library I had free rein, where he taught me the alphabets of three languages and told me stories until the day he died, my childhood ended, and the library sold off soon after by his sons; Fr. G. K. Carlson of the Society of Jesus, who fed me wonderful books and daring ideas in the otherwise sterile school years; Amal Bhattacharji at Presidency College, who ignored the plodding syllabi and swept me through Dante in the first great travel of my life; A. N. Kaul, at Delhi University, and Brijraj Singh, who was my mentor and colleague when I began to teach at St. Stephen's College in Delhi. I was enriched by the numerous chats over poems and novels and bad English department coffee in Rochester, New York, with George Ford and Anthony Hecht, who taught me that the rigours of prose were no less than those of poetry.

To the numerous books of history, memoirs, and journals

that I used in my novel, my debt is incalculable. Just a small sampling will suggest the deep soil in which I planted my branching story of the various diaspora, identity, and hybridity. I found Cecil Woodham-Smith's *The Great Hunger* a marvelous starting point; her insights are unfailingly sharp and clear. These were balanced by Thomas Campbell Foster, *Letters on the Condition of the People of Ireland* (1846), *Leaders of Public Opinion in Ireland* by W. E. H. Lecky, De Beaumont's *Ireland* (1839), T. W. Freeman's *Pre-Famine Ireland*, and Liam O'Flaherty's novels. Nassau Senior's nineteenth-century oeuvre *Journals, Conversations and Essays Relating to Ireland* was full of information, as were Edward Wakefield's *Ireland: Statistical and Political (1812 Vol. I)*, Sir Charles Trevelyan's *The Irish Crisis* reprinted in *Edinburgh Review* (1850), and Sir George Nicholls's *A History of the Irish Poor Law* (1856). I ploughed through Alfred Smee's *The Potato Plant, Its Uses and Properties* (1846) for an insight into contemporary understanding of the problem. An earlier work, Arthur Young's *A Tour in Ireland* (1780), made for compelling reading. This is just a small sampling of what became a much larger bibliography.

For a period of six months, before writing the Ireland segment of my novel, I immersed myself in reading contemporary journals from the 1840s, such publications as *Freemen's Journal; Nation,* which was founded in 1842 by Daniel O'Connell himself; *The Times of London,* which had not yet spawned its many namesakes in various parts of the world; *The Famine in the Land* (1847), written by Isaac Butt, who was a friend of W. B. Yeats's father; Sir Robert Peel's *Memoirs* (1856); W. J. Fitzpatrick's *Correspondence of Daniel O'Connell;* and a veritable pile of contemporary pamphlets and posters. Later historical research often corrected contemporary perceptions of events, but I needed to keep in mind that for a novelist, the first reactions, even rumours—especially early rumours—are of prime value and must dye the tempera of the narrative.

I spent many hours, often with a magnifying glass in hand, peering into Victorian-era cityscapes of Dublin and, like Brendan Aherne, at Irish landscapes of that period. So I did at photographic archives of Bengal in general, and Calcutta in particular, for use in the later segments of my novel. I mourn the destruction by fire of the extensive and irreplaceable photo archives of Bourne & Shepherd in Calcutta, parts of which I had the good fortune to look at years ago.

For the Indian sections, apart from English language sources, I delved into a wide variety of vernacular books, newspapers, reminiscences—too numerous to set down in the context of a work of fiction. Anyone who researches my novel will find these multiple roots that fed the narrative. "Truth flourishes where the student's lamp has shown, and there alone . . . ," as Yeats himself put it.

I shall not belabour the point that considerable research went into imagining New York City in the 1910s. Again, archival photographs in various libraries were invaluable, as were books such as Kathie Friedman-Kasaba's *Memories of Migration: Gender, Ethnicity, and Work in the Lives of Jewish and Italian Women in New York 1870–1924*. Before writing about the Triangle Shirtwaist Factory fire, I read and re-read Leon Stein's definitive *The Triangle Fire*, excerpts from the trial testimony of *People of the State of New York vs. Isaac Harris and Max Blanck*, and David Von Drehle's *Triangle*, a fine synoptic book. I was thus enabled to use the backgrounds of each worker I mentioned in my narrative although, of course, Bibi Sztolberg and Ijjybijjy Malouf and the cause of the fire are my invention. Josephine Grunwald is part fiction, as she is modelled on my friend Rosalind Fischell's aunt Josephine Greenwood.

For the exigencies of the fictional narrative, I pulled some events closer together or placed a historical figure in a place where he, in fact, was not, but I have been mindful that the essential truth of the times was not tampered. The most unlikely events, however, are based on actual events, such as the foundering of the fictional ship *Rose of Erin* on an iceberg and the subsequent rescue; O'Dwyer's assassination by a massacre survivor; the eruption of Vesuvius and the resultant devastation around it. Boscotrecase has now recovered, rebuilt; when I last went there, I cast a wary eye on the implacable bulk of Vesuvius.

Needless to say, different segments of research needed to be done in several countries, and without the help of librarians in each, I would have been stuck at dead ends or shut doors on three continents. I salute their separate but related tribes.

Mr. Neal O'Brien, former Member of Parliament, welcomed me to his home in Calcutta and his journal resources. He reminisced about his Anglo-Indian childhood and youth, while Mrs. O'Brien graciously added her comments on typical Anglo-Indian recipes and festivities. I recounted anecdotes of my Anglo-Indian teachers and classmates at Miss B. Hartley's School, the first magical classroom I attended before being transferred to the mercy of the Jesuits at St. Lawrence School.

I wish to thank a number of individuals on three separate continents for their unflagging interest and faith in my work: Eugene Datta, Rosalind Fischell, Tuli Banerjee, Ethan Shapiro, Rama Lohani and Philip Chase, Dona and Dipanjan Chatterjee, Kunal Basu, Anjali Singh, Carol Zook Shapiro, Janet Eber, Geetali Basu, Deb Dimatteo, John Murray who passed away before he could see *No Country* in print, and, in particular, Gillian Stern in London. In India, my debts to people are too many to enumerate. Suffice it to say that I shall thank them individually, preferably over dinner. And if it is possible to thank a much-maligned city—exciting, maddening, nurturing—I want to thank Calcutta for continuing to be itself, a difficult mother.

My bi-continental agent Elizabeth Sheinkman is brilliant, discerning, and a striking beauty. None of these attributes prevented her from doling out measures of tough love when necessary. I also wish to thank Millicent Bennett in New York, who graciously took *No Country* under her wing; Alexandra Pringle in London has been a delight to work with, and her teams, headed in India by Diya Kar Hazra, and in Australia by Hannah Temby, have given me much-appreciated support.

At home, my elegant and intelligent wife, Aparna Sen, my first reader, endured untidy desks (on both continents), piles of papers and books, and my absent-mindedness, yet found it in her heart to love and support me steadfastly through the years, reading the chapters and all my revisions with a keen eye.